M000310471

WHAT SIMON DIDN'T SAY

LUNAR TOWER PRESS

Joy M. Copeland

ISBN: 099973170X
ISBN 13: 9780999731703
Library of Congress Control Number: 2017919284
Lunar Tower Press, Oak Hill, VA

AUTHOR'S NOTE

This is a work of fiction. Names, characters, places, and incidents are the product of the author's imagination or are used fictitiously. Any resemblance to real people, living or dead, or to real locales is coincidental.

Lunar Tower Press
Oak Hill, Virginia

flowed efficiently, cleaning the street of garbage on its way to the nearby gutter. She spotted a place where the water looked wide but less deep. *Now or never,* she thought. With her head bowed under the umbrella, she extended her leg to leave the curb. Before her foot could touch the street, she was snatched backward and lifted like a rag doll, out of the path of a black Mercedes turning onto K Street. At first she was confused, but then she realized that someone had rescued her. She was secure on the sidewalk but shaken. Although the car hadn't hit her, it managed to drench her with a giant splash.

"Are you okay, miss?" The voice asking was deep and seemed to come from far away.

She suspected it had come from a face blocked from view by her umbrella. Looking down, she saw a pair of rain-soaked Oxfords and dark baggy trousers.

"Thank you," she said, rubbing her neck. "I'll be fine." Her wet pantsuit and a bare foot drew her attention. "My shoe! My shoe! Do you see it?"

She scanned the wet pavement, the curb, and the street around her. Then she spotted her missing heel. It was a ways down the street, bobbing in the swirling water above the sewer, fighting the river of rain that wanted to wash it down.

"Don't worry, miss." This message came from a different voice.

A second man, tattered with a wild head full of dreads, sprang from nowhere. With ape-like moves, the second man leaped into the street, retrieved the shoe, and then disappeared.

"Hey! Where's he taking my shoe?"

"Come on, miss." It was that deep voice again. By now Zoie could see its source, a rich dark-chocolate face framed by a rain-soaked newsboy cap. The speaker's eyes examined her. In a shoeless hobble, she offered no resistance as he guided her to the protection of a nearby awning. There the wild man waited with her rescued shoe. He seemed a little older than the other

CHAPTER 1

YOU'RE A WINNER

The walk from the Farragut North Metro Station to the Crayton Foundation's offices on K Street should have been an easy one. Alas, the weather had conspired against Zoie Taylor on that day. She heard the rain forecast on WTOP but never heard how hard it would pour. Remnants of an offshore storm would swamp the city in the morning in a fashion usually reserved for DC's late-afternoon thunderstorms.

"Who knew?" she said, sighing.

She struggled with her tiny umbrella. It proved no match for the storm's ferocity. The umbrella, which she held low over her head, barely protected her hair and shoulders. There was no way around getting wet. The blowing rain threatened to drench her cream-colored pantsuit and to give new life to the alligator DNA in her pencil-thin heels. In a defensive move, she lowered the umbrella to shield her face from the rain's sting. "Just a couple more blocks," she muttered in an attempt to convince herself that her mini-ordeal would be over soon.

At the corner of busy Sixteenth Street, Zoie scanned the street for a puddle-free place to cross. A small river had developed. It

ACKNOWLEDGMENTS

I'd like to thank my writers' workshop crew for "keeping it real" with your critiques, encouragement, and fellowship. Valerie Jean, Sherryle Jackson, Ellon Walker, Christina Northern, and Earl Best—you're all wonderful writers. Over the years I've learned a great deal about the craft of writing from our interactions. Writing, by its nature, is a lonely endeavor. Our Saturday workshops have made it less so. Roger Newell, you read most of this novel before you departed this earth. I speak for the group: we miss you.

Diane Dix, thanks for your inspired title twist.

Dennis, I'm grateful for your love, patience, and encouragement, plus your great editing support—things that kept me on track.

And to Lee, my wonderful daughter, I so appreciate your consistent, enthusiastic support for my writing projects. With you in my corner, I'm always a winner.

one—or was it the aging that comes with life on the street? Zoie closed her umbrella and took her shoe from him. "God, it's ruined," she said, stroking its soggy leather.

"Simon, the girl's right. 'Cept no point telling God. God already knows the shoe's ruined. Don't know why she's telling God what he already knows. That shoe doesn't want to be wet. Alligators only like water when they're alive." He held his stomach and squealed with delight at his own joke. Still laughing, he leaned into the dry corner created by the awning next to an overloaded shopping cart.

Zoie didn't laugh. Neither did the younger man, who responded to his associate's display of amusement with a shrug. Then he offered, "Miss, he don't mean no harm. He ain't the fool you think he is."

With her long-strapped briefcase slung over her shoulder, Zoie balanced herself against the shop window, put on her shoe, and wrung the excess water from the bottoms of her pants. "Thanks for saving me...Simon, is it?"

The younger man nodded, the corners of his mouth turning up in a slight smile.

"And thank you too," she said, turning to the older man, who had claimed the driest spot under the awning. "I don't believe I got your name."

He ceased laughing, buried his chin in his chest, and mumbled to himself.

For a second Zoie stared at him. He avoided her eyes by staring at the pavement. "Anyway, thank you both," she said, turning away. She noticed a red donation can marked "Help" against the wall. *The homeless.* It seemed DC had as many homeless as New York. She fumbled in her bag for her wallet, pulled out a twenty, and put it in the can.

"Thank you, miss." It was the younger man's deep voice again. This time his face bore a broad grin. He grabbed her free hand

and pressed a piece of paper into her palm and then forced her fingers to form a fist around it. His grip was cold and hard, his hand more steel-like than flesh and bone. Fearful of possible aggression, Zoie pulled away. Some months ago she had seen a headline in the *New York Post*: "Attacks by Street People on the Rise." They were needy for sure but sometimes dangerous.

"What did you give me?" she said, looking at the folded paper, which was now damp from her still-wet palm.

"Read it," he insisted.

Zoie closed her hand around the paper and glanced at her watch. She was now officially annoyed and running late for her 9:00 a.m. meeting. In New York, attorney business didn't start until ten in the morning. But DC, the nation's capital, was an early riser city, even for attorneys.

"Read it," he repeated, his tone more commanding and a little scary.

"I will!" She stuffed the paper into her pocket. "But later. Right now I'm in a hurry."

"Humph," the wild man interjected from his corner. "Hurrying is what almost turned you into mocha mush." He broke into a sickly sounding fit of laughter.

Things had become too weird. Zoie decided to make a quick exit. "Got to go," she said. With her umbrella ready, she stepped from under the awning, half-prepared to fight if they attempted to pull her back. In the still pouring rain, her umbrella did what it could to protect her, which wasn't much. She moved fast, covering the remaining two blocks to her office in long strides. She was late, and she wanted to put distance between her and the scene of her near accident—distance between her and those creepy guys. All the while, her feet squished uncomfortably in her waterlogged shoes. She never looked back.

At work Zoie checked her cream-colored pantsuit for signs, other than wetness, of the morning incident. Fortunately there were none. The waterlogged shoe that had sailed to the gutter was definitely darker than its mate. It would survive the day. She borrowed a hair dryer from a colleague to dry her pants and walked into the 9:00 a.m. meeting thirty minutes late, offering a "Sorry!" but no further explanation.

Instinct told her not to mention her mishap. She was embarrassed about her carelessness and didn't like to dwell on ugly thoughts of death or injury. The possibility of her death—of leaving Nikki parentless—haunted her at times. She couldn't deal with those thoughts today. It was not until she was alone in her office after the meeting that she remembered the paper that Simon had pressed into her palm.

"It's probably a biblical reference," she told herself, pulling it from her pocket. The paper was a little larger than the strips found in fortune cookies. The message, handwritten in crisp black lettering, had been unaffected by the moisture—"You're a Winner."

"A winner, huh? Oh, boy, I wish." She hadn't played the lottery or anything else that would make her a winner and didn't plan to. At least the message was positive. Not being hit by that car was positive. She tossed the paper on her desk and recalled her other close calls, like the near drowning at Virginia Beach when she was fifteen. She was trying to calculate what remained of her nine lives when her thoughts were interrupted.

"Here's the last three years of grant procedures," said Regina. Her young assistant placed the ominous stack of folders on the corner of Zoie's desk. "Oh, and e-mail's back up," she added pushing back her short precision cut hair.

"Oh, I didn't realize it was down. Thanks, Regina."

Regina turned to leave.

"Regina, wait. Can I ask you something?"

"Sure."

"Are Crayton meetings always so dry?"

"Bored already, huh? Zoie, you've only been here three weeks. You can't be bored already."

"Who said I was bored?" Zoie replied.

"I can tell. You're having second thoughts about this place. Missing that big-time New York law firm, huh?"

"Am I missing sixty- to seventy-hour workweeks...I don't think so."

"Yeah, but you're missing something."

"I'll admit this is different for me." Zoie spun around once in her chair, responding when she again faced Regina. "Yeah, it's a little *slow*...I mean compared with the pace that I'm used to."

"I hear you," Regina fired back.

"Then maybe it's the lack of good-looking guys."

The two giggled. It wasn't as though Zoie had dated often in New York. But her retort sounded good.

"Ooh. That's cold," Regina said, gazing at the ceiling. "Haven't seen anybody here, huh?"

"Right." Zoie drummed her pale pink nails on the desk.

"I know what you mean."

"Don't get me wrong," Zoie said, attempting to explain. "I wanted it this way. Things to be slower, I mean. I need more time for Nikki."

"Isn't she out of town or something?"

"Just until school starts."

"Oh, to be child-free for a month," Regina said with a sigh. Like Zoie, Regina was a single parent.

Regina turned to leave but pivoted back. "Wait—I forgot! Here's some excitement for you."

"What?" Zoie leaned across her desk expecting to hear some of Regina's juicy gossip.

"*You* won the baby pool!"

"Me? Win something? No way!" Zoie sat up in her chair with new energy.

"Rachel's baby was born last night—a girl," Regina said, batting her lashes, as proud as if the new child were her very own. "Right on the day you picked. Three days before the actual due date, at eleven at night, just like you guessed. Even your pick for the baby's weight was close. She weighed seven pounds, six ounces, and you guessed seven, seven."

"Are you sure that I won?" Zoie asked with a disbelieving frown.

"You are ZT, aren't you? There are no other ZTs in this office."

"Wow! What d'ya know!"

Regina grinned. "What's freaky is Rachel went out on maternity just before you started."

It was true. Zoie hadn't laid eyes on Rachel. She hadn't sized up the woman's belly, if that made a difference. As a newbie she signed up for the baby pool to show support for the office's social activities—a five-dollar investment for the cause of group acceptance. Somehow, now that she'd won, it seemed unfair to take the money.

"The pot's seventy dollars," Regina continued. "I'll get your money."

Her assistant gone, Zoie again whirled in her chair. Whether the prize was five dollars or seventy, it felt wonderful to win. As far as she could remember, she'd never won anything. Long ago she'd convinced herself that things only came her way from hard work. Luck or divine intervention had nothing to do with anything. Zoie retrieved the paper fortune from her desk and stared at its message—"You're a Winner."

"Wow! What a coincidence. I really won something."

CHAPTER 2

DAUGHTERS, DADDIES, AND DOGS

Zoie keyed into her Connecticut Avenue apartment. She unloaded her briefcase and the grocery bag she'd lugged from the health-food store onto the kitchen counter, then kicked off her heels, and poured a glass of cold water. Leaning against the sink, she sipped the water and allowed herself to be mesmerized by the suspended dust moving in the last rays of the sun, which flooded her top-floor window.

This apartment pleased her. It was larger than her Manhattan place, four blocks from the Metro, with easy access to her grandmother's house on Brandywine. Best of all, the Smithsonian's National Zoo was a few blocks away, something that especially pleased Nikki.

Zoie unpacked her groceries and stared at the kitchen's blank white walls. So far she hadn't bothered to personalize the place. Not a picture or a calendar on the wall. No window treatment blocked the daylight or the dark, with the exception of the yellowing shades in her bedroom. Decorating wasn't her priority. Decorating implied commitment—commitment to her new job, to her new life, and to staying in DC. She missed New York's excitement, that feeling that caused her blood to move faster and her walk to be more deliberate. Despite that it was her hometown, Washington, DC, could be a sleepy place. The city's political aura was like tuning into CNN more than anything real. She'd never plugged in to the political scene. Her move back to DC was more about Nikki. DC was slower paced and it was near family—what little family she and Nikki had left.

It had been two weeks since Zoie had driven Nikki to Ohio to spend the summer with Elliot's folks, the Benjamins. The plan was simple. With Nikki away Zoie would have time to settle into her Foundation job and to find after-school care for Nikki, who would start attending the first grade in late August. Zoie never counted on the teary goodbye on the Benjamins' manicured lawn. During the first hundred miles of the drive back to DC, she almost turned the car around. But as it often did with Zoie, the logic of the situation prevailed. Leaving Nikki in Ohio for the summer was for the best. Still, Zoie longed to hear her daughter's elfin jabber and feel her thin-armed hugs.

Zoie knew Celeste and Phillip Benjamin to be decent, caring people. Perrysburg, Ohio, their home, was a picturesque town near Toledo, where Elliot spent his childhood and Phillip Benjamin operated a successful optometry practice. Celeste was a professional volunteer. The Benjamins tried their best to compensate for Elliot's abdication of parental responsibility. They used every opportunity to see Nikki, staying in a hotel not far from Zoie's Upper West Side apartment, taking their granddaughter on outings around the city. Every week Celeste telephoned Nikki, and every few months a package of toys and clothing would arrive. They'd even established a generous college fund for Nikki. The Benjamins were Nikki's only grandparents, and Nikki adored them.

It was strange the way the relationship with the Benjamins had worked out. At first Zoie had been reluctant to intertwine her life and Nikki's with Elliot's parents, but their love for Nikki and interest in her welfare seemed genuine. The couple was always delighted to see Nikki but avoided looking Zoie in the eye and certainly never mentioned their son, Elliot, in Zoie's presence. The Benjamins' other child, a daughter, had converted from Judaism to Catholicism right after high school. Much to her parents' dismay, at age twenty-one she joined a convent. Elliot's declaration that he didn't want children threatened to seal-off the Benjamin bloodline—until Nikki came along.

In a moment of weakness, Zoie consented to give Nikki the Benjamin name. Nothing required it. Certainly not the years she and Elliot had lived together. Certainly not Elliot's actions. "This was your doing," he said to her, the day he moved out. His stance on child support was simple. "I'm not paying. This wasn't supposed to happen."

Elliot walked away that day as if she and Nikki were something he could scrape from his shoe. Anger saw her through Nikki's delivery and the months after. It wasn't as if Zoie needed financial assistance to raise a child, although every bit helped. It was the principle of the thing. She was prepared for a court battle over child support when Elliot's parents stepped in with an informal arrangement. Thereafter, support checks appeared as reliably as moon phases, all handled with discretion by a third party, on behalf of Elliot.

It was time for her daily call to Ohio. Zoie selected the Benjamins' number. It rang several times.

"Hello." It was Celeste's high-pitched voice.

"Celeste, it's Zoie."

"Oh...hi Zoie...I thought it might be you."

Celeste sounded distant, more so than usual. No matter how many times the two women talked, awkwardness always loomed.

"How's everything going? How's Nikki?"

"Fine. Fine." There was a pause. "We went out for dinner. Nikki had chicken fingers."

"Oh, good. I'm glad you took a break from cooking."

"I don't mind cooking, really. Just that there's a fair in town... that's where we've been all day. Didn't get a chance to cook."

"A fair!" Zoie exclaimed, feigning enthusiasm. "I bet Nikki loved that."

"She sure did," Celeste said.

There was silence.

"Celeste, Nikki's not wearing you out, is she?" Zoie asked. A six-year-old in constant motion could exhaust anyone.

"I'm keeping up. You know we love having Nikki."

"Let me talk to her."

She heard Celeste call Nikki to the phone. Zoie knew something was up. Something was different in Celeste's tone.

An out-of-breath little girl took the phone. "Mommy, Mommy, I knew you'd call."

"Don't I call everyday, baby?"

"Yeah, but I couldn't wait. I've got so much to tell you."

"Have you been running?"

"Yeah, a little," the child said. "I was in the basement with the puppies. Nellie has five of them, you know."

"That's wonderful, sweetie."

"Yeah, Mommy, and you know what's even more wonderful?"

"What, baby?"

"Grandma says I can have a puppy. Isn't that wonderful, Mommy? My own puppy!"

Puppy! Puppy! Visions of newspapers on the floor, chewed furniture, and late-night walks in the cold swirled in Zoie's head. Nellie, a sweet dog, was a black lab. Her cute puppies would grow large—large and hairy. Their lives didn't have room for a dog. And Celeste had no right to make such a commitment without

checking first. *Now what?* Nikki was thrilled. Saying no was going to be difficult, especially saying no long distance.

"I don't know, Nikki," said Zoie, unable to muster anything else. "Mommy has to think about it, sweetie. You know a puppy takes a lot of care. And we're not home all day." Zoie bit her lip, waiting for her daughter's response.

"I know, Mommy," the child moaned. "But I've already picked the one I want."

"Mommy said that she'd think about it." It was Zoie's weak attempt to credit the probable no to a third-person arbiter called "Mommy." It wasn't that Zoie didn't like pets. She just wasn't ready to be responsible for an animal.

"Well, Mommy, you got to think hard," the child commanded. "I named my puppy Biscuit 'cause I know he'll like biscuits when he gets bigger." The child giggled in the bubbly way she did when something thrilled her.

"Okay, I will." Zoie sighed, her irritation with Celeste growing. "So what else did you, Grandma, and Grandpa do today?"

"Well, we went to the fair. I rode the Ferris wheel with Grandpa. And I had some cotton candy."

"Cool."

"And guess what, Mommy!"

"What, sweetie?"

"Daddy's here."

"Huh?" Zoie thought she'd heard the word *daddy*—which was a foreign term to her. Whose daddy? Her daddy? Nikki's daddy? A daddy hadn't been part of any picture in Zoie's life for a long time.

"Mommy, are you listening? Mommy, did you hear me? I said my daddy is here."

"Oh, he is?" Blood rushed to Zoie's ears.

"And you know what, Mommy? Daddy's new wife is here too."

The word *wife* slipped into Zoie's brain just as her ears were shutting down. "Oh."

The child continued. "Daddy says I'm going to have a new brother or sister."

So that's why Celeste sounded so strange. She never mentioned that Elliot would be visiting. Elliot lived in California. He actually hated Ohio. *Elliot in Ohio?*

"Nikki, let me talk to your grandmother," Zoie said, rubbing her neck. Heat crept from the base of her skull up to the top of her head, the way it did when she stayed too long in the sun. Everything in the kitchen took on a pink-tinged blur.

"But, Mommy, what about my puppy?"

"Mommy's still thinking about it, Nikki. Now please let me talk to your grandmother!" said Zoie, fighting to control her anger. There was going to be an outburst, but it was wrong to direct her anger at Nikki.

"Grandma! Grandma! Mommy wants to talk to you! Grandma, Mommy is thinking about the puppy!"

Zoie closed her eyes and took a deep breath. She promised herself that she wouldn't scream at the woman. It seemed like forever before Celeste took the receiver. Zoie could hear voices in the background, but she couldn't make out to whom the voices belonged. When Celeste finally picked up the phone, Zoie concentrated her anger into a harsh whisper. "Celeste! What's going on? What's this about Elliot? You know I don't want him around my child!"

"Zoie, he just showed up. I swear, I didn't know he was coming," Celeste pleaded.

"People just don't show up in Ohio all the way from California."

"When he called, they were already at the airport. What could I do?"

"Celeste, how could you? I trusted you with my child."

"Zoie, calm down. Nikki's fine. They're getting along."

"Getting along! That bastard shows up to say hello to a child he hasn't set eyes on since she was three months old, and you tell me that Nikki's just fine!"

"Zoie, you're not being fair. We can't control Elliot's comings and goings. After all, this is his home." Celeste's last remark hung in the air like a breath on a frosty morning.

"Celeste, I'm coming to get Nikki this weekend. I'd like you to have her packed and ready."

"Zoie, please don't take this out on Nikki. Let the child stay as we planned. Elliot's leaving tomorrow." Then Celeste's voice dropped to a whisper. "Zoie...I can't talk right now. Nikki just came back into the room. They're in the living room."

They? Remnants of Nikki's information streamed back from Zoie's subconscious. Nikki *had* mentioned a wife. And a new brother or sister. *Elliot married? A pregnant wife? A child on the way?* Elliot never wanted children. Not wanting children had been his reason for walking out on her. The nausea that often accompanied thoughts of Elliot hit Zoie full force. Elliot was having a child with another woman and sneaking to see the daughter he didn't want. Or had Celeste been staging these reunions all along? No, Celeste couldn't have pulled that off. Nikki was too bright a child. Nikki couldn't keep secrets.

"Celeste, expect me on Saturday." Zoie slammed down the phone. It had occurred to her that one day Eliot might try to contact Nikki. She'd filed the thought away, never expecting it to happen. Now he'd reentered Nikki's life, only to put her in second place, behind some new baby—one he obviously wanted.

Silent tears streamed down Zoie's face. Faint childhood memories emerged, bringing that familiar sinking sensation. In the shadows of her mind, she could see her father. He was walking away again, growing smaller as he moved down a narrow corridor. "Daddy, Daddy!" she called. He didn't turn. He just disappeared.

Memories she'd kept carefully locked away overflowed. Zoie sank to the kitchen floor. She felt like a child again, deserted and unloved by the man most important in her life.

It was dark when Zoie moved from the kitchen floor. In the morning she would check on flights to Toledo. Better still, she would arrange for a rental car. It was an eight-hour, 475-mile drive to Perrysburg. Having a car might be wise, in case she needed to bring home a puppy.

CHAPTER 3

THANK YOU, BROTHERS AND SISTERS—GOD LOVES YOU

The sidewalk in front of the bank building on Fourteenth Street was unoccupied. From a distance Maynard scoped out the area. No one loomed near his target spot. Satisfied that the path was clear, he bolted the hundred yards up the block, his shopping cart in tow and shifting wildly. Everything he owned was in that cart: flattened cardboard stuffed lengthwise, three pill-covered blankets, an empty red coffee can, several green trash bags that bulged against their knots, and his binder, innocent looking with its frayed cover. Having any more stuff would have made his life more complicated. The few things he owned already proved cumbersome, especially when events required him to move with speed. More things meant more to track. More to protect.

He sorted through his cardboard collection and selected a folded piece with faded red letters that read Fragile. He spread the cardboard on the sidewalk, forming a four-foot pallet on the warm pavement. Then, with his jagged nails, he picked the knot of a plastic sack, freeing a bottle of water, a blackened banana, and a partial roll of toilet paper. He arranged these items along one side of his makeshift seat and placed his coffee can and a crude placard against the bank wall. In heavy black lettering, the placard read, "Thank You, Brothers and Sisters." His rigorous testing proved that that message inspired people to give more than the message on his alternate placard, which read, "God Loves You." Maynard never understood why the mention of God upset some people. In his many conversations with heaven over the years, he'd found the Almighty to be quite reasonable, though sometimes downright pushy. Demons were the real problem.

Yesterday had been a good day. Situated in the same spot, he'd collected over twenty-five dollars, a decent sum, though by no means what he could collect on his best days. His best days came at Christmastime. Filled with holiday spirit, people sometimes dropped a twenty-dollar bill in his can, smugly believing their charitable act would buy them passes for their souls.

Situated on his pallet, Maynard leaned into the wall. The bank's digital clock read 8:30 a.m. It was too early for tourists and already hot. No matter the temperature, he remained clothed in his dark hooded sweatshirt and navy skullcap. Ignoring the legs passing in front of him, he didn't see the little girl approach until he heard the clang of coins hitting his can. She was no taller than his cart. Biting her finger, she stared at him. When he lifted his hand in a gesture of thanks, a rather large woman in white shorts snatched the girl away by the shirt. "But, Mommy, you said I could put the money in the bucket!"

"I know, honey. You did good. Now we've got to go."

"Mommy, why is that man so dirty?" the child asked, as her mother dragged her down the street. They'd moved away so fast that Maynard never heard the mother's answer.

Although it was only morning, his thoughts shifted to where he'd sleep that night. Warm weather made for more choices. He settled on Franklin Square, right up Fourteenth Street, with its benches, grass and trees, and druggies, dealers, and thieves. It was still better than most shelters. Having his stuff stolen by other residents was the least of his worries. During his last stay, the Shelter staff had taken his binder, and he suspected that they had poisoned his food. Why else would he have puked his guts out all that night? Several times they called him by his full name, Maynard Frick—a definite red flag. Being called Maynard or, even worse, Mr. Frick always signaled that something dreadful was about to happen—a nightmare complete with hypodermics and barred windows. Years at St. Elizabeth's had taught him that much.

The staff at the clinic where he'd received his risperidone therapy (which lasted until six months ago) called him Mr. Frick. The medication made his voices go away. It had been lonely without God, and as frightening as they could sometimes be, he missed the other voices too. The voices made him do bad things, like the time they told him to pee on the Chinaman who'd shooed him from the back of the restaurant. There was no use hiding. No matter where, those voices would find him.

Simon called him Maynard, but he didn't mind. The truth of it was that Simon never said much of anything. Sharing a corner with Simon was fine. Somehow the younger man attracted the cash. When Simon was around, which wasn't that often, donations picked up. Maybe it was Simon's bold approach—he would go right up to people as they passed—or the fact that he didn't look disheveled. Then, at the end of the day, Simon always went his own way. Simon had been there on the day of his largest take. No, he didn't mind Simon at all. Simon might be somebody whom Maynard could tell about what happened at the Shelter. *Simon won't breathe a word.*

Maynard wiped his hands with a wad of wet toilet tissue and then stuck the dirty tissue ball under the edge of his mat. He pulled four more sheets from the toilet roll and placed them on his lap as a napkin for his black banana. The clanking of metal hitting metal caught his attention. He looked up to see whom to thank, but the person was now just a shadow of a rear end. As he stuffed the banana mush into his mouth, a familiar, gritty voice filled his head. He swallowed and frowned.

Maynard you need to make a copy of all the material in your binder and hide it.

"How?" Maynard answered aloud. "Copies of all that paper? Huh. And if I did, where in the hell am I going to put it?"

You're a smart boy, Maynard. How many degrees do you have? Figure it out!

Maynard winced at the loud voice in his head. "Yeah, that's money. Copies cost a bit. So does a safe-deposit box," he mumbled under his breath.

Don't get fresh with me, boy! Did I say anything about a safety-deposit box, nummy? I said hide it! Don't you know they read your notes! They know that you're on to them. Don't be stupid!

Maynard wished that he hadn't been at the Shelter that night and that he hadn't overheard their conversation. He couldn't go to the police. The police would lock him up again, as they did when he told them about the plot to poison the cherry trees on the Mall. That was serious business. Imagine DC's big tourist attraction dying off. He couldn't risk St. Elizabeth's again. No, telling was too dangerous. Maybe they didn't have time to read what was in his binder. The binder had been out of his sight for only a minute...or had it been hours?

Maynard leaned forward, scanned the street, and shrank into the wall. Those Shelter people cruised in vans, picking folks up from the street, just like the cops did. *Isn't that how it started with the Jews in Poland?* He hid his eyes in his hands.

Have you been listening at all, asshole? You blew it!

"I didn't know."

Of course you didn't know. You're too fucking stupid to know!

"Please don't call me that." With eyes closed and knees to his chest, he used both hands to cover his ears. "Please don't call me stupid!"

Okay, then how about dumb ass? Maynard is a dumb ass! sang the voice.

"No! No!"

Maynard felt pressure on his shoulder. Someone or something was touching him. He opened his eyes to see dark trousers and a light-blue shirt. It was a woman, and she was using her baton to push his shoulder.

"Eeeek!" he screamed and jerked backward, knocking his head on the bank's outer wall.

"Mister, are you all right?"

There it was—that *mister*. Was it the mister that preceded Frick? Maynard's bottom lip quivered. Through his gooey eyes, everything was blurred.

"Mister, do you hear me? Are you all right?"

Ooh, that mister again! Maybe it's that anonymous mister. Mr. Anybody.

His breathing slowed. They hadn't found him, but it was close. The woman standing over him was nearer than anyone had been to him in days. He could see the radio attached to her shirt, and the gun holstered at her hip. He kept his head low so that their eyes couldn't meet. He tried to make himself small.

"Sir, do you need assistance? Do you want to go to the hospital? I can call the shelter to come pick you up."

Thank God. She was now calling him sir and not mister. "No! No! I'm fine," he said.

"Well, you really shouldn't be here. I've got to ask you to move on."

Where was the cop that usually patrolled this street—the one who never bothered him? That cop never looked down. Never used his baton to touch him.

"Did you hear me? I said you need to move!"

"Okay, okay." He unwound his arms from his tingling legs and rose from the pallet. He began to fold his cardboard pallet and put it in his shopping cart. The baton lady didn't wait for him to finish gathering his possessions. She was the one moving on. He watched her stroll south as he emptied his puny take from the coffee can—two dollars and seventy-five cents. He stuffed the rest of his belongings into the cart and wheeled it in the opposite direction. Things weren't going well. Being forced to move wasn't a good way to start the day. He hadn't heard from heaven in a couple of days. *Where's God when you need him?*

CHAPTER 4

FRANCES WOODS

"Now why you go and do that?" asked Queen, with her thick Jamaican accent, scooping up all of Frances Woods's ninety-six pounds from the floor. "I told you that when you wanna go to the toilet, you call me. You okay?" Queen placed the trembling older woman gently on the plastic-backed pad on the bed and went to inspect the spot where she had fallen.

"Yeah," answered Frances Woods begrudgingly. "It was a slow collapse, not a fall. I couldn't wait. I had to pee. Anyway, I don't have enough breath to call you when you're downstairs." Frances Woods hacked a few times. The coughs caused her to tremble. She tried to take a deep breath and hacked some more.

"So you pee on the floor," said Queen, standing with her hands on her hips, peering over the small puddle on the wood floor. By anyone's measurements, Queen was a big, strong woman. Strong legs showed from beneath her yellow-print housedress, like crusty black tree trunks rising up from her mannish slippers. She wore a red-knit cap, part of her year-round attire, along with the dishtowel that hung from her pocket. "You gotta use the walker," said Queen, pointing to the apparatus on the wall, next to the bed table. Her tone was calm but firm. "Now I gotta take care of this mess. And get you cleaned. Sit still. I'll be right back. If you get the urge to pee, pee on that pad." Queen shook her head. "Looks like we gonna have to go back to diapers."

"Humph! You know I couldn't help it. I thought I could make it," said Frances Woods, mustering enough breath to yell after her caregiver, who'd already left the room. She hacked again and then snorted and mumbled to herself. She hated the walker. The thought of adult diapers was particularly distressing. She hated the feeling of helplessness and the feeling of being trapped in her own home. She hated being scolded most of all.

With emotions cycling from anger to embarrassment, Frances Woods sat in her urine-soaked gown. She folded her arms tightly, using most of her strength. She needed to be angry with some-one. The trouble was she didn't know whom to target. Almost anybody would do at this point. *Queen,* she guessed. *Whoever heard of naming a child after the queen of England? Maybe that's what makes Queen so uppity.*

As her wet gown grew cold, she tried to undress herself, grum-bling and struggling to remove the soiled gown. Her right arm got caught in the sleeve when she tried to lift the gown over her head. The garment partially hid her face as Queen returned to the room with a pail, a sponge, and the Lysol spray.

"Couldn't wait like I asked you?" Queen said, seeing Frances Woods's face half-buried in the garment. "I only got two hands," she continued in her singsong inflection. Queen put down the cleaning supplies and assisted her charge in taking off the wet gown and panties. Then she left the room again to fetch a pan of water, washcloth, and towel.

With arms crossed tightly against her bare chest, Frances Woods hunched to hide her nakedness. But there was no one in the room to see her sagging skin, no one with whom modesty would matter. Queen had bathed and changed her numerous times in the eighteen months since her foot missed the second step on her way downstairs. Since Calvin's death no males had come to the house, except for repairmen, like Queen's brother.

"Queen, I'm getting cold," Frances Woods barked in a raspy voice. A series of hacking coughs followed, vibrating in her bare chest.

Queen was back in a flash, this time with a pan of warm soapy water, a washcloth, and a towel. "You best quiet down, or you'll go to spasms," she said. She gently washed the old woman's thighs between her bony legs, dried her, and powdered her gray-tinged skin; then she helped her change into a pair of white cotton panties and a pale-pink gown.

Frances Woods felt a good deal better. A weak thank-you punctuated with a hiss pushed passed her lips, almost as an involuntary action.

"Mrs. Woods, you think I'm two maids round here. I need to find another place to work and leave you here to bark at yourself."

"There are plenty more people willing to take your place," Frances Woods snorted.

"Go ahead. See what you get if you replace me. The agency will send you one of them African gals. Then you'll see how nice I've been to you," Queen said as she fluffed her charge's pillows and arranged the bedclothes.

"Humph."

"You won't like it. Sometimes them African gals smell. And their food puts a fire in your belly."

"Queen, your food's no picnic."

Queen stopped fussing with the bed and put her hands on her hips. "So! Now y'ah don't like my cooking! You eat it all! Every time!" Queen said with a laugh.

"I have to. I have no choice."

"The agency will send you a body that can cook. One of those gals from El Salvador...cooks with the chilies...won't speak a word of English. You'll be sorry."

Frances Woods managed to snicker. She wasn't about to raise the ante on this argument over who could and couldn't speak English, though after many months she understood Queen's thickly accented English perfectly.

The doorbell rang.

"Oh Lawd, who's that now?" Queen asked with a groan.

"Zoie's got her own key."

"It's Sunday. It must be your friend."

Queen headed down the wide staircase and across the formal foyer with its mirrored credenza. She opened the door and recognized the little old woman standing on the porch as Ida Bascomb. The old woman was huffing and puffing from climbing the seventeen stairs from the street to the porch. She was dressed in a grape-colored suit that hung like a potato sack on the hanger that was her bony frame. Two circles of pink rouge highlighted her dusty beige face. Her thick white wig, reminiscent of an English barrister style, made her purple hat ride high on her head. Even with this extra height, Ida Bascomb came only as high as Queen's chest. Yes, Ida Bascomb was as frail as Frances Woods. On a gusty day, without the weight of her clothes, a good wind could have blown her back down the stairs to the street. Today there was no breeze. Ida Bascomb carried her usual black umbrella, even though there wasn't a cloud in the sky. It served as a substitute cane and, if need be, a weapon.

"Afternoon, Ms. Bascomb," Queen said, looking down at the woman.

"Good afternoon, Queen. I've come to see Frances," Ida said, stepping in the door and handing her umbrella to Queen. "How's she doing?"

"She's ornery when she feels good. I think today she's feels *real* good."

Queen looked out the door and surveyed the street to locate the old woman's vintage Chrysler. She was glad to see the car parked safely down the street and not in the driveway behind her own red Nissan.

"Mrs. Woods is awake. Can I help you up the steps?" Queen asked.

"No, I'm fine. I can make it on my own. Just a little out of breath from those stairs."

All the houses on that part of Brandywine Street required a good pair of legs to get to their front doors. "I could use some water, if you don't mind."

Ida Bascomb visited Frances Woods after church on every other Sunday. She'd drive from Calvary Cross Baptist to Brandywine Street and then back home again, without hitting major traffic.

"Mrs. Woods, Ms. Bascomb is here to see you," Queen yelled up the stairs as the smaller woman started her climb, pulling herself up the first step with both hands on the banister. Queen watched awhile and then shook her head and went to get the water. She couldn't believe that this woman, who was a good deal older than Frances Woods, was still driving and making it up all those stairs on her own. When Queen returned from the kitchen with a tray carrying two slices of pound cake and two glasses of ice water, she found Ida Bascomb seated on the bench on the staircase landing.

"Just got to rest a bit," she said.

Queen passed her and continued up the stairs. "Take your time, Ms. Bascomb."

"Frances," Ida Bascomb called as she started her trek up the rest of the stairs, "I told you long a time ago you should have moved to a rambler."

Queen set up a TV tray and chair for Ida next to Frances Woods's bed. Then she left the room to give the friends some privacy, going down the stairs and passing Ida Bascomb still in her climb.

By the time Ida Bascomb entered the room, Frances Woods's earlier anger had disappeared. She was sitting up in her bed, propped up by her two large pillows. Ida shuffled to her bedside. The two hugged.

"I do believe you get thinner each time I see you," Ida Bascomb told her friend.

"Now look who's talking. You could fit another person with you in that suit."

The older woman smoothed the air pockets from her blouse to reveal a perfectly flat chest. "You know my theory: less weight, less to carry. Makes it easier to get around," Ida said with a smile.

"I wished I had learned that before I slipped down those stairs. Now look at me."

"I thought I'd find Zoie and Nikki here," Ida said as she sat in the chair that Queen had provided. She took a sip of the cold water and picked at the cake. "I haven't seen that child since your Laurel died. Zoie was still pregnant."

"Yeah, that was a bad year, with Laurel's passing and Zoie's breaking up with that jerk. I didn't think Zoie wanted to come back to DC after that."

"I was surprised when you told me that she was moving back. What made her do it? A man?" Ida Bascomb said with a mischievous smile.

"Something tells me this has nothing to do with a man."

"A man—a good man—is what she needs. That white guy she hooked up with in New York, now he was what you call a scalawag," Ida said. "I hated to hear her getting hurt like that."

"White, black, green—all men can be dogs. Look what happened to my Laurel." Frances Woods coughed.

Ida and Frances Woods had been friends for fifty years. Ida knew all of Frances Woods's secrets, and Frances Woods thought she knew all of Ida's.

"I'd like to see Nikki. Frances, you know I've never seen that baby."

"Whose fault is that? I invited you to come with me to New York after Nikki was born. She's not a baby anymore."

"I know."

"Now that Zoie's back in town, you'll see her. Right now Nikki is in Ohio for the summer, with Elliot's parents."

"The father's parents? I know you're joking!"

"His parents offered, and Zoie needed the break."

"I got to give it to her: she's a better person than I could be, letting his folks keep Nikki like that, after all that unpleasantness."

"Humph," said Frances Woods, not caring to say more.

The two friends prattled on for almost an hour. Ida did most of the talking, while Frances Woods rested her voice. The usual topics prevailed: church gossip, each other's aches and pains, prescriptions, doctors, and disputes over health-insurance claims. Frances Woods wanted to tell Ida her latest complaints about Queen but thought better of starting that discussion, just in case Queen sashayed back into the room.

Ida, as usual, was worried about money. Her husband, Coleman Bascomb, had died without an insurance policy or a pension. With only Social Security and a small pension due upon her retirement, Ida had stayed on at the DC Public Library as long as she could. The way she told it, every last penny was committed to some bill or other, with just five dollars to spare.

"Frances, I can't tell you how fortunate you are that Calvin left you well off."

"I thank the Lord every day," said Frances Woods, holding her chest. Calvin, bless his soul, had invested wisely. Between the money he'd made as a postal worker and her salary as a vice principal of a high school, plus the windfalls they'd received some forty years ago, her money—if handled wisely—was something she didn't have to worry about. With Calvin and her daughter

Laurel gone, there was only Zoie. Zoie and Nikki. And when she was gone, all of what was left would go to them. She began to cough again. The cough came from deep in her chest.

"Frances, you don't sound well *at all*."

At first Frances Woods couldn't catch her breath to respond. She wanted to say that she already knew that she didn't sound good. Ida gave her some water.

"When I get these coughing spells…I'm so drained," Frances Woods said between hacks.

"When are you going to see the doctor?"

"Thursday," Frances Woods whispered with a wheeze.

"You get Queen or Zoie to take you before Thursday."

Frances Woods waved her right hand dismissively while covering her mouth with the left.

"Frances, you're as hard headed as they come," Ida told her.

Frances Woods waved her hand again. She was trying to quiet the coughs by keeping her mouth closed. She saw the concern in her friend's eyes.

"Okay, you get some rest," said Ida. "I'll call you tomorrow." She picked up her bag and left the room.

Minutes later Frances Woods heard the heavy front door close. Her coughing subsided as she lay perfectly still, her head back on the pillow, her eyes directed at the leaf-patterned relief in the center of the ceiling. This room, which she had so lovingly decorated with rose-patterned wallpaper and champagne-colored curtains, had turned into her prison. Its four walls and the bathroom down the hall were now the extent of her world. Her thoughts drifted to her dear Laurel and Calvin and other friends and family she had lost over the years. Gone, all gone. Somewhere in heaven they were waiting for her. She was glad they couldn't see her now. She'd always been such a strong woman. At least that's what everybody told her. In heaven she would be strong again. They all would be there. *What about Gabriel? Is he in heaven too? How did I lose him all those years ago?* There'd been no word from him in fifty-four years. He had to be dead. She had tried not to think of him, especially when Calvin was alive. These days thoughts of him entered her mind more often—his beautiful dark face, those loving eyes, that mouth that could consume hers with the kind of kisses reserved for the young. It might be crowded in heaven with both Calvin and Gabriel. She smiled. She'd have to deal with that when her time came.

The house was so large and so empty, except for Queen. Francis Woods was disappointed upon learning that Zoie had decided to get an apartment rather than move in to share the place. There was plenty of room. After all, the house was going to be Zoie's one day. Maybe sooner than later.

CHAPTER 5

BE CAREFUL WHAT
YOU WISH FOR

Glass in hand, Jahi Khalfani weaved through the crowd at the Washington Hyatt. The high-ceiling reception room was filled to capacity with attendees from donor companies and their anxious recipients. The mayor, city-council members, and prominent business leaders—not to mention a small contingent from Capitol Hill—waited to have their pictures taken. Their black-tie uniforms made them look like penguins *from National Geographic*'s "Life in the Arctic." Tonight, in a rented tux, Jahi was one of them.

So far he hadn't seen Ray Gaddis, his main contact at the Crayton Foundation. *Ray will turn up soon enough*, Jahi thought, continuing to make his way through a tight pack of people vying for hors d'oeuvres. Jahi tolerated these events. Attendance was de facto mandatory, at least for active nonprofits. He needed to be there to promote the Crayton Foundation's crucial support for his mission: Mahali Salaam, or "Shelter for the Homeless."

Angling his broad shoulders, Jahi forged a path through the crowd. "Pardon me, coming through," he announced. And like a biblical sea, those around him parted so he could pass. Across the room a clearing next to a column beckoned him. He had almost reached his destination when a woman backed into his path. Focused on telling a tale to a mesmerized audience, the woman was oblivious to his presence. Her arms flailed dangerously close to his glass. Jahi steadied his wine. In a mischievous moment, he considered simply allowing the mishap to take place. As if reading a script, he envisioned an accident scene: wine splashing on the woman's bare shoulder, the red eruption catching his shirt, the onlookers moaning, and a flurry of napkins dabbing to save the woman's dress. Of course, he would offer his heartfelt apologies and don his best imitation of embarrassment. Everyone, including the Crayton folks, would understand the reason for his departure—a badly stained shirt. The foolhardy notion of a staged calamity quickly faded.

"Excuse me," he said. The woman who was blocking his way still didn't notice him. "Please excuse me," he said again, this time leaning into her ear, his whispered request leaving his breath on her neck.

She snatched her head around. Her tight lips that had initially greeted him transformed into a soft smile. "Oh," she said.

"Sorry, I just need to get by," he said, smiling back.

"Oh, of course," she responded and stepped aside.

The spot by the column was still available. Having claimed it, he looked back at the crowd, sipping his wine and pondering the grand event. Here he was, in the seat of global power, Washington, DC, where citizens slept on the sidewalks only blocks from the White House. How could the nation dare to solve the deeper problems facing the world without handling those at home? A call from a familiar voice interrupted his thoughts.

"Jahi! Jahi! There you are." The voice was unmistakable. Its vocal cords were affected by incomplete puberty. Their owner, Milton Page.

Be nice, Jahi reminded himself. "Ah, Milton," he said when the somewhat breathless man with carrot-red hair styled as "unkempt chic" appeared at his side.

"Jahi, someone told me you'd arrived. I've been searching for you. Nice turnout, huh?" Milton turned to view the attendees.

"Always is."

"Crayton has three tables, as usual."

"Where's Ray?"

"Ooh, Ray couldn't make it. Something came up at the last minute."

"Gee, that's too bad." In a phone call just two days prior, Ray Gaddis assured him that the Foundation would be making its usual contribution to the Shelter, pending the Board's confirmation, of course. Ray had also intimated that that confirmation step was a fait accompli. "I hope everything is okay," Jahi said.

"Sorry, last minute change. He really didn't explain," Milton said with a nonchalant flick of his wrist. "You'll be sitting with one of our new Foundation members. Just down from New York. Come on. I want to introduce you."

Jahi let Milton lead him along the edge of the crowd and to the opposite corner of the room, where a woman was waiting. With military precision Jahi made mental notes about the Foundation's newest staff member. Standing alone, she appeared aloof. In a navy-blue business suit, she was underdressed for the black-tie affair. He guessed that she was Ray's last minute fill-in. The drink she held looked like seltzer. She wasn't much on make-up or jewelry—in fact, nothing on her sparkled. She was plain with keen features, what his father would have described as a *handsome* woman. Petite but not cutesy. As he shifted his glance to avoid staring, her dark eyes caught his. She was not afraid to look at him.

"Jahi Khalfani, I'd like you to meet Zoie Taylor. Zoie is our new staff attorney," Milton said. "And this morning Zoie was elected the Foundation's new Board Secretary."

"Congratulations, Ms. Taylor," Jahi said, gesturing with a slight bow of his head. She had not extended her hand.

"Thank you, Mr. Khalfani."

"Zoie, Jahi here is one of our repeat grantees. He's done marvelous things for the homeless over at the Mahali Salaam Shelter."

Jahi could feel her surveying his dreadlocks. Women always seemed to be fascinated by his hair.

"Oh, yes, I remember reading about your work in our annual report," she said.

"It seems that Ms. Taylor has done her homework," Jahi said, turning to Milton.

"She's on the ball, all right. The Board took to her right away," said Milton, but then his attention shifted to someone across the crowded room. "I'll let you two get acquainted. I need to catch up with an old friend. See you at dinner."

The two stood silently and side by side as Milton's red top disappeared back into the crowd. Out of the corner of his eye, Jahi could see Zoie's fingers drumming against her glass. He checked his watch. Dinner was still thirty minutes off.

"Do you do this often? The cocktail parties, the banquets?" he asked.

"Not really. But I'm afraid I'm going to be doing this more than I expected." She sniffed as if she were getting a cold. "What about you?"

"I'm on a tight budget. I attend when Crayton or one of our other sponsors pays my way, and then I can rent a tux for half the price."

"I imagine these events don't jive with feeding and sheltering the homeless."

"What this place scrapes off the plates tonight could feed my Shelter's residents for several days. At least we've arranged for the untouched leftovers to go to our kitchen for tomorrow's meal."

"Glad to hear it," she said.

"The funds spent on this shindig could underwrite another shelter."

She turned and looked at him. "You're obviously passionate about you work. This must be awkward for you...I mean your being here."

Had he said too much? They had just met. He had to be careful.

"Ms. Taylor..."

"Please call me Zoie. 'Ms. Taylor' makes me sound like a schoolteacher."

"By all means, Zoie," He bit his lip. The name didn't fit her conservative dress. "Zoie, maybe one day you and I can bring the absurdity of it all to the attention of the dinner's sponsors."

"Is Crayton a sponsor?"

"Of course. And you're in a prominent position to effect change. It'll take some time to change that thinking. In the meantime I'm here to network with the people important to my project."

"Like who?"

"Well, like people from other organizations that represent the homeless."

"Like?"

"Other shelters in the DC area."

"Aren't they your competitors?"

"I'd like to think that we work cooperatively."

"But aren't you all vying for the same scarce grant dollars?"

"Aren't you the inquisitor!"

"Sorry," she said with a deep sigh. "I'm learning this whole corporate-charity thing. Charitable giving as an industry is very new for me."

Industry—she hit it right on the head, he thought.

"Questioning is the way I learn," she continued.

"The Socratic method, huh?"

"I guess so."

"Well, I'm glad you explained yourself. I was beginning to think I was on the witness stand. Does the Crayton Foundation realize it has hired a trial attorney?"

They both laughed. Her broad smile revealed a beautiful set of teeth.

Ah! That smile is her sparkle. "Well, I hope I can help," Jahi continued. "It's important to have informed members on the Foundation's Board. Now to answer your question about my network, Ms. Taylor—I mean *Zoie*—there are representatives here from all aspects of my business: private and government social service agencies that send us the clients, as well as the job banks and psychiatric and medical services to which we refer clients. Including drug programs."

"And you feed your clients and provide them a place to sleep?"

"In a nutshell, we try our best to keep them from dying."

"Oh," she said, looking into her glass. "I'd really like to understand more. Maybe I could have a tour of your operation."

"The Foundation folks came over in May."

"Sorry, that was before I started. Oh, I don't need anything special."

"Well, sure, a tour can be arranged. But tell me about yourself," he said. "How did you land at the Crayton Foundation?"

"Well, I was at a New York firm—Fairday and Winston. I don't suppose you've heard of them?"

"Can't say that I have," he answered, scratching his lip.

"The work was mostly administrative and dealt with corporate law. We handled the overflow cases from in-house attorneys. I was involved in a number of suits filed by our clients' own employees. Really dry, textbook stuff. I needed a change."

"And you think that charity board work is going to prove more exciting?"

"You say that as though you don't think it's possible."

"You see I'm biased. I prefer action to—pardon the term—paper pushing. I like to help people. I like to see it actually happen. I know we have to jump through the political hoops to get funding and all. Naturally, I do the political stuff so that the Shelter gets what it needs. But I'd rather leave fund raising to somebody else." He took a final sip from his glass.

She was following his every word and hadn't touched her own drink. "I'm hoping my part of this process will be interesting. And I'm hoping that I can make a difference. But I'd like to hear your story. Tell me, how did you start the Shelter?"

Jahi was about to give his canned speech—the one aimed at donors, the one that revealed his having been homeless in the past—when he felt a tap on his shoulder.

"Jahi, I thought that was you."

The woman standing next to him was molded into her gown. Her hair was pulled back from her tan face in an elegant bun. Her dress was a shade of mesmerizing purple, a color whose name he couldn't recall or maybe he didn't know. He was surprised.

"Why, Jahi, it hasn't been that long," she said in a sultry voice, probably deepened by drinks she'd had earlier in the evening.

"Lena!"

"That's better. I'm in no mood for rejection. Rejection can be a bitch. Isn't that right, Jahi," Lena said, rubbing her gown's heavy beadwork against his thigh.

The scene was awkward. Taking her cue from her nonintroduction, Zoie moved to make her exit. "Jahi, I'll see you later at our table."

"Wait, don't go," Lena said. She was now hanging on Jahi's arm. "Don't I know you?"

Zoie shrugged.

"No, really, your face is so familiar." Lena's face contorted while she searched her fuzzy memory bank.

"Lena, this is…"

"Shhhh, Jahi. Don't tell me. Just give me a second."

Jahi looked up at the ceiling, and Zoie sighed.

"Bingo! You're Zoie Taylor."

"You got me," said Zoie, who was actually surprised. This person knew her, but she was baffled.

"You don't remember me, do you? Lena…Lena Christian."

Zoie raised her brow. "Forgive me. I can't place you."

"Zoie's new in town," Jahi explained, trying to be helpful.

"New my ass!" Lena said. "We went to high school together. Woodrow Wilson."

Jahi turned to Zoie. "So you're a DC girl?"

"Yep. Born and raised. I left for college," said Zoie.

Jahi let that new information about Zoie sink in while continuing to slip from Lena's grip. Her preoccupation with an old classmate rather than him was just the opportunity he needed.

"We were in several classes together," said Lena, "gym and something else. We graduated the same year. We even attended the same church. Don't you remember?"

"It'll come back. I'm a little hazy tonight," Zoie answered.

"Listen, ladies, I see someone I need to talk to over there." Jahi was making his escape, but Lena was still clutching his arm. She whined. "Stay, Jahi. How often do I get to see you?"

Zoie rolled her eyes and sipped from her drink.

Lena turned her attention back to Zoie. "I remember you were one of the smartest kids in school. Jahi, this girl was "Ms. It's Academic." But didn't some guy beat you out for valedictorian? You had it, and then you lost it, or something crazy like that happened."

"It was a technicality," Zoie explained.

"Yeah, technically you didn't get it."

"Lena, Zoie was about to tell us the real story." Somehow Jahi managed to loosen Lena's hold. He wished Lena would disappear or, better still, he could disappear. But on second thought, he considered the risk of leaving Lena alone to spew venom about him at a key member of the Foundation's Board. Obviously, Lena had had a few too many. Who knew what she might say?

"I'm only saying what I know to be true," Lena insisted. I also heard you went off to Yale."

"Boston University," said Zoie, correcting her.

Jahi added, "Then she went to law school at—"

"Columbia," said Zoie.

"And now she's on the Crayton Foundation's Board," Jahi said. As soon as the words left his mouth, he was sorry. He knew this information only added fuel to Lena's sarcasm.

"Well, la dee da," Lena exclaimed. "I'm just a city reporter for the *Washington Times*. And you don't remember me. But Jahi here remembers me—don't you, baby? Jahi and I are products of local academics—UDC." She fiddled with the end of one of his long locks while stretching her hand with her wine glass behind her. "Jahi, you better watch out for this one. If she's the Zoie Taylor I remember, she's too smart for her own good."

Jahi surmised that Lena's words ranked as high school jealousy mixed with liquor. Still, he made a mental note of Lena's warning.

What transpired next was a bad dream on steroids. A hurrying waiter balancing a tray of refreshments sideswiped Lena's outstretched arm, sending her teetering on her stilettos. The waiter struggled to regain control of his heavy tray; in the process he stepped on the hem of Lena's gown. Battling gravity, Lena grabbed a fistful of Jahi's dreads, but instead of saving herself, she pulled Jahi to the floor along with her. Within seconds bystanders helped the two to their feet. The distressed waiter pleaded for mercy in broken English in at least two other languages and then ran for towels. The incident happened so quickly, and it appeared that only the people in the immediate vicinity even noticed.

A little stunned, hobbling on one heel, Lena circled the mess while scanning the floor for her missing shoe. A bystander retrieved the shoe for her.

In stone-faced disgust Jahi brushed greasy scallops wrapped in bacon from his tux. "Lena, are you okay?" he asked.

"Yeah, now that I've got my shoe back," she said. Miraculously the greasy food had missed her dress. "Some night, huh! I always thought we'd be together again, but not like this."

A few feet away, Jahi spotted Zoie. She'd dodged the whole mess. With a hand covering her mouth, it was clear that she was laughing.

"Jahi, are you all right?" said Zoie, managing to say the question between giggles, and tears rolling down her cheek. "I wish I had a camera. It all happened so fast. She had you in an incredible headlock."

"Well, Ms. Taylor, I'm glad you enjoyed it." Jahi assessed the damage to his shirt. "As you can see, I've already had my dinner."

"But that was just the appetizer," Zoie said in a new round of giggles.

He didn't smile. "Please give my apologies to Milton and the other Crayton folks. I'm sure you'll provide them with the full account of this evening's events."

Zoie opened her mouth to say something, but he didn't wait to hear her words. He turned and walked away.

CHAPTER 6

THE LIFE AND DEATH TEST

The meeting of the Crayton Foundation's Board was into its third hour. And they were still fifty thousand over budget. Zoie crossed her legs and rubbed her hands under the table. The attention of the seven-member Board was fading fast. Only Dylan Ross and Ray Gaddis were fully engaged.

"Dylan, I do understand your point about the Village Green Reading Program," Ray said, his face a little red, his mouth still locked in a forced smile. "I wish we could give money to every program. But I'm questioning the wisdom of funding a start-up program at the expense of things that we know work already."

"You mean the Shelter's program?" Dylan Ross said. He was an entrepreneur in the Internet world. He'd been on the Board just six months and was still enthusiastic about his role.

"Well, yes," Ray responded.

"We keep giving that place more money," Dylan said emphatically. "Wasn't it during the last meeting that we voted to shift our focus to children at risk?"

Several of the Board members nodded.

"Dylan, I think what Ray is saying is let's not make one of our most successful grantees suffer because of our philosophical move." It was Hilda Kaufman, a Crayton Industries' vice president Hilda was in her third term on the Foundation's Board.

"Our funding cap is identical to last year. If we're serious about changing our charitable focus, something's got to give. Someone's program has to get less," said Dylan, leaning back and twiddling his thumbs in his lap.

Zoie bit her bottom lip as she gauged the group's reactions. The disengaged members were either slouched in their chairs or doodling. Ray, the Board's chair, sat with curled lips, stroking the loose skin on this throat.

Keith Pastori, by all accounts the lowest-ranking member of the group, spoke up. "The Shelter aids homeless children. That fits our new theme."

"Keith, dear, you missed the tour," Hilda said, fingering a strand of her platinum hair. "Their mission is strictly homeless adults—of which ninety percent are men."

"Oh! That doesn't fit the new profile," Keith said, acknowledging his error.

"Bingo!" Dylan said, his blue eyes sending off sparks. There was a loud silence. He turned to Zoie. "What's your opinion on this? Should we continue to fund existing grantees who don't fit the direction we want to head?"

Zoie took a deep breath. She'd hoped to make it through this second Board meeting as the board secretary by staying on the periphery—listening, observing, and *not* making enemies. She glanced at Ray, whose lips were still curled.

"Well, it's a difficult choice," she started, waiting for the right words. "I think cutting Mahali Salaam's grant might be a dangerous move." She was now the center of attention.

"Dangerous? How so?" Dylan asked.

"It could put more homeless back on the streets this winter. By comparison I just don't see anything that compelling or urgent in the reading program."

Ray broke out in a broad smile and banged his palm on the table. "Exactly! That's exactly what I've been getting at. The decision we make today may affect life and death. Our zealousness for this new direction could cost lives. When and if we cut Mahali's funding, they'll need adequate notice. Time to seek replacement funds. They depend on us."

Other members nodded their heads in agreement.

"Well...I've said my piece," Dylan sighed. "I guess the reading program doesn't stand up to the 'life and death' test—if that's the measure we're using."

"And neither does the senior's day-care center," Hilda added. "That should go."

"By my count we're still over by ten thousand—that is, unless someone here wants to make a private donation?" The voice was coming from Lloyd Story, a grocery-chain executive. His mention of private donations caused the others to mumble, bow their heads, and shuffle papers.

"Lloyd, don't worry. I'll take care of it. I'll shave a few dollars from each grant," Ray said. There were no objections. "Now I'd like to close this with a vote. All in favor of the slate of proposed grantees, with the adjusted amounts we just discussed."

Zoie was surprised to see Dylan raise his hand with the others.

"Great. It's unanimous," Ray said. "Lunch is being served in the dining room. We'll resume at one thirty."

"Thank God," Hilda said. "I didn't think my bladder was going to make it."

"Don't forget that this afternoon we'll discuss our new PR campaign," Ray called after them, as they exited.

"Why bother?" Dylan said. He had hung back and was fumbling with his cell phone. "Ray, how can we put out public-service announcements touting our support for children when that's not where we've directed the bulk of the Foundation's grants?"

43

"Dylan, Dylan, I understand your frustration. Transition takes time. We can't rush these things," Ray said. "The PR campaign is for the future."

Avoiding the conversation, Zoie brushed by the two men and headed to her office. Milton Page, though not a Board member, had sat in on the meeting. He caught her in the hall.

"Excellent save, Zoie," said Milton, grimacing. "Ole Ray was about to bust a gut."

"He did look a little 'pee o'd," she said.

"Ray's not accustomed to being challenged on his grant recommendations."

"Really, why not?"

"The Board members are usually comfortable with his judgment. They come for lunch, listen to his speeches, get their little stipends, and then go home."

"So we're supposed to be a rubber stamp, huh?" she asked.

"No, not like that. Ray briefs everyone before the meeting and gets buy-in," Milton explained.

"Well, he didn't talk to me. And I doubt he got to Dylan."

"Now, Zoie, you're a Crayton employee. I guess you're supposed to understand the legwork that goes into our recommendations and our reviewing and investigating applicants." Then Milton's voice dropped to a whisper. "The Board members are lazy. You saw how unprepared they were. Nobody even read the material we sent them."

"I bet Dylan Ross read his packet. Based on what he was saying, I thought he'd abstain."

"But *you* stopped that. You were brilliant. 'Life and death,'" Milton said, waving a finger as though he were conducting a mini-symphony.

"Those, my friend, were *not* my words," Zoie retorted.

"No, but you led Ray and then Dylan right to them. Brilliant! Did Ray thank you?"

"No, but…"

"Don't worry. He will."

Milton left her standing in the hall. She was mentally replaying the boardroom scene. Zoie wasn't sure that she wanted credit for scuttling the fledgling reading program or for contributing to the demise of the seniors' day care. As a mother and a granddaughter, she could relate to those programs. But homelessness, the desperation of living on the street, was something foreign.

Zoie reached into her pocket for the ladies' room key. She'd made a habit of stopping by the spot where the homeless men who'd saved her life hung out to leave small donations. She felt the latest small folded paper that Simon had thrust at her just that morning. She unfolded it. It read, "You must be wary of what you say when life and death is the game you play."

Of course this is another fluke. A coincidence. But even if she'd read its message earlier, she wouldn't have changed a thing she'd said or done that day. "Too weird," she said, stuffing the paper back into her pocket.

Coming out of the ladies' room, she ran into Ray Gaddis. "Zoie, I'm glad I caught you." He was a head taller than she was, but then most men were. "Thank you for your support with the Board, just now." His all-purpose plastic smile had returned.

"No problem. Your arguments made sense."

"I'm glad you could see that. The Board needs to understand. Disrupting the Shelter's funding could send the place into a tailspin. Replacement money for nonprofits is hard to come by, with government cutbacks and all."

"Yes, it'll be difficult for the Shelter as we transition," she said.

"Well, yes." He paused and took on a more serious air. "For now let's assume that *somehow* we'll continue to support Mahali. We'll have to figure out a way to preserve their grant in the next round. Are you with me?"

His question surprised her. "I guess...I really don't know much about the place." What else could she say?

"That's easily solved. Call Jahi Khalfani. He'll arrange a tour of the Shelter. You'll be up to speed in no time."

"I'll do that." With a hand in her pocket, she crushed the strip of paper with its warning.

"Khalfani can be a little bullheaded, but you'll find that he's very accommodating when it comes to the Foundation." Ray stroked his neck and then looked at his watch. "I've got to go spend quality time with these people," he said, referring to the Board members. "See you at lunch, but remember to keep thinking about a strategy." He walked away.

Zoie's expression was blank. *A strategy?* What had she gotten herself into?

CHAPTER 7
NOT ENOUGH LOVE

Frances Woods lay in her bed. Shadows crossed her room as the moon tried to hide behind the trees outside her window. She sighed with relief. She'd had another coughing spell. Now her breath was finally calm, and Gabe was on her mind again.

Thoughts of Gabe had been vivid in recent days. His image had been clear. The scene of the day she told him she was leaving played in her head. His eyes had a glow, a flickering light that sparkled like a firecracker at a summer fair when he was excited. They shimmered like moonlight on a river when he was deep in thought. On that day his eyes were deep, dark, and still. It was as though he knew what she was going to tell him before the words found her mouth. How would she break the news? How could she break his heart as well as her own?

"What's wrong, Francee?"

"Gabe," she'd sputtered, her voice weak, her eyes searching for a place to settle on the floor, rather than looking into his. "I'm going away."

"I knew something bad was coming," he said, shaking his head.

She cried. She'd figured that she could tell him without tears, but she hadn't understood how much she would miss him until then. He was a part of her heart.

"Gabe, I wanted to tell you before someone else did."

"Where you goin'?"

"Baltimore," she sighed. "To live with a cousin."

"Why? I don't understand."

"Gabe, it's complicated."

"It don't have to be complicated. Francee, I got a job now, over at Tuck's Cabinets. I wanted to tell you. It don't pay much, not while I'm an apprentice. But it will later. Carpentry pays good. Folks always need a good carpenter, especially a cabinetmaker."

"That's not it, Gabe."

"Francee, let me finish. After a year or two, we can get married. I'll save up. Do some extra work on the side."

She hadn't planned to tell him about the seed growing inside of her. It didn't seem fair, now that her parents were sending her away from prying eyes and snickering. But the child inside of her had a mind of its own. It wanted to be recognized. Somehow it reached beyond her will and used her mouth to make the announcement.

"Gabe, I'm going to have a baby."

There—she'd said it. She'd told him and had not turned to dust.

He grabbed her hands and kissed her palms; then he gently stroked her face with one of his big hands. He was quiet, but his tears spoke the words of his heart. For a second, he even smiled. Then that solemn stare returned, as if he'd just realized that he wouldn't be allowed to be a father.

"It's our child I'm having."

"I know that, Francee."

"So you see our getting married in one or two years, well, would be too late."

"Francee, we'll marry sooner. I'll do anything. I'll work two jobs. We can live in Luckit at my Aunt Ruth's. She's got an extra room behind the kitchen. She wouldn't charge much."

The truth was that even two years was too soon. *Any time was too soon.* Her parents would never have agreed to her union with a man like Gabe, a man with skin as smooth and dark as her mother's mahogany table. Closing her eyes, she bit her lip to feel the pain. There was no point in telling him the extent of her parents' disapproval, no use adding that rusty nail. He needn't know the whole truth of it. But then maybe deep down he already understood.

"Gabe, don't you see? That won't work. I mean to go to college. I mean to be a teacher. Remember, just as I talked about."

"God, Francee! You ain't giving me a chance. I thought you loved me."

What did she know about love? Only that she couldn't sleep thinking about their next meeting. Only that her mind wandered, causing her to put salt in the sugar jar and the cornmeal in the flour bin. At eighteen she had kissed only one other boy and only because of a dare. What did she know about love when she couldn't think straight half the time and with a baby pushing on her insides, making her queasy, sleepy, and cross?

Her father made his pronouncement, after church. "You're going to Cousin Mabel's up in Baltimore—*no ifs, ands, or buts.* No daughter of mine is going to parade around town flaunting a belly." His pale skin, with its ruddy sun blotches, was brick red from the heat of his anger. Wisps of the hair on his balding head stood erect like fur on a mad dog. "Cousin Mabel will take good care of you. I'll send money. You have to understand, Frances, we're not deserting you."

No matter his words, to Frances Woods his edict felt like desertion. She dared not say a word. Her father could be loose with his hands. She looked to her mother, who'd been quiet through her father's tirade. She could see her mother's acceptance. Celia Moore never questioned her husband's judgment.

"This is for your own good. Cousin Mabel will introduce you to some decent fellow." *Decent* was her father's code word for "light skinned, preferably college educated." After all, Joseph Moore, of the Moores of Ricetown, principal of Ricetown Colored School—thank you very much—had a position in the community to uphold.

Frances Woods tried to move her position in the bed. A pain shot through her hip as intense as the day of her fall. She lay still, afraid to move again, not wanting to call Queen, not wanting to end her reverie. The pain gripped her leg. She tried to ignore it. She let her mind drift again. She couldn't seem to stay in the here and now. Thoughts of Gabe—sweet, though sad—somehow dulled the pain. The pain seemed to transfer from her legs and her hip to her heart, a heart that had borne a secret pain all these years.

She could hear Gabe's words again. "God, Francee! You're not giving me a chance to make this right. I mean to take care of you and the child."

He promised to come to Baltimore to be with her. After he put some money together, he would catch up. She tried to dissuade him, though she never actually said, "No, don't come."

"I thought you loved me." Those words haunted her when everything was still and she could hear her own heartbeat. "I thought you loved me," he said again, between the beats, his voice soft, not angry, though he had every right to be.

"Gabe, I do love you," she answered. What she didn't say was, *I love you but not enough to run away with you. Not enough to live in the spare room behind your aunt's kitchen, down in Luckit. Not enough to disobey my father or to give up my dream of becoming a teacher, even if that dream is now second to holding the child inside me.*

Frances Woods's leg cramped. "Damn it." The leg had a mind of its own. When she wanted to walk, the leg acted as if it belonged to someone else, but when the leg wanted to hurt, the pain was all hers. Grunting, she pushed herself up on her elbows, reached down, and pushed her leg to the side until it fell in flat on the bed. She massaged her upper thigh, the only part of her leg she could reach. Thankfully, the cramp passed. Exhausted, she fell back on her high pillows.

Only God could judge her. Things were complicated back in the good ole days. They just seemed to be simpler since no one talked about the complications. It wasn't polite. She always felt guilty that she hadn't loved Gabe enough or given him the chance to make things right, the chance that he had asked for.

She had written him several times and given him Cousin Mabel's address in Baltimore. Deep in her heart of hearts, she expected him to come for her or at least to hear from him, especially after the letter in which she told him that she had given birth to a girl. "Dear Gabe," she wrote. "The child is here. Her name is Laurel. She has your eyes." In that same letter, she mentioned that she had met a kind gentleman from DC, a Howard University graduate. He wanted to marry her, to help her with the child, and even to help her get a degree from DC's Teachers College.

Her dear Calvin Woods, her savoir, treated Laurel as his own, though folks wondered how Laurel came to have her wonderful dark cinnamon complexion when both of her parents were so light. "Who does she favor?" they'd ask, expecting to hear a convoluted story, like the one most people told about their Cherokee ancestry, their white grandfathers, and the like.

Calvin, a man of few words, put an end to all their inquiries. "My people have more color than I do," he'd tell them, pointing to his pale skin. "Guess not as many rapes in that part of the family."

Frances Woods would stifle a laugh and beam with pride. Who couldn't love Calvin Woods? Over time she'd come to love him. That love was different than what she had felt for Gabe. But it was still love; she was sure of that.

The last time she set eyes on Gabe was at the Ricetown rail station. Her parents were putting her on the train. She could see Gabe standing behind the post at the end of the platform, that cap he always wore shading his eyes. He stayed at the end of the platform, away from her family. For a moment she thought he might come forward, but he didn't. As the train pulled away, she hung at the window. Their eyes met for a second. And that was it.

She was the one that left. She was the one who didn't love him enough to runaway. "Laurel had your eyes, dear Gabe. Wherever you are. Laurel had your eyes. Zoie, her daughter, has them too. Oh, I wish you could see them. If you've left this earth, I hope Laurel is with you."

"Mrs. Woods," Queen called from downstairs, "Zoie is here."

CHAPTER 8

THE CHOICE: SPIKE LEE OR YOUR NOSE

Zoie loved the Brandywine house, the house of her child-hood. Looking at it now, she thought the staircase some-how looked less grand than it had through her child eyes, its dark banisters not as wide, the ascent to the landing not as steep. The staircase landing once served as Zoie's official playhouse. It was better than a tree house, where the rain and the caterpillars could interfere with a tea party. Better than the dark crawl space under the lattice on the side of the house, with its worms and spider nests. That landing had been her castle, a place where she had spent hours humming nonsensical tunes, arranging her dolls neatly atop the upholstered bench, or sprawling across it while reading a favorite book. As a child she could wedge her-self under that bench and become hidden from adult view. The sound of her mother's voice was still clear. "Zoie! Zoie! You can hide if you want to. You're still going to clean your room—even if it takes until midnight."

Her grandmother's house was a place of simpler times, though her father's leaving left a deep and complex scar on the child who had played on those stairs. Reeling from the news about Elliot, Zoie the child was coming home to Grandma for answers. Elliot married? Expecting a child? Wasn't her daughter good enough for him?

Tonight Zoie wanted to curl up, to force her body under that bench, and to hide from the world. Being thirty-six, her body wouldn't fit.

"Zoie, we weren't expecting you," Queen said, coming from the kitchen. The big woman wiped her hands on her dishtowel and grinned. Queen always seemed pleasant enough. Zoie couldn't understand why there was such a rift between her grandmother and this woman, who seemed so caring.

"Hope I didn't alarm you."

"I guessed it was you. You're the only other one with a key. If you'd been somebody else, I'da cracked you on the head." Queen pointed to a baseball bat handle rising above the rim of its home—the umbrella stand.

"Oh, I should've called. I decided I needed to see her," Zoie said, handing Queen a bag with a couple of heavy bottles.

Queen peered into the bag. "Ah! Fruit juice. She likes good juice. Not too sweet."

"How's she doing?"

"You know. So so. She's a little depressed."

"Depressed about what?"

"Just moody, that's all. She gets that way," Queen explained. "Seeing you will do her good."

"Seeing her will do *me* good." After that dreadful phone call to Ohio and three hours sitting on the floor of her dark kitchen, Zoie needed to talk. She'd tried her friend Tina first, but Tina had gone incommunicado. Grandma was her next best choice.

"Go on up," Queen said. "She's awake. I tell you she'll be glad to see you."

Halfway up the stairs, Zoie's nose zeroed in on the faint scent of disinfectant. The scent grew stronger as she entered her grandmother's dark room. In the room, lit only by moonlight, she could make out part of her grandmother's profile. The older woman was sitting up in bed, propped by thick pillows, her head tilting toward the window.

"Grandma, what are you doing here in the dark?"

"Thinking."

"Thinking about what?"

"Nothing in particular. At my age thinking is about all a body can do...thinking and watching that boob tube." The television sat dark atop the bureau.

"Anything worth watching tonight?"

"Nah. It's all violence. I can't stand all that violence."

"Grandma, you should get cable."

"What for? To pay to see more shooting and killing?"

Zoie tried another tact. "What about reading? You love to read."

"I can't seem to follow a book these days. My eyes don't want to cooperate."

"Some light might help," Zoie said, groping for the switch under the shade of a tall pole lamp.

For the first time since Zoie entered the room, her grandmother faced her. "Don't go turning on the light. The dark is just fine."

"Okay. Okay." *Perhaps tonight's visit was a bad idea.* Now that Zoie was there, she was obliged to stay for a while. "Grandma, how are you feeling?"

"I'm well enough. I just have to stop this hacking." Her grandmother again gazed out the window, mesmerized by the dark sky, as if searching for something. Maybe a shooting star.

When the old woman turned again, Zoie's eyes had adjusted enough to make out her grandmother's keen features, still padded by soft cream-colored skin, which looked gray and shadowy in the dim moonlight.

"Zo, is this the weekend? I can't tell anymore." For just a moment, her grandmother sounded unsure, fragile, like someone truly lost.

"No, Grandma. It's only Wednesday."

"Wednesday, huh. What brings you over this way on a weeknight?"

"You, Grandma."

"Humph!" Her edge was back. Once again her grandmother turned to the sky, to whatever distant star she was waiting to see.

"Grandma!"

"Guess Queen told you to come. Told you I was on my death bed, didn't she?"

"No. In fact, Queen said you were doing fine."

"Now there's another lie. That woman either has me up dancing or lying in the grave."

Zoie threw up her hands. "I wish you wouldn't talk that way." She positioned herself to settle on the bed, careful not to sit on her grandmother's leg.

"Unexpected visit, huh? That means something's wrong."

"I need your advice."

"Umm, sounds ominous."

"Surreal is more like it."

"Okay, give it to me." Frances Woods pushed herself up with her elbows and relaxed into her pillows.

Zoie searched for the words. It would be the first telling of the story. Maybe the Ohio phone call had been a dream. If saying the words out loud made it real, she'd be better off keeping her mouth shut. Finally, she blurted, "That bastard Elliot showed up in Ohio to see Nikki."

"Lord, the Phoenix has risen." One of the old woman's hands flew to her mouth to stifle any further utterance. Her eyes glowed like a sponge that had absorbed what little light there was in the room.

"Phoenix? Phoenix, my ass," Zoie said in disgust. "Why are you talking about Elliot as if he were some second coming? You hated Elliot."

"Honey, how many times have I told you that hate takes too much energy?" Frances Woods coughed. "I never said I hated him—never even said I disliked him. He could have washed that curly hair of his more often, though." She made herself laugh and triggered more coughing. Grabbing a handful of tissues from a nearby box, she covered her mouth. Her action only muffled the sound of the string of coughs that followed.

"Grandma, anything I can do?"

Frances Woods waved a tissue to indicate no, then clutched another tissue to her mouth.

Dismayed, Zoie could only wait and watch as her grandmother settled down. After a few minutes, the old woman could take a long, slow breath. When she began to speak again, it was in a whisper. "Zo, honey, I just said I didn't think that guy was right for you."

"You hardly knew him."

"True. True enough. I don't have to know a person to pick up on their vibe. And what I picked up was that your vibe and his vibe didn't mesh."

"I wish you'd said something back then. Told me to watch out."

"Zo, you wouldn't have listened. You were all starry eyed. Anyway, don't you remember? During the time you were with him, your mother got sick."

The mention of her mother imposed a moment's quiet.

"Anyway, if you two hadn't hooked up, you wouldn't have Nikki."

Life without Nikki was too bleak for Zoie to consider. Nikki was the one good thing that came from it all. "He's got some nerve, showing up to see his daughter," Zoie said, her venom thick.

"Thank God he's got nerve."

"Grandma, you don't see the wrong in this? He abandoned her."

"Wrong? No. I admit it is awkward. Yeah, awkward, for sure. But wrong? That's a judgment I'll leave to the man upstairs."

"Grandma, I don't believe you." Zoie slapped her thighs so hard the bed shook. She jumped up and paced the dark room like a caged animal.

"Zoie, calm down. You have to let go of this rage. If you don't, it will eat you up."

"I told Elliot's mother that I was coming to get Nikki this weekend."

"I thought you arranged for Nikki to stay for the summer."

"That was the plan. But after this…how can I let her stay there?"

"Now I guess Elliot's parents are wrong too?"

"They let this happen." Zoie stopped pacing to emphasize her statement.

"What are they supposed to do?" Her grandmother's voice was weak. To hear her Zoie moved closer, settling on the bed again. "Whatever else they may feel about the situation, Elliot *is* their son."

"That's what Celeste said."

"Zoie, what's bringing Nikki home now going to prove? That you're still angry because five years ago…"

"Six."

"How many ever years ago." Frances Woods coughed. "Elliot acted totally immature."

"Immature! He's an asshole!"

"I prefer fool."

"Humph!"

"You must still have feelings for him. Otherwise, you wouldn't be so angry."

"Grandma, I don't have feelings for Elliot. Elliot's married. They're expecting a child."

"Oh, you didn't tell me that part." Her grandmother's voice was a high-pitched whisper of disbelief.

"That's not why I want to bring Nikki home."

"So you're punishing the child for seeing her father?" her grandmother asked. "Don't you think she has the right to know him?"

"Why does this always come back to me? Why am I the villain?"

"Honey, you're not a villain, but you have the power to make this a better situation. You're intelligent, and quiet as kept, you've got a heart, a good heart. Though it's hard to tell sometimes since it's trapped under your law books."

"Gee, thanks." Zoie sucked her teeth.

"Zo, I'm not telling you anything you don't already know."

"So what should I do?"

"You're looking for me to tell you what to do. You're a grown woman. Do what your conscience tells you."

"*Grandma*," Zoie whined.

"You know what you have to do. You knew before you came over here. Do the right thing. Zoie, don't be so proud. Don't cut off your nose to spite that pretty face."

All the talking triggered more coughs. Zoie gave her grandmother some water and called out for Queen. Queen arrived with a concoction of tea and honey. Her grandmother took a few sips, then collapsed into her high pillows. When the spasm subsided, Zoie brushed her grandmother's hair from her clammy forehead and kissed her brow.

Concerned by her grandmother's spasm, Zoie forgot to think about Elliot. On the way home in a cab, her grandmother's words came back. "Do the right thing." Wasn't that the name of the

Spike Lee movie? What was the right thing, anyway? Right, according to her grandmother, might not be right for her and Nikki. How could her grandmother defend Elliot? No matter what her grandmother had said, Elliot was an asshole.

Do the right thing, huh? She was supposed to take the high ground, whatever that was. Even as she considered it, trying to reach that place and leaving her ego behind were not going to happen. The hurt he had caused her wouldn't let go.

"Zoie, don't be so proud. Don't you cut off your nose to spite that pretty face," her grandmother had said. Those words appealed to Zoie's sense of logic. As a practical matter, she hadn't arranged for any summer day care in DC. At the moment she had zilch. Bringing Nikki back early from Ohio would create a major problem: what would she do with Nikki until she found appropriate care? Making good on her promise to Celeste to come get Nikki meant that Zoie would have to stay home from work until she found someone to care for her child. If that wasn't "biting off her nose," she didn't know what was.

By the time the cab pulled up in front of her building, Zoie's head felt like a water balloon about to explode. Eyes closed, she didn't even notice that the car had stopped moving.

"Is this it, lady?" the driver asked.

"Oh, yeah, this is it."

She paid the driver and decided to deal with her new trauma drama in the morning.

CHAPTER 9
I APOLOGIZE—WELL, SORT OF

Zoie started the office copier, her mind drifting between the morning's major events: the pseudo-apologetic call to Celeste Benjamin and the mental preparation for her afternoon meeting with a representative of Trinity Elder Day Care. The copier's dull hum intensified her semi-stupor.

That morning she called Celeste Benjamin. "Celeste, I've changed my mind. I'm not coming to get Nikki this weekend."

"Oh!" said Celeste. "Zoie, are you sure? The other night you sounded so *definite*." Celeste was not her usual Saccharin sweet self.

"Yes, I've had a change of mind." Indeed, Zoie's decision to let Nikki stay the remainder of the summer in Ohio was a change of *mind*, not *heart*. "You said Elliot was leaving today."

"That's right. They're leaving in a couple of hours." Celeste wasn't even trying to make conversation. She wasn't going to make this easy.

"Fine then. Nikki can stay." There was an uncomfortable silence. "That is, if you'll still have her."

"Of course Nikki can stay. We're delighted that you've changed your mind." Celeste's voice was still cold but had hints of cracks in the ice. At least Celeste wasn't asking why Zoie had changed her mind.

"Did you say anything to Nikki? About coming home early?" Zoie asked.

"No. I was waiting for your call."

"Good. Nikki sounds like she's having a good time there." That was the most concession that Zoie was going to give the woman. *I have to get along with this woman*, Zoie thought. *This woman is taking care of my child.*

"She's having fun. Do you want to talk to her?"

Suddenly Zoie remembered the whole puppy issue. She envisioned the puppy trailing behind her daughter as if it already belonged to her. And she envisioned it pooping on her living-room rug. Nikki would surely pressure her for an answer about bringing the dog home. Not prepared to deliver the bad news, Zoie could only stall. *Please. No more drama. The dog question will have to wait.*

"That's okay, Celeste. Don't get Nikki now. I'll call her tonight."

The conversation had gone quickly. Zoie had managed to keep her voice calm, making no mention of Elliot's wife or expectant child. It had been awkward, as far as awkward things go, but Zoie was satisfied. Upon hanging up she breathed a long sigh of relief.

Zoie added paper to the copier tray. The machine started its second round. The Trinity rep was coming at 1:00 p.m., leaving her a little over an hour to do her research. From what she knew, the Trinity issue seemed straightforward. Trinity, a former grantee, had continued to cite the Crayton Foundation as one of its major sponsors on its brochures long after Crayton had severed ties with the program.

"We don't need that kind of negative publicity," Ray had ranted, referring to Trinity's battle with the IRS. Trinity was about to lose its most valuable asset—its nonprofit status. "I want the Foundation's name off anything to do with Trinity."

Was this a case of negligence or simply an organization's failure to update its media material? Stupidity, maybe. But stupidity wasn't the same as fraud. At 1:00 p.m. she'd find out. *This won't be difficult,* she thought as she read the top page of the stack of documents, while rounding the corner and heading to her office.

Combat boots were the last things she remembered before the collision. Head first she went full contact into his chest, the smack knocking her back, shaking loose the top layer of her documents. Dazed and embarrassed, she looked up to find none other than Jahi Khalfani.

"What are doing here?" she asked, her tone indignant.

"Why, Ms. Taylor, is this place off limits to the likes of me?"

"No. No. I'm sorry. It's just that I...I didn't expect to run into you."

"But you did...*literally.*" He smiled, seeming self-satisfied. "Please, no more accidents. Our meetings are becoming dangerous." He picked up her fallen documents and laid them on the stack in her arms. "Good thing it wasn't coffee."

"I'm sorry. I should pay attention. But why are you here?" she asked, gathering her wits.

"Oh, the questions again." He waited a second before answering. "If you must know, I'm here to sign some papers."

She wanted to ask which papers, but having been called to task for her inquiring mind (or, as some called it, her grand inquisitor style), she suppressed the urge. "I was going to call you."

"*Really.* Is there something we need to talk about?"

"Yes. But first I'd like to apologize for my awful behavior at the charity dinner last week."

"Oh, that," he said, rolling his eyes and sighing. "That was quite an evening. I'm happy to have provided you with some entertainment." He bowed his head in jest.

Zoie smiled. The comic scene at the reception had provided a good laugh. Even now the thought of it—Jahi and his lady friend, both dressed in their finest, sprawled on the floor, drenched in greasy food and booze—still tickled her funny bone but made her feel guilty.

"Don't make fun of other people's misfortunes," her grandmother told her long ago, when she laughed at her cousin Ralph, who was being spanked on his bare bottom. That happened when she was six or seven. But her grandmother's warning voice had stuck with her. Having the self-control to obey it was a different story.

"Obviously, the entertainment continues," Jahi said, reacting to her expression of amusement, the rise of color in her high cheeks.

Zoie bit her bottom lip and fought to stifle any laugh that might follow. "I'm sorry. You must think I'm terrible."

He shrugged. "Don't be so hard on yourself, Ms. Taylor. And, please, no more apologies. I don't know what I'll do if you apologize to me one more time."

She didn't know how she'd gotten there, but she had—that uncomfortable apology zone, the one brought on by continuing to do or say the wrong things, better known as "putting one's foot in one's mouth." She was about to say *sorry* yet again but caught herself. "Remember, you can call me Zoie."

"Right, Zoie. You told me that last week. Everything got washed away in that disaster."

They laughed.

"Zoie." Her name somehow sounded different when he said it, as if the name she'd always thought as cutesy, playful, and childish became serious, substantial, and womanly when spoken from his mouth.

"How can I make it up to you?" she asked.

"There's nothing to make up. That night wasn't my night. Bad karma, I guess," he said, sighing.

"Was your *lady* friend the 'bad karma'?"

"You mean Lena? Lena Christian? Not at all."

Zoie smirked and looked away.

"Yes, Lena is a lady and just a friend," he continued, "albeit, a friend who had too much to drink that night."

"Seems your friend is also my former classmate."

"True. And it appears she has some fond memories of you," he added.

"Look, I don't want to get into your business. But it's obvious that Lena thinks your relationship is more than a friendship."

"Well, Zoie, since you *don't* want to get into my business, we'll just leave that alone."

"Right," she said, shutting her mouth as tightly as she could. An awkward silence followed, a time warp in which Zoie became aware of the office's background noises: telephones ringing, printers chugging, and the elevator's bell dinging. How could she be so stupid? What made her say that about Lena? It was unprofessional. She wished that she could escape or melt into the floor like the witch in the *Wizard of Oz*. She'd managed to not say sorry again, though this latest faux pas screamed for an apology.

Why was she doing this? Something about Jahi made her feel uncomfortable. Somehow her sense of confidence—the rudder that always stabilized her in rough corporate waters—had gone missing. This was not a corporate situation. She was at a loss for words. Her usual quick comebacks were on a hiatus. Whatever was coming out of her mouth was coming out wrong.

"Ms. Taylor—I mean Zoie—was the other night's fiasco what you wanted to talk to me about?" Jahi asked, his tone more serious.

She needed to ask for a tour of Mahali Salaam. Asking for the tour shouldn't be such a big deal. "Yes, the apology part, but…"

Just then Regina walked by. Her mouth was agape, and the younger woman's eyes gave Jahi a once-over. It was a shameless sexual exchange, like behavior attributed to some men on the street, minus the catcalls.

"You're Jahi Khalfani, aren't you?" Regina asked, ignoring the fact that she'd just interrupted her boss's conversation. "I've seen your name on documents around here, and I've seen you in the paper and on TV."

"Regina Bullock, meet Jahi Khalfani," Zoie said, trying to salvage some dignity after witnessing the shameful display. Her irritation with the young woman was apparent.

Like a princess at a ball, Regina extended her hand.

"Hello, Regina," Jahi said. He held her hand between his hands as if caressing a small bird, while staring admiringly into the young woman's eyes.

Regina, the temptress, had been tamed. She blushed and giggled like a schoolgirl.

Not cool, girlfriend. Not cool at all, Zoie thought, observing the pair. Hopefully, Regina was putting on an act. This streetwise young woman couldn't have been less subtle. Zoie wondered when she had missed the news flash declaring that Jahi Khalfani had rock-star status.

"Regina!" said Zoie, an edge to her voice. "Mr. Khalfani and I need to talk business."

"Oh, goodness! Did I interrupt? My bad." Still blushing, Regina backed away and, in doing so, almost collided with the watercooler. Regina turned and moved down the hall, her hips swaying in what Zoie was sure was the most sensuous walk the young woman could muster. Regina peeked back and gave the two a little wave. Incredulous, Zoie waited until Regina was out of sight to resume the conversation.

Zoie spoke first. "Jahi, sorry about that."

"There you go again. You have no control over that woman."

"Okay, okay, I'll stop apologizing for anything or anybody. But I do have a question," Zoie said. "Do you always have that effect on women?"

Jahi blushed. This time he was the one at a loss for words. But then he spoke. His voice was low and sexy, and his eyes gazed unflinchingly into Zoie's. "Obviously, not all women."

The cell phone attached to Zoie's hip played its familiar baroque fugue, a tune out of date with the pop downloads many people were using. Zoie was glad for the interruption.

Zoie identified her caller: Tina. She was probably returning last night's distress call about Elliot. It took her only a second to look at her phone, but that second was all it took for Jahi to disappear. She caught a glimpse of him turning the corner that led to the Foundation's other wing, the wing where Ray's office was located.

Twenty minutes later Regina stopped by Zoie's office. Zoie was trying to put the latest scene with Jahi behind her. She needed to concentrate on the stack of papers in front of her.

"Need anything?" Regina asked. "I'm headed to lunch. I could bring you back something."

"No. I'll step out after my meeting."

"Okay."

"Regina, what was that all about out there?"

"What?" said the young woman, feigning innocence.

"That thing with you and Jahi Khalfani."

"Oh, that." Regina was glowing. "He's hot—that's all. Reminds me of Eric Benet. You know, like Halle Berry's ex, only taller with more muscle."

"Girl, you're ridiculous," Zoie responded, rolling her eyes.

"Don't tell me he doesn't do anything for you?"

"Is he still around?" Zoie said, shifting the conversation. "We didn't finish our business."

"Nope. Picked up his check from Marge and took off."

"What check?"

"Ray authorized an advance on the Shelter's grant," Regina explained. "I guess they were running low on funds."

"Does that happen often? I mean grantees getting advances?" Zoie asked with a raised brow.

"Not really. They know they have to wait until later in the month. It's not like the Shelter's getting anything additional. They're just getting their money sooner."

Zoie thought about what Regina said. Certainly it was compassionate to give an early allocation to the Shelter if it needed the money to maintain smooth operations. After all, the Board had approved its funds. The rest was administrative red tape. But anything that smacked of special treatment, for whatever reason, bothered her. It exposed the Foundation to possible complaints. Though the chances that a grantee would complain—in essence, "bite the hand that feeds it"—were slim. She was sure that if other grantees knew that it was possible to request funds sooner, there would be a run on the place. It was prudent to stick to the published-awards schedule to avoid any criticism. To avoid possible lawsuits.

"Regina, when you get back from lunch, I need you to make an appointment for me."

"Shoot."

"I'll give you the details when you get back, but I need a tour of Mahali Salaam."

"You're going to Jahi Khalfani's place?" Regina asked with excited interest.

"Ray wants me to see it. Apparently I missed the tour a few weeks back with the other Board members."

"Uh huh," Regina said, her tone both solemn and disbelieving. "I wish I could go."

CHAPTER 10

THE MOUTH OF THE METRO CAVE

Propped against the entrance wall of the Metro station, Maynard dropped his head almost between his knees. Hunched, he was like an animal waiting for its prey. His eyes and skullcap were the only visible parts of his head.

Maynard, however, wasn't planning to pounce on anyone or anything. In truth, he was exhausted. As usual he had slept the previous night with one eye opened. Doing so had given him little rest. There had been the voices. One voice in particular yelled obscenities in his head, each expletive like the blast of an air horn.

In the shadow of the massive government building, Maynard found some respite from the afternoon sun. At one point he'd considered riding the dragon's tongue, the escalator, which went deep into the dark Metro cave. Underground it was always twenty degrees cooler. But the cave could be treacherous—at least that's what his voices warned. Escape from the heat might not be worth the danger. And then there was the issue of his cart, always within easy reach. Those meticulously tied green garbage bags were the neatest thing about him. When Simon was around, he guarded the cart. Nothing was ever missing. Simon was probably the only one Maynard could trust, but in the last few days, Simon hadn't been around. Better stated, Simon had disappeared *again*. Going to "who knows where" or the "ask me no questions, and I'll tell you no lies" place. Wherever that was. That place would suck you up and spit you back out. That place would spit Simon back out, but there was no telling when.

Foot traffic entering the Metro cave was light. With his coffee can close by, Maynard watched beleaguered Metro riders descend into the cave via the dragon's tongue. Few riders offered donations. Money-wise, it was going to be a so-so day. He let his eyes narrow. His need for sleep was defeating his attempt to stay alert. With arms resting on his knees, he drifted into semi-consciousness.

Whether it was Coach's voice in his head shouting, *Wake up, nummy!* that alerted him or his slit-eyed peripheral vision that spotted the hand creeping toward his bag, his reaction was the same. He sprang to his haunches, falling forward on his hands, against the gritty pavement, looking like an attack dog.

"Stop!" Maynard screamed, his voice sounding more like a foghorn than a human voice. "Stop, you fucker!"

Two kids. Junior hoodlums. The worst kind. The one behind him reached for the coffee can. The other one lifted a green bag from the cart while his feet did the "Ali shuffle." The kid had the top bag, the one with Maynard's binder.

Get him, nummy! Coach bellowed. *Get the little fuck!*

Rising to his feet, Maynard sprang for the kid with his bag. He grabbed the kid's baggy pants and held on to his leg. In the struggle to free himself, the kid lost his shoe. That was Maynard's opening. Maynard buried his teeth into the kid's stinky sock.

"Aghhhh! Get off me, muthafucka! Aghhhhh!" The kid dropped the bag. Hopping on one leg, the kid fought to stay erect. "Vick! Help me!"

With a violent tug, Maynard pulled the kid down, the boy's butt landing hard on the pavement. In a flash the second kid was on Maynard's back.

Teeth still engaged, Maynard reached behind and sank his claw-like fingernails into his aggressor's neck. With a jerk he threw the aggressor off. Maynard was a mad dog on the attack. He growled as his teeth clamped down again on the boy's foot.

"Aghhhhhhhh!"

A small crowd had gathered but kept its distance.

"Vick, get this muthafucka off me! This nigga's killing me!"

Scrambling for his freedom, the kid managed to remove Maynard's skullcap. Free from the sweaty cap, Maynard's matted hair rose like a giant rat's nest. The boy bent forward, grabbed Maynard's hair with both hands, wedged his free foot against Maynard's shoulder for leverage, and pulled. Maynard's scalp burned. Further angered, he tightened his jaw.

"Agghhhhh! My foot. Help! Somebody help me!"

Vick, who'd been stunned by Maynard's wrestler move, which had sent him flying in an overhead crash, began to stir again.

As sure as he could recognize the sound of coins hitting his coffee can, Maynard recognized the click of a switchblade. There was an "oooooooh!" from the gathering.

Get the other bastard, nummy! said Coach, cheering inside his head.

Maynard released his mouth's grip on the first kid, turned, and rammed head first into the second kid's midsection, knocking the boy backward, to the pavement. On his knees Maynard grabbed the hand that held the blade. He bent the boy's wrist back until the hand released it.

"Aghhhh!"

Nice work, nummy. Now get his balls, the voice instructed. The voice laughed. It was a screeching laugh, like a parrot being strangled.

Obeying the new command, Maynard put an elbow in the boy's stomach, pulled his legs apart, buried his head in the boy's smelly crotch, and bit down.

"Awwwwwwwwwwwwwwwwwwwwww!" the kid screamed.

"Grrrrrrr," said Maynard, his growl muffled.

Back arched, the boy flopped like a fish on a boat deck. "Get off me! Muthafucking pervert! Get him off me! Awwwwwwww!"

"Hey, you! Let him go! I said to let him go!" The new instructions weren't coming from Coach, an angel, or even God. The voice had Coach's commanding tone. "Let him go, I said!"

Maynard felt a hand tugging at his collar and a large stick pressed against his face. Quick to follow orders, Maynard released his mouth's lock on the boy's crotch fabric. "Don't hit me. Don't hit me," said Maynard, begging, throwing his hands in the air. He stopped begging long enough to spit lint.

Tears rolled down the boy's face. "That muthafucka damaged my nuts," the boy cried, holding his crotch.

"Child abuse! Child abuse!" said his one-shoe friend, cheering from the sideline.

Stone faced, eyes down, Maynard sat back on his heels, his hands still in the air. He was trembling and sweating. From the corner of his eye, he spotted his bag. It was about ten feet away.

The victim of Maynard's crotch attack dragged himself on his elbows along the pavement, distancing himself from his attacker. The victim of the foot attack removed his sock and inspected the bite marks. "Look at that!" he said. "He's got fangs." With one bare foot, he limped toward Maynard. While the policeman fumbled with his radio, the kid used his good foot to give Maynard a swift kick in the ribs.

Maynard groaned and reached for the kid's foot. This time the boy was too fast.

"Kid, stay over there," the policeman ordered.

"Little jackass! Cockroach! Rat poop!" Maynard yelled at the kid.

You tell them, nummy! Coach said, continuing his private instructions.

"Keep quiet!" ordered the policeman, his voice decibels louder than the one giving orders in Maynard's head.

Keep quiet, nummy. Don't say anything. It was Coach again, speaking this time with a loud whisper that pierced Maynard's brain like a train whistle. Maynard grabbed his ears to smother it.

"Hands down!" the officer ordered. He forced Maynard's hands away from his ears. "Behind your back! Behind your back, I said!"

Maynard complied.

With precision the policeman bent down and fitted Maynard with plastic cuffs.

"I didn't do anything," Maynard said.

"Liar! Officer, that fool attacked us," the young kicker announced.

"Hold on. I'll get your story in a minute." The officer pressed a button on his shoulder-mounted radio and spoke in code. The crackled reply was so much static. The only thing that was clear was that backup was on the way.

"Okay, what happened here?" the officer asked, directing his question not to the kid most anxious to talk but to the one still moaning on the ground and holding his crotch.

"That crazy muthafucka attacked me. He's a pervert," moaned the boy on the ground, his tears mixing with dust and sweat.

"Yeah, he attacked us. He jumped us. He's crazy!" said the other boy, his statement accompanied by hopping and wild arm gestures.

"Not!" Maynard bellowed, his eyes blazing. He grunted.

Nummy, they're not going to listen to you. They're going to put you away again.

"You calm down," the officer said, pressing his baton into Maynard's shoulder, as if the pressure of the baton could hold him in place. Maynard flinched.

Nummy, you don't listen. Quiet! Bide your time. Later you'll get them. Later you can pee on them.

"But I got to talk. Those little bastards tried to steal my bag," Maynard said, talking out loud to his personal coach, wanting everyone to hear.

The audience that had gathered had all but dispersed. About twenty feet away, a straggler witness, a man with a mid-fifties paunch and a newspaper, lingered in the building's archway.

"Hey, you! Did you see anything?" the officer called to him.

"It looked as if the kid pulled a knife on him," the witness replied, pointing to the kid on the ground.

"Is that right, kid?"

"Naw. No way. That fucker attacked us."

"Sir, may I get a statement from you?"

The man raised his hand and shook his head, signaling that the answer was no. Then he walked away.

Without changing his position, the officer's eyes scanned the pavement. If there *had* been a knife, it was missing.

"Look at my foot," said the victim of the foot attack, pointing to the red teeth marks. "He's a damn werewolf. I could get rabies."

"You have to come down to the station and press charges," the officer said.

The standing boy looked at the pavement and did a kind of shuffle. The eyes of the boy on the ground widened.

"The car will be here in a minute. I'll take you and your friend to the station to fill out the papers."

The boy cut an eye to his friend, who still seemed in too much pain to stand.

"Naw. We don't wanna press charges. He's a crazy fuck, but we don't wanna press no charges. Right, Vick?"

Vick shook his head in agreement.

Quickly the kid pulled on his sock and then his shoe.

"Don't be in such a hurry, boys. Both of you should get some medical attention."

"Naw," answered one of the boys.

The officer turned to the boy on the ground. "Hey, kid. What about you? You want to see a doctor?"

"Umm, no," the kid answered. He murmured something under his breath, still loud enough for all to hear: "He messed with my balls. God, I hope they still work."

"Groin injuries can be serious. Let a doctor look at it," the officer said.

"Should never have messed with my things," Maynard barked. Then he laughed, a laugh so wicked it caused both kids to flinch.

Lights flashing, a patrol car pulled up. Two officers were inside. A tall thin officer came around from the driver's side. He approached Maynard, who was still handcuffed and kneeling. The second officer emerged from the passenger's side. Arms folded, he leaned against the car.

"Looks as if you got it under control, Bob," said the tall officer.

"These two decided to not press charges. Is that right, boys?" said the first officer on the scene. He looked each kid in the eye.

Each said, "Yeah, that's right."

The kid on the ground struggled to his feet. He staggered a few steps, his hand cupping his crotch.

"We can drive you boys home. Talk to your parents. Maybe they'll want to file charges on your behalf."

"Ahh, no," they said in unison.

Maynard growled.

"You pipe down," the first officer told Maynard, pressing the baton against his shoulder again. "I want to take this one in. No telling what he'll do out here."

The kid who was hopping went over to his friend to help him walk. "We gotta go."

"If you're not pressing charges, we don't need you. Hey, you with the crotch injury!"

The boy stopped moving.

"Tell your mom to take you to a doctor."

The boy nodded as his friend hurried him along.

Maynard watched the two disappear into the Metro cave.

You got him good. Hee hee hee, said a voice in Maynard's head.

Maynard laughed his wicked laugh again. He wasn't laughing at the officer's jokes. He had another scenario going on in his head. This scenario involved his young attackers and what would happen to them down in the Metro cave.

"Let's go, buddy!"

Two of the officers pulled Maynard to his feet. They pushed him up against the car. The third officer frisked him and made the pronouncement "He's clean."

"My gut tells me those punks instigated this," the tall officer said.

"Probably. But now what?"

"Let's not take chances. He's agitated. All we need is for him to attack some tourist."

"You off your meds?" one of the officers asked Maynard as the side of his face lay against the hot metal of the car's roof. Maynard's only response was to turn away.

"Let's take him in."

"My things," Maynard pleaded.

"Quiet down," instructed the officer.

The beat cop retrieved the green bag from the pavement and then pushed Maynard's cart over to the curb. With gloved hands he transferred the three garbage bags and the folded cart into the police vehicle's trunk.

"We should leave that crap," his colleague said. "It's probably infested with something."

"It's probably all he's got. Where's your compassion?" the tall officer said.

"Waiting for Christmas," the officer answered sarcastically.

"What are you going to charge him with?"

"Loitering, disturbing the peace...I'll think of something."

CHAPTER 11

MAHALI SALAAM MEANS
SAFE PLACE

The Shelter was a mostly windowless brick structure, solid, and industrial. It consumed a full square block in depressed NE, an area probably in some developer's plan to become prime DC real estate in the near future. Gentrification of city neighborhoods was pushing toward the northeast. As Zoie looked at the building, she wondered how the Shelter would survive the speculative onslaught. It wouldn't.

A group of homeless men congregated near the Shelter's entrance. Their shabby clothes and vacant looks were unmistakable.

Several men mumbled unintelligible greetings and stepped aside to let Zoie pass. Others extended open palms, seeking change, a dollar, or a cigarette. One man tipped his hat before extending his hand. In New York she'd learned the drill: ignore them if you can. The guilt that plagued her as she passed was quieted by the knowledge that she'd given regular contributions to the two homeless characters who frequented the streets near the Foundation, the men who'd saved her life.

Close to the Shelter's entrance, more men were camped on the hard sidewalk, their backs supported by the building's wall. A lone man slept sprawled across a solitary bench, next to the building. No one seemed to mind that he'd taken the whole bench for himself.

On any other day, Zoie would have crossed the street to avoid this weird congregation. They were not like the young men whose menacing presence caused trepidation when she passed certain street corners. Neither were they innocuous like the men who gathered to play checkers. She fortified her walk. She was there on official business, there to help. One way to help was to gain more knowledge about their plight in order to be an effective advocate on their behalf.

Zoie tugged at the cathedral-sized entrance door. It didn't budge. She tried again, this time with her briefcase bag slung over her shoulder and pulling with two arms. As she angled her foot and leaned into the pull, a dark hand appeared above hers on the door's handle. Its knuckles strained in a tight grip. With a single pull, the door opened. She caught the weight of the door to keep it open and then looked back to see who had come to her aid. "Thanks," she said faintly, but her helper had quickly disappeared into the small crowd before she could see him.

The Shelter's reception hall had the same industrial feel as the building's exterior. Its walls were painted a dreadful green, a mixture of mint and swamp, if swamp were a color. Wooden benches, the kind used as church pews, lined the walls. A tall reception desk, like the ones found in police stations, occupied the far end of the hall.

Zoie headed to the high desk, where a bearded man was busy shuffling papers, unaware of her presence.

"Excuse me," she said to get his attention.

Head down, the bearded man continued to perform what looked like filing.

She tried again, this time louder. "Excuse me!"

Again, there was no reaction.

Frustrated, Zoie raised a fist to bang on the high counter, but before she had a chance, she heard her name called from across the hall.

"Ms. Taylor. Ms. Taylor?"

She spun around. "Yes."

The call had come from a young man. He looked as if he were in his early twenties. With a quick step, he made his way to where Zoie was standing and extended his hand. "Hello, I'm Tarik," he said with a voice as upbeat as his smile. "Jahi thought you might be here by now."

Tall and thin, he had a runner's body. Tight, wooly curls drifted over his cocoa-colored forehead. The dark shadows under his black eyes gave him an exotic look. *Ethiopian*, Zoie guessed, though she'd detected no accent.

"Have you been waiting long?" he asked.

"No, I just arrived." She looked back at the bearded man and wondered what his problem had been.

As if reading her mind, Tarik said, "You're wondering about Carl—he's deaf. We shouldn't have him solo on the desk, but it's been a rough week. Several of our volunteers called in sick."

"I see," she said.

"Jahi's in his office," Tarik continued. "He's on a call. I'll take you there."

Tarik headed out of the hall and down a long corridor. Zoie followed a few steps behind, going deeper into a labyrinth of halls and doors. Except for a few posters plastered here and there, the place was void of decoration. The posters warned of AIDS. One portrayed men sharing hypodermics, but a giant *X* covered the scene. She recognized one poster as the famous food pyramid, the one with bread and pasta as the foundation foods. It was out of date. Somehow the poster seemed absurd in a homeless shelter. While eating healthy was an admirable goal, how about the goal of *just eating*?

Zoie was trying to take it all in, but Tarik moved fast. She stretched her legs to keep up with his strides. Many doors lined their path; most were closed. There was no time to look behind them. Their signs read Laundry, First Aid, Social Services, and Legal Aid. Perhaps she would see what was behind these doors as part of her tour.

Jahi's office was far from the entrance, deep in the bowels of the place. As they continued down the hall, the place was surprisingly quiet, a quiet broken only by the clicks of her tiny-heeled sandals on the tiled floor. She noticed that Tarik's soft loafers made no sound. En route she saw a few men shuffling in the halls. They, too, were quiet. But other than those few people, the place seemed deserted. She wanted to ask, where's everyone? But she didn't get a chance.

"Here we are," Tarik said, stopping at a door with a milky glass pane, with a stencil that read Director. "I hope he's off the phone."

Tarik reached for the knob.

"Hey! I'm next!" said a man seated on another pew-style bench, the kind she'd seen everywhere. It was as if the place had been furnished after raiding a church. The man making the complaint looked to be in his mid-forties. He was dressed in a faded camouflage t-shirt, black pants, and worn high-top sneakers. He leaned forward and restated his claim. "I'm first. I've been waiting." His furrowed brow signaled that he was not too happy.

Zoie looked at Tarik, bewildered. "No problem. I can wait," she said.

"No. I'll handle this," Tarik said before turning to the man. "Frank, what are you doing here? Remember what Jahi told you?"

With lips in a defiant twist, the man shrugged and looked down the vacant corridor.

"Frank, are you listening? Jahi said he'd see you only if you wrote down what you wanted to talk about," said Tarik, his tone stern. "Did you do it?"

"Humph. I'm not talking to you. You're not the boss of me. I'm talking to Jahi. What I've got to say is important."

"Well, if it's so important, why can't you remember? Jahi doesn't have time to waste."

To watch Tarik talk to the grown man as if he were talking to a child made Zoie cringe.

Frank didn't respond, but his defiant expression transformed into confusion. It was as if he hadn't comprehended a word of what Tarik had said, as if English were a foreign tongue. With a gentle tug of her arm, Tarik pulled Zoie a few feet away.

"Ms. Taylor, this is Frank's usual modus operandi."

"Do you really have to treat him like that?" she asked with a challenging tone.

"I know I sound harsh. Unfortunately, when some of our residents act like children, we have to treat them like children. Frank continually demands to see Jahi."

"It must be to tell him something important. Does Jahi ever talk to him?"

"Sure. But when he's in Jahi's office, Frank just freezes." Tarik shook his head. "He can't remember what he came to say."

"I see," Zoie said with a sigh.

"Jahi had to put a stop to it. He told Frank that he'd only see him if he wrote down what he wanted to talk about."

"Seems fair."

"Except that Frank won't do it."

"I see. Maybe he's not capable," Zoie said.

"I doubt that. I believe Frank used to be a teacher."

"Goodness."

"Some of our residents have mental challenges. Don't feel guilty about Frank."

"Okay," she answered with a raised brow, before gesturing with her head and eyes toward Jahi's door. "Look now."

Tarik turned around. Frank had taken up a position in front of Jahi's door.

"Frank, move. Go ahead now," Tarik commanded, shooing the man away. "Go around to the kitchen, and get some lunch."

"Can't. They're closed. Stopped serving," Frank grumbled, but he stepped away from the door.

"Tell whoever is down there that I sent you." Tarik took out a small pad, scribbled a note, and handed it to Frank. "Give them this. They'll give you something to eat."

Frank read the note and grumbled under his breath. Reluctantly he headed down the hall, in the direction from which Zoie had just come. He looked back at Zoie with a look that made her a little afraid.

With Zoie behind him, Tarik knocked before opening Jahi's door.

Jahi was behind his desk, his combat-booted feet propped on a disarray of paper. His cell phone seemed glued to his ear. He motioned for his visitors to enter.

Zoie and Tarik entered. There were two chairs in front of the desk, but they chose to stand. Zoie's eyes scanned the small office. There were more AIDS posters, tattered and yellowing memos tacked to a cork bulletin board, and stacks of files on what looked like a folding table. Jahi sat with his back to a large window, which looked as if it hadn't been washed in recent years. Through the window's smudge and haze, Zoie saw what looked like an inner courtyard with a loading dock.

Zoie could feel Jahi watching her, though he kept the phone close to his ear. He offered an "uh huh" here and there but seemed to be doing more listening than talking.

"Okay, we can talk more later. I've got to go," said Jahi, finally ending his phone conversation. Then he jumped up to greet his visitors. "Ms. Taylor, welcome to Mahali Salaam."

Zoie extended her hand for a business handshake, but Jahi took her hand and held it between his two in the manner he'd done with Regina that day at the Foundation's office. He fixed his eyes on hers.

Unlike Regina, Zoie neither blushed nor giggled. Having witnessed the Regina episode, she was fully in control, fully ready to resist whatever extra charm he dished out. Nonetheless, Zoie felt the power of Jahi's eyes. They seemed more intense than that night at the charity dinner or the time she bumped into him at the Foundation. Maybe the intensity was due to his being in his element, on his own turf.

"Tarik, thanks for seeing Ms. Taylor to my office," he said, turning to the young man.

"No problem, boss."

"Are you going to be around later?" Jahi asked.

"Sure, I'm here for the afternoon," Tarik answered.

"Good. I may need you later."

"Okay," the young man answered, though seeming disinclined to leave.

"Tarik, it's all right. I've got it from here."

The Mahali Salaam facility was a three-story building, but the second and third floors were sealed off, pending future development. The place was a former bread factory and regional headquarters for a major distributor of baked goods. Zoie imagined that when the place had been in operation, the fragrance of baking bread probably permeated the neighborhood. That smell had long faded. The scent of industrial disinfectant had replaced it.

"Jahi, where is everyone?" Zoie asked as they walked the Shelter's corridors, during her private tour.

"Most of the staff come in around four. Right now folks are in the kitchen, cleaning up from lunch and preparing for dinner."

"No, I mean the residents."

"Zoie, remember we're an emergency shelter." He looked at her as if that explanation meant something, but it didn't, so he continued. "Emergency shelters are shelters of last resort. A place to sleep and to catch a shower and a meal. The men can't leave their possessions here over night. Registration for a bed for the night starts at five. Between five and six, they'll be lined up outside to register for the night. Since it's July and not raining, we'll run at half-capacity. In the winter this place will bulge to its limits."

"So you mean the homeless have to go back out on the street during the day?"

Jahi sighed. "Yes, that's the way it works, unfortunately. Checkout, as we call it, is at ten in the morning. I wish it could be otherwise. We have services, including a mailing address, that they can sign up for. They can come back in for a specific appointment. Look, I'd like nothing better than to put these guys under a permanent roof."

"Are you working toward that?" Zoie asked.

"We're working toward a separate short-term-stay facility, like the one we have for the women."

"And when will that happen?"

"I can get you more details on our plan. It all takes money. That's where Crayton comes in. And it takes the city's cooperation."

"I guess these men will be glad to have something more permanent," Zoie said.

"Zoie, you'd be surprised. Some will; some won't. You're not going to believe this, but a lot of men actually like living in the streets."

Zoie frowned.

"Oh, yes," he continued with a half smile. "You see, the street represents freedom—a life without rules. Or so they think. However, every environment has rules, just different rules. Out there they're at the mercy of the hoodlums and even the police, not to mention hunger, the elements, and deteriorating health. Many of these guys really belong in a mental-health facility. You see, our clientele are mostly what is known as the chronically homeless. Quite a few of the men are veterans who have been without permanent addresses for years. Stop me if I'm preaching."

"No, go on. I'm fascinated," she said, tilting her head. "I'm here to learn and understand."

"Well, good. We need for folks to understand. A lot of people just want to write checks without knowing the sordid details. They don't want to get their hands dirty. They want to keep the horror of homelessness at a distance."

Zoie looked at the floor, hoping his bitter remarks weren't directed at her.

"Don't let me get started," he said. "Let me show you the dorms."

What Jahi called the dorms was room after room of bunk beds. Some rooms had space for twelve occupants; some rooms were more intimate, able to hold only eight people. From college Zoie had known dorms to be wild and crazy places, the rooms often as distinct as the students themselves. These rooms were stark. Their only decorations were more posters warning of the dangers of HIV and AIDS and a placard near the light switches spelling out the Shelter's rules: "No Smoking, No Fighting, No Weapons, No Loud Music, and No Yelling. Lights out at 11:00 p.m."

Similar to a military style, each bed's sheets were tight with a single blanket. There was nothing homey about this place for the homeless. It was a place with a roof, away from the cold and the rain, but an institution, nevertheless.

"I know what you're thinking," Jahi said in an eerie mind-reader fashion. "It's Spartan."

Zoie nodded. "I suppose it's like a barracks." She clung to her briefcase as if she expected someone to emerge from the vacant corridors and grab it.

"Yes, it's Spartan—but clean and safe," he continued. "Every day we change the sheets and put out fresh towels. Every day we clean this place from top to bottom. Folks who live in the street can carry diseases. We can't be too careful. We must protect the health of the other residents and the staff."

They took the back stairs down to the kitchen.

"The men line up on the side of the building near the kitchen entrance. They don't have to register for a night's stay to get a meal," Jahi explained.

A double door opened to a large cafeteria-style facility with about twenty picnic-style tables, each of which was covered with a plastic gingham tablecloth. A large white board hung on the wall, listing the day's menu. In the background Zoie could hear the clatter of pots and pans and a radio blasting Beyoncé.

Jahi and Zoie passed through the swinging door and into the Shelter's industrial kitchen, a place alive with activity. Based on Zoie's quick count, at least seven people were busy with various culinary tasks. Each cook was dressed in a white chef coat and disposable head coverings. The peeling of the potatoes, the snapping of the beans, the scrubbing of humungous vats—such things created a general rhythm. No one seemed to notice Jahi and Zoie's arrival until a short Hispanic-looking man, who was tying up some garbage, looked up and greeted Jahi with a smile. "Hey, boss. Looking for Hank?"

"Yeah, Rico. Where is he?" Jahi's voice was loud against the radio's blare.

"I think in the storeroom."

"Ask him to come out for a second. There's someone I'd like him to meet."

"Sure." Rico left to find Hank.

Zoie walked deeper into the room, doing a 360, but being careful not to get in the way of the work in progress. "I'm impressed," she said, moving back toward Jahi, who had not gone much farther than the door. "This is quite an operation."

"Yeah, it's pretty much nonstop. We serve food three times a day."

"Amazing operation," Zoie said wide eyed.

"With the exception of Hank and Rico, our staff are all volunteers."

For the first time, Zoie saw women. Each acknowledged Zoie's presence with a nod and continued with her task.

Hank came out to greet them. He was a tall man, almost Jahi's height. "Hey, man. What goes?" he said.

He and Jahi exchanged the "black power" handshake, which Zoie found curious since Hank was a white brother.

"Hank, this is Zoie Taylor. You have to be nice to her. She's our hookup with the money."

"Oh, a dignitary!" said Hank, extending his hand. With curly brown hair, a moustache, and a full-length apron, he could've been a bartender at an Irish pub. "A pleasure to meet you. Jahi here didn't need to mention the money hookup. Visitors are always welcomed—especially those that want to come help out in the kitchen."

"Hank's always recruiting," Jahi said with a smile.

"You've got quite a job," Zoie said, addressing Hank.

Hank sighed. "It's a lot of hard work, but it doesn't tax the brain. I get to sleep nights, unlike my buddy Jahi here. He's the one who has to deal with the fundraising and political BS."

"Hank may not be political, but he does sinful things with a peach cobbler," Jahi said, placing a hand on Hank's shoulder, without looking his way.

Hank beamed as if he had received a medal. "You all staying for dinner? Tonight it's baked chicken, collards, sweet potatoes, and peach cobbler."

Zoie's nose couldn't distinguish the chicken from the sweet potatoes or cobbler. The blended aroma reminded her of old days at her grandmother's house at Thanksgiving: the combined food fragrances stirred emotions that said, "You're safe and loved."

"Thanks. Maybe another time," Zoie said.

"Not tonight," Jahi answered.

Hank was about to explain the intricacies of preparing large quantities of food when Jahi got a call. Jahi excused himself and moved to the far corner of the kitchen, away from the clanging of pots and the radio's blare.

"First time visiting Mahali Salaam?" Hank asked, making small talk in Jahi's absence.

"Yes, it's my first time to this shelter or any shelter, for that matter," Zoie answered. "I'm overwhelmed. The amount of work. The organization. Mostly volunteers, you said?"

"Did I say that?" Hank asked, his square face looking puzzled. "Maybe Jahi said it. But if he told you that, it's true. You can count on Jahi." Hank fumbled with the strings of his apron. He was clearly more at home with his stove than with chitchat with "political types."

Jahi finished his call and joined Hank and Zoie closer to the kitchen's main action. Hank seemed relieved to turn Zoie back over to his boss.

"Zoie, I've got a situation," Jahi said with a frown. "I have to go. I've arranged for Tarik to finish your tour."

"Oh. Maybe I should come back another time?" she said, though she had set aside her entire afternoon for this tour.

"Really, Tarik will take care of you. I might even be back before you leave," Jahi said.

Zoie really didn't want to abort the tour. Ray had already inquired several times as to whether she had scheduled the visit.

He seemed particularly interested in Mahali. She knew that when she returned to the office, he'd ask questions: Did you see this? Did you see that? Information was her power, and she wanted to be able to answer Ray's questions in earnest. She would stay. But Jahi left without her confirmation.

CHAPTER 12

THE MAN IN THE NAVY SKULLCAP

Jahi's entering the police station brought little attention. He'd been there on a number of occasions to rescue homeless pickups but hadn't been there in recent years. The police were unequipped to deal with these vagrants, half of them out of their minds, driven further into madness by club-wielding threats.

At the day officer's desk, a hassled uniform-type worked the phone and thumbed the pages of an oversized logbook. Before a word could pass Jahi's lips, the desk officer raised a single finger, signaling him to wait.

It seemed to Jahi that he had been standing there for an eternity before the officer set down the receiver and once more looked up at him with squinting eyes. "Now what can I do for you?" The officer's tone had been cordial and businesslike.

"I'm Jahi Khalfani. Here to see Officer Gleason."

The desk clerk pointed his pencil to a uniformed threesome huddled near a soda machine across the room. "Hey, Mike. You have a visitor!"

Until then Jahi hadn't connected the caller's name or voice with this face. Gleason was a friendly face from the past. Five years had passed since the unforgettable winter with its two weeks of near-zero temperatures, a cold spell atypical for DC. Those winter weeks yielded three corpses, street people who'd failed to heed the warning to seek shelter. As each body was discovered, the police summoned someone from Mahali to the morgue to help identify the victims. Jahi volunteered himself for the sad duty. In those days he knew the Mahali regulars by sight. He'd also been curious for a glimpse of death by freezing. It was amazing to see how one's rich brown skin turned the color of wet cement when chilled to that degree. But seeing just one was enough. That crazy winter they scrambled to get the homeless off the streets. Gleason had been there. Jahi knew him as one of the good guys.

Jahi approached the three men. Gleason, the tallest, hovered over the others like a giraffe conversing with ostriches.

"Long time no see," Jahi said, extending his hand to Gleason.

"Khalfani, thanks for coming," said Gleason, greeting him with a smile as he completed the handshake. "Sorry for the rush."

The two uniformed types who had been chatting with Gleason moved away.

A tall man himself, Jahi was unaccustomed to looking up at anyone. Gleason towered over him by more than a couple of inches. The officer's pale-brown eyes fixed on him from a face framed by light-brown hair. His milk-white complexion was heavily freckled. It was a complexion that reminded Jahi of his paler relatives.

"So what you got? Where's this guy?" Jahi asked.

"He's in the holding room. I didn't want to put him in a cell. He's already freaked."

Jahi followed Gleason down a short hall. Behind a one-way glass wall, a man was seated at a small table, with his slightly lifted head pressed to the wall. He was watching something on the ceiling. A halo of ragged dreads framed his face like a lion's

mane. He could've been fortyish or older, but then it was difficult to tell. Life on the street aged people.

"Who is he?" Jahi asked, staring through the glass, trying to
remember whether he had seen this one before.

"I was hoping you could tell me. There's nothing to identify
him."

"What does he say when you ask him?"

"'None of your damn business,' followed by a string of profanity. We picked him up on Thirteenth Street, next to the Metro.
He attacked two young punks. Bit them both. Had one in a
crotch-lock that would've made the WWF proud."

"Yikes," Jahi replied with a frown.

Gleason scratched his head. "They might have deserved it.
Could've been trying to steal from him. He was probably defend-
ing his property."

"Two against one, huh?"

"Yep, but I wouldn't want to get on his bad side in any fight."

The man behind the glass picked at his hair and then waved
his hands as if he were swatting flies. He was talking to himself,
but they didn't turn on the room's speakers.

"So what's he in for?" Jahi asked.

"Nothing at the moment. The kids didn't press charges."

"Then why is he here?"

"He's very agitated. We've been holding him for his protection and the public's."

"I see. So you want me to take him?"

"Right. Let him cool off at the Shelter for the night," Gleason
said with a shrug. "Otherwise, we'll have to book him. And you
know what that means."

Jahi weighed the merits of complying with Gleason's request. The man's fate, should he be kept in jail overnight, was
dim. Taking him was the right political move, a way to maintain good relations with this particular officer. Having another

law-enforcement type on one's side was always wise. One never knew when such a relationship would come in handy.

"Who's he talking to?" Jahi asked.

Behind the glass the man was in full conversation mode, gesturing to an invisible companion.

"I heard him refer to someone named 'Coach.' I figure he's off his meds, if he ever was taking any to begin with."

"You know I can't force him to come with me," Jahi said, his thick eyebrows raised.

"At least talk to him. See what you can do."

When Jahi and Gleason walked into the small room, the man's solo conversation and scratching stopped. Head half-bowed, the man's eyes tracked them as they settled in the two chairs in front of the table. Jahi felt that there was something familiar about the man. Jahi leaned forward, trying to look into his eyes, but the man shifted away.

"Do I know you?" Jahi asked in a low tone.

"Tell us your name, buddy. Maybe we can help you," Gleason chimed in.

"Did you check his prints?" Jahi asked.

At the mention of prints, the man winced.

"No. Remember, we didn't book him. I'm trying to slide this one under the radar. You know, I want to keep the paperwork down."

"Understood," Jahi said.

"So you'll take him?"

"Yeah, I can take him, but only if he wants to go. You or I can't force him."

"Buddy, Mr. Khalfani here is going to take you to a shelter."

"No!" the man screamed.

"At least he's talking to us," Jahi said.

"Yeah, remember the *Exorcist*?"

Jahi smirked. "You know, maybe he needs more than a bed. How about a hospital?"

"You mean the loony bin," Gleason replied.

"Careful, Gleason," Jahi warned. "He's not doing much talking, but he hears and understands what's going on—up to a point."

"Well, nix the hospital idea. I'm not going through the admissions' ordeal." Gleason turned to the man, again. "Buddy, here's your choice: either you go with Mr. Khalfani to the Shelter and get a bed and a meal, or we'll have to lock you up. Do you understand?"

The man winced again, indicating an understanding that something unpleasant was about to happen to him. After a few long seconds, he asked, "Where are my things? Where's my hat?"

"Guess that means he's agreed to go," Gleason said, directing his remarks to Jahi.

"He wore a hat?" Jahi asked.

"A navy or black skullcap. Guess it got lost in the shuffle. Why? Does a hat ring a bell?"

Jahi put it together. No wonder the guy seemed so familiar. The night he saw him, his lion's mane was hidden beneath the cap—a cap pulled down nearly to his eyebrows. It had been at the Shelter about a month ago.

Jahi shrugged. "Not sure. Just wondering. I took the Metro to get here. I have another stop to make before returning to the Shelter. I'll send one of my staff over right away with the van to pick him up."

Gleason turned to the man. "See, buddy. You'll get your things. Go to the Shelter. Everything will be fine."

The man's eyes rolled to the ceiling. " Oh, God, where are you?"

CHAPTER 13

A ROSE BY ANY OTHER NAME

Zoie and Tarik were back in the Shelter's reception hall when Jahi returned.

"Good, I caught you," Jahi said, smiling as he strode over to where they stood by the high counter desk. In Jahi's presence the younger man's lanky body stood taller and straighter. He was quick with answers to Jahi's inquiries about the tour. Ever the gentleman, Tarik turned to Zoie to say goodbye.

"Thank you for being my stand-in guide," she said, extending her hand to him, only to have his limp handshake in return. He was a nice-looking kid, even if the handshake was a disappointment. She made a mental note.

"An impressive young man," Zoie told Jahi, after Tarik had left. "Is he a volunteer?"

"Oh, no. We pay him. Surely not what he's worth, though," Jahi explained. "Don't let his youth fool you. He's wise beyond his years and quite reliable. Especially lately. He's my right hand. I lean on him a lot. With a little more schooling in people skills, he could run this place."

Jahi's dark eyes threatened to capture hers if she looked into them any longer. She turned from his gaze. She had a million questions about the Shelter but had forgotten them all.

"Did the rest of the tour go to your satisfaction?" he asked.

"Yes. Tarik was a wonderful guide. You have quite an operation here."

"Counselor, this is not like you. You must still have questions." His seriousness had returned.

She blushed at his reference to her inquisitor mode.

"Are you in a hurry?" he asked.

"No."

"Then let's go around the corner to a coffee shop I know. We can talk there."

Jahi's version of "around the corner" turned out to be a three-block walk in the hot late-afternoon sun. In route he seemed to know everyone, or at least they knew him. "Hey, Brother Jahi," various people would say. There was an old man with a slow, stiff walk, a mother with a pile of laundry and a gaggle of children, and a truck driver unloading soda in front of a small grocery store. From what Zoie could make out, Jahi was a local celebrity.

She noticed the number of men lining the streets. They gathered close to the building to capture the shade. Some were sitting on folding chairs; some were standing. They were men just hanging around as if they had no place to go and no jobs, just the street in all this heat. But these men were not homeless.

The walk, which might have been considered short, if not for the heat, brought Zoie and Jahi to a "hole in the wall" type of place. The white lettering on the faded green awning read Sunrise Café—named as such, as Jahi explained, because it opened at 6:00 a.m., a tradition started before *Starbucks* hit the scene, in nearby neighborhoods.

Under the protection of the café's awning, a serious game of chess was in progress. With arms pressed against the rickety table, the two street strategists looked up long enough to acknowledge Jahi and Zoie, before sinking back into intense concentration. Zoie removed her sunglasses as she entered, letting her eyes adjust.

The Sunrise Café was a narrow establishment in which ten simultaneous customers would have constituted a crowd. Five faux leather booths lined one side of the place, and a long wooden counter stretched across the other. It was a definite neighborhood throwback, worn but clean. In contrast to the bright afternoon sun, the place was dark. Its only lighting emanated from the picture window and its opened door, both in the restaurant's front. With no air conditioning, Zoie wondered whether the restaurant's proprietor had paid the electric bill. But the hum of the large overhead fan and a radio announcing itself as Cool Jazz 105 were indications that he had.

Zoie and Jahi were the only customers. Zoie looked around, her face not hiding her skepticism about the place.

"Don't let its looks deceive you," Jahi said. "The food here is pretty good. We're just here in the off hours."

"It's your neighborhood. You're in the lead," Zoie answered.

They sat in the middle booth, away from the opened door, but where there was still enough light to read the plastic-covered menus, which they pulled from behind the napkin holder.

A small man with a nicely trimmed beard, white apron, and a towel thrown over his shoulder emerged from somewhere in the back. Judging by his smooth face and weathered hands, both of which contrasted with each other, Zoie thought he could have been anywhere from forty to sixty.

"Jahi, my man! Where you been?" said the man, greeting them with both delight and a rasp in his voice, signs that marked him as someone who'd spent many years in smoke-filled rooms. He whipped out a hand to grasp Jahi's.

"Zoie, meet Stan. Stan's the man. He runs this place."

"Pleased to meet you, Stan," Zoie said, exchanging a handshake across the table. Unlike Tarik's soft touch, Stan's hand was both rough and solid.

"Glad to meet you too, pretty lady."

Zoie blushed. It was the second time that day she had felt a warm flush on her cheeks.

"Brother Jahi, you've been hidin' out on me. I know you're busy and all, but you could take time to come see an old friend."

Jahi offered a half-guilty shrug. "Stan, you know how it is. Mahali keeps me busy. And lately there's been all that other stuff."

"Helter, skelter, shelter. I know how much work that place is. But sometimes work is an excuse for not living your life," Stan chided. "Everybody's got to eat and shoot the breeze once in a while."

"True enough," Jahi said, taking in his friend's scolding with pouty lips, while he focused on the gray laminate table.

"Miss, I hope you can talk some sense into this brother. I know he's getting to be a big shot and all, but you ought to make him take a break sometime."

Zoie, puzzled, responded wide eyed. Obviously, Stan had confused her relationship with Jahi as something more than it was. She wanted to correct him, to tell him that they were only business associates, when a clandestine wink from Jahi, the signal to be silent, caught her attention.

"Now that I've said my piece, what can I get you folks?" Stan said.

They both ordered ice coffee, and Jahi order blueberry pie.

Zoie waited until Stan had moved toward the back and then whispered, "I thought that you were going to go back to the Shelter to eat some of Hank's peach cobbler."

"Are you keeping tabs on my calorie count, Counselor? Two pieces of pie in one day. Somehow I'll manage." He patted his upper abdomen. She imagined his abs to be as flat as an ironing board.

"You see Stan?" said Jahi, gesturing toward his friend, who was behind the counter. "He's one of our success stories."

"I had a feeling that he either lived or worked at the Shelter."

"Very good, Counselor. Yeah, Stan was on the street for about seven years. Then one day he decided to pull it together."

"He's quite a character," she said, scanning the rest of the restaurant's décor, which comprised pictures of roosters and chickens, and those pictures were mixed in with African prints. "Does he own this place?"

"No, he doesn't own it, but he might as well. He does almost everything, except sign the checks. I got him this gig a few years ago. He would sleep at the Shelter and then work here during the day. The owner relies on him completely. Gave Stan a room in the back. It's small, but it's a place of his own."

"That's a great story."

"Yeah, Stan's one in a million." Jahi sighed again. "His kind of rescue doesn't happen often. A lot of our residents are mentally ill or addicts. They need more than a job. Without medication, rehabilitation, or someone to watch out for them, their chances of transitioning into permanent, stable housing are slim."

"Then there are the ones who want to stay on the street, right?" Zoie asked.

"Yes, that too. But they want that because the alternatives, like institutionalization, are too gruesome."

"Don't you ever feel helpless or frustrated? As if all you're doing is for naught?"

Jahi shook his head and gave a quick laugh. "I'd be lying if I said no, but then I think about the once-in-a-blue-moon case like Stan's. And the ones who could've died if we hadn't pulled them in from the bitter cold. As little as it may seem, I know I'm making a difference."

"It's not a little difference. It's *huge*," Zoie said. She wasn't in the habit of throwing out empty compliments. She knew that she probably could have gone further in business had she cultivated that habit. Clients needed to be schmoozed, and schmoozing was something that she wasn't good at. Jahi's commitment genuinely impressed her. How many people who were passionate about helping others did she know? All of her male acquaintances were passionate men, all right—passionate about one thing: making money. She remembered how Elliot's face would light up after he'd pulled off a big deal. He would be happy for his clients and even happier for the subsequent commission.

"Counselor, you have something on your mind. Spit it out."

"Jahi, remember the charity dinner?" she asked, her finger making smudge circles on the table's smooth surface.

"The dinner. How could I forget?" he said, grimacing.

"Before the accident you were about to tell me how you started the Shelter."

"Was I?" said Jahi, adjusting himself in the seat. "You have a good memory. Much about that night is a blur to me." He took a deep breath as if he had to reach deep for the story. Maybe he was tired of telling it. "I'll give you the short version."

"Okay." She sank back in her seat, keeping her hands clasped on the table, ready to listen.

"Well, after the Gulf War…you do remember that one, right?"

"Don't be silly. It wasn't that long ago. CNN's live coverage of our soldiers in action."

"Gee, you put a strange twist on things. I never thought of the war as a TV event. I was definitely on the wrong side of that transmission."

"Where?"

"In the US Marines. Semper Fi and all that good stuff. Can't you see me with the uniform and an almost-skinned head?"

She shook her head.

"Then I decided I wasn't going to make a career out of the war thing. So I returned home, not knowing quite what to do with myself."

"I see." She smiled, trying to picture him without his mystical dreads—Sampson without his hair. Jahi was as non-establishment as you could get. The military image didn't fit.

He frowned. "It's a wonder that Hank didn't tell you."

"Is Hank your biographer?"

"No. Hank and I served together. He was my unit's cook."

"So that's how you got into the Shelter business—playing off Hank's skills with the hungry masses."

"Counselor, you make it sound like a plan. This thing just happened. But first I had to experience what it was to be homeless. Not on purpose, of course."

"You were homeless?" said Zoie, sitting up straight.

"Yeah. I left the service and had a two-bit part-time job. I was in school and staying with my aunt. And then she died. I tried to hang on to her place. Next thing I knew, they had repoed my ride—a nice red convertible," he said, shaking his head.

Zoie snickered.

"How is homelessness funny?" he asked with feigned indignation.

"I'm sorry." She wiped her eyes. "I'm still trying to picture you without dreads, in this bright red car. Somehow the vision isn't working."

He shrugged. "People change. I sure did."

"If you say so. But I want to hear the rest of your story."

"Anyway, I stayed with friends and other family until I wore out my welcome. My credit was so bad that no landlord dealing 'on the books' would deal with me. And the ones dealing 'off the books' wanted upfront cash that I didn't have."

"Goodness," she said.

"Then I started sleeping at the place where I worked," he continued. "Actually, I was attending UDC and worked part time so I could take classes."

"Did they know you were staying there? The place where you worked, I mean?"

"My boss found the box where I kept my blanket, pillow, and some clothes. He let me stay. Anthony Rupe was his name, a decent guy. He died a few years ago."

"Then you had a place to stay, so technically you weren't homeless."

"Counselor, a couch in a storage room where you have to hide your belongings from the other employees hardly qualifies as a home." His eyes widened as he spoke.

"Right," she answered, feeling stupid for making the insensitive remark.

"I was one of the working poor. Granted, my situation was different from most Mahali residents. I did the 'under the stars' thing for about a week. It's not nice."

"I expect not." She frowned.

Jahi in no way seemed meek or needy. Even without the dreads, Zoie was having difficulty thinking of him as not being in control, as being someone who'd lost his way, like the men whom she'd seen on route to the café. Like her homeless acquaintances near her office.

"Then I got involved with a group at UDC," he continued. "We were organized and ready to change the world. We started doing things to help the homeless. We started small, doing things like collecting clothes and food drives. A lot of the group dropped off over the years."

"But you stuck with it?"

"That's it. There's nothing like not knowing where to rest your hat or where your next meal is coming from. If anyone ever tries to convince you that it's liberating to be penniless or that it's a romantic adventure to sleep under the stars, you tell them to come see me."

Their conversation was interrupted when Stan returned with two tall iced coffees and Jahi's pie.

The cool coffee was just what she needed. She sipped slowly as they chatted about how he had been able to set up the corporation that runs the Shelter and about his ongoing battles with the city and the community. He had a lot of irons in the fire. Other groups around the city expected his assistance. He had to maintain multiple quid pro quo relationships to support his cause. The politics of coalitions kept him on the go.

"I've been meaning to ask you something," Zoie said, so taken with his discourse that she had forgotten her follow-up questions about Mahali. "Where are you from?"

"DC."

"I mean your family."

"DC by way of the Carolinas. I changed my name after I returned from the Gulf."

"And what was your 'slave name'? Is that what you call it?"

"You mean the name that was a legacy of the master. I'll tell you, but you have to promise you won't laugh."

Promising was something she'd made a habit of not doing. Promises were easily broken, not taken seriously. But this wasn't serious. She just wanted to know his name, the one before he researched his new one in the Swahili name book. Curiosity had the best of her. The only way she was going to find out his other name was to promise.

He waited for her answer.

"Okay, I promise," she said, raising her hand above the table, in an oath-like fashion.

"Oswald Smoot."

Zoie took a sip of her drink. She felt the cold beverage head for her nostrils. She put a napkin to her face and managed to control the gross physical result of her nosiness. She coughed, sputtered, and turned red with embarrassment.

"Are you okay?" he asked rather calmly, considering that his name was the brunt of her amusement. "I'm sorry that my name choked you."

It was the charity dinner deja vu. With napkin covering her nose and mouth, she shook her head. Summoning what little dignity remained, she repeated the name in disbelief. "*Oswald Smoot.*" It sounded even funnier than the first time. She fought to restrain her giggles. "No way!"

Seeming not offended, though not smiling, Jahi leaned on the table and folded his hands. "Counselor, it's actually Oswald Smoot the third. I tried to warn you. That's exactly why I don't tell most people. That's exactly why I changed it."

"Oh my goodness," she blurted, still trying to control herself.

"Before my mother passed, she apologized for labeling me like that. She even congratulated me for changing it." He smiled.

Thank God he's not angry.

"Yeah, old Oswald the third has been retired," he continued.

"I'm so sorry. Please, no more." Tears of laughter rolled down Zoie's cheek. She dabbed them with the napkin that had saved her from complete embarrassment. Then she took several deep breaths and fanned her face. "Well, I like the name you chose," she said in a lame effort to repair the damage.

"It's a world of difference from..."

"No, don't say it!" Even in her embarrassment, she knew that if she heard the name again, it would trigger another round of laughter. She sniffed, patted the tears from her face once more, and wiped her nose.

"Yeah, the original Smoot was a big-time plantation owner on the Eastern Shore. Don't ask me how my folks ended up in North Carolina. Sold down there, I guess. Don't ask me where the *Oswald* came from. But if it's easier for you to accept, know that prior to the name change, my friends called me Ossie."

"Oh, like Ossie Davis. That's not bad."

"Counselor, there's one thing I know about you."

"What's that?"

"I know how to make you laugh."

CHAPTER 14

EQUAL-OPPORTUNITY
HARASSMENT

At the Sunrise Café, neutral territory, Zoie felt relaxed in Jahi's presence. *Some* of her professional guard seemed to be melting away. She still needed to follow up on the Foundation's business. But before she could ask her questions about the Shelter, another phone call beckoned him away.

Jahi didn't explain his new emergency, nor did he explain the earlier call that had pulled him away during the tour. He did stay with her outside the café until a cab came to take her back to her office.

"Counselor, I regret that our meetings are always interrupted," he said. "I would like to see you again." He couldn't contain a smile. "Maybe for some more iced coffee? Doesn't have to be at the Sunrise. You pick the place."

"Would I be meeting you as the Crayton Foundation's representative?" she asked with a coy smile.

He laughed. "I'll leave that up to you."

She hesitated, but in a moment of weakness, she agreed. She wanted to see him again. The electricity between them couldn't be denied. As thoughts of a potential conflict of interest wafted through her mind, she shrugged them off. *It's only to chat*, she told herself. *I'll deal with conflict matters later if things go any further.*

"What about a movie?" she proposed boldly.

He raised an eyebrow as if the thought of a movie was an outlandish concept. "You mean a movie...in a theater...with other people?"

"Uh-huh. Not a private showing. What would you say to *Star Wars: Attack of the Clones*? The Uptown on Connecticut is having a *Star Wars* reprise. I missed out on the *Attack of the Clones*. Those movies just aren't the same on the small screen."

Jahi rubbed his chin as he considered her proposal. "Counselor, you're full of surprises. Okay, with iced coffee afterward. I guess that will work."

They agreed to set the date for the coming weekend, before The Uptown ended its showings.

Visiting the Shelter had been worthwhile. On the ride back to her office, Zoie couldn't decide what part of the afternoon had been more fascinating, the Shelter itself or her chat with its director. Certainly the revelation of Jahi's former name topped the bill. The café scene where she had lost her cool played over and over in her head, and that name still tickled her funny bone.

It was late afternoon, and the Washington sun was still blazing when Zoie exited the cab, near her office building. She took a slow walk, stopping at a boutique stationary store to buy a birthday card for her dear friend, Tina. Then she purchased an ice-cream cup from a street vendor before entering the building.

Ray had been right about one thing: she *did* need to see the Shelter's mode of operation to become its useful advocate. Certain things about the Shelter hadn't clicked from reading the reports—like the fact that it only housed the homeless for the night. Safe shelter was a temporary thing. The lives of the homeless were fragile and unstable. Never again would she look at her lifesavers, Simon and his profane friend, in quite the same light. When she saw them again, she would urge them to go to Mahali, now that she had real connections there. She scanned both sides of K Street, thinking she might spot them. They hadn't been in any of their usual places that morning, and they weren't there now.

As Zoie neared her office, the business aspects of her visit to the Shelter came rushing back. Several things about the place still disturbed her. Jahi, with his funny name; Stan, the man; and her own giddiness had distracted her. Her concerns about the Shelter were not about what she'd seen there but more about what she hadn't seen.

For one thing, the women's wing was off limits. "I can't take you there without Sister Te's permission," Tarik told her. "Men aren't allowed inside."

"I'm not a man," she reminded him.

"But, Ms. Taylor, you need a female escort. And currently no female escorts are available."

How did he know that no one was available? Zoie wondered. She didn't see him check.

Then there was the missing van. Tarik took her out back, to the loading dock, which was in a courtyard off the back alley. There she saw two vans, and neither looked that new. She could have sworn that Mahali's annual report listed the recent purchase of a used van, a $22,000 line item, meant to replace one of two unreliable vehicles. In the same report, she recalled something about the installation of a new security system, one featuring panic buttons in each room. At the time she read it, the panic buttons sounded important—not because of the $19,000 price tag but because it added protection for the Shelter's residents, especially the women. She asked Tarik about the system, but he seemed clueless. She made a mental to note to follow-up with Jahi.

Perhaps she was confused. Perhaps these items were proposed improvements, things for the future. Perhaps her mind
had wandered while going through those reports. After all, she
read about those things during her first days on the job, in the
days when she was still navigating the office space—when she
was still mapping her way to the pantry and to the restroom. She
might be wrong about what the reports said, but she was rarely
wrong about such things. She had a knack for detail, a brain that
noticed bits that others missed. It was a skill that served her well
in contract law. However, rechecking the report would ease her
mind.

Back at the Foundation's office, Zoie found Regina with her
bag draped on her shoulder, preparing to depart.

"Hey, Regina."

"You came back," her young assistant said. "I wasn't expecting
you."

"I know," Zoie said, sounding weary.

"You should've gone home. Everyone else does after a field
trip."

"Well, good for them. I still have work to do."

Regina set her trashcan at the entrance to her cubicle for the
cleaning crew. "How was the Shelter? Did you see him?"

"If you mean Mr. Khalfani, of course I saw him."

"Can I go next time?" Regina asked in a begging tone reminiscent of Nikki.

"I don't know that there'll be a next time."

"So that's not a no—it's a maybe?"

Zoie wagged her finger to say no. Regina took the hint and
moved to finish her tasks. Zoie watched as Regina efficiently put
her phone on forward, arranged her papers into neat piles, and
turned off her desk light. Regina was in a hurry.

However, Zoie wanted those Mahali reports. Her mind
would churn about those questionable items until she checked

her facts. Having not mastered the Foundation's filing system, she needed Regina's help to locate the folders. She followed her assistant to the elevator. She certainly understood the need for a parent to leave work on time. If DC childcare establishments operated as they did in New York, the cost of overtime care was prohibitive.

"Zoie, gotta go." The elevator wasn't coming, so Regina decided to take the stairs. It was only six flights.

"Please, just one last favor before you escape," Zoie pleaded.

"Okay, make it quick."

"I need to look at the Mahali Salaam files again."

Regina looked at her watch. "Listen, Zoie, is it all right if I get them for you tomorrow?"

"I can get them myself. Just point me in the right direction," Zoie said.

"Gee," Regina said, thinking for a minute. "I'm pretty sure Ray has those files."

"Why would he have them?"

"Ray? He's the interim account manager for Mahali Salaam and several other grantees."

Zoie wondered why she didn't know that. Before, when she'd read the file, she hadn't paid attention to the account manager's name. Still new, she might not have thought to look for an account manager. Or maybe it was that the account manager's name was missing altogether.

"I didn't think Ray handled any accounts."

"He didn't, well, not until a year ago. When Carmen Silva left, he took over some of her accounts."

"Carmen Silva. I don't think I've ever heard that name."

"Probably not. She's before your time. She only lasted six months," Regina said. One of her hands was pressed against the exit to the stairway.

"Six months. That was fast."

"Right. I don't think she liked it here. She and Ray did *not* get along." As Regina talked, the young woman's urgent need to exit seemed to disappear. She lowered her voice, indicating that what she was about to disclose was "privileged" information. Early on, Zoie had learned that she could count on Regina for the office gossip. Thus far Zoie found Regina's tendency to gossip useful. She liked her young assistant but couldn't help wondering what the young woman said about her behind her back.

"So Ray and this Carmen didn't hit it off, huh?" Zoie said, fanning the flames.

"Those two were oil and water." Regina laughed and rested her heavy bag on the floor. "Carmen tried to tell Ray things, but Ray just wouldn't listen."

"What kinds of things?"

"I'm not quite sure. Carmen was young, a smart dresser like you. Attractive. She knew her stuff—not like some of the others around here, if you know what I mean."

"No, I don't," Zoie said with a raised eyebrow.

Regina looked around to see if anyone was in listening range. "Stick around long enough, you'll see. I'm not sure what the final straw was with Carmen. She never discussed her disagreements with Ray. But everyone knew something was up. One day I caught her crying in her office. She told me it had to do with a death in the family. She didn't want to talk about it. I know it didn't have anything to do with anyone dying. Hear what I'm saying?"

"I hear you," Zoie said.

"Who knows? She probably turned him down."

All kinds of visions went through Zoie's head. Was Regina talking sex?

Regina continued. "Then a couple of days later, Carmen packs up and leaves. Wouldn't even come back for the little going-away party."

Sexual harassment? Was it possible that Ray had been harassing Carmen? Zoie had dealt with plenty of those cases. Attractive young women, older men, sometimes young men too. Actually, it didn't matter what the women looked like. Sexual harassment, like rape, was about power and control—not sexual gratification. Naïve corporations shelled out millions on these cases, most often settling out of court. They spent fortunes because of the uncontrolled egos and overexcited gonads of the higher-ups. Call it "hush money." The strange thing about it was that only some of the perpetrators were ever fired. Since the settlements carried no admissions of guilt and used nondisclosure agreements, the perpetrators often folded quietly, back into the corporate ranks. They were allowed to stick around to offend another day. But no matter how much a company tried to keep a thing like that under wraps, it always leaked.

Plastic-smile Ray seemed a little sleazy, but so far he'd given no indication that he was an office predator. Maybe Ray wasn't an equal-opportunity harasser. Maybe she hadn't been there long enough. Or maybe Ray was careful in picking his victims. Maybe he knew better than to mess with an attorney who knew a lot about harassment cases.

"So what happened to Carmen?" Zoie asked. "Where did she go?"

"Florida. She's got family there. I've got her forwarding address for personal mail."

"Huh. Too strange."

"This place is strange. All I know is Ray's a lot happier without Carmen around," Regina said.

Part of Zoie wanted to press her assistant for more details. Given the opportunity, Regina would gush gossip like water from an open hydrant. But Zoie thought about Regina's child, a darling two-year-old, whose picture Regina displayed prominently in her workspace.

"Hey, aren't you going to be late for your son?"

Regina checked her watch. "Damn! The Red Line better be running right today. Zoie, about those files," Regina said, backing through the exit door, "Ray's in Bethesda, and I know he keeps his door locked. I'll get them for you in the morning."

"Okay. I guess I'll have to wait."

CHAPTER 15
ATTACK OF THE CLONES

Zoie and Jahi's pseudo-date happened the weekend after they'd shared iced coffee at Sunrise Café. She walked the twenty blocks from her apartment to Uptown Theater, heading up Connecticut Avenue. A block from the theater, she spotted Jahi outside the theater. She wiped the sweat from her brow and lengthened her stride. She was late.

"Sorry," she called to him from ten yards away.

"This was the time we agreed to meet?" Jahi dipped his eyes to check his watch. "The movie is about to start."

It was *Star Wars: Episode II, Attack of the Clones,* playing on the big screen. When Jahi had suggested getting together, Zoie had hesitated. Mahali was a client, and Jahi was the head of it. Perhaps that was a conflict. He wasn't her usual type, but something about him intrigued her, an attraction beyond the physical—although the physical wasn't bad. From college onward her experience dating black men was limited. White guys, not brothers, always sought her out. Part of her wanted to know if a relationship with a brother could work. A movie seemed a safe way to start, especially since it wasn't supposed to be a real date. *Right.*

"Forgive me. Some last minute family business," Zoie said, slightly out of breath from her fast walk. She patted her damp face with a balled-up tissue.

Jahi didn't respond. At least he wasn't frowning. He was dressed in the same casual manner as at the Shelter. He was wearing an oversized T-shirt, which advertised an image of Miles Davis, and jeans. The thick soles of his combat boots added at least an inch to his already-tall height.

"At least there's no line," Zoie said, looking around.

"That's because everybody is already inside," he said.

"Sorry. I'm usually punctual."

"Uh-huh," he said, this time smiling. "Two for the eight o'clock show." He pushed two tens through the ticket booth's small slot without looking at the cashier.

Zoie took note. Elliot had never shelled out money for her. She and Elliot had made the agreement to always go "Dutch" early in their relationship. At the time the arrangement made sense. Elliot was a well-paid securities broker; she, an equally well-paid attorney. Why shouldn't they cover their own expenses? In their seven years together, except for Christmas and her birthdays, Elliot never offered to pay for anything. Looking back, she noticed clues to his lack of commitment had always been there. She'd chosen to ignore them.

"Sir, the total prices is twenty-two dollars," said the young cashier, drumming his fingers on the counter.

"What!" Jahi said, his head darting to the theater's price chart behind the cashier.

"Twenty-two," the cashier repeated, "eleven a piece."

"When did movies get so pricey?" Jahi asked.

"It's still cheaper than New York," Zoie said, offering him a ten.

"No, that's all right." Jahi opened his wallet and fingered its remaining bills. "Guess it's been a long time since I've been to a movie."

"Here, take it. I can't let you pay my way," Zoie insisted.

"Why?"

"Because I can afford to pay my own way."

"And I can't afford to pay for you?" he asked, seeming indignant.

The truth was that she did know how much he made. The Shelter's grant package listed his compensation along with other Shelter expenses. "Don't get all sensitive on me now," she said.

"I should be insulted. But you're right. I don't make attorney money. Is that a problem?"

"No," she answered quickly. "My covering my own expenses avoids any impropriety."

"I'm not going to fight you about this. But eleven dollars is hardly a bribe!"

"It can't even have the appearance," she insisted.

"Jeez!"

"Sir, do you want the tickets or not?" asked the irritated cashier.

"Yeah. Okay, okay." Jahi took Zoie's ten, bought the tickets, and kept the change.

"Tell you what," she said. "You can buy me an ice cream after the show."

Inside Jahi bought his own popcorn, and she bought a bottle of water. The theater was packed, and it was dark. The flickering light of the coming attractions provided enough light for Zoie to see that some people had come in *Star Wars* costumes. Jahi spotted two empty seats down in the front.

"This is pretty close. I usually sit in the back or at least the middle," Zoie told him after they had climbed over several people to settle in their seats.

"Well, I usually sit on my sofa and watch a DVD," he responded.

When the *Star Wars* theme music started, the enthusiastic crowd let out a loud cheer.

Perhaps this is going to be all right, Zoie thought as she looked to her right, where Jahi appeared ready to enjoy the movie. But about fifteen minutes into the movie, he began shifting nervously in his seat.

"What's wrong?" she whispered.

"The dude behind me is kicking my seat," Jahi whispered back. Then he turned to face the culprit. In a low, firm voice he said, "Settle down, boys. We're all here to enjoy this movie."

Zoie swung around to see three snickering adolescents, huddled together like the hyena trio in the *Lion King,* a movie she'd watched twenty times with Nikki. The kid directly behind Jahi had a red pimply face and spiked hair. His defiant eyes labeled him the ringleader.

Jahi continued to monitor them with a fierce stare until their snickering stopped; then he turned back to the movie. The peace lasted all of ten minutes before the snickering started again.

Zoie closed her eyes and prayed under her breath. "God, please make this go away."

Her prayer was too late. Jahi rose from his seat and faced the boys. "Goddammit! Who do you little fools think you're messing with?"

"Sit down up there! You're blocking the screen!" came the cry from somewhere in the back.

"Yeah, sit down!" was the command from another part of the theater.

Jahi ignored these protests.

"What's your problem?" asked the pimple-faced kid as he squirmed further into his seat.

"You're my problem." His face contorting with anger, Jahi leaned over and grabbed the kid's collar. He twisted it tightly against the boy's throat and yanked the boy from his seat.

"Let me go," said the kid, managing only a throaty whimper.

"Hey, man—let him go!" cried another of the three, a greasy-looking short teenager, who was bouncing as if he were about to wet himself. "Man you're choking him! Let him go!"

Jahi seemed to not hear the kids' loud protests or the continued calls from onlookers. With his one-handed grip, he pulled the kid's face close to his. The boy coughed and struggled to pull free, his efforts as hopeless as an antelope in the grip of a lion. For all their histrionics, neither of his buddies lifted a hand to rescue him.

"Somebody call the police," cried another person in the theater.

Zoie was on her feet. "Let him go! Let him go!"

"You little bastard! I ought to wring your neck like a chicken!" Jahi growled, causing the kid to pee in his pants.

"Jahi, listen. This kid is a brat. Whatever he's done, it's not worth it." Zoie grabbed Jahi's straining bicep, and her doing so seemed to trigger the release of Jahi's grip. The boy fell back into his seat with a bang.

"Little bastard," Jahi said, massaging his hand.

A small crowd had gathered at the end of their aisle. "Where's the police?" an onlooker cried out.

"Let's get out of here. We can do without this publicity," said Zoie, grabbing her bag and Jahi's arm. She led him past the patrons, who backed away as they passed.

Outside the theater it was dusk. A light drizzle had started. Zoie and Jahi quickly crossed busy Connecticut Avenue and headed down the block at a good pace. As far as Zoie could tell, no one was following them. Jahi seemed unconcerned. They stopped under the awning of a Greek restaurant, at the corner. Zoie looked back at the theater. Two police cruisers pulled up in front of the theater, and the officers went inside.

"Oh, God. Just what I need—a night with you in DC jail," Zoie said, breathing heavily, her heart racing.

"And your purpose there would be to serve as my attorney," Jahi said, his tone more appropriate for candlelight cocktails than the frantic scene they'd just escaped. "Don't worry. I know these guys. DC cops have better things to do than to come after us. Do you want to go back?"

"You must be kidding! What I want to know is what the hell happened back there?"

"You were there! You saw!" Jahi said in falsetto.

Zoie was exasperated. "I saw teenagers horsing around. That's no reason to choke anyone."

"I assure you that I was not choking that bastard. If I'd wanted to choke him, he'd be dead."

Zoie was at a loss for words. Arms crossed, she tapped her foot while contemplating her next move. Guys she had dated in the past were never so physical, so hot tempered. Bullying kids was not being brave. It was time to go home, time to call it a night. She shook her head and looked over to see Jahi groping his locks.

"I think those little bastards did something to my hair."

"Let me see," Zoie said with a huff. In the fading light, she could make out spots of gray mass in the already-matted hair. The stuff was soft and sticky. "Oh, God, it's gum. All stuck in your hair."

Jahi pulled his locks forward to see for himself. "Damn! Damn! What did I tell you?"

"The only way I know to get gum out is to cut it out."

"Damn, I want to sue! You see, Counselor, it was self-defense!"

CHAPTER 16
DON'T BE AFRAID TO LIVE

Life was good, even without someone like Jahi Khalfani in it—albeit a little boring. The summer was slow. Thus far Zoie hadn't made good use of her solo time. She'd intended to do all sorts of things while Nikki was in Ohio. Somehow the time slipped away. At thirty-six her life had become predictable and passionless. Like a child on playground equipment, Zoie spun in her black leather chair, lifting her shoeless feet from the floor as she propelled herself round and round. On each go-round her eyes avoided the ten-inch pile of folders on her desk, which represented at least five hours of dry reading.

Two weeks had passed since she and Jahi had attempted to see the *Stars Wars* movie; their date of sorts had been sabotaged by pimply punks and Jahi's quick temper. Whatever the reason, their evening had been wrecked. She was angry with Jahi and not the boy. After all, Jahi was the adult. She'd witnessed his temper. She could still see the boy's face filled with fear as Jahi's fingers tightened his collar. Never had she imagined that Jahi was capable of such fury. Yes, it had been two weeks since she and Jahi had scurried down Connecticut Avenue to avoid the police.

That night her heart pounded. The whole thing was maddening, childish, and even frightening. Still, in the midst of it, she felt alive. She hadn't experienced anything that exciting in a while. Zoie took a deep breath, blew it out, and whirled again.

The intercom buzzed. It was Regina. "Mr. Khalfani on line two. You want to be in?"

Zoie hadn't talked to Jahi since that night. Zoie thought for a moment. *He could be calling about business.*

"It's okay, Regina. I'll pick up." Zoie closed her eyes and took another deep breath. It was as if God had answered her unspoken prayer and sent her a spark, something to wake her up. Still, she needed to be careful. What God had sent her was not a spark. It was fire.

She tempered her voice to be strong and businesslike. "Mr. Khalfani, how can I help you?"

"Zoie, don't be that way."

"Is this call about Foundation business?" she asked.

"If I said yes, would that make it easier? Would you talk to me?" he asked.

"Business is business. If I remember correctly, the last time we had a conversation you almost ended up needing me to represent you in court. Let's see...felony assault? Assault on a minor?"

He sighed. "And you would have been fabulous in court. But I do believe that little snot was at least eighteen."

"Let's not quibble," she shot back.

"You know you've been on my mind a lot." His voice was low and calm. "I realize how wrong I was. How can I apologize? How can I make this up to you?"

"How can I trust you not to attack anyone again?" she replied. There was silence. He sounded so sincere. Part of her wanted to believe him, but he wasn't getting off that easy. "You don't seem to handle the general public very well, Mr. Khalfani."

"I know I have issues. It's a long story. Perhaps one day you'll allow me to explain. None of it, however, is an excuse for not controlling my temper."

His deep voice sounded so good. Her heart fluttered. Her resolve to be careful was failing fast.

"Tell you what," he continued persuasively. "I'd like to fix dinner for you. Away from the general public, as you say. Then we can talk without interruption."

Alone with Jahi? Should I dare it? "Whoa! How did we get from criminal court to dinner at your place?"

He laughed. "Well, actually, not at my place. I have a humble abode. I'm house sitting for a friend who's on a three-month assignment overseas, for the State Department. So some days I stay at his place on Capitol Hill. I get to use his gourmet kitchen. What do you say?"

"I thought your friend at the Shelter did all the cooking."

"Hank is the master of cooking for the masses, but for more-intimate dinners, I'm not so bad, if I do say so myself."

Zoie made little circles with her finger on her desk. "And you promise there'll be no teenage boys?"

"I promise."

<hr />

Zoie didn't know quite what to expect when she arrived at the row house on Eighth Street SE, several days later. She rang the bell, and Jahi was immediately at the door, his dreads pulled back in a sort of ponytail, wearing a black silk-looking shirt and light-colored slacks, both of which were protected by a cook's apron. *What a change.*

"Greetings, Ms. Taylor," he said, taking the bottle of wine she offered. He gave her a peck on the cheek.

"I didn't even ask what you were fixing, so I just guessed red."

"Perfect. My budget always says chicken. You do eat poultry?" he asked, waiting for a reply.

"Yes. I'm a sometime vegetarian but not this week. I would have warned you."

Zoie wandered into the living room as Jahi headed into the kitchen. The place seemed nice enough. It was filled with pictures and books. It was comfortable and clean. The owner had kept the best of the building's original feel, like the heavy crown molding and built-in bookcases, and that original feel was set off by very modern furniture. She reminded herself that this home didn't belong to Jahi. It was on loan. She wondered what his place looked like.

Jahi served dinner in the small dining room, which had huge curtainless windows. He'd fixed a wonderful chicken fricassee, something she hadn't had in years. She was careful not to lick her fingers, though she really wanted to. She praised him profusely and listened as he talked about life in the US Marines, his aunt, and his take on the music scene. She offered to help him clean up the kitchen, but he wouldn't hear of it. They finished the bottle of red wine she brought; then he pulled out another. With a slight buzz, she was relaxed and comfortable. She wondered what had happened to the Jahi she'd seen at the movie two weeks before. Where was the Jahi who headed up the Shelter? Neither persona seemed to be there that evening. *This* man was altogether different—gentle, caring, and strong. She was intrigued.

He turned on some soft jazz, and they settled on the sectional sofa in the living room. As she was finishing her first glass from the second bottle, she said, "You haven't mentioned one thing about the Shelter tonight."

"On purpose," he answered quickly. "I have to stop myself thinking about that place. Most days I eat and sleep the concerns of the homeless. Tonight I just want to be a normal human being without that weight on me. Does that sound selfish?"

Did his eyes twinkle, or was it just the wine? "No, that's not selfish," she answered. "I know you're dedicated, but everyone needs a break."

"It's like this place. I couldn't afford this. But it's good to take a break and let go of the misery for a while. Sometimes I dream about those poor guys out there on the streets, the ones I've found dead. I do what I can." There was anguish in his voice. "There's only so much I can do." He bowed his shaking head.

"I understand—I really do," she said. Moving closer, she took his hand and held it between her own to comfort him. The touch of his skin was electric.

He lifted his head, pulled her toward him and put his mouth on hers. Her head spun. She felt herself sinking into a slow whirlpool. "And what do you want?" he asked when they came up for air. "Zoie, I know what I want. What do you want?"

Her answer was silent: *I want to feel alive.*

Without hearing an answer, he understood.

CHAPTER 17

YOU OUGHT TO KNOW

One day in early August, a call came from Tommy Vance. Zoie was glad to hear the friendly voice from her recent past. "How are things down in the capital?" Tommy asked with his thick Brooklyn accent.

Tommy was a senior partner at Fairday and Winston, her former New York firm. He was a decent sort, as far as corporate wheelers and dealers went. He'd served as her mentor. She counted him among her true friends. But what did he want?

"Let me see…how are things down here?" she said, echoing Tommy's question. *Better not say too much.* She'd left the firm on good terms. Perhaps they wanted her back. "Hot. Real hot."

"You are talking weather?" Tommy asked, his tone playful.

"Tommy, behave!"

He laughed. "So tell me something. Do you miss us?" he asked.

Is he trying to feel me out?

"Sure, I miss the city, but I don't miss those crazy hours. Now my busy week is forty-five hours max." She didn't want to admit that most days the slower-paced Foundation work bored her to tears or that those forty-five hours were more like forty. And some of those forty hours she spent just twiddling her thumbs. *Give it a chance*, she kept telling herself. *You might even be able to have a life.* But if Fairday and Winston wanted her back, she'd at least consider it.

"Wow! Forty-five hours! Sounds like a picnic," Tommy said.

"I wouldn't call it that. It's different. Sometimes the office politics makes one hour seem like two."

"If I remember correctly, you didn't have time for office politics here. You didn't care for the politics part at all. Hey, you're not getting yourself in trouble down there, are you? You know how you can be when you start on a crusade."

"You know me too well. But no, no crusading this week."

"Good."

"Now, Tommy, it's good to hear from you, but I know you didn't call just to 'shoot the breeze.'"

"Zoie, you're right as usual. Still all business, huh? Look, I need a favor."

So this is not about coming back to Fairday and Winston. Just as well. She owed Tommy several times over for getting her out of jams at the firm. She could always count on his being on her side or his giving her a good reference if she needed it. There was only one thing to say: "Glad to be of service—what can I do for you?"

"That's my Zoie. Look, I have a friend down there by the name of Sy Rosen. Sy's an old law-school bud. He's doing some pro bono work for a nonprofit. Some reading program."

"So you want me to advise him on how the program can apply for a grant from the Crayton Foundation?"

"No," Tommy answered, "seems they applied last year."

"From your tone it sounds as if they were unsuccessful."

"Yeah. And I know *you* can't get them the grant, but if you could just meet with Sy and hear him out...he's one of the good guys. Having someone listen to his situation may satisfy the whole thing."

Internally all kinds of alarms were going off. "Okay," she answered but with hesitation.

"Just hear him out."

"That's probably all I can do anyway," Zoie said, setting low expectations for her ability to help this Rosen.

"Don't worry—if listening is all you can do, well, that's all you can do. Zoie, you're a peach. You should be getting a call."

Later that afternoon Zoie got the call. Sy Rosen seemed pleasant enough but made it clear that he didn't want to discuss his client's situation on the phone. Nor did he want to come to the Foundation's office. She offered to stop by his office, but he suggested that they meet the next morning at the Starbucks on K Street, which was halfway between their offices.

Zoie was on time, exactly at 10:30 a.m. It was past the morning coffee rush and too early for the lunch crowd. She'd done preliminary research on Rosen. No one matching the picture she'd seen on LinkedIn was in the place. She ordered an iced coffee and then settled at a corner table away from the K Street windows but with a view of the door. She took out her cell phone and read her e-mails.

A few minutes later, a thin man with a shock of Einstein-like hair came over to her. "Ms. Taylor?"

"Mr. Rosen?"

"Sorry—I'm a little late," Rosen said, out of breath. He plopped in the chair across from her as if he had just finished a run. His LinkedIn photo was obviously from some years back. When compared with Tommy, he showed a lot of wear and tear, but then she always suspected that Tommy—being the vain preppy that he was—had undergone some facial restoration.

"No problem," she said to his apology for tardiness. "It gave me a chance to catch up on some e-mails." Zoie put her phone away and folded her hands on the table. "Now, Mr. Rosen, fill me in. Why did you want to talk to me?"

"Tommy said you were good looking," Rosen said with a crooked smile. "He also said you were all business."

"Well, thank you for the compliment. And, yes, I have that reputation."

"Tommy probably never said anything to you about your looks when you worked with him. That would have been out of line. So now that you don't work there anymore, just thought I'd pass that on."

"*Okay.* So, Mr. Rosen, what's this about?"

"Call me Sy."

"Okay, Sy, tell me your client's story. I understand it has something to do with the Crayton Foundation and an unsuccessful grant application."

"Mind if I call you Zoie?"

"No, not at all."

"Then, Zoie, what I'm about to tell you should go no further. This is just between you and me. I want your take on things. And I don't want to put you in an awkward position with Crayton."

"Believe me, Sy, I don't intend to do anything that would put me in that position."

"Okay then." He took a deep breath. "My client, Magnum Youth Literacy, has been operating successfully for twelve years. It has two arms: a for-profit program for children whose parents pay for reading tutoring and the like, and a 501(c)(3) arm, a separate entity that serves children whose parents can't afford to pay. In fact, the needy children make up the bulk of the program's participants."

"So the corporations are separate?"

"Yes and no. They share a building, and they share the teachers, who are paid by the hour. The teachers can work for either corporation. They get separate checks based on the number of hours working for either Magnum or Magnum Plus Reading, the entity that serves the need-qualified students. Simple enough, huh?"

"Seems so. Go on."

He handed her the colorful Magnum brochure. Then he continued in a quiet voice. "For the last three years, Magnum Plus has been receiving grant funds from the Crayton Foundation and from several other foundations. Last year the grant advisor from Crayton told Magnum Plus that its application for a continuing grant was in order. Though the advisor could not promise future funds—based on a recent program review, in which Magnum Plus received an A—she thought it likely that Magnum would get another grant."

"I know that Magnum didn't get the grant, so what happened?" Zoie asked, equally as quiet.

"Magnum Plus was notified that it was a finalist for last year's funding cycle. And then nothing happened." Rosen threw up his arms.

"What do you mean 'nothing'?"

"No funding. No explanation as to why Magnum had missed out."

Zoie took a deep breath and then said, "The Foundation can't give any grantee a guarantee of ongoing funding."

"Thank you, Ms. Taylor, for stating the obvious. The bottom line is that the Foundation can do what it wants to do. I understand that. My client understands that. But what puzzled my client was how it all went down so last minute. Then, to top it off, Magnum was strongly dissuaded from appealing through the official appeals process."

Zoie frowned. "What do you mean 'strongly dissuaded'?"

"The Crayton grant advisor told Maxwell Bynum, he's Magnum's CEO, that Magnum should be satisfied with the good run of grants it had received in previous years. Furthermore, the advisor said that Magnum should accept the decision and not fight it, especially if it ever wanted to be considered for a grant in the future."

"That was rather blunt."

"I'd call it threatening."

"Okay, okay, so what happened?"

"Maxwell Bynum decided to appeal anyway. He's bullheaded, in a good way. He followed the application-based appeal process." Rosen waved his hand dismissively. "It's all out there on the Foundation's website. The next thing you know, the IRS is pulling audits on Magnum and Magnum Plus. Then the Foundation's response to Magnum's appeal is that it cannot consider grants for any organization under an IRS audit."

"But you can't connect the IRS audit to the Foundation, can you? If that's what you're insinuating..."

"The timing is all too coincidental. Someone sicked the feds on Magnum. You see, Maxwell wasn't going to take no for an answer, not without a good explanation. Based on the expectation of further funding, Maxwell had kids lined up and ready to start the program. He had instructors on the hook."

"Then that's on him," Zoie said. "He took a risk, and it didn't work out."

"True, but his risk was well calculated. His operation was clean as a whistle. You can say a lot about Maxwell, but he was determined...persistent. So he started questioning his grant advisor about how the funding had gone. If you look at the grants for that funding cycle, Mahali Salaam made out like a bandit. Have you heard of them?"

"Of course. They're one of our premier grant recipients."

Rosen wiped his brow and continued. "I'm all for helping the homeless. But this time the process smells.

"Sy, I don't know what to tell you. How did your client do in the audit?"

"Came through with flying colors," Sy said, waving his hand in the air like a symphony conductor. "There was a preliminary finding that the IRS actually owed Magnum a few thousand dollars. And as far as Magnum Plus goes, its nonprofit status was upheld with no problems.

"Magnum had to scale down. Kids had to be turned away. A bunch of teachers lost their part-time jobs. This year Magnum is seeking other sources of funding. But it's too late for those other kids," Rosen said with a sigh.

"Sorry to hear that." Zoie had been listening intently and drawing small circles on the table with her index finger. She stopped.

"Where does that leave us?" he asked.

Zoie felt sorry for the kids who missed out on the tutoring and for the teachers, but what could she do? Had there been real malfeasance or just lousy process management? It sounded as if Rosen had no proof of wrongdoing. It would be Rosen's word against the Foundation's, her employer, *her client.*

"Considering the clean audit, sounds as if Magnum is in good standing to apply again."

"I don't think Maxwell wants anything more to do with the Crayton Foundation. Look, when Tommy told me that someone he used to work with had gone to work for the Crayton Foundation, I just thought I'd give that person an earful and then put the situation to bed. I don't think Magnum can expect justice without a thorough investigation and without throwing a lot of money at trying to fight the situation. Maybe some other small-time nonprofit out there can save itself some time and effort. Seems that if another nonprofit wants to get funding from Crayton, they will need an *in.*"

Zoie didn't know what to say.

"Thank you, Zoie, for hearing me out, for letting me get this off my chest. Keep your eyes open."

Rosen left, and Zoie sipped what was left of her diluted ice coffee. Her thoughts were consumed by the strange meeting that had just transpired. *Sometimes life isn't fair,* she thought. And if the Shelter managed to get more money but Magnum lost out, that wasn't the Shelter's fault. The Foundation, on the other hand, needed to be careful.

Why had Tommy wanted her to talk to Sy Rosen? Tommy must have known she couldn't do anything. No, she was supposed to listen to Sy Rosen. This was Tommy being Tommy; he was still looking out for her. Tommy was sending her a warning.

CHAPTER 18

ZEN AND NOW

When Zoie arrived at Nora's on Florida Avenue, she found Tina already seated and sipping something in a tall glass. In a yellow terry-cloth jogging outfit, trimmed with white piping, Tina looked like a marshmallow chick, the kind kids find in their Easter baskets. Still, Tina made the outfit look elegant, not that it took much. Tina was a beautiful woman, one of the ones who'd look good in most any type of clothing. She had a glow about her. Zoie figured it had to do with Tina's inner peace. Something Zoie wanted but didn't have.

"Happy birthday, sweetie," Zoie said, giving her friend a peck on the cheek and plopping a gold gift bag billowing with pink tissue on the table in front of her friend.

"Zo, how pretty! Thank you," Tina said, gushing.

As soon as Zoie situated herself at the table, a waitress in a white blouse and tailored black slacks appeared.

"Hello, ladies," she said as she slid a menu in front of Zoie. "What may I get you to drink?"

"Have you ordered yet?" Zoie asked, noticing Tina's menu tucked under her beverage plate.

"No food. I was waiting for you."

Turning to the waitress, Zoie pointed to Tina's frosty glass. "What's that?"

"Lemon-ginger iced tea."

"Sounds wonderful. I'll have one of those, please. And maybe later some wine."

"Sure, no problem," the waitress said, leaving the two friends to talk.

Tina beamed. The hint of pink on her brown cheeks looked natural. Reaching into her gift bag, she pulled out a large ivory candle and brought it to her nose.

"It's coconut, but there's more," Zoie told her.

Indeed, there was a large orange one and one the color of raspberry Kool-Aid.

"They're wonderful," Tina said, savoring the scent of each. "I especially love the coconut."

"I'm glad you like them—just don't set yourself on fire," Zoie said half-teasingly. She'd been to Tina's condo on more than one occasion and witnessed the place ablaze in candlelight. Tina's place reminded Zoie of church, its atmosphere mystical yet ripe for disaster.

The efficient waitress returned with Zoie's iced tea and placed it in front of her.

"We're not ready yet," Zoie said, picking up her menu for the first time.

"Don't rush. I'll come back," the waitress said, leaving them.

Zoie toasted Tina's birthday. Their glasses clinked.

"Well, we finally got together," Zoie sighed as she settled into her chair and pushed her briefcase against the table leg. Even though it was early, Nora's was busy. The popular organic restaurant drew a good crowd throughout dinner. Tina had arranged the six o'clock reservation because, in her words, "late dinners are tough on the digestion."

"I move back to DC, and now I see you less than when I was in New York," Zoie said with a frown.

"I know," Tina began. "I've been a lousy friend. So much for getting you reacclimated to the DC groove, huh?" Tina stirred her tea with her straw.

"There's a groove here?" Zoie asked in a mocking tone. "I forgot."

They both laughed. The two had been friends since their days at Boston University. Though their lives had diverged, they stayed best buds. Tina got her Harvard MBA the year before Zoie finished Columbia Law. Then after years in business in a series of high-profile, high-paying positions, Tina just dropped out. She jettisoned the corporate rat race and the daily grind. Call it a crash, a burnout, or a nervous breakdown—the result was the same: no more pinstriped pantsuits and martini lunches. She'd managed to squirrel away enough to extend her affluent lifestyle beyond what her new career—yoga instructor – could support.

"No groove. That's bad," Tina said.

"Yep. Really, though, for now I want it that way. I could be out there ripping and running, especially with Nikki out of town, but I'm not."

"By the way, how's my goddaughter?"

"Nikki's fine," Zoie said unconvincingly. "I'll have to catch you up on the puppy saga."

"You're getting a puppy?"

"Not if I can help it," Zoie answered quickly.

"Oh, I see. So what *have* you been doing?"

"Reading, working…getting upset at Elliot."

"Yeah, you told me about that thing with Elliot on the phone. You said something about a new wife. You said, '*He's back!*'"

"*Please.* You sound like my grandmother." Zoie's eyes narrowed.

"Okay, no Elliot talk. Now you just have to replace all those hours you used to work with something different. Something fulfilling."

"Well...I have been seeing this guy," Zoie said with a sly smile.

"Girl, you've been holding out on me. Who is he? What's he like?"

"Let's see. How should I describe him?" Zoie drummed two fingers on her lips as she thought. "The word *edgy* comes to mind."

"Edgy, like in freaky?"

"*Noooo.* Different. A little intense. Sometimes funny. Just someone I thought I'd never go out with. Not my usual type."

"Oh, a brother," Tina said with a smirk.

"Yes, for a change. And he's smart and interesting."

"Uh-huh."

"And he has dreads and...empty pockets."

"What a riot! You with someone with empty pockets? Well, good for you."

"I don't know how good it is. Elliot had money. But if you remember, he didn't spend it on me."

"Yeah, I forgot about that ridiculous arrangement you two had," Tina said.

"Well, with this one, on our first date we split the tab. But overall it ended rather badly," Zoie sighed. "He had a serious run-in with a kid."

"Define *run-in*," Tina said with a furrowed brow.

Tina was all-ears as Zoie recounted the incident at Uptown Theater.

"My, my...the brother has a temper," Tina said.

"Tina, I've never witnessed anything like it. When he had this kid by the throat, it was as if he were in a trance or something."

"Were you scared?"

"Only scared he was going to hurt the kid. Scared he was going to be arrested."

"A wild one, huh. Sounds like a Jekyll and Hyde situation," Tina said, taking a sip of her iced tea.

"But he didn't harm the kid. Those kids were way out of line, putting gum in his hair."

"You know that I'm not a violent person, but if some kid put gum in my hair, I might've slapped him myself." Tina fingered her natural short curls. "Sounds as if you've got past that incident."

"Pretty much. There's certainly still a question mark there. Still, there's a lot about him that's so compelling."

"Like what?"

"Well, for one thing, he's gorgeous," Zoie said with a sly smile, looking to the ceiling for more inspiration. "He's funny and dynamic. He's performing a worthwhile service to the community. And…"

"And what?"

"He's not bad in the sack."

"My, my…you're a goner."

Zoie played with the napkin near her glass of ice tea. "But the theater incident keeps replaying in my mind. It's as if I were waiting for this Hyde character, as you called him, to reappear."

"Well, keep him away from movie theaters. And from teens."

"Yeah," Zoie said, laughing.

"So what's this community service?"

"Advocacy for the homeless. He operates a shelter. You might have seen him on TV or in the newspaper."

"You know I watch TV as little as possible. And my copies of the *Washington Post* just pile up unread. In fact, I'm about to drop my subscription." Tina played with the pink paper on her package. "So where's this thing with this guy going?"

"Who knows? I walked away disgusted after the movie incident. Maybe that should have been the sign that it wasn't right. But then I've been seeing him again. And speaking of signs, I've been meaning to tell you that I've also been receiving messages from this homeless guy."

"I leave you to yourself for a few weeks, and you go off the deep end," Tina said with a smile.

"Tina, listen to this. This stuff is right up your alley. This homeless man saved my life. I was about to step into the path of a car, but he stopped me."

"Thank goodness."

"Actually, there're two of them. But the one guy in particular, whenever I see him, he passes me a message on a scrap of paper, like the ones in fortune cookies, only handwritten.

"And?" Tina's interest was piqued. She got excited whenever their conversations turned to the mystical, which wasn't that often.

"So I get a message and sure enough something happens to me or around me that's in line with the message." Zoie explained the series of events where the messages had proved to be true, starting with the day she won the office pool.

"Zo, that's wonderful. It's the universe sending you messages."

"Literally. At first I thought the whole thing was just repeating coincidences."

"But, Zo, you know there's no such thing as a coincidence. Everything happens for a reason."

"Believe me that I believe it now."

"The stars have lined up and are pointing in your direction. The universe is telling you something."

"The question is, what?"

"No, the question is, are you listening?" Tina said. "Because if you are, you'll know the what."

The waitress returned, ready to take their orders. Tina, a vegetarian, ordered the fettuccini with squash, basil, and goat cheese. Zoie couldn't decide between the salmon and the soft-shell crabs. At the waitress's suggestion, she ordered the crabs.

"So tell me more about this job of yours," Tina said.

"Oh, the Foundation." Zoie lowered her voice. "After a big law firm, the place is a little lame for my tastes."

"Are we surprised? We already know you're a New York snob," Tina said with a snicker, "even though you were born here in Chuck Brown Town. No DC firm is ever going to live up to your hard-driving standards. Anyway, it's a nonprofit. No money to be made."

"No, it's not that." Zoie explained some of the weird goings-on, like the fact that a grantee could get a payout ahead of schedule, and the disturbing happenings around the reading program's grant. "I can't go into more detail. All I can say is that things happen there without procedures."

"Hmm. You're being nice. I smell a lawsuit," Tina said, sounding sure of her judgment.

Tight lipped, Zoie shrugged. Perhaps she'd already shared too much.

"Obviously, you're not going to explain. I understand," Tina said. "At least now this Foundation has you to keep it out of trouble."

"I'll do my best. I do believe the members' hearts are in the right place."

"But you know what they say about good intentions," Tina said, stroking her frosted glass.

"That road to hell thing. Exactly," Zoie said.

"Zo, be careful. Watch yourself. Listen to your gut."

"These days I've got more than my gut telling me stuff." Not wanting to delve deeper in her client's business, Zoie changed the subject. "Tina, when are we going to do something fun?"

"Speaking of fun, I'll be out of town for a month. Maybe longer."

Zoie was surprised and a little sadden by this news. "Where are you going?"

"Fort Lauderdale."

"Florida? In the summer? You have all the sun you could ever want right here in DC."

Tina smiled. "Yes, I could sit out at the mall and get my vitamin D, but the reflecting pool is hardly a beach. Plus, I've met someone—someone who's going to produce and direct my latest endeavor: a video I'm calling *Yoga for Seniors*."

"Fort Lauderdale? Wow! A video?"

"Walt's got a particular seniors group in mind. Plus, he lives there. Walt is the backer and the filmmaker. I met him at a yoga conference. He liked my idea, and so here goes nothin'."

"Just like that? Wow. That means I won't see you for the rest of the summer," Zoie said somberly. "I thought we could hang out. You know, before Nikki returns."

There was a long silence. Even Tina, normally upbeat, looked sad.

The waitress showed up with their orders. Zoie was glad because she was hungry; the crab, covered with some light-brown sauce, looked wonderful.

"Hey, I've got an idea," Tina said, picking at her pasta plate. "Why don't you come down to Fort Lauderdale with me at the end of the week? I've reserved a little efficiency not far from the beach."

"Fly to Florida for the weekend? I don't know."

There was nothing really stopping Zoie. And what else was she going to do this weekend? Jahi hadn't called.

Zoie thought about Carmen Silva, the defunct Crayton Foundation grant officer, whom Regina had talked about. Supposedly Carmen had relocated somewhere near Fort Lauderdale. Going to see Tina could be the opportunity to pay the woman a visit, her chance to get the real scoop on Ray Gaddis and the situation at the Foundation—that is, if this Carmen person would talk to her.

"Okay, okay. This may work out," Zoie answered. "There's actually somebody in the Fort Lauderdale area I need to look up."

"Not Elliot's aunt?" Tina asked. Tina knew all about the Benjamin family condo in Fort Lauderdale."

"*Please.* No, this person is work related. I can't say anymore."

"You're investigating something, and you're doing it on your own, aren't you? The company's not asking you to go see this person."

"Bingo." Tina was very perceptive. Sometimes Zoie felt as if Tina could read her mind.

"You're bored, so you're snooping around to spice things up."

"I never thought of it that way. But I just need to follow up on something I heard."

"Now see, Zo—you were fated to go to Florida, and I just happened to provide the opportunity. I told you, the universe sends you things right when you need them. Everything happens for a reason."

"If you say so."

CHAPTER 19

DOG DAYS

Zoie's Delta flight from Reagan Airport to Fort Lauderdale bumped down and glided to a full stop. Pausing for a second, it turned and then moved slowly toward what everyone aboard thought would be the gate. So engrossed in her inch-thick brief, Zoie hardly noticed that she was now safely on the ground. Her ability to focus on dry material, no matter the distractions, had been her edge through law school. Others had found uncanny her ability to wall off personal worries while focusing on the law. This ability had seen her through more than one tough exam, even as her mother lay dying miles away.

"We're twenty minutes early," said the confident voice of the pilot, over the plane's loudspeaker. A few minutes later, his pronouncement was followed by a disappointing update: "Unfortunately, we've got to wait here. You may use your electronic devices, including cell phones, but I ask that you remain seated with your seat belts fastened until we arrive at a gate."

Flying fast didn't count when no gate was available.

The pilot's message brought a chorus of groans from the captives on the crowded plane, Zoie among them. With a punctuating

sigh, she looked past her two row mates, whom she'd barely acknowledged the entire trip, to view the scene on the busy runway.
Baggage carts sprinted back and forth like Disney World trams,
and thin plumes of steam rose from the tarmac, looking like
miniature volcanoes. She was going into a Florida steam bath.
Florida in August. Ugh.

Zoie pulled out her cell phone to check in with Celeste
Benjamin. In the rush to leave town, she'd neglected to inform
the woman entrusted with her daughter that she'd left DC.

"Celeste, it's Zoie."

"Oh, Zoie. This is a terrible connection. I can barely hear
you."

"Sorry. I'm on a plane. I've just landed in Florida," Zoie said
in a raised voice, which brought a grimace from the passenger
next to her.

"Oh," said Celeste, responding flatly.

Perhaps Celeste's "oh" simply meant she was surprised. When
it came to interpreting conversations with Celeste, Zoie's mind
was forever on hyperdrive—each word was analyzed and then
reanalyzed for hidden meanings.

When Zoie was fifteen and announced that she wanted to
be an attorney, her grandmother sounded relieved. "Hmm. I
thought you were headed for private investigator," she said, referring to Zoie's super-inquisitive nature and tendency to analyze
the hell out of things. "You're going to turn everything inside out
until you make two and two come out five."

"Isn't that what attorneys do?" she asked her grandmother.

Celeste broke the long silence. "Are you on business?"

"No, I'm here for the weekend to visit a friend. I wanted to
make sure you had this number, in case anything came up."

"According to the caller ID, it's your cell phone," Celeste confirmed. "Not to worry. Things are fine."

"Just checking," Zoie replied with a snap to her voice. No matter how nice she tried to be, there was always something irritating in Celeste's tone or at least in the way Zoie heard it.

From her aisle seat, Zoie could see other restless passengers with cell phones to their ears. Their collective conversation plus the plane engine's drone and the fact that Zoie's ears hadn't cleared further strained the already-tense conversation. "Is Nikki around?" Zoie asked at a volume meant to overcome the noise. It took every ounce of control for Zoie to restrain from asking whether Elliot and his new lady had departed as planned.

"Nikki's next door with my neighbor's kids. They're having a *Lion King* movie marathon," Celeste responded with a hint of glee in her voice.

"Good." Zoie knew what Nikki's movie marathons were like.

"Zoie, do you want me to have her call when she returns?" asked Celeste, sounding more like Nikki's personal secretary than the child's grandmother.

"No," Zoie answered, hesitant. In the four weeks since Nikki had gone to Ohio, Zoie hadn't missed a night of talking to her daughter. A twinge of guilt tried to make her change her mind. Then in an instant, she convinced herself that not talking to her daughter for one night wouldn't make her a bad mother. Confident in her decision, she said, "No, that's okay, Celeste. Tell her I said hi and that I'll call her tomorrow."

"Whatever works for you," Celeste said, her tone cool.

Zoie ended the call and bit her lip. She turned away from the annoyed glance of the passenger next her.

Though Zoie loved hearing her daughter's voice, this time she was relieved. It would be good to have a day without Nikki's detailed rundown of puppy activities. And what was more, she could use a day without being hit with Nikki's perpetual question: "*Mommy*, when are you going to make the decision about Biscuit?"

The child's whine had become almost unbearable. Zoie's pat answer—"I'm still thinking about it, sweetie"—now lacked credibility. Paralyzed by parental cowardice, she couldn't bring herself to tell Nikki that there would be no Biscuit residing at their Connecticut Avenue apartment. However, to delay telling Nikki the truth was only prolonging the agony. Zoie knew that each day Nikki grew more attached to the animal, which only increased the magnitude of betrayal Nikki would feel when Zoie finally delivered the bad news.

Recently Zoie had been using her last best excuse: "Nikki, I have to check with the building's management."

"Why?" the child asked, using the one-word questioning method she'd adeptly developed as a toddler.

"Because the apartment management makes the rules, and sometimes the rules say people can't have pets."

"But, Mommy, everybody had dogs when we lived in New York." The child was right, or so it seemed. On the Upper West Side, dog owners were usually out in force, often juggling two leashes with one hand and a pooper-scooper and plastic bags with the other. Living in an apartment didn't prevent pet owner-ship. Purina relied on it.

"We don't live in New York anymore, sweetie. I don't know what this apartment building management will allow."

But the building-management decision was a delay ploy. Zoie had made up her mind after considerable thought. She'd never owned a dog and had no interest in owning one. At the same time, she tried to be thorough in her analysis of the situation, for Nikki's sake. The cons couldn't be denied: dog hair, chewed furniture, and guilt about having a large animal penned up in an apartment, not to mention leaving the poor creature alone all day. But then there were ways around some of those cons. Other people managed to own dogs. She could manage her way through all the impediments with money, extra cleaning, and proper dog training. Yes, everything about owning a dog was manageable—until it came to the walks. It was there that Zoie's decision solidified. Morning walks would be difficult since mornings were already mini-ordeals: racing to comb Nikki's hair, to fix her breakfast before school, and to get her dressed. Then, of course, Zoie had to get herself ready for work. Night walks would be an equal challenge. She pictured herself in the dark, the rain, and the cold, toting a pooper-scooper and plastic bag, with an animal on a leash. Nikki would have to stay inside, asleep and alone upstairs. No, it wouldn't work. The negatives outweighed any positives. In fact, she couldn't think of any positives, except for maybe her daughter's happiness.

Feeling guilty that she'd made her decision too quickly, Zoie actually checked with the apartment's management. There were certainly dogs in the building. She'd seen several tenants leaving the premises with dogs in tow. Deep down she hoped that the apartment management would bear the "bad guy" mantle by nixing her request. When she called the Madison House's business office, the young man who answered the phone was very accommodating. "Sure, Ms. Taylor, you can have a dog. We do have a building pet quota. Right now there are two slots open for dogs—one for seventy-five pounds or less and one for twenty-five pounds or less." The apartment management seemed to welcome dogs according to the projected pounds of poop. "It's on a first-come basis," the young man said.

"Oh," Zoie answered, disappointed. She'd hoped that a simple no would end the matter.

"Now you mentioned a lab. For large dogs there's a nonrefundable $500 deposit and a monthly rent surcharge of $40."

"Forty dollars! You're kidding!" Zoie replied, obliged to be incensed about the additional cost, in case the cost became the issue she would use with Nikki.

"You did say a lab. A lab's a big dog."

"But right now it's a puppy."

"Oh! Puppies are the worse. They can be very destructive, and they do grow up. And we'll have to do a flea treatment when you vacate. That would be another $200."

There had been a long silence during which Zoie thought not about what to say to the guy on the phone but about what to say to Nikki. She'd gambled on a tidy no and lost.

"Do you want me to add a pet addendum to your lease?"

"No," Zoie told the clerk. "I'm still considering it."

"Well, I can't promise that the slots will be there tomorrow."

"I understand," she answered, now counting on the time lapse to solve her problem. Somehow she would have to break the bad news to Nikki.

Zoie's anger toward Celeste smoldered like the last log in a fireplace. That Celeste had told Nikki she could have that "damn puppy" without first checking with Zoie sat like a puppy poop in a punch bowl. She'd been so rattled by news of Elliot's reappearance that she neglected to confront Celeste about the dog.

Zoie had sought her grandmother's counsel. "Grandma, what am I supposed to do? She is promising Nikki things I can't deliver on."

"Let it go, honey," her grandmother advised. "In the scheme of things, that woman's misjudgment is just a nit. You're acting as if she were some kind of demon. A little misguided maybe, but certainly no demon. You wouldn't let a demon take Nikki, would you? Zo, you can't let the small stuff ruffle you so. If you get all unpinned about the small stuff, what will you ever do when the big stuff comes around?"

As always her grandmother had a point.

"Ladies and gentlemen, thank you for your patience," came the pilot's voice over the loudspeaker. "They've assigned us a gate. Note that the seat-belt light is still on. We're headed to gate B-12."

CHAPTER 20
EVERYBODY CHANGES

In a perfectly timed rendezvous, Zoie exited the terminal as Tina pulled up in a nondescript white rental car. Tina had flown down earlier, checked into her efficiency apartment, and returned to the airport to pick up Zoie. They hugged, and then Zoie stuffed her carry-on bag into the car's back seat.

Fort Lauderdale, like DC, was hot and humid, but all similarities between the cities ended there. Unlike the capital city, traffic on the flat stretch of Florida highway was moderate, not jammed. The breeze from the ocean brought a scent that told Zoie, "You're at the beach."

Tina's efficiency was one block from the ocean, on the fifth floor of a pink-stucco midrise building. The place came with assigned parking underneath.

After the slow ride up the creaking elevator, Tina opened the door to the small apartment. The first thing that Zoie noticed was the smell of fresh limes, which masked a hint of mildew. From the vantage point of two steps inside the door, Zoie's eyes did a quick survey of the place. The place was adorable. Its furnishings, in that Florida-rental style, looked almost new. And leave it to Tina to find a place with live plants.

"A balcony too," Zoie said, pulling back the sliding glass door and stepping onto the concrete slab with wrought-iron balusters. There was a partially obstructed view of the Atlantic, which in the sun's glare shimmered like silvery gray mercury.

"Don't you love it?" Tina asked, giddy, which was not one of her typical emotions. She galloped around the small place, pointing out its features before collapsing onto a big white sofa.

"It's great. How did you find this place?" Zoie asked.

"Walt," Tina replied as if she'd known this Walt forever and expected Zoie to make the same instant connection. "It's a condo. Walt's friend owns this one and several others in this building. I got a good deal on the rent."

Zoie made a mental note. She'd have to meet this Walt, who'd lured her friend down to Fort Lauderdale for the yoga project.

"Hope you don't mind sharing a sofa bed," Tina said. "It's a queen."

"Fine. I sleep pretty still."

Tina served herbal iced tea. Zoie plopped on the sofa next to her friend, kicked off her shoes, and let her feet join Tina's on the pine coffee table.

"Yeah! We made it," Tina said in a toast of subdued excitement.

"At last," Zoie said, clinking her glass with Tina's and sighing.

"Zo, you sound like you're down for the count. It's too early to crash."

"I know."

"Don't crash on me now. Come on. What are you up for?"

To Zoie, changing into a lounging outfit and curling up with a glass of wine sounded perfect. She'd be satisfied with spending the evening in catch-up girl talk, with a background of soft jazz and an ocean breeze.

"I know what to do—let's hit South Beach," Tina said, sitting up straight to dispel the low energy that was about to put them both to sleep.

"South Beach, huh? I guess I could pull myself together," Zoie said.

"Zo, you're in the lead. You know your way around here better than I do."

"Tina, it's been seven years."

"Didn't you come down here all the time? It'll come back to you."

An hour later the two had pulled themselves together to go out for the night. Tina did the driving, but Zoie guided her. Zoie remembered. The route to South Beach came back like a bad dream. On other visits Elliot had always done the driving. Indeed, South Beach had changed. Whatever had been in South Miami seven years ago had doubled and spread like a garden growing under a landscaper's care: more shops, more bars, more restaurants, and more people.

Decked out in minidresses, Zoie and Tina made their way to several clubs. At each place they stopped long enough to dance a couple of dances with eager partners, have a drink, survey the crowd, and depart. Their consensus of each crowd was the same: young and very Hollywood. Always there seemed to be the types of men who were ready and eager to sit at their table and buy them drinks. One over-eager beaver even stroked Tina's bare arm until she reminded him to "keep his hands to himself."

"Ugh," Tina said when the last of the latest tangle of vipers at the Dolphin Club slinked back into the crowd. "Zoie, tell me something: Is it just me, or are they all wearing Italian designers?"

"Tina, it's not you," Zoie said, looking out at the crowd. "You know that there's something about pretty men that turns me off."

"I guess we asked for it; after all, we showed up at the meat market, dressed as choice cuts. What should we expect to attract?"

"Dogs!" they said in unison, before breaking into rounds of laughter. Their giddiness seemed to keep the men at bay.

As the designated driver, Tina nursed tonic water with lime. Zoie, on the other hand, occupied herself with spearing the olive in her third martini. Florida reminded her too much of Elliot. The martinis were helping her forget.

"Speaking of dogs," Tina said. "So Elliot's come around, huh?"

Zoie looked surprised. "I don't know about 'come around.' What he did was show up."

"Well, that's a start."

"Tina, the thing is I'm not actually sure he meant to see his daughter."

"What do you mean?" Tina looked puzzled.

"I think Elliot came to visit his parents. His running into Nikki might have been a coincidence."

"Remember…"

"I know what you're going to say: there are *no* coincidences."

"Bingo." Tina took a long sip of tonic water. "He may not have known that Nikki was going to be there. But the universe put those two together, because that's what the universe does."

Zoie rolled her eyes.

"Elliot was meant to hook up with his daughter," Tina continued. "He needed to reconcile with being a father, even if it had to happen in his subconscious."

"Uh-huh. I don't know how much reconciling went on. I didn't ask," Zoie said, stirring her now olive-less drink with the saber pick. The tempo of the music changed.

"I'm sure Elliot melted once he saw Nikki," Tina said. "How could anyone resist her?"

"Maybe." Zoie shrugged, her mouth contorted in an unattractive twist.

"And this woman he's with…she's his wife, right?"

"Supposed to be. I really don't know. I haven't had that conversation with him or his mother." Zoie stared into her drink before picking it up and downing it.

"Well, maybe this woman is a positive influence on him. Maybe the man has changed."

"Come on, Tina. Do you really believe people change?"

"Yeah, I do. Everybody goes through a stupid period. For some people adolescence extends well into midlife."

"Then Elliot's working on stupid 'til death," Zoie retorted.

"People do change. Look at me. I've changed. Haven't I?"

It was a rhetorical question. To anyone who knew Tina, her change had been unbelievable, a metamorphosis of epic proportions: she went from being a high-powered, kick-ass executive type to a mellow, off-the-chart spiritual guru. And she still liked to party.

The club's DJ picked up the pace as Tina tried to finish her thought. "Change doesn't happen all at once. Folks transition. They seek enlightenment in stages—unless some cataclysmic event, like a near-death experience, forces the change."

"Oh, yeah," Zoie answered. She was finding it difficult to camouflage her irritation. Things had been going well until Tina used the word *enlightenment.* Zoie didn't care to hear one of Tina's preachy enlightenment speeches.

"And I'm not saying everyone makes that journey," Tina continued.

Luckily the increasing volume of the music drowned out further discussion of spiritual journeys, right at the point where Zoie was going to zone out.

"Tina, I must be getting old," Zoie shouted over the base thunder. "We'll both lose our hearing if we stay here."

"Then let's move."

The two friends weaved their way through the crowd, toward the club's entrance. A few yards from their goal, the club's large glass doors, several guys blocked their exit.

"Hello, ladies," said the tallest of the three, who was wearing a Tommy Bahamas–style shirt. His hair was slicked back like Don Johnson's in *Miami Vice.* The other two, one black and the other Hispanic looking, hung back as the self-elected white spokesman for the trio stepped closer to Zoie. A little too close. "Can't leave now, ladies. The party's just getting started!" he shouted over the booming music.

Zoie gave him a lopsided smile and her best New York–schooled, all-purpose stare. "Sorry, guys—we're in a hurry." From behind she grabbed Tina's hand and gave her a "come on" tug. With a wide side step, they passed the guys and were out the door in seconds. The glass door swung closed, muffling the eardrum shattering *boom boom* inside.

In the warm Miami air, Zoie took a long, deep breath. "Girl, I can't hang anymore. Ten years ago I would have closed the place and danced each of those dudes into the floor. But now even if I could, I don't want to."

"I know what you mean," Tina sighed.

It was a respectable two o'clock when they rolled into the condo's parking space.

The next morning, Tina was up, dressed, and rushing to meet Walt at nine. Fingering her curly, close-cut coif, she explained that Walt was anxious to show her his studio. He had arranged for her to meet the seniors who'd volunteered to be in the yoga video. Volunteering didn't mean they were automatically in. They had to audition.

"How am I going to tell an eager eighty-year-old, 'You didn't make the cut'?" Tina asked Zoie, who lingered in bed, her eyes half-closed, as Tina dressed.

Zoie didn't answer. She was in the first stage of martini recuperation. Drinking had never been her thing. Why hadn't she remembered that last night? She covered her eyes with her arm, wishing that the bright sun from the balcony doors would go away. "Do we have to get up?" she moaned.

"I do, but you don't. Sleep in. Walt's picking me up downstairs in a few minutes. There's herb tea in the cupboard, bran muffins on the counter, and cut-up fruit in the fridge."

"Thanks," Zoie managed, although the act of speaking was painful.

"And I'm leaving the car keys and an extra door key on the table. But the way you look, I doubt you'll be going anywhere."

To Zoie's throbbing ears, the keys hitting the table sounded like empty trash cans being overturned in an alley.

Zoie made her mouth move. "I'll get up. I told you I'm going to Boca." The forearm she'd been using to shield the sun's rays from her eyes dropped away. Through her headache blur, she could see Tina's silhouette at the foot of the bed. Her friend was shaking her head. "Why don't you wait? Wait until I get back. Then I'll go to Boca with you. I'll make sure Walt gets me back by one."

For a second Zoie felt waiting for Tina sounded like a plan. Despite her fogged brain, her better judgment set in. This was going to be her opportunity to check out her hunch about potential improprieties at the Foundation.

"That's okay. I'd rather do this alone," Zoie explained. "I don't want to cut into our beach time. I want to get this over with." Zoie was about to add that if they showed up together at Carmen Silva's door, they might scare the woman into silence. But then again Tina wouldn't understand the delicacies of the situation without a long explanation. And Zoie's brain hurt too much for long explanations.

Thank goodness that Tina didn't push the issue. Once more Zoie closed her eyes and opened them again when she heard a thud near her head.

"Here's Tylenol, and a glass of water is on the table next to the bed," Tina said.

"Thanks," Zoie groaned.

"And I've got your cell number, and you've got mine."

Zoie opened her eyes long enough to see Tina using her fingers to indicate the completion of items on her mental checklist.

"Do me a favor," Zoie said, her voice low and hoarse like a longtime smoker.

"What? Did I forget something?"

"Turn on your phone."

"Oh." Tina smirked. She had the habit of keeping her cell phone off. Often it was impossible to reach her directly. The new Tina had severed the electronic appendage that used to hang from her ear. Even in a detached state, she kept phones at a distance—unconnected.

"What's the point of having your number if I can't get in touch?" Zoie said, straining to get her voice beyond a gravelly whisper.

"Okay, Ms. Leftover Martini, I'll turn it on."

"Tina, don't be mean. In this condition I can't fight back."

"I know. It hurts. Drink water, and think about what you want to do tonight. If you need to stay in, that's fine with me."

"Definitely no martinis."

"I'm surprised you can form the word." Tina turned and left.

CHAPTER 21

CARMEN SILVA

Not since her college days had Zoie been so hungover. At one point in the early morning, the pain above her eyes was so brutal that she fantasized about the therapeutic benefits of decapitation—of having a body free of its damaged head. Thanks to two more hours of sleep and some blessed Tylenol, the pulsing pain in Zoie's temple finally subsided. She extended her arms and lifted her shoulders and managed a gentle stretch. Yes, life was still worth living, but going forward, it would be lived without martinis.

After downing two glasses of water as Tina had instructed and a quiet wait of twenty minutes, she pronounced herself well enough to proceed with her plan to visit the mysterious Carmen Silva.

She showered and dressed at a leisurely pace and then settled on a stool next to the tall counter, which separated the kitchenette area from the rest of the place. The earlier havoc in her head hadn't affected her stomach. She made a cup of hot tea and, in a matter of minutes, devoured the muffin and fruit lovingly left by Tina.

Her time in Florida would be short, and the day hadn't started well. Talking to Carmen Silva was a now-or-never matter. Zoie's best instincts told her that her conversation with this Silva woman had to be in person. Sensitive topics didn't make for phone discussions, especially between strangers. She checked her notepad for the page where she'd scribbled Carmen Silva's address. Smiling smugly, she recalled her amateur sleuth activities, in which she had rummaged through Regina's desk during the after hours to obtain it.

Going to Boca without calling first to check if someone would even be home was indeed a folly. But then the whole thing was folly. Even if Carmen was home, it was a long shot that this woman would be willing to talk to a stranger. The whole thing could backfire. The woman could complain to the Foundation. Still, something drove Zoie on. She had to go through with her plan.

In the building's parking lot, Tina's car looked like every other small white rental vehicle, except that Tina had added her own means of ID: a neon-pink pompom. Zoie spotted the fuzzy ball hanging from the car's rearview mirror.

The Florida sun's tropical intensity had heated up the car, even though it was parked in the shade of the building. She cranked down the driver's side window to release the hot air. The car door felt as hollow as an empty sardine can. Definitely this car qualified as basic transportation when compared to Tina's BMW, which sat idle in its DC parking space. Zoie turned the key in the ignition and set the air conditioner on full blast. After a few jerky stops, she steered the vehicle onto the main road.

The trek to Boca would be Zoie's first time heading north from Fort Lauderdale. In her previous trips with Elliot, their destinations always had been south, down in Miami, and one time to the Keys. She followed I-95 North, rehearsing what she'd say to Carmen Silva when they stood face to face. From Regina's description Carmen sounded like a kindred spirit, someone who took her job seriously, and whose recommendations and expertise might have been ignored. Zoie could hardly claim that her experience was the same. Since coming to work at the Foundation, everyone there had embraced her. Hadn't she been made a member of the Foundation's board? As far as she could tell, Ray and Milton had been bringing her in on significant decisions, but Ray had been patronizing. He wanted her involved, all right, in the way a parent wants a child to be involved—there to listen and follow directions, not to ask probing questions. Perhaps Carmen would understand and at least offer Zoie some insights on their work environment and maybe more.

Distracted, Zoie nearly missed her exit from I-95. Thank goodness that traffic was light. She steered the small car across two lanes, just in time to make the right-hand ramp marked Yamato Road West. Now intent on following her MapQuest instructions, printed two days prior, she performed several more maneuvers that put her at the gated entrance of Tara Palms.

Pulling up to the small guard shack, she found no guard in sight and the gate raised. She hesitated, expecting some uniformed person to appear, but then drove through.

"Some security."

With red tile roofs and white stucco exteriors, the homes of Tara Palms were typical Floridian-Spanish style. These homes were not mansions but were larger than most, situated close to the street, dwarfing their small front lawns and extra-wide driveways. Zoie noticed that the neighborhood was immaculate. The streets looked as if they had been power washed—if not by man or machine, then by a torrential Florida downpour.

It was Saturday, a day when people were supposed to be home. Surprised, Zoie found the streets deserted. A few cars sat in their driveways. A little way down the street, a child's bike equipped with training wheels lay ditched on a patch of thick lawn. The place felt like a ghost town, as if all its residents had been evacuated. Perhaps it was just that the residents knew better than to linger outside in the scorching heat of mid-day.

Zoie made slow progress, checking each curbside address while being vigilant to the possibilities that a child—perhaps the one belonging to the bike—might dash from behind a palm at any moment. Carmen Silva's address was about three blocks into the development. A purple car, looking like a giant misplaced eggplant, sat in the driveway. The car gave her hope that somebody was home.

Zoie parked and sat with the engine still running. A remnant of the hangover shot to her right temple, the pain vanishing quickly over her eye. Perhaps the resurrected headache was an omen about the bizarre meeting about to occur. She slumped into the steering wheel, resting her head on its upper edge. Part of her wanted to pull away from the curb, to turn the car around, and to forget the wrongheaded idea that had brought her to this house. But she'd come this far. She would regret it if she didn't go through with it.

The car's air conditioner whined as it continued to pump out cool air. Zoie lingered in its breeze, reconsidering her little speech meant to persuade Carmen to talk.

Minutes ticked by. Perhaps the woman had already looked out her window and was wondering why this car had parked in front of her house. It was time to move. Zoie dreaded abandoning the cool comfort of the car almost as much as she dreaded meeting this woman without a reasonable explanation as to why. In a final step to prepare, she checked her hair and makeup in the visor mirror, grabbed her bag from the passenger's seat, and entered Florida's perpetual sauna.

At the residence's double doors, she found the bell, rang it, and waited under the shade of a small overhang. It seemed as if many minutes passed before a woman—short and round, dressed in white shorts and a bright-pink top—opened the door.

"Yes," the woman said, her face expressionless, her skin seeping a scent like bubblegum.

"Is Carmen Silva in?"

"She is. Who's calling?" The voice was deep for such a small woman; her few words were laced with a thick Spanish accent.

"Mommy, who is it?" A younger woman said, preempting the older one from behind. This one was tall and had big dark eyes and short dark hair done in an attractive feather cut. "Mommy, por favor, check on Joey for me. I'll handle this."

Oh, thought Zoie. *Already I'm something to be handled, and I haven't even started.*

The older woman didn't respond immediately to the woman who was obviously her daughter. She stayed at the door for a moment, staring at Zoie before retreating into the cool darkness of the house.

"I'm Carmen Silva," the younger woman said, stepping on to the walkway and pulling the door almost closed, thus denying Zoie a view into the house.

"Hello, Ms. Silva," Zoie said, offering a hand and a perky smile worthy of a prize distributor working for Publishers Clearing House.

Clearly suspicious, the woman returned the handshake. "Look, miss, I don't know what you're selling, but right now I'm in the middle of something."

Knowing that if she didn't talk fast the door would be shut her face, Zoie said in rapid fire, "I'm not selling anything. I just need a few minutes. My name is Zoie Taylor. I work at Crayton Industry."

At the mention of Crayton, the woman's eyes went wide and then quickly narrowed. "Who sent you?"

"No one."

"It's the Foundation, isn't it? The Foundation sent you."

"I work for the Foundation, but—"

"I knew it." The woman backed into her door. This time the door was in motion and about to close.

"Wait! Please!" Zoie stepped closer as if preparing to use her body to maintain the door's gap.

"I have nothing to say to you."

"But wait, please!"

The woman hesitated long enough for Zoie to make her plea. "Give me a second, please," said Zoie. "I came because I was in the area. I swear. No one sent me. I'm not here officially."

Carmen waited, her head peeking from behind the door.

"I need to talk to you. Regina told me about you," Zoie explained. "You remember Regina Bullock. She spoke so highly of you. Said you were a real professional." It was Zoie's half-assed attempt to follow her planned script, the one that was supposed to break the ice.

"Regina promised not to give out my address."

"Ugh, she didn't. Not directly anyway," Zoie said with an apologetic shrug, hoping not to have to explain how she'd come to have it.

"Look, I left the Foundation because I was tired of talking. Talking with no one listening. I've done my talking," Carmen said.

"I understand, but I swear that no one sent me. I just started at the Foundation this summer."

"I bet they still tell stories about me, huh?" Carmen said, smirking as she clung to the half-closed door.

"No, not at all. At least not to me."

"Then why are you here?" Carmen stepped from behind the door but still clung to it, prepared for a quick retreat.

"If you'd give me a few minutes, I'll explain…"

From inside, Zoie heard a child's cry. Carmen's head jerked around behind the door. "Joey! Listen to Abuela!" Clearly anxious, she turned back to Zoie and gave a hard stare. "What were you saying?"

"I was saying that since I was in the area, I thought I'd come over to ask a few questions," Zoie said.

"Ask me questions? Why?" Carmen was clearly irritated. "I don't work there anymore. I've been gone from that place for eighteen months."

"You're right. Perhaps I shouldn't have come."

Zoie's willingness to leave seemed to do the trick. The woman's defenses relaxed as she thought for a second. Inside the house the child's cries grew louder. She stuck her head back behind the door and called. "Mommy, que pasa con Joey?"

"I can see this is not a good time," Zoie said.

"It's never a good time," Carmen responded, sighing. "I guess I have a second. Come in."

"Thank you."

The child had stopped crying. Carmen sighed again as if thankful for the silence. She ushered Zoie to a wide hall.

Zoie took stock of her surroundings. The home's exterior had been deceptive. She wasn't quite sure what she expected. Nonetheless, she was impressed. The entryway opened to a magnificent living room, offering a spectacular view of a lake through a wall of windows that were two stories tall. "Your home is lovely," Zoie said with an admiring gaze.

"Thank you," Carmen said, but as soon as she had spoken again, the silence was broken—this time the child was screaming. With a look of disgust, Carmen closed her eyes for a second to gain her composure. She didn't go running to check as parents do when their children screamed. Zoie surmised that the event must happen often.

"I hope the child's okay," Zoie said, unable to keep from butting in.

"Please, wait here."

Carmen disappeared into the house, leaving Zoie standing in the hall. Zoie wanted to wander into the living room but thought it would be presumptuous. Instead, she let the view of the lake draw her eyes from where she stood. The child's wail not withstanding, the room had a palpable calm about it, a serenity she'd disturbed with her visit.

Carmen was gone for a good five minutes, returning only when the child's crying had stopped. Noticeably less irritated, she apologized for leaving Zoie standing there.

Zoie followed her barefooted hostess across the beige tile floor and into a living room, where she was directed to one of two white armchairs angled with a view of the lake.

Carmen situated herself on an opposite couch and clasped her hands between her knees. "Sorry about that. My mother wants to use the old ways with my son. He's only three. She wants to smack him on the bottom when he doesn't do what she tells him right away. That's the way my siblings and I were raised. But I don't want to raise my son like that." She looked bewildered, as if she was trying to convince herself that her way was right.

Zoie was silent.

"I didn't get your name."

"Zoie Taylor."

"Ms. Taylor, do you have children?"

"Yes, a daughter. Nikki. She's six."

"Then you understand."

"About discipline? Yes, I understand, though I wish my mother were around to help with Nikki. My mother and daughter never met. She died before Nikki was born." Zoie stared off at the lake. It had been a long time since she'd discussed her mother with anyone, except her grandmother. From the corner of her eye, she caught a glimpse of Carmen's face. The woman's angry face had softened. Although Zoie hadn't planned it, talking about her mother seemed to break the ice.

"I'm sorry to hear about your mother," Carmen said after some silence. "I complain about my mother, but actually I don't know what I'd do without her. We're very close. My husband is a pilot, and she stays with me when he's out of town."

"I see. I really appreciate you're taking the time to talk to me."

"I'm sorry I've been so abrupt. It's just that anything to do with the Crayton Foundation sets me off. That place was another lifetime—one I'd rather forget."

"This is new for me. I've only worked there a couple of months. I'm still trying to figure the place out."

"Good luck," Carmen said with short snort, looking away.

"Ms. Silva, why did you leave?"

"Why did I leave Crayton? Why did I leave?" Carmen looked up at the two-story ceiling as if to call on heaven for the answer. "You want the official reason?"

"Whatever reason you want to give me." Happy that Carmen was talking, Zoie didn't want to pressure her.

Carmen sighed. "I don't know what people have told you, but I left because my husband's job relocated to Miami."

"That's the official story?"

"Yes." Carmen was now wearing her poker face and keeping her hands folded in her lap.

Carmen was going to play coy or at least attempt it. Zoie had seen these signals before from witnesses, people giving depositions. Body language spoke volumes over what came from people's mouths. So she waited. There was no need to push. This woman wanted to talk, and eventually she would. "I see," Zoie said.

"But even if he hadn't relocated, I would have left anyway," Carmen continued.

"You weren't happy at the Foundation?"

"That's an understatement." Nervously Carmen rubbed her palms into her denim-clad thighs as if she were trying to remove dirt from them. "I'm not surprised you're finding it difficult. I've never worked at such an unprofessional place."

Zoie was on the edge of her seat. She could tell, with just gentle pressure, that what she wanted to know from Carmen Silva was about to come pouring out. "How so?"

"Ms. Taylor, you're the grant advisor who took my place, right?"

"Actually, no. As far as I know, Ray never replaced you." Zoie reached into her bag and pulled out a business card. Stretching forward, she handed it to Carmen.

Carmen glanced at the card. "An attorney, huh. So the Foundation finally got its own attorney. It needs one...perhaps I've said enough."

"I swear my reasons for being here are strictly personal. Whatever you tell me will remain confidential. Think of it as an attorney-client privilege."

"I hope I have no need for an attorney, Ms. Taylor. And according to your business card, the Foundation *is* your client."

"You're absolutely right," Zoie said. "But at present I'm not here in that capacity."

"Hmm." Carmen looked at the card again. "Says here you're also the board secretary. You're in pretty deep." She threw the card on the coffee table. It spun like a pinwheel on the glass surface, coming to rest against an exquisite pottery vase with a single pink bloom.

Zoie's eyes followed the spinning. Then she squirmed in her seat at Carmen's accusatory tone. "I'm not sure what you mean."

"Ms. Taylor, you're part of the Foundation's inner sanctum. Me, I was only a peon, an outsider. I was never in on the big meetings."

"Ms. Silva, did Ray ever make sexual advances toward you?" Zoie hadn't intended to be so blunt.

Carmen's eyes widened. "Wow!"

"Sorry. Don't answer if it makes you uncomfortable," Zoie said quickly. The nonpushy tactic had worked before. Maybe it would work again.

For a second Carmen looked puzzled. With arms folded she pushed back into the couch and then began to speak. "'Uncomfortable' isn't quite the way I'd describe it. More like funny." Carmen snickered and rolled her eyes. "You think Ray... Ray Gaddis and me? What a thought."

"I didn't mean to imply that *you* were interested in him."

"You're right about that." Carmen adjusted her position. "Ms. Taylor, don't tell me Ray has been coming on to you."

"Thankfully, no. I thought maybe that's why you left the Foundation."

"You think sexual harassment drove me out?" Carmen couldn't contain her laughter. It was haunting as it echoed off the high ceiling and vibrated in the otherwise quiet room. Carmen leaned forward, retrieved the business card, and looked at it again. "May I call you Zoie?"

"By all means."

"Well, Zoie, the truth is...I'm hardly Ray's type. Neither are you. Ray is gay."

Now it was Zoie's turn to be stunned. "Ray? No way. He's married. He has kids."

Tight mouthed, Carmen shrugged.

The thought of Ray being gay hadn't crossed Zoie's mind. Not that his sexual preference bothered her one way or the other, except that this new information destroyed her whole theory about him being a womanizer. How did this woman know this kind of information?

"I'm finding this hard to believe."

"Believe it. I'm telling you that he is," Carmen continued.

"Are you just speculating, or do you know this for sure?" Zoie looked the woman in the eye.

At first Carmen barely blinked. Then she fingered her dark feathered hair, bit her bottom lip, and looked down as if considering what to say. "Listen, you've come to find out something, but the something you've found out isn't what you expected."

"Yes, you're right. I sure wasn't expecting to hear that Ray is gay."

"Granted, he's not obvious at all. Then I guess I should explain how I know."

With Zoie all ears, Carmen shifted on the couch and started her explanation slowly, in a voice not quite a whisper. "I was working late one night. I used to work a lot of late hours. I seemed to be the only one who did, but that's another story. One night I needed to finish a report. That place could be creepy, especially in the winter, when it gets dark early. Anyway, being alone I was a little skittish. I heard noises coming from the file room down the hall."

"The room near the copy machine?"

"Yes, you know the one. Well, the cleaning crew had already been through for the evening. I figured one of them had come back. At least I was hoping that was what it was. As I got closer, I heard these low grunts. I peeked in, expecting to see the cleaning crew. And there they were."

"The cleaning crew messing around?"

"No, Ray and Milton. Going at it."

"Oh my God!" Zoie grimaced and covered her eyes with her hands as if to do so would protect her from the mental images of the file-room scene.

"You asked how I know," Carmen said in a matter-of-fact tone.

"What did they say to you?"

"They didn't see me or hear me, as far as I know. They were too involved. Humph."

"So what did you do?"

"I got out of there pronto. Went home. Had a drink. Actually two drinks."

"My goodness." Zoie took a deep breath. "I'm having a hard time with this."

"How do you think I felt?"

Zoie pictured an imaginary headline in the business section of the *Washington Post*: "Crayton Foundation Head Fired. Details on p. F-2." Well, maybe not the headline but one of the stories for sure. She frowned. "I don't know what to say. This is unbelievable."

"Believe it," Carmen said emphatically.

"So you kept this quiet?"

"Not exactly. I told my mother, my husband, my sister…and now you."

"You didn't tell Regina?"

"Oh, no. If I had told Regina, you'd already know the details. I guess the whole world would know. You may have noticed she can't keep a secret." Carmen sucked her teeth in disgust. "I specifically asked her to *not* give out my address and to use it only to send me personal mail."

"In fairness to Regina," Zoie confessed, "she didn't give me your address. I found your address among her things."

It was Carmen's turn to frown. "Well, that's not good either. As for Ray, other than the people that I've mentioned, I haven't told anyone. Frankly I don't know why I'm telling you now," Carmen said, rubbing her hands together, appearing nervous.

In the long silence that followed, Zoie tried to comprehend all that she had heard. Carmen was right. Zoie had come on a fact-finding mission, expecting that she already knew the answers. She couldn't stop shaking her head in disbelief. There had been no hint of Ray's being gay, let alone of his having a relationship with Milton, other than that of the boss and the "golden boy." Milton functioned as the de facto second in command. Everyone knew he was Ray's confidant. That was reason enough for their frequent closed-door meetings, not that she had been counting. She'd adopted a policy of keeping meetings with Ray to a minimum. It wasn't that she disliked Ray—dislike was too strong a word. Her feeling was better expressed in a childhood expression: she found him *icky*. She, like Carmen, now knew Ray's secret—a secret that was icky *and* volatile.

"I never suspected," Zoie said, nearly whispering, continuing to shake her head. "Milton and Ray?"

"I didn't know either until I saw them with my own eyes. In retrospect there were signs," Carmen said, sitting up. "But I never put them all together. I mean that Milton is obvious, but by itself that means nothing."

Zoie found her composure to speak. "Then you left the Foundation because of this knowledge. This incident made you uncomfortable?"

"My God! Talk about awkward!" Carmen held both cheeks. "It's hard to look people in the eye when you've seen them with their pants down." She smiled. "In the days following, I don't know what was worse—running into Milton or Ray or seeing them together in meetings."

"I can imagine," Zoie said, trying to not smile too hard since she couldn't help but picture the uncomfortable incidents.

"I wouldn't leave a job because of someone's sexual preference."

"Of course not, but what about the fact that having sex in the office violates standards of appropriate office behavior? I don't care whether the sex is homosexual or heterosexual, let alone that Ray is an officer at Crayton."

"Yeah, I know. Right. It was serious stuff. But that's not what did it for me," Carmen continued.

"Then why *did* you leave the Foundation?"

Carmen sighed and clasped her hands. "I left because Ray was an asshole. No pun intended."

Zoie smiled with clinched teeth and a raised brow. "He was being stupid. You caught him. Others could do the same." *Another stupid executive*, Zoie thought.

"It was more than that," Carmen said with a frown distorting her attractive face. "That place was sleazy. Ray was sleazy. Milton was sleazy." She hesitated, trying to think of what to say. "Have you witnessed how the grants are given out?"

"Huh?"

"You must have wondered! Didn't grant season just pass?"

"If you mean how grants are given out procedurally, yeah, it's a little loose." Zoie didn't want to be more specific. Having approached Carmen, Zoie was already on the ethical fringe.

"A little loose! You didn't notice how Ray dishes out funding? He treats the Foundation's funds like his personal treasure chest. King Ray likes to grant wishes to his personal favorites."

"But the Board has the final say," Zoie said.

"I've never attended one of the Foundation's Board meetings. Remember, I was a peon. All I know is whatever Ray recommended to the Board is what the members okayed."

Zoie smirked. "Humph."

"Ray calls the shots," Carmen continued. "Then he struts like a peacock when he gets his way."

"I see." Zoie's voice was hushed.

"Don't tell me you haven't noticed. Isn't that what really brought you here?"

"I just happened to be in Fort Lauderdale for the weekend. It wasn't a special trip," Zoie answered in defense of her actions.

"Uh-huh. And you just came to see me because you had nothing else to do? Ms. Taylor, don't fool yourself. You suspect something. You know something."

"I do have concerns. Part of my job is to keep the Foundation from being sued."

"Good luck," Carmen said in a snappy tone.

"You're insinuating that there's hanky panky beyond sex in the office. Help me, please. Give me a clue here. Obviously, you know a lot."

There was a long silence while Carmen considered how much she should say. She got up and walked to the picture windows and stared out at the lake. Then she turned to face Zoie. "Okay, let's say…you've noticed the same things that I did. Maybe that's your concern."

"Could you be more specific?"

"Maybe you noticed some irregularities in the way some of Ray's favorite grantees are handled or in how these grantees account for their spending."

Zoie sat back in her chair. "Could be," she answered.

"And maybe you've noticed how Ray always pressures for a particular grantee."

"You mean Mahali Salaam?"

Carmen shrugged and, with a Cheshire smile, tilted her head to indicate agreement.

Zoie said, "That homeless shelter seems to be a worthwhile investment for the Foundation."

Carmen smiled. "I've nothing against the homeless, but when other successful, innovative programs are being cut…" she said, returning to the couch.

"Which programs are you talking about? Which one did Ray cut?"

"I try to forget this stuff."

"Let me help you. Was it Magnum Youth Literacy?"

"At least that one."

"Did you ever tell Ray about your concerns?"

"Yes," Carmen said emphatically, "both before and after the file-room incident—though God knows dealing with him after was difficult." Carmen rolled her eyes.

"What did Ray say?"

"Humph. He told me I was making a 'mountain out of a molehill.' He called me a nitpicker and said that I was letting bureaucratic details get in the way of providing service to the community. What a bunch of bull." Carmen rolled her eyes again. "I told him I thought it was my job to look thoroughly into our grantee operations and to make recommendations. Then he accused me of not being a team player." As she spoke, Carmen's sun-kissed cheeks grew red. "He told me if I couldn't go along with the *changed agenda*, then I should move on."

"Is that what you did?"

"That's right. I moved on."

"Whoa!" Zoie said.

"I'm surprised that an audit hasn't uncovered this stuff. One day it's going to hit the newspapers. It won't make the papers here in Florida."

"And I don't want to be part of a news story," Zoie whispered.

There was another long silence, which was broken by a sharp cry coming from upstairs. This time the cry was different: it signaled a hurt child, not an irritated one. Carmen jumped up from the couch and stormed from the room, her bare feet pounding the ceramic tiles, sounding like a four-hundred-pound sumo wrestler.

After a while the crying subsided, but the quiet was soon broken by the loud voices of two women squabbling in Spanish. The child's screams joined the raucous. For Zoie the distraction of the noise from upstairs was momentary. The potential consequences of her new knowledge preoccupied her mind. Was what she had heard about Ray and the Foundation true? There was no reason to believe that Carmen was lying or to attribute her damaging allegations to the ramblings of a disgruntled employee. As an officer of the Foundation, Zoie was duty bound to act. It was the right thing to do, and if something came out later, she could be implicated and deemed negligent if she failed to take action to remedy the situation. But which situation? The in-office fornication or the alleged misappropriation of the Foundation's funds? She was sitting on a ticking time bomb.

Anxious to leave, Zoie checked her watch. It was one o'clock, the time Tina expected to be back at the apartment. Zoie retrieved her cell from her bag and pressed the programmed number for Tina. The line rang several times until Tina's automated voice chimed in and urged the caller to leave a message. "Figures," Zoie said.

Carmen reentered the room. "Sorry about that. My son decided to jump off my bed. He thinks he's Spiderman, but he hasn't learned to land."

"I've heard that boys are more active than girls." Zoie thought of Nikki. The truth was she could envision Nikki doing the exact same thing. Zoie smiled and stood. "I better go."

"Ms. Taylor, we've talked about a lot of things today. I've probably said *way more* than I should have. I need to know something: What do you intend to do with what I've told you?"

"I'm not sure," Zoie answered, gazing at the floor.

Carmen winced, her slender body becoming tense. "Please don't pull me into anything to do with Crayton. I won't give any official statements."

"I understand." During her years at Fairday and Winston, Zoie had encountered many people whose accounts of unsavory or illicit acts were given only with the promise that their disclosures would remain off the record. Having witnessed such events, most people didn't want to get sucked further into the mire. Cautious witnesses clammed up, a tendency that benefited her corporate clients and left prosecutors frustrated.

"I won't give an official statement about anything," Carmen repeated.

"It may end here."

"No, I have a strong feeling that it's not over for you," Carmen said.

Not sure of what to say, Zoie just shrugged.

Carmen walked Zoie to the door. Zoie stepped down the single step to the walkway and turned to face her host. "Again, thank you for your time and for being so frank."

"Perhaps I've put a light on some things for you," Carmen said as she clung to the door. Then with a matter-of-fact tone, as if she were ordering meat at the butcher's, she said, "I wish you luck in your quest, but I must ask that you don't contact me again. And I will deny anything that I've told you today. I'm sorry, but that's the way it has to be."

Before Zoie could utter a word, the door closed.

CHAPTER 22
GUILTY UNTIL PROVEN INNOCENT

On the drive from Boca back to Fort Lauderdale, Zoie's head whirled from Carmen's revelations. She felt stung by the meeting's abrupt ending. Naively she'd begun to consider Carmen Silva an ally—someone she could count on, someone who could help interpret further findings. However, Carmen made it clear that she wouldn't come forward to make any official statements and that she wanted no more contact.

Zoie parked Tina's rental car in its designated spot and made her way into the elevator. The heavy afternoon heat followed her through the passageway until she keyed into the air-conditioned efficiency. Tina hadn't returned from the yoga auditions and as usual was incommunicado.

Zoie cut a slice of carrot cake, grabbed a glass of iced herb tea, and plopped in a lounge chair on the covered balcony. The ocean breeze on the building's balcony side made it cooler. Staring into the distance, Zoie was oblivious to the buildings blocking her ocean view. Her mind was elsewhere as she recounted Carmen's every word: the unfortunate sex scene featuring Ray and Milton,

Carmen's concerns about the grants, and Ray's invitation to her to leave. Of course, Carmen could have been exaggerating, even making the whole thing up. A wounded ex-employee could easily fabricate a whopper of a tale. Zoie had seen it before: employee retaliation with months of out-of-court negotiations, usually ending in eventual settlements with nondisclosure agreements. But the more Zoie considered Carmen Silva, the more she believed the woman. She seemed straightforward and not motivated by money; she was not someone seeking revenge. She wasn't out to make more trouble for the Foundation. No suit was pending or about to be filed. This woman wanted no part of the Foundation. Carmen Silva had told the truth.

Zoie shoved a chunk of the carrot cake into her mouth and swallowed it, failing to chew first. Its uncomfortable dryness stuck in her throat until she downed it with a swig of tea. What was she going to do? So this was why Ray had pressured her to support funding for the Shelter. His boundless enthusiasm for Mahali Salaam had always seemed a little fishy, exceeding what one might simply think of as altruistic sponsorship. He was selling Mahali like a used-car salesman promoting a prized lemon.

And where was the Shelter's money going, money that was supposed to be there for that truck, that alarm system, and God only knows what else? But all those things were on the Shelter's end. Was Ray covering for them?

Then there was Jahi, serious and dedicated. She didn't want to believe that he could be caught up in something crooked. It was only fair that she confront him and give him the opportunity to tell her that she was wrong. As for Ray she'd give him that same benefit of the doubt. His office indiscretions were a separate issue. Or were they? The possibilities of what else could be happening frightened her, things like embezzlement, extortion, and kickbacks.

Her thoughts of fraud possibilities bounced from bad to worse. Maybe she'd been reading too many crime novels. After all, this was happening in real life, not in a book, a movie, or a TV show. As sloppy as the Foundation's practices were, she'd always felt that the lack of a process was because everyone was anxious to make things simpler and more convenient for the grantees, an attitude that the grantees were there to do good work for the community, not to dot i's and to cross t's. Why couldn't it end there? With everyone squeaky clean, a little loose and a little unstructured, but certainly well intentioned.

The sky's brightness bore heavy on her eyes. Her eyes, which had been staring at nothing yet seeing everything, closed.

Zoie didn't know how long she'd been asleep on the balcony when Tina startled her. Her friend was glowing with excitement.

"Tina, don't sneak up on me like that."

"I'm sorry. You were having such a nice nap."

"Where's Walt?" Zoie asked, still trying to get a fix on the time, the day, and the planet.

"Don't worry. You'll meet him. He had an appointment. He said he would stop by and take us to lunch tomorrow, before your plane."

Zoie came out of her stupor. "So how were the auditions?"

"Well, we didn't get that far. But it's definitely workable. Walt's studio is small. We thought we could shoot it there or maybe at the community clubhouse at this senior citizens' complex."

"I thought you wanted to do the video on the beach? You know, water, sand, sky."

"Right…that's still under consideration. We'd have to build a solid platform. I don't think these folks could do yoga moves in the sand," Tina said as she pressed her hands together in a prayer position and balanced on one leg. Tina came out of the pose and pulled up a chair next to Zoie. "And what about you? Did you lounge all morning?"

"No, I made it to Boca."

"You did?" Tina looked surprised.

"Hey, remind me to stay away from anything with alcohol."

Tina grinned, but Zoie's face was dead serious.

"No problem. I'll remind you. So what's up with this woman in Boca? You made it sound so mysterious. Like CIA stuff or something."

"Girlfriend, you've been living in DC too long," Zoie said.

"Nothing juicy like that, huh?"

"Oh, it's juicy all right. I wish it wasn't," Zoie replied, her lips twisting.

"Zo, this must be serious. So tell me. You know I can keep my mouth shut. Who would I tell anyway?"

"Walt!"

"Tsk. No! Seriously, mum's the word. Okay."

There was a long silence as Zoie considered her friend's trustworthiness. This was privileged corporate information with significant ramifications. In truth, however, she had to tell someone. She needed a sanity check and some advice.

"Well, do you want me to guess?" Tina asked.

Zoie wasn't ready for twenty questions. "Okay, I'll tell you, but you're sworn to secrecy."

In a mock swearing in, Tina raised her right hand. "Okay, out with it. And after all this formality, this better be good."

Zoie leaned toward Tina, her lightweight lounge chair creaking. "Well, this woman named Carmen used to work at the Foundation," Zoie said, starting slowly, aware that Tina was hanging on to her every word. "She told me that the Foundation's president, Ray Gaddis, is gay."

Tina looked disappointed. "*Okay*. Big deal. So why do you care?"

"I don't. Well, I mean that's not the whole of it. She caught Ray and this other guy I work with having sex in the office."

"Ooh!"

"And that's not all. She confirmed my suspicions about the whole flakey-funding thing."

"Zo, you never told me any details. Actually, I don't know if I want to know." Tina bit her bottom lip and frowned. "This sounds serious."

"It is."

"What are you going to do?"

"I don't know."

Overhead a flock of birds passed through the condo canyon, honking in the breeze.

"Don't get dragged in. I don't want to read about you in the paper."

Fleeting thoughts of Enron and the scandal at United Way some years back filled Zoie's head. "Don't you think I've thought about that?" Zoie sighed. "Seems I'm damned if I do and damned if I don't."

"Wait a second. Do you trust this woman?"

Zoie put her hand to her mouth and waited to answer. "I don't think she lied. She's hiding. She wants nothing to do with Crayton Industries or the Foundation."

"What's she afraid of?" Tina said.

"I'm not sure."

"Maybe someone is after her."

"No, I think she's hiding from bad memories."

"Hmmm," Tina said, making a face. "She's not hiding very well if you found her."

"She's disgusted. Of course, I need to verify what she told me."

"Gee, Zo, I'm sorry. You know if this stuff is true, you'll have to get out of there."

Zoie frowned. She hadn't thought that far ahead. "Maybe," she said, hesitating. "It's not as if I'm in love with the place." She wondered if she should tell Tina that Carmen's revelations implicated Jahi and the Shelter but without mentioning Jahi by name.

"I think I believe her," Zoie continued. "She went out on a limb by telling me as much as she did."

"So what does your gut tell you?" Tina asked.

"What about a fact-based analysis? A person is innocent until proven guilty." Zoie's mind held images of both Ray and Jahi. "What's with this gut stuff? You sound like Carmen."

"Maybe," Tina said with raised brows. "I think I like this Carmen. She sounds like a smart lady."

"I've got to believe that something else is going on here," Zoie said.

"Zo, you're taking in all kinds of information. It goes to your subconscious. You know stuff you don't even know that you know."

"Are you trying to recite that old Arabian proverb? 'He who knows, knows not that he knows'—etcetera, etcetera…'"

"I know the saying, but this is different. This has to do with things you pick up without realizing it. Good old intuition. Your subconscious is working overtime. It knows stuff. And you know stuff at a cellular level—like the gut. That's where all those sayings about the gut come from."

"Tina, I *do* understand about 'going with your gut,'" Zoie said, annoyed by her friend's lecture.

"Sooooo what does your gut tell you now?"

Zoie felt like a reluctant witness giving a deposition. She sighed and thought for a second. "I guess my gut tells me it's true. Something is very wrong at that place. I've known it from the first. I just wish it would all go away."

"Stuff like this doesn't go away. Dirty secrets have a way of coming out, whether it's you blowing the whistle or not."

"I know," Zoie replied, sullen. "I'd just rather not be around when everything blows up. Anyway, I can't go around blowing the whistle without proof. That would be reckless, not to mention career limiting."

Tina shrugged. "Then what are you going to do?"

Zoie knew she needed to act before the situation acted on her. But all she could say was, "I don't know."

CHAPTER 23

IS HANKY PANKY
A LEGAL TERM?

"Sorry, Zoie, but Ray's schedule is extremely tight today," Arleen said as she scrolled through Ray's online calendar. "There's no way I can fit you in, unless it's an emergency."

It was serious, but Zoie wasn't about to wave the red flag. Looking over Arleen's shoulder, she tried to read the computer screen, hoping that she'd spot an opening that Arleen had overlooked. Indeed, the screen was filled with yellow blocks denoting committed times.

Arleen sighed, threw up her hands, and slapped her thighs. She was an affable woman, stuck somewhere in the Fifties, in her clean and crisp style. She was a dead ringer for Queen Elizabeth, minus a decade or two, and by all accounts, she was fiercely loyal to Ray. She turned to face Zoie and placed her folded hands on the only spot on her desktop not consumed by the shrine to her seven grandchildren. "The best I can do is Monday at eleven, for a half hour," she continued. "He needs time to get to his noon lunch appointment."

"I see," Zoie said, not at all pleased. She bit her bottom lip as a check on verbal sparring. Monday was four whole days away. That was too long to wait. She had to talk to him before she lost her nerve.

In the most pleasant voice she could muster, Zoie made her plea. "Arleen, it's urgent. Doesn't he have *anything* sooner?"

"Well," said Arleen, being more accommodating, "he's supposed to come back to sign some papers this evening. You never can tell. He might wait until morning to sign them. Can Milton Page help you? He's around today."

"No," Zoie blurted in a way she instantly recognized as being too quick. "It's Ray I really need to talk to."

Zoie realized she was getting nowhere with Ray's assistant. Arleen wanted to know the topic of the urgency, and Zoie wasn't prepared to tell her.

"I'll just catch him later," Zoie said nonchalantly. She headed down the hall to her own office, leaving Arleen somewhat bewildered.

An hour later Milton Page's bright red hair lit up Zoie's doorway.

"Zoie, what's up? Arleen said you might need me."

"Milton! Did Arleen say that? *Hmmmm.* Actually, I was looking for Ray." *Arleen is being much too efficient.* Zoie avoided looking directly into Milton's blue-gray eyes. He was handsome in a peculiar way, like a freckled-faced, grown-up Opie from *The Andy Griffith Show.* Since learning of his tryst with Ray, like Carmen, she felt uncomfortable in his presence. Milton was now officially a "junior icky."

Milton moved from the doorway and closer to her desk. "Ray may not have time to see you. He's swamped these days, but if I can be of help…"

Zoie cut him short. "What's got Ray so tied up?"

"Crayton's business side," Milton said vaguely.

"I see. But thanks for stopping by. I need to see Ray. I'll call you if I need you." She disliked getting the brush-off, the push-down to the second-tier management, to resolve her issues. There was no need to be unpleasant with Milton. He had no idea how serious the matter was. Or did he?

"Just checking," Milton said with a quizzical look. Then he turned and left.

By six in the evening, the Foundation's office had cleared out. With the Auction for the Homeless over and the Charity Walk still forty-five days away, staff didn't need to hang around. A two-person cleaning crew rolled in with a small dumpster and began emptying wastebaskets. After years among New York's corporate workaholics, Zoie felt that leaving work before 6:00 p.m. was like cheating. Today she wasn't leaving because she was trying to catch Ray.

At the end of the hall of executive suites, Arleen's workspace was dark, except for the low light of a small desk lamp, which shone like an eternal candle over her shrine of family photos. From the cracked office door belonging to Ray Gaddis, the light was more than daylight. Zoie knocked to ensure no surprises. "Ray, it's Zoie. May I come in?"

"Zoie. Um, come in," Ray said, his voice muffled.

In three months on the job, Zoie had only been in Ray's office a few times. Meetings usually took place in the conference rooms. She entered the spacious office, elegant with its black leather, chrome items, and antique oriental carpet. Next to the black leather sofa, there was an expensive-looking vase the size of a child. She took a quick scan of the blindingly white walls, bare except for the two small pieces of corporate art, the large mahogany bookcase, and the few personal pictures. Ray was behind his glass desk, seemingly ignoring her, as he busily shuffled through a pile of papers.

He looked up from his work. His brow was furrowed, and he was missing his plastic smile. He looked tired. "Arleen left me a message that you were looking for me," he said in a voice neither anxious nor inviting.

"Your assistant is very efficient," Zoie said.

"Yes, Arleen's a crackerjack. She's been with me a long time. She's like family." He pressed some buttons on his phone, turned back to Zoie, and then folded his hands on the pile. "So how can I help you? I hope it's something quick."

"Ray, it could take some time. I thought we needed to talk."

"Well, my dear, I'm afraid you've caught me at a bad time for long discussions. I have a dinner engagement."

Zoie frowned. "Then I don't want to keep you. But I think you'll find what I have to say very important."

"Hmmm. Sounds ominous. By all means tell me what's on your mind." Now he looked concerned. He gestured for her to sit in one of the leather chairs facing the desk.

She felt unprepared. She hadn't thought about just how she'd relay the information. It was unusual for Zoie not to rehearse for an important discussion. She was counting on her best attorney instincts to kick in. The key was to not accuse him, to not make it about him. She needed to emphasize her concern for the Foundation, its reputation, its grantees, and Crayton Industries overall. She didn't want to put him on the defensive.

"I'll get right to the point," she started. "Over the last few weeks, I've uncovered some disturbing information about a grantee."

"Oh," Ray said. His sleepy eyes widened as he rested his elbows on the desk. "This sounds serious."

"It is." Zoie leaned closer to the desk. "Ray, I believe there is some hanky panky going on with at least one of our grantees."

"Hanky panky? Is that a legal term? Do you mean anything like fraud?"

"Funds misappropriated, perhaps more."

"Ms. Taylor, that's quite a charge. What evidence do you have to back up your allegation?"

The fact that he hadn't asked her *which* grantee caused her to hesitate. His omission of that question was strange—damning. "I do have evidence," she continued. "Enough to warrant a full-scale investigation."

Ray laughed as if the whole thing were a joke. "Zoie, a full-scale investigation? Isn't that a bit drastic? Do you realize the consequences of such an action?"

"Yes, I think if the Foundation takes decisive action, we can't be accused of either negligence or complicity." Still, she hadn't mentioned the grantee's name, and he hadn't asked. Clearly, he already knew.

There was a long silence. Ray rose from his chair. He turned and faced his picture window, which looked out to the infamous Needle Park, where the homeless congregated. "See those poor devils down there?" he said. "They need us. Frivolous accusations or overzealous lawyering could send shock waves through the Foundation. Through Crayton Industries, for that matter. Affect all our grantees. Disrupt the flow of funds. The media attention alone could prevent us from fulfilling our mission."

"Ray, I take offense! You think I'd make these charges frivolously?"

"You're making serious accusations, Ms. Taylor," Ray said, still with his back to her.

"You're damn right they're serious!" she shot back. It felt weird talking to his back.

A loud silence hung in the air like a heavy cloak. Ray continued to stare out the window at the park. He was either afraid to face her or pondering his next best lie. It was Zoie who broke the silence. "Ray, do you realize...you haven't even asked me *which* grantee I'm talking about?"

"Oh, yeah," he sighed as if all the air had been let out of his sails. He finally turned back to face her. "Which one is it?"

"Mahali Salaam."

Ray said nothing. He was usually full of himself, never at a loss for words.

Zoie wondered how she should proceed. Her evidence was circumstantial, but Ray didn't know that. She couldn't mention her meeting with Carmen Silva. The anomalies in the Shelter's accounting were enough to warrant calling for an investigation. Perhaps the Foundation and Mahali Salaam could survive this. But if the corruption ran deep, nothing would protect them. Unfortunately, Jahi, his dream, and the people that the Shelter served might all be victims of this corruption. *Coming forward is doing the right thing.*

Ray was now staring at his desk. He seemed stunned. She chose her next words carefully. She spoke slowly and forcefully. "Ray, I have proof. We must go to the Board."

"The Board!"

"Yes. There are numerous irregularities in the records of Mahali Salaam. And in my meeting with Sy Rosen, who represents Magnum Youth Literacy..."

"Huh! You met with those pansies. They're always bellyaching about something. They were cut because of tax problems," Ray said, groaning, his words almost unintelligible because his forefingers covered his lips.

"But the Board's decision to cut them came a full three weeks before the IRS notified them of a pending audit. I checked the dates in the files."

Ray was again silent.

"Ray, ever since I've been here, you've pressured me to be a strong advocate for the Shelter, over other worthy grant recipients."

"*Pressured* is a strong word. I wanted you to understand the value in the Shelter's work." Ray now played with a pen on his desk, spinning it like a top. "Have you mentioned your suspicions to Khalfani?"

Zoie bowed her head. "Not really. I pointed out some errors to him in the Shelter's annual report."

"And?"

"He apologized. In fact, he seemed embarrassed. He promised to look into it."

"Now see here, Zoie—does that sound like someone who is misappropriating funds?"

"Everything is not what it seems." She'd used the exact words from Simon's last prophecy. "I'm asking that you call an emergency Board meeting."

"The Board—pssssssssssh! I don't need the Board to handle this," Ray said, bellowing like a trumpet. "That is, if there's really anything to handle."

"Ray, I'm serious about this. We need the Board's involvement. We need full Board support."

"I don't need Board approval to initiate an investigative audit."

"I don't think *you* should call the audit. The audit has to be independent of you."

"What!" Ray sat straight in his chair.

Zoie hesitated, not sure that she should continue, but the words kept coming as if her mouth was on automatic pilot. Her voice was fearless and clear, her righteous persona preempting her fear of losing her job.

"I strongly recommend you use the Board," she continued. "The Board should ask for the investigation, and any investigative findings should be reported directly to all members. Look, Ray—as chair of the Board, you'll know what's going on. You'll be part of the whole thing."

"Ms. Taylor, I think you have overstepped your position in this."

"I thought I was hired to give you my best legal judgment, and I must tell you that if you don't do as I am recommending...I'll be forced to go directly to Crayton's general counsel."

"How dare you!" Ray pounded a fist on his glass desk. The glass held, but the items on it rattled.

Zoie flinched. Ray's face was red, and he was huffing like a bull. She was out on a limb, even though she hadn't laid all her cards on the table. There was no going back. One way or the other, she was leaving the Foundation. She couldn't sit around and wait, as Tina had put it, for the "boom to fall."

She rose to leave.

"Zoie, wait. Perhaps I've been too hasty. You're a very bright woman," he sputtered, his tone lowered. "I shouldn't underestimate your good intentions here. Err, your legal expertise in these matters. I understand that sometimes attorneys have to get tough with their clients. You're just trying to protect the Foundation. I appreciate that."

Zoie listened, her lips tight. His words hadn't offended her. They'd only revealed his stupidity and possibly desperation.

"If you could just hold off," he continued, "just hold off any action for twenty-four hours."

"Ray, I don't understand. What will twenty-four hours buy us?" In an attempt to keep him calm, using *us* put her back on his team. She watched as beads of sweat gathered on his forehead. If he were involved, as she now suspected, in twenty-four hours he could destroy any incriminating records.

"It's my career on the line here, as well as the Foundation's reputation, of course," he blurted. "Sensitive things like this have to be handled with care. I'm asking for twenty-four hours. I would like to work out a presentation on this for the Board. I'll need your help, of course. Anyway, we can't call a Board meeting that quickly."

"Oh," she replied. What he was saying was partly true. Such a matter needed to be handled in a face-to-face Board meeting, not an e-mail proxy meeting or even a video-conference call. The Board members all had busy schedules. Board members couldn't be expected to drop everything and run to the Crayton Foundation, unless it was really a matter of life or death. So far this hadn't approached that scale. Had she forced Ray into a sudden change of heart? She didn't know quite what to think.

"We'll send out a notice for an urgent meeting next week. They're going to ask lots of questions…we need to be prepared." Ray was regaining his air of authority.

"Ray, I've already gathered some material."

He winced. "Well, good. Good! I'd like the twenty-four hours to go over that material and consider my—I mean *our*—next steps before we send the notice to the Board."

"Then we should meet tomorrow. Same time?"

"Yes, but I'll be in Bethesda all day. Crayton officers' meeting. A mandatory event."

"The sooner we do this, the better, Ray."

"I'm sure," he responded. "Look, I have a black-tie appearance tomorrow evening. It's also up in Bethesda. After the officer's meeting, I have to run home and get dressed. Could you meet me at my home in Potomac?"

"Well…I suppose." She thought of using Tina's car, which had been sitting idly in its parking spot. She had the keys, and Tina had urged her to use it if needed.

"Then that's what we'll do. We can brainstorm on it tomorrow at six." Ray grabbed a sheet of paper and scribbled his address.

"And for the time being, let's keep this to ourselves. Right? Say nothing more to Khalfani or his crew or anyone else."

What could possibly change in twenty-four hours? Ray was going to go about his normal work schedule. "Okay," she answered. "I'll bring the material with me. Tomorrow I'll be at your house at six."

"Thank you, Zoie."

Zoie left his office, hoping that on the way to the Metro she'd run into Simon. Maybe he'd have another message for her—a less cryptic message. However, neither Simon nor his weird buddy was at their usual spot. Part of her wanted to warn Jahi. But for now she had to keep her mouth shut. He could be involved.

⊷ ⊶

From behind his glass desk, Ray Gaddis stared at the black-framed picture of his prize, the *Bonnie Princess*. The shot was taken the day he sailed her up to Annapolis. His fifty-foot sailboat was his dream of a lifetime. But most weekends the boat stayed docked. Time to sail was at a premium. What would happen to the *Bonnie Princess* if he had to serve time?

Ray tapped his wedding band on the arm of his chair. Over the last year, his nervous tapping had badly scarred the chrome. Things had been going well. To some degree the financial rock he'd been under was lifted. He'd mastered juggling the funds for boat payments and tuition at Brown and Yale for his twin sons, Gavin and Glen. The hefty mortgage on his ten-thousand-square-foot home on Benniford Lane, in Potomac, was still doable. Ray sighed. Money was tight, but he was surviving.

"Ahh. How did life get so complicated?" He moaned.

Four more years at the Foundation was his rough calculation of the time left before he could comfortably retire. Then he'd say

193

adios to all those Crayton bastards—the ones who grated on his nerves with their disingenuous pats on the back, the ones who'd pushed him into the dead-end Foundation job with a cut in salary and no bonuses, and the ones for whom he'd perfected his famous Gaddis smile. Now this nosey little legal bitch was going to mess it all up.

The Crayton rumor mill had it that Anthony Clarke would personally ask him to resume his old position as head of Operations. The inner sanctum had put out feelers: "Ray Gaddis back in the saddle over in Operations—what do you think?" They even sent a flunky—Deputy General Council Jeffries—to feel him out.

"Ray, we know you like the Foundation job, but we may need you back in Operations. How would you feel if Tony asked you to step in again? Take the reins of Operations? It would only be temporary, until we could find someone."

"Don't know. I'd have to give it some thought," he'd answered. "You know I'll do what's right for the company."

That night Ray met a young man at a Capitol Hill bar. It was the best damn sex he'd had in over a year. In the subsequent days, he strutted like a rooster. It was all he could do to stifle his smiles of victory. He planned how he'd turn down Clarke's official offer. *The nerve of them,* Ray thought. They expected him to bail Crayton out after unceremoniously kicking him to the curb.

A real offer, however, never materialized. All Ray could think was that Anthony really hated him. The feeling was mutual.

Now serious clouds threatened the skies. He might go to jail. Maybe they'd put him in an executive-style, minimum-security prison, in a country-club lockup for white-collar criminals.

Ray pulled out a bottle of John Walker Blue Label from the credenza and poured a half glass. He gulped it down and poured another. Then he picked up the phone to make the call that he'd been dreading. After several rings it was answered.

"Yeah."

"It's me," Ray said.

"I know who it is. Yeah, what's up? I don't like you calling me."

"Well, I wouldn't if I didn't have to. We have a serious problem."

"Oh?"

"That Taylor woman snooped around and found something."

"Like *what?*"

"Irregularities. Enough that she's demanding that I tell the Board."

"Or what?"

Ray gulped. "Or she'll go to the corporate authorities." His voice trailed.

"Damn, Ray! How could you be so careless?"

"What do you mean? She's a nosey bitch." Ray drained his glass.

"You take care of things."

"I have been. She's too smart for her own good," Ray said. "I told her to give me twenty-four hours to respond to her."

Ray grabbed a wad of tissues from a box on his desk and wiped new sweat from his forehead.

"What a fuck up. Has she told anyone else about her suspicions?"

"I don't think so."

"This time I'll take care of it."

"What does 'take care of it' mean?" Ray asked.

"Don't worry. Let me handle it from here."

"Look, I don't want to get involved in anything heavy duty."

"Ray, you're already involved. Did you forget the pictures?"

For a second Ray had forgotten. Somehow he'd turned attempts to extort him into even more lucrative kickbacks, a scheme that put money in his pockets in a quid pro quo arrangement. In the switch he'd forgotten all about the pictures. Now the whole scheme was out of control. They had evidence of his infidelity, his homosexual encounters. The pictures could get him fired from Crayton and out him to his wife, family, and friends. But pictures alone couldn't put him in jail. In the light of this new trauma, those pictures were a weak threat. Despite his feeling of desperation, he wasn't stupid.

"Pictures? No, I haven't forgotten," he answered.

"Good. When do you see the Taylor woman?"

"Tomorrow. Tomorrow at six, at my home."

"I'll be in touch. Go about your business as if nothing has happened. Understand?"

"Yeah, yeah."

Ray poured his third glass of Johnny Walker. He was mesmerized by the amber liquid, which promised to calm his fears. There had to be another way, a way he could fix it all. He thought about going down to the marina. He could stay on his boat for the night or even sail away. But he wouldn't have time to make arrangements. It was an hour's drive, and Joan was out of town, so were the kids. He needed a crew. Plus, driving that far with the liquor he'd consumed didn't make sense.

"Shit," he said. "Might as well just bite the bullet." He could confess to the Board. Yes, confess and ask for mercy. Repay the funds. He had until tomorrow to think about it. In the meantime he'd go home and gather some things, in case he would have to make a quick exit.

CHAPTER 24
ANYBODY HOME?

Zoie was coming. His twenty-four hours were up. Scotch in hand, Ray paced the narrow aisle of his dimly lit media center. The length of the theater-style room measured fifteen of his large steps. In an hour he'd made the journey enough times to wear a spot in the carpet.

Ray liked the room's techno-corporate feel. It radiated power. But today the feeling of corporate power failed him. His actions mimicked those of a madman, not an executive, as he trudged endlessly in the hole that he'd dug for himself.

On the next pass, he knocked a chair out of place, but he didn't adjust his course. He trudged ahead, colliding with another chair, brutalizing that chair with his hip in an almost deliberate act to punish himself. His legs, disconnected from his mind, moved under demonic control, oblivious to fatigue. Fear had taken hold, suspending rational behavior and thinking. Fear gave him increased energy but no real answers. The message his subconscious relayed to his conscious mind was loud and clear: *Your goose is cooked!*

The media room was the only room in the house without windows. Who knew what or who could be watching his activities from the thick woods, which surrounded the place? He'd always enjoyed the privacy of his woodland, which provided peacefulness and distance from the corporate grind. Except for today, the isolation was worrisome. Earlier he looked out at the woods and thought he'd seen eyes looking back at him.

Joan was visiting her sister and not due back for a week. The boys were in Nags Head with friends. Just as well. They didn't need to be in town when the hell was unleashed. While sitting through the officer meetings all day, he'd pondered the hell that was coming. He almost decided to take the "fessing up" route— not because he felt guilt or remorse but because he couldn't stand his growing panic, his fear of getting caught. The tension was eating him alive. *I can't do time,* he thought. *Life's too short.* If he made a deal, maybe the powers that be would let him off easy. He could offer the name of his accomplice in exchange for leniency.

He stood still for the first time in many minutes. Putting a hand to his face, he felt its dampness from his crazy exercise. He'd lost count of his Scotch refills. He was supposed to attend the officers' banquet at eight. How could he possibly drive? What did it matter anyway? His world was about to unravel. In forty-eight hours the people who had smiled at him and patted him on the back at the earlier meeting would distance themselves from his personal and professional train wreck.

He looked at his watch. Where was that Taylor woman? He couldn't remember whether he'd told her five thirty or six. He moved from the media room's solid walls to his very open foyer. Through the glass panels adjacent to his double doors, his eyes scanned the driveway's tree-lined perimeter. This time no eyes real or imagined gazed back. He chalked up his previous sighting to his foggy brain.

He was about to head to his office to wait when he saw a car making its way from the main road and down the long driveway.

The vehicle was a dusty gray and devoid of shine, a late model of something or other. The car made its way slowly into the circular driveway. Instead of stopping in front of the door, it continued around the circle, pulling into the short connector, with the separate garage building. Ray couldn't make out the identity of the driver. For longer than seemed appropriate, the car sat motionless. The car didn't fit the image of something that Zoie Taylor would drive. The nosey bitch was a classy dresser, likely to drive a classy car. *On what we pay her, she certainly can afford something better,* Ray thought, still trying to figure out what was going on. Freelance workmen often trolled the area searching for trees to cut and brush to clear, but the good ole boys always came in trucks. No one else he knew would be caught dead in such a vehicle. His address was too far off the beaten path for the casual drop-in. Perhaps Joan had set up some service appointment and had forgotten to tell him. Having regained his composure, he stepped out onto his flagstone porch, Scotch in hand, ready to greet and then quickly dismiss the car's occupant.

Finally a woman emerged.

No, it wasn't Zoie, though like Zoie this woman was black, but she was taller. She wore tight jeans and a sapphire-blue fitted shirt, which matched the color and iridescence of her ethnic head wrap. She carried a worn leather satchel, like the ones carried by old college professors. *Maybe she's one of Joan's charity contacts,* he thought, irritated by the intrusion in the midst of his personal trauma. *Why the fuck did she park so far away?*

"Can I help you?" he yelled out to the woman, who moved toward him with a slow swaying, being careful on the cobblestone drive.

When she was within a few steps, she said, "Mr. Ray Gaddis?"

"No, my wife is not home. You'll have to come back when she's around."

"I'm looking for you. You are Mr. Ray Gaddis?"

Attempting to decipher the hint of her accent, he acknowledged his identity with a nod and then immediately regretted doing so.

"I've got a message for you."

At close contact his eyes locked on the woman's dark eyes. Those eyes looked straight into his and seemed to not blink. Their deep blackness picked up the hint of sapphire blue from her blouse. Like deep dark pools, they invited him to take a plunge. It wasn't about sex. Women weren't his thing. Entranced, Ray didn't see the man who came from around the tall thin evergreen topiary, which adorned his flagstone porch. The man grabbed him from the side and covered Ray's mouth with a large gloved hand. Stunned, Ray didn't think to bite. It was all happening so quickly. He was being dragged inside. The front door slammed so hard it shook the vase on the foyer table. The next thing Ray knew, he was gagged, and his hands were bound behind him. His eyes batted back the sweat as the two forced him into his study and shoved him into a chair. He strained to say something, but what came out sounded like grunts.

The man wore a ski mask, had a wiry build, and was obviously strong. The man held Ray in the chair while the woman pulled some rubber tubing from her briefcase, pushed up Ray's sleeve, and tied it around his bare arm. The two were moving fast, using signals rather than words to communicate. The woman filled a syringe from a small vial. As Ray squirmed in his chair under the man's strong grip, she searched for a vein. Ray's eyes went wild, and they filled with sweat. Then he felt a pop. As the cool liquid entered his arm, he stopped squirming. With droopy eyes he watched the woman dab with a cotton ball the place on his arm where the needle had entered. The man released his grip.

Ray saw the man pull off his mask. But by now his two captors were fuzzy shadows. Ray's neck could no longer support his heavy head. He was so tired. His eyes could no longer stay open.

His heart felt like a bowling ball, too heavy to beat another beat. With eyes closed he could still think, but thinking—like breathing—was no longer important. The cares of the world were lifted. Perhaps this was better than prison. Finally understanding what was taking place, he thought he should have known they would cover their tracks. On the horizon Ray saw his boat, the *Bonnie Princess. Sail away. Sail away.*

Ray's house in upper Potomac proved difficult to find. Not sure how to use the GPS in Tina's car, Zoie had printed the MapQuest directions and had them on the seat next to her. But the directions leading from point A to point B proved worthless after she'd gone off course. More than once she backtracked after missing a turn. Hassled and frustrated, she pulled into a gas station at a busy intersection to seek help. From behind the counter of the station's small convenience store, a quick-tongued attendant rattled off a series of driving maneuvers, in Asian-accented English. Zoie asked him twice to repeat the instructions, trying to tune her ear to the rhythm of his English with minimum success. Not bothering to ask him a third time, she thanked him and left, understanding only two maneuvers. Her wandering through Potomac was over when she spotted a parkway sign that indicated that she was back on the right road.

Zoie was prepared for this meeting. She'd reworked her write-up of the situation and prepared slides for a Board presentation. *I'll let him do what he wants with the stuff,* she decided. She just wanted to get the meeting over with and get home before the evening thunderstorm rolled in.

It had been only twenty-four hours since she alerted Ray to her suspicions of fraud. Now he wanted to put his spin on things before going to the Board. Had she let herself be duped? What could have changed in twenty-four hours that would cause a better outcome? Or was this little meeting a ploy to delay the inevitable? She thought about Jahi. Part of her wanted to warn him, but she had promised not to say anything to him.

Zoie arrived at Ray's house ten minutes late—not bad for all the trouble she'd had finding it. The house was close to what she had expected: grander than grand, a country estate. "Chateau is not my style, but this will do for a weekend getaway," Zoie said, laughing as she rounded the driveway. She parked in front, grabbed her briefcase, and went up to the door. She rang the bell and waited and waited; then she rang the bell again. She knocked a number of times and then pressed her face against the glass panel beside the door to look inside. There was a large foyer and a curving staircase with a wrought-iron railing. She went to the side of the house, going into the flowerbeds in her heels. She found another window and looked in. What she saw looked like an office, but all seemed quiet in there.

"Ray, where are you? I know you didn't dare stand me up," she shouted defiantly. Irritated that she'd made the drive at his request, she pulled out her cell phone and scanned through her contacts. Ray's cell or home number wasn't there. She could call Milton, but Milton would want to know why she was looking for Ray. She'd promised Ray not to say anything to anyone. But if Ray didn't show, all bets would be off on that promise.

Zoie sat in Tina's car for another thirty minutes. The air was muggy and strangely still, the sky growing dark. "Even full professors only get twenty minutes," she said to the trees, recalling her college days.

Disgusted, she drove away.

CHAPTER 25

DOG EAT DOG

For someone who'd gone in circles searching for Ray's house in the burbs, Zoie found the route back to the city with surprising ease. Tina's car seemed to find its own way. It was if the car knew that the mind of the person behind its wheel was otherwise engaged.

Zoie cursed Ray a hundred times, first for standing her up and then for being a general scum bucket—not to mention a likely felon. Not since the days following her breakup with Elliot had she used such foul language or damned so thoroughly a fellow soul. She raged on as if someone were listening, and she slapped the wheel to emphasize her points. But the worst of it came when she began to curse herself. With lips finally quiet, she noticed a bitter taste on her tongue—a bitterness caused by her own stupidity. She'd fallen into Ray's little trap and listened to his plea to work things his way. She should have followed her instincts to do what she knew to be right. Why had she given the bastard the benefit of the doubt? He'd bought another whole day of scheming with the knowledge that she was onto him.

The rush hour was almost over, but the traffic was still heavy on the Washington Beltway. Coming from the right like a low-flying comet, a silver sports car moved suddenly into Zoie's lane and cut her off. She braked, slowing the BMW from sixty-five to twenty-five, in an instant that seemed more like a lifetime. The offending car quickly darted into the far-left lane and then rocketed out of sight.

Zoie's heart was in her throat. She couldn't curse because she'd used up all the choice words on Ray. "Thank God these brakes are working," she murmured as the blood drained from her head to her feet. "Thank God the car behind me wasn't tailgating."

The incident brought Zoie's attention back to the road and to thoughts of what would happen to Nikki if anything were to happen to her. She had discussed raising Nikki with Tina, and Tina had agreed to take on the responsibility should it ever come to that. But since that conversation, Zoie hadn't taken the necessary steps to finalize her wishes. If anything happened to her, the Benjamins would seek custody of Nikki on Elliot's behalf. After all, officially he was paying child support. Zoie shook her head, trying to remove the morbid thoughts of her death and the uncertain fate of her child in those circumstances. It was all too gruesome, too complicated to fathom. The best way to handle it was not to die.

As she exited the Beltway at Connecticut Avenue, Zoie decided that she would go to her grandmother's house since she had the car. She calmed her nerves after the close call on the Beltway. But thus far the day's events stacked high in the negative column. She spent the early part of the day cataloguing her hunches and converting her fraud theory into analytic substance. She prepared a presentation tailored for a Board audience—a high-level presentation with clear decision points, one that could focus the members' thinking and lead them to take action. Nowhere did she point a finger. But anyone with any intelligence could name the likely culprits. These were the things she was prepared to discuss with Ray that evening. Although Ray had admitted nothing, his behavior was that of someone who was guilty. He was someone who already knew the details of his shady dealings and didn't need further elaboration.

With a sad shrug, Zoie resolved that she'd done what she could. It was a shame about Jahi. She so wanted to trust him, to hear from his own lips that he was innocent. Now she felt free to call him.

A distant flash of lightning lit up an early dark sky as the BMW pulled up in front of her grandmother's house. Zoie looked up at the formidable structure on the upscale city block. She often wondered how her grandparents had been able to afford such a place or how welcomed they'd felt when they first came to the neighborhood. Back in those days, the block was predominately white. Zoie saw a light in the second-floor room that used to be her mother's. The room was now Queen's. A pale honey glow beamed from the oval window over the front door.

As Zoie exited the car, the trees swayed with unease, signaling that wind and heavy rain were not far off. A warm gust caught Zoie's gauze jacket, ballooning it into a miniature parachute. She headed up the steep uneven steps to the covered porch. Deciding not to dig for the house keys hiding somewhere at the bottom of her bag, she was about to ring the bell when the wide door seemed to open on its own. Queen was standing in the doorway with a half smile. "Zoie, I wasn't expecting you."

"Hello, Queen. Sorry, but I didn't call before coming. I made up my mind to stop by at the last minute."

"No problem. We're home."

"How did you know I was here?"

"I've got elephant ears," Queen replied with a wide grin. "Except for the cars heading to the park, sometimes it gets so quiet around here. I get creeped out. That's why I keep this." Queen pulled a baseball bat from the umbrella stand.

"Oh!" said Zoie. "It's awful dark out here. The porch light is out."

"I can get my brother to take a look at it," Queen said.

Zoie heard stories about caregivers who took advantage of their elderly charges. But from everything that she'd witnessed so far, Queen was one of the better ones. Frances Woods's body might have failed her, but her mind remained clear and decisive. If there had been any difficulty with the situation, her grandmother, a strong-willed woman, would have made it known.

"Come on in," Queen said.

"How's she doing?" Zoie asked, gazing up the stairs to where she'd find her grandmother.

"Pretty well. No bad coughing spells today. She's eating okay," the woman answered with a sigh of mild fatigue. "Guess that medicine the doctor gave her for the cough is working. Go on up. She should be awake."

Without further discussion, Queen disappeared in the direction of the kitchen. Zoie climbed the grand staircase, listening for its familiar groans. *No one could ever sneak up these stairs without being heard.* Stopping at the landing, she reminisced about the time when the landing and its bench had served as her very special hiding place—her pretend castle on a pretend mountain. A place where she felt safe. Things were simpler in those days. At least they appeared to be. Her mother and grandmother had hid life's painful details as best they could, but children knew when things weren't right. Some things just couldn't be hidden. Zoie wanted that feeling of safety for Nikki, a shelter from life's distress. There was no need for a six-year-old to know all the details that complicated her existence.

Zoie found her grandmother in the bed, slouching in a seated position. Her head was slumped forward, her chin braced awkwardly against her chest, with her reading glasses precariously askew on her nose. With rhythmic snoring her grandmother looked uncomfortable but, at the same time, sort of peaceful. At first Zoie considered not waking her, but she wanted to adjust her grandmother's head.

She came close to the bed and gently shook her grandmother's arm. "Grandma."

"Huh!" the older woman said, giving off a short snort, signifying that a good snore had been interrupted. She lifted her head slowly and in apparent disorientation swatted at the glasses. The glasses tumbled to the bed.

"Sorry. I didn't mean to startle you," Zoie said.

Almost ignoring that Zoie was in the room, Frances Woods looked down and closed the book in her lap, marking her effort with a deep sigh and two fingers left pressed between its pages to serve as a bookmark. "Whoa, I can't seem to make it past a couple of pages without dozing."

Zoie bent over and kissed her grandmother on the forehead and then smoothed the woman's thick ruffled hair, a mass of light-brown hay dominated by silver. "So what are you reading?"

"Oh, some dry history about Beaufort County, North Carolina."

"Ooh. No wonder you're dozing off. You should try a good mystery."

"This is a little dense. Ida got it for me. She knows I hail from the Beaufort region. And you know she's got those library connections. If she thinks I haven't read it, she will be upset with me."

"Gotcha. Tell her to bring you a mystery next time." Thinking of skinny old Ms. Bascomb, Zoie smiled to herself and maneuvered the small carved chair kept by the bed so that she could face her grandmother. The chair, undoubtedly an antique, was regular height, but its seat was better suited to a child or someone with a tiny rear end. Zoie could feel her grandmother's eyes inspecting her, but she did not pass judgment on what Zoie was wearing or how her hair looked. Tonight there were no such comments.

"I wasn't expecting you," her grandmother said finally.

"Are you sorry I came?"

"Now you know I'm always glad to see you. I'm just surprised… that's all. What brings you out tonight?" The wheeze that followed made it clear that the old woman was running out of breath. She strained to contain the cough that was about to erupt and to deliver her last few words before lapsing into a spasm. Zoie cringed. On her last visit, she witnessed her grandmother's scary hacking fit. How her grandmother's body withstood the fits, Zoie couldn't understand, except to know that Frances Woods was one strong woman.

This time the coughs sounded less severe. The rumble deep in her grandmother's chest indicated that the congestion was loose. Zoie waited for the coughs to subside before attempting further conversation.

"You okay?" Zoie finally asked as she offered her grandmother a sip of water from a bedside glass.

"Yeah, yeah," her grandmother replied after swallowing a bit of water and seeming to have regained control over her breathing. Her voice was still hoarse.

"You asked why I came by. Well, I have my friend's car today and figured I'd use it to come here," said Zoie. "But how are you doing?"

"Doing better. Thank the Lord. Doctor's got me on a bunch of new stuff for this cough. The different medicines are not too nasty. Queen's got the whole protocol timed to the minute for when I take each medicine." She pointed to a tray on the side table, which was lined with medicine bottles big and small. "Taking all this stuff makes me sleepy."

Zoie examined the labels on several bottles.

"Tell me when am I going to see my great-granddaughter, Nikki?" her grandmother asked.

"It's just two more weeks. Two more weeks and then I go get her."

"You miss her, don't you?"

"Yeah, I do," Zoie answered in a soft voice, thinking of her daughter's hug.

"So did you get in much socializing while she was away? You've been a free woman this summer."

Zoie's mind skipped to thoughts of Jahi and the few times they'd been together over the past month. Jahi had always been a question mark. Now he was more so. She smiled at her grandmother. "Socially it's been a quiet summer. It doesn't seem to matter whether Nikki is here or not. My love life is still on hiatus."

"You're too young to be on hiatus or whatever you're calling it." Her grandmother tossed the book aside, seeming not to care that she was freeing her fingers from bookmark duty. "Well, I miss Nikki too. Please bring her by before school starts."

"I've got to call Nikki tonight. I call her most every night, but tonight's going to be tough."

"What now?" said her grandmother.

"I told you about the dog situation."

Her grandmother looked bewildered and then said, "You mean that thing between you and your ex-mother-in-law?"

"Ex-nothing. Remember, Elliot and I were never married."

"Well, you lived together for years. Nikki is the women's grandchild. Call it what you want, but you two have a family relationship."

Zoie smirked.

Her grandmother continued. "Does this mean you haven't told that child your decision about the dog?"

"Right," Zoie answered, her voice dropping off, bowing her head.

"So Nikki still thinks she's bringing the dog home?"

"What she thinks is that I'm still considering it. But, yes, I admit it. I've been too chicken to tell her." Zoie rubbed her arm nervously.

"My, my. Shame on you, Zo."

"Grandma, there's been so much else going on." Zoie sighed.

"How about bringing the dog here? Letting it stay here?"

"You mean so Queen can take care of it? Anyway, it's not even a dog yet. It's a puppy. No, Grandma. Thanks, but *that* would not be a good idea."

Her grandmother put her finger to her chin and gazed off. "Well, you've got to do what you got to do."

"Believe me. I've thought this through."

"Zo, I just didn't want to see my little Nikki disappointed. But the sooner you break the news to her, the better. She's really bonded with that dog by now. That dog is her best friend."

After all of Zoie's soul searching, guilt still washed over her, but the guilt wasn't powerful enough to make her change her mind. There'd be no dog in their DC apartment. Tonight she'd bite the bullet and tell her daughter her decision.

"It's not just this dog thing that's clouding your life, is it?" her grandmother asked, putting her age-freckled hand on Zoie's.

"Things have been pretty crazy, especially the last couple of weeks." There was a long silence. She considered how much to share with her grandmother. "I think the Foundation may be in some serious trouble. We could be having a mini-Watergate."

"Humph! Folks can't even do right when they're giving funds to the needy."

"I can't tell you any more," Zoie said, wondering if she should have said anything at all.

"That's okay. All I need to know is that you're not involved," her grandmother said. "But since you're their lawyer, you have to be involved."

"I'm not involved directly. As the Foundation's attorney, I'm trying to work it out. But there's only so much I can do."

"Friends of yours involved?" asked her grandmother.

"Possibly." Zoie answered, thinking of Jahi.

"Mmm...well, you do the right thing. Don't go trying to change the world singlehandedly. Remember Don Quixote?"

"Of course. You and mom took me to the play when I was a kid. Batting at windmills."

"And you can't make everyone else's problem yours either," her grandmother continued. "You've got your good reputation to protect and Nikki to worry about."

"When this hits the fan, I might not have a job."

"Don't let that stop you from doing the right thing. You and Nikki can come and live here with me. I offered that to you before. This place is going to be yours anyway when I'm gone."

Providing words of wisdom sapped her grandmother's precious energy. After a few more exchanges, Frances Woods's voice was just a mumble. Her heavy lids shut over her tired eyes. Zoie picked up the tallest brown glass bottle from the bed table and held it under the lamp. Its prescription label confirmed her suspicion: cough medicine with codeine. Codeine wasn't exactly a bad thing when the alternative was a coughing fit. But the drug was a sedative.

Zoie went to the window to see if the rain had come and gone. The roof wasn't wet at all. Perhaps the storm had passed them by.

Zoie lowered her grandmother's pillows and saw to it that she was resting comfortably. Then she gave the sleeping woman a kiss on the forehead. On the way out of the house, Zoie spoke to Queen briefly about the cough medicine. Queen said, "I'm just going by the doctor's instructions."

After dropping off the car at Tina's parking spot in Adams Morgan, Zoie walked home. The walk helped clear her head. She was dreading talking to Nikki. "Let me get this over with," she said, once back in her apartment. With shoes off and a glass of red wine in hand, she called the Benjamins' home. As usual it was Celeste's sugary voice that answered.

"Oh, hello Zoie."

"How are things?"

"Great. Today we went to the library to get some easy reading. We've been practicing, so she'll be ready for first grade."

"Good, good," Zoie said, feeling a little guilty that she hadn't lately made an effort to advance Nikki's reading skills. The private kindergarten Nikki had attended in New York was very advanced, offering a curriculum that encompassed a lot of the first grade. Relying heavily on that instruction, she'd neglected to think about Nikki getting rusty over the summer.

"I hope I didn't call too late." It was another faint hope for further delay. Perhaps Nikki had fallen asleep.

"Nikki's in her pjs, but she knew you'd call. Hold on...Nikki! It's your mom!"

Celeste apparently put the phone down, because she was no longer attempting to make conversation. Zoie took two large sips of her wine as she waited for her daughter to take the phone. After a minute she could hear little screams of glee and the sound of the running steps coming from a forty-pound body.

"Mommy, Mommy," came Nikki's high-pitched voice, full of joyful exuberance. "I've been waiting for you to call. Why did you take so long?"

"Sorry, baby. I had some business to take care of for the office, and then I went to see your great-grandma."

"Oh. I hope she's getting better, 'cause I don't want her to die or something like that."

"Me neither, baby."

"My friend Mark's grandmother died, and he had to go see her dead body."

"How sad," Zoie replied. They'd discussed death and dying several times over the years, and certainly they would cover it several times more.

"Yeah, I don't want to be sad like that," Nikki said.

"So tell me what you did today," Zoie said, changing the subject.

"Grandma took me to the library. I borrowed twenty-five books."

"Wow. Twenty-five books?"

"Uh-huh. The library trusts us. I just have to careful to keep them away from Biscuit because he might eat them."

It was time to tell her. No further waiting.

"About Biscuit, baby."

"Mommy, did you know that Grandma and Grandpa have given away all the puppies? But they're not giving away Biscuit because he's mine and I need to take him home with me and I'm teaching him not to eat the books or my shoes. When are you coming to get us?"

Zoie gulped the last of her wine. She expected it to be a difficult conversation, but it was on the path to being even worse than she had imagined.

"Listen, baby, we need to talk about Biscuit." She tried to sound serious but to still keep her tone light. "You can't bring Biscuit home with you."

"But you promised," Nikki said, whining.

"Nikki, now you know I never promised that you could keep that dog. I said I would think about."

"You said that you would check with the building management to see if they would let me have Biscuit. Did they say no?"

Oh, God, I cannot lie. With other animals in the building, Nikki will figure it out. She'll just have to understand the facts of life. "I'm sorry,

Nikki, but we can't keep a dog. It's not the building management. I've thought about it a lot and, well...it's just that it's...too difficult."

"Mommy, what do you mean?"

"I mean we can't have a dog. Who's going to walk him three times a day? Who's going to feed him and clean up after him when he makes a mess?" Zoie could hear low sobs.

"But, Mommy, Biscuit is my friend!" Nikki said, choking back sobs. "I'll teach him not to make messes. What will happen to him? He's only got me to take care of him."

"Maybe when you're older, Nikki. Then you can do more to help take care of a dog. That'll be the time to get one. But right now, baby, having a dog is too much to handle."

Zoie covered her mouth, not knowing what else to say. Her daughter's soft sobs distressed her, but she had to hold firm. "Look, baby, I'll be there in another couple of weeks to bring you home. Don't worry about Biscuit. Your Grandma Celeste will find him a nice home."

"But that's not fair. He's my dog," Nikki answered, her tone defiant.

"Nikki..."

"No," Nikki said with the harshness of a two-year-old in the midst of a tantrum.

"I'm sorry, baby. That's the way it has to be."

"I won't let them give away my dog."

"Nikki, I'm sorry..." Zoie heard a click in the connection. It was as if the line had dropped. "Nikki, are you there? Nikki?" Indeed, they were no longer connected. Was she cut off or was what had happened more serious? Zoie let the phone fall into her lap and stared into the distance, her mouth wide in disbelief.

"My child hung up on me!"

CHAPTER 26

BAD MOMMY

Later that night, counting on Nikki's being asleep, Zoie called the Benjamins. Phillip Benjamin answered the phone. After a frosty "Hello, Zoie," he left Zoie hanging in silence while he fetched his wife. Celeste took the phone without her usual pleasantries. She dived right into an account of the upheaval at the Benjamins' home.

"It's been a mess," Celeste reported, punctuating her comment with a heavy sigh.

Clutching the phone, Zoie winced. She sensed her blood pressure rising. In the past Celeste's accounts of Nikki's visits were covered with powdered sugar. *Too contrived,* Zoie remembered thinking. *No child could be that happy—not all the time.* Her Nikki was a good child, but she had a temper and could pout for hours in the best tradition of willful six-year-olds. Knowing this, Zoie was usually prepared to hear the bad news along with the good. A normal account. Tonight Zoie just wanted to hear that things had settled down.

"Nikki's been sobbing nonstop. The poor puppy is whining right along with her," Celeste continued.

Zoie bit her lip. "Well, what about now?" Zoie asked. "How is she?"

Celeste's dramatic long sigh told more of the story. "At first the poor child just couldn't be consoled. You know how kids cry so hard that they can't catch their breath. She wore herself out. She curled up with Biscuit in her bed and cried herself to sleep."

The phone pressed to her ear, Zoie rolled her eyes and paced the floor. She was concerned for her child, and at the same time, she wondered whether Celeste was overdramatizing her account. *Anything to make me feel guilty!*

"She's devastated," Celeste continued.

The tension was palpable. Zoie could no longer hold her tongue. "Celeste, this would have *never* happened if you hadn't promised Nikki that dog!" Zoie blasted. "You should have talked to me first!"

"I'm sorry. Obviously, you think I've overstepped," Celeste answered, her stiff tone accompanied by sniffles. "I was only trying to make a lonely little girl happy."

Celeste's words stung. Zoie never considered her daughter to be a "lonely little girl." An only child, yes. *But* only *doesn't equate to* lonely, Zoie thought.

"I wish you could see how happy the two of them are together; then you'd understand."

"You got Nikki's hopes up," Zoie snapped. "I don't live in a house with a white picket fence. I have a full-time job. And in case you forgot, I'm raising Nikki as a solo parent. Right now there's no room in our lives for a dog!"

Celeste offered neither further defense of her actions nor apologies. There was only a long silence. "When Nicki leaves, we'll find the puppy a home. It won't be hard. Families want labs because they're good with children."

Not this family, Zoie thought. "Okay, okay, Celeste. I just don't want my baby's feelings hurt anymore with promises of things that can't be fulfilled." There was no point in making threats about retrieving Nikki earlier than planned. "I'll call tomorrow. Maybe she'll have calmed down by then."

The call ended without further angry words. Zoie knew Nikki's disappointment would linger. She was counting on time to heal her daughter's hurt feelings and mend the mother-daughter relationship. Once school started Nikki would be caught up in the excitement of the first grade—new friends and new knowledge. *In time Nikki will forget the dog,* Zoie thought.

Parenting at a distance was proving unfeasible. She couldn't give Nikki a reassuring hug. It wasn't every day that a six-year-old hung up on a parent. Part of Zoie wanted to reach across the airwaves and give Nikki a good shake, but the other part of her felt her child's pain. She understood Nikki's sadness and frustration at the prospect of being separated from something or someone she loved. She could even feel it as if it were happening to her. A tear rolled down Zoie's cheek. She closed her eyes and hugged her shoulders to sooth her longing to hold her daughter. Nikki was her family. Besides her grandmother, Nikki was pretty much the only close family she had left. In nine more days, they'd reunite. The lonely little girl and her sometimes lonely mom.

That night Zoie tossed and turned. The next morning she remembered her dream. It was about a frolicking black puppy and a little girl. Running late, she called into work.

"Regina, is anyone looking for me this morning?"

"No, but things are hectic here. We're getting ready for the charity walk for the homeless. I'm scheduled to staff one of the refreshment stands. And we penned you in for the registration desk. Is that okay?"

"Yeah, I forgot. Sure, I'll work registration," Zoie said, remembering that she was committing to a Saturday weeks in the future, but a whole lot could happen before then. "Have you seen Ray?"

"No. Do you need him? I can check with Arleen."

"No, don't bother. I'll contact him directly. If anyone else is looking for me, tell them I have an appointment this morning. I'll be in later."

CHAPTER 27
FAMILY SECRETS

Frances Woods was oblivious to the hum of the window air conditioner and to the chatter interspersed with laughter coming from the rabbit-eared TV atop the bureau. She inspected her breakfast tray. Today the oatmeal seemed thicker than usual. The white liquid floating over the oatmeal was a watery substance, not anything from a cow.

"Humph," Frances Woods complained, though Queen was not there to hear her. On her tray was also a cup of plain tea and her usual piece of toast. The toast was cold, though the greasy spot at its center was evidence that Queen had buttered it when it was hot. She frowned at the bowl and then sighed. Her life had become bland like the oatmeal.

Last night both Gabe and Calvin appeared in her dreams. Calvin looked old and tired, the way he had during the last years of his life, as the cancer sapped his vitality. Why hadn't he appeared to her young and spry like Gabe? Gabe looked the same. His face had been the same one etched in her memory from all those years ago. Appearing together in her dream, the two men, close in age, could have been grandfather and grandson. She laughed at the thought of such an unlikely relationship. Both men whom she loved—loved in different ways. Ways only a heart could explain.

Staring out the window at the morning light, she pondered Gabe's fate. His whereabouts were a mystery. In truth, she didn't know whether he was dead or alive. Would she appear in heaven as she did now—wrinkled and gray? Or would she be that thin-waist girl of years gone by? Heaven had to be a complicated place. The Lord would surely work it out.

In her dream Gabe and Calvin delivered an important message: "It is not your time." Calvin did the talking. Gabe stood smiling that broad smile of his, the smile that could light up a room. *Hallelujah!* Life on earth was not over...not yet, anyway. The news that her death wasn't imminent was its own magic tonic, an auxiliary to the medicine the doctor had prescribed. Or maybe it was the other way around.

Her attention shifted to the twenty-year-old tube she called a TV. There was no sense in buying a new set when this one still worked. Even though its rabbit ears delivered fuzzy images, the sound was still good.

Queen entered the room, alert and stately, carrying her own bowl of the same oatmeal. The small chair next to Frances Woods's bed groaned as the big woman sat down.

"What's the matter? Don't it taste good?" Queen asked, stretching to peer at her charge's unfinished meal.

Frances Woods used her half-eaten toast to point inside her bowl. "What's this on the oatmeal?"

Queen gave a hearty laugh. "Mrs. Woods, you're too funny. You think I'm trying to poison you? Ha!"

Frances Woods smirked and waited for a real answer.

"Didn't fool you, huh? The doctor said keep you away from dairy 'cause it makes mucous and congestion in your chest. That's rice milk," Queen explained with a proud smile.

"Oh. I'm eating it," Frances Woods said, sighing. "I just wish I had something good and greasy. Some bacon or sausage—something with some flavor."

"Okay, I'll fix something good and greasy for you tomorrow. But you know what your doctor said: we got to watch your cholesterol."

"Cholesterol…congestion…and I've got ten other things wrong with me to boot. Everybody has to die of something," Frances Woods barked.

Queen laughed a laugh as melodic as her accent. "You right about that. But while I'm here, *ain't nobody dying.*"

Even if she had wanted to die, Frances Woods now knew that Queen would not have permitted it. She was in good hands, even if Queen sometimes riled her "last nerve." Frances Woods pointed at the TV with her toast. "Look at him," she said, changing the subject. Al Roker was hosting a cooking segment on the *Today Show.* "Now that man had an operation to reduce the size of his stomach to lose weight, and they turn around and make him taste food. Doesn't make a bit of sense."

"You right about that. Looks as if he's putting that weight back on," said Queen. "Is your tea cold?" Rather than waiting for Frances Woods to respond, Queen reached over and felt the cup. "I'm gonna heat it up."

"Thank you," Frances Woods said. "And can you bring me some lemon, since I can't have the milk?"

"Sure."

Queen was quick to return with the heated cup and lemon. "You've got a mornin' visitor."

"Zo!" Frances Woods said as her granddaughter's face peeked out from behind Queen.

"Morning, Grandma." Zoie bent down and kissed her on the cheek.

"My goodness, you were here just last night. Why aren't you at work? You're dressed as if you're going to work," Frances Woods said, referring to her granddaughter's summer weight gray pantsuit.

"You said I could come to see you anytime," Zoie answered.

"Zoie, want me to fix you some oatmeal?" Queen asked.

Zoie looked down at her grandmother's almost empty bowl. "Nah! I mean no thanks, Queen," she said. "But I'll have some toast and tea if you don't mind."

With Queen's departure, Frances Woods picked up the TV remote from the folds of her sheet and muted the TV to ready herself for a serious conversation. "Zo, you usually don't visit on a weekday and never in the early morning. What's wrong?"

"It didn't go well last night. Well, nothing went well yesterday." Zoie rolled her eyes. "I talked to Nikki."

"Oh, the dog thing!"

"Nikki didn't take it well when I told her she couldn't keep that dog."

"Well, Zo, honey, you knew that was coming. Did you talk to Elliot's mother?"

"Celeste? Yeah, I talked to her. Gave her a piece of my mind for raising Nikki's hopes and making *me* look like the bad guy."

"Ooh. Sounds ugly."

"It was awful. Now Nikki doesn't want to speak to me. I'm the bad parent."

"Zo, I'm sorry that things turned out that way. She'll get over it. Give her time."

"Yeah, Celeste said that Nikki cried herself to sleep. Curled up with the dog in her bed, of course."

A thud from the window interrupted their conversation. It was the air conditioner's compressor kicking in. "That thing keeps turning on," her grandmother said.

"How old is it?" Zoie asked. "Sounds as if it's on its last leg. Did you ever consider putting in central air?"

"Now, Zo, you're talking big bucks and lots of disruption to this house. When you inherit this place, you can do whatever you want."

"Since you and grandfather could afford this house, I thought maybe you could afford to upgrade some things."

"Yes, we worked hard. And we saved. And we were blessed," Frances Woods said. "I guess your mother never told you the story of our good fortune."

"What story are you talking about?"

"The one about how Calvin and I were able to buy this house." Frances Woods pushed her bowl back farther on the tray and held her tea mug steady.

"No, Mom never mentioned anything about this house. I guess I never knew how expensive property in this neighborhood could be."

"It's always been pricy right here, off the park."

"Well, how did you and Grandpa manage it? I mean an assistant principal and a postal worker? Did you inherit some money?"

"Now who on either side of this family have you ever heard of having more money than they needed to live on from day to day?"

Zoie's eyes widened as she considered the question. "No one."

"That's right. To go to college, your grandfather had a scholarship. Then he worked to pay my way," Frances Woods said with pride in her voice.

"Then how *did* you manage it?"

"Hold on, now. I'm going to tell you. But this isn't for broadcasting."

"Grandma! Did Grandpa steal the money?"

"Lord, no! Zo, why did you go there? Calvin stealing money— what a foolish idea."

Zoie looked down sheepishly.

"So are you going to let me tell you, or are you going to guess?" Frances Woods said.

Zoie put her hand to her mouth and stayed quiet.

"Okay. You know that your grandfather had that mail route over in Shaw for many years. Well, there was this guy who lived on the streets over there. Your grandfather used to bring him food. Give him lunches. For some reason Calvin was always thinking about this guy."

"A homeless man?"

"Yeah, a homeless man."

"So what does this have to do with getting this house?"

"I'm getting to it," Frances Woods said. "One day this guy told your grandfather to play some numbers. Gave him the numbers on a piece of paper and said, 'Play these.' You know this was before the legal numbers. Now don't turn up your nose. Those 'illegal' numbers were how people hit the lottery before there were legal lotteries."

"Grandma, I understand. Really."

"Well, your grandfather was not a regular numbers player. He dabbled now and then. Just a few dollars. Least that's all I knew about. We were saving up for a house to get out of that basement apartment over on Gerard. Somehow this homeless guy convinced your grandfather to put a lot of money on these special numbers. Even told him to play with several different bookies."

"How much did he play?"

"Oh, baby, I don't know those details," Francis Woods said, sounding irritated. "I think it was a lot. He never told me. Actually, I never asked. As churchgoing people we weren't supposed to gamble."

"And the number hit?"

"Glad we sent you to college, Zo," Frances Woods said, rolling her eyes before continuing her story. "Your grandfather hit it straight. I've never seen so much cash. Of course, your mother was a kid, but later I explained it to her. I'm surprised she never told you how we got our windfall."

"And the money was enough to buy this house?"

"Sure was. Of course, we gave money to the church. And your grandfather got himself a decent car. And we made sure that Laurel had money for college, and we put some away for a rainy day."

"And what about the homeless guy?"

"Your grandfather tried to give him some money, but he never could find him again. That man disappeared...it was the strangest thing," Frances Woods said in almost a whisper.

"Grandma, that's some story."

"If anybody asked how we could afford this or that, we were always vague. Later, when I was an assistant principal and your grandfather had finally gotten the promotion in the post office, where he didn't have to walk the streets, we were in a position to actually afford this place on our own. People just stopped asking questions." Frances Woods took a deep breath. "Guess folks figured like you did: that it was an inheritance. Poor Calvin. He was so honest. He worried that someone might think he got rich stealing the mail. You can't be too careful."

"A homeless man, huh? I wonder why this man didn't play the numbers himself," Zoie said.

"Who knows? Maybe he did. Maybe that's why we never saw him again." Frances Woods shrugged her shoulders and gave a quizzical look.

"But how?" Zoie said, unable to utter the complete question.

"Some things just never make *our* kind of sense. The older I get, the more I know that everything doesn't get a logical explanation. Some things are best left in God's hands, and he works in mysterious ways."

Frances Woods turned back to the muted TV and its fuzzy picture. Zoie's eyes followed. A channel-four newscaster was discussing the man whose picture was plastered on one side of the screen. The person in the picture was a good-looking brown-skinned fellow with dreads. For a second Frances Woods thought she might have seen him on TV before but couldn't place him.

"Grandma! Turn it up! I want to hear what they're saying."

"Oh," said Frances Woods, fumbling for the TV remote in the bed covers. "Zo, is he someone you know?" She patted the covers without success.

Anxious, Zoie reached across her grandmother, almost overturning the dishes on the bed tray.

"My goodness, Zo. Calm down."

"Sorry, Grandma," Zoie said, coming up with the device. She canceled the mute, but it was too late. "Ahhhhhhhh! I missed the story. I know that guy."

"Is he a criminal or something?"

Zoie took a deep breath. "I hope not. I *sure* hope not."

CHAPTER 28
CAPITAL HAPPENINGS

I t was Jahi's face that had filled her grandmother's small TV screen. Despite the sullen pose and blurred picture, his sculpted cheeks and mounds of locks were unmistakable. In the confusion of the moment, Zoie missed the words accompanying his image. What could put Jahi on the news? Had he been arrested or in an accident? There were less-dire reasons for his being in the news. There was the Shelter. After all, he was a public figure. It could be anything, not necessarily something bad—though her suspicions about him had grown by the hour.

She needed to find out what was going on with Jahi. He was certainly linked to the Shelter and Ray and possibly the shenanigans. "What's really going on?" she asked out loud as she walked home. Folks on Connecticut Avenue ignored her. They couldn't answer her question. She'd have to find the answer on her own.

Over the past two days, Jahi hadn't returned her calls. She was going to ask him about the Shelter's accounting again, but that was before Ray asked her not to talk to him. With Ray's non-appearance last night, all bets were off. She left another message, asking that he make contact. "It's urgent," she said. "It's business." She understood he was busy, but then she was too. Not returning her call wasn't like the Jahi she knew, the Jahi who cared about the Shelter and, so it seemed, about her. In the days when they were discovering each other, she came to count on the sound of his voice, if not his presence. Her logical brain pushed aside her romantic folly. The several nights they spent together gave her no rights to know his every whereabouts. She really didn't know Jahi that well—certainly not well enough to trust him without question.

A half block from her apartment, Zoie stopped at the little coffee shop. She placed her order for iced coffee and picked up a copy of *The Washington Post*. *There's bound to be a story in there about Jahi*, she thought. Its banner headline blasted the Iraq War. She turned a cold eye to the story and scanned the page. *Nothing.* Before she could open the Metro section, the young woman signaled that her coffee was ready. Zoie was about to turn away to retrieve the coffee, when the *Washington Times*, a paper she'd never bothered to look at, caught her attention. It wasn't that she had anything against the *Times*, but why get a copy of it—a paper known for its right-wing leanings—when the *Post* was available?

"I'll take this and this one too," Zoie said, paying for both papers and her coffee.

At the entrance to her building, Zoie pulled her cell phone from her pocket and checked the missed-call log. Nothing from Jahi. Disgusted, she stuffed the phone back into her pocket.

Steps away, a woman exiting her building held the heavy door as her small dog passed under her arm. Zoie thought of the previous night's dog drama—the one that had left Nikki angry at the world and, most of all, angry with her mother. Zoie watched as the proud short-haired pooch trotted by as if it owned the place. Yes, indeed, the Madison House accepted dogs. And when Nikki came home in a couple of weeks, there'd be plenty of pet-owning tenants going to and from the building, which would point out that fact.

Zoie passed the reception window and glanced in. Head bowed, the desk clerk was hunched over a magazine. There wasn't the usual greeting—"Hello, Ms. Taylor." Zoie wasn't even sure whether the mop of dark curls belonged to the building's regular guy or some replacement. Wanting to read the papers, Zoie headed straight to the waiting elevator, not stopping at her mailbox. On the ride to the sixth floor, she had an uneasy feeling. She'd entered the building without keying in or even being seen. That wasn't good.

Once in her apartment, she kicked off her shoes, gulped her iced coffee, and opened the newspapers on her coffee table. In a quick review of the *Post*'s Metro section, she found nothing about Jahi or the Shelter. Unfamiliar with the *Times*'s layout, she approached checking it with more care. The *Times* carried more local stories than the *Post*. Again her search came up short. She considered calling the TV station to ask what the story was about or simply checking online, until she spotted a small picture of a familiar face on page K-2 of the *Times*. It was Lena Christian, her "friend" of sorts and certainly a friend of Jahi's. Her last encounter with Lena had been at a DC charity dinner, earlier in the summer, the event where she first met Jahi. The column Capital Happenings carried Lena's byline.

"Oh, yeah," said Zoie, her mind working to make sense of the Lena-Jahi connection. Lena Christian surely could answer questions about Jahi. She'd know why he had made the TV news. With a few well-placed calls, Zoie could find out what she needed to know. But what she really needed from Lena was more than this latest Jahi story. She needed someone who knew Jahi and who could explain missing pieces about him. She'd have to be careful in how she approached Lena. Lena was definitely a Jahi fan, as evidenced by the scene at the dinner.

But first she tried calling the Shelter, one more time.

A gruff voice answered, chewing the name Mahali Salaam as if it were a piece of gum.

"Jahi Khalfani, please," Zoie said.

"I don't think he's back there, but I'll connect you with his voice mail."

"No, that's okay," she answered. "Do you happen to know where he is?"

"I just heard that he'd be out all day. He keeps his own schedule."

"I see," she replied. "Well, do you know anything about this morning's news story about him?"

There was a long pause. She heard the guy she was talking to call out, "Hey, Boots. You know anything about Jahi being on the news? This woman on the phone here wants to know."

The response was faint, but she heard it clearly. "He's on the news all the time. We ain't no press room. We're here to shelter the homeless. Take a message, and tell her he'll get back to her."

Before the man could repeat the message, Zoie said, "I heard."

Her frustration mounting, Zoie tried to reach Lena at her at the *Washington Times*'s office but was told that Lena Christian was off on Thursdays. So far Zoie was batting zero.

The Lena Christian lead was too important to let a little "Thursday off" thwart Zoie. She checked the DC white pages, but there was no listing for a Lena Christian. As was the case with many single woman, Lena's number was probably unlisted, just like Zoie's. She wasn't even sure that Lena still lived in the district. Zoie recalled that Lena's aunt was a longtime member of her grandmother's church, Calvary Cross Baptist. In fact, Zoie and Lena had first met at the church long before high school. Perhaps she could get Lena's home phone number from her aunt.

Zoie called her grandmother and asked for Lena's aunt's phone number.

"Child, what are you up to?" her grandmother asked.

Zoie gave her a story about a friend knowing a friend and how she needed to catch up with Lena, a mostly true story, but one designed to hide her real intention. Her grandmother said, "Okay. Queen, hand me my address book on the bureau." After her grandmother gave her Blanche McCarthy's phone number, Zoie wasted no time in making the next call.

"Oh, how sweet of you," cooed Blanche McCarthy in a light southern drawl, more syrupy than her grandmother's, though both women hailed from North Carolina. "I heard you moved back. It's so nice that you're thinking of my Lena. You know my Lena's a reporter now. She's at the *Washington Times*."

The pride in the woman's voice gave Zoie a twinge of guilt. She'd have to lie. "Yes, I saw her column this morning, and it made me think of her." That part was true. "You must be proud."

"Yes, I am. She made something of herself, after all."

The qualified compliment caught Zoie off guard. How could someone be proud but then cancel that pride with an *after all?*

"You know that I always wanted you two to be friends," Blanche McCarthy continued.

"Well, I'm calling because I need her address and phone number. I want to send her an invitation to a get-together I'm having in a few weeks. A housewarming thing."

"Wonderful!"

"Wonderful!" Zoie mimicked after the call ended. Having secured Lena's address, Zoie took a moment to reflect on the comment of Lena's aunt about wanting her to be friends with Lena. At the charity affair, Zoie hadn't even recognized Lena. Lena had been just another woman, a tipsy one clinging to Jahi. That night Lena was what her grandmother called a "brazen hussy." Still, Lena recognized Zoie. And it was clear through all the alcohol that Lena despised her.

The two girls had been thrown together on numerous occasions. They shared a church pew. They were dragged as a pair to see the Nutcracker ballet at the Kennedy Center. There had always been a stark contrast between them. Lena was tall and shapely. Her bosom and hips developed beyond her preteen years. Zoie was boyish and petite, the perfect candidate for Peter Pan in the middle school play. Mrs. McCarthy's incessant push for their friendship achieved the opposite effect. She once committed the ultimate faux pas: complimenting Zoie on her glowing academic record and, almost in the same breath, saying to Lena, "Why don't you try to be more like Zoie?"—insensitive words that, even at a young age, caused Zoie to cringe. She could only imagine how poor Lena felt. Yes, the chances for friendship back then were slim and shattered by an ignorant but well-meaning adult.

Lena lived in the up and coming DC area known as the M Street Corridor, a Southeast neighborhood near the Navy Yard. A woman with a child in stroller exited the building and let Zoie catch the open door. Zoie slipped into the Stafford East Condos without using the buzzer or a key. She took a deep breath before knocking on apartment 707G.

"Who is it?"

"Lena, it's Zoie, Zoie Taylor." Zoie could see an eye behind the peephole.

"Huh," said Lena when the door swung open moments later. Standing guard at her threshold, she donned a silky yellow head wrap, matching halter top, and skimpy jean shorts. "My goodness! One never knows who or what one might find outside the door."

Zoie gave an innocent shrug.

"What brings you here?" Lena asked, clinching her mouth in a tight smirk. "And how did you get in without buzzing?"

Zoie was about to explain, but Lena waved her off. "Never mind, I know." Lena quickly looked in both directions down the hallway to see whether other surprises awaited her. Satisfied that it was just the two of them, she opened her door wider and gestured for Zoie to enter. "I should have read my horoscope this morning. It would have warned me."

"Hello, Lena," said Zoie as she stood in the apartment's small foyer.

"Let me see," Lena said, holding her fingers to her chin. "Last time we saw each other, I was looking up, and you were standing over me laughing. Wasn't that when Jahi and I landed on the floor at the Hilton?"

"Unfortunately, yes. And that was rude of me," Zoie said, thinking that Lena's account of that night wasn't quite the way it happened.

"By the way, from here on it's shoe-free," Lena said, pointing to the shoe rack near the door.

Zoie made up her mind: no matter how much Lena egged her on, she wasn't going to succumb to trading insults. She was counting on Lena to be reasonable.

Zoie placed her small heel sandals in the rack and moved to the plush carpet, following the lead of her hostess. The path before her was a spectacle in white, what she imagined a polar bear's cave would be like, minus the chill. A white sectional sofa filled half the room. Without legs it was indistinguishable from the snowy carpet on which it sat. White lumps, probably pillows, were here and there like moguls on a ski slope. Zoie spotted a hint of pale pink in the form of a single flower in a glass globe, which seemed to float above the rimless glass coffee table. Other than the flower and a magazine opened on the table, there was little else to tell Zoie that she wasn't at the North Pole.

Through an opening in the gauzy white curtain, Zoie could see the Capitol dome. *What a view! This place is prime real estate.* Lena had done well. *Good for her.*

Lena stood by with folded arms, watching her childhood acquaintance check out the apartment.

"Nice place," Zoie said in genuine admiration.

"Thank you. I find it comfortable." Lena's face continued to show agitation. "But you didn't come by to see my place."

"True, true," Zoie responded. She was about to explain the reason for her visit, but an impatient Lena interrupted.

"So tell me how did you find me? Did Jahi give you my address?"

"No," Zoie quickly replied. "Your aunt gave it to me, the one who attends Calvary Cross Baptist."

Lena let out a cynical laugh. "Dear Aunt Blanche. She's still trying to hook us up. I don't know what kind of game you were playing that night. Acting like I was some alien."

"Lena, I'm truly sorry. That night I had brain fog. I really couldn't place you." Zoie sensed Lena's mood softening, the tension subsiding.

"So to what do I owe this visit?"

"I wanted to talk to you about Jahi," Zoie said as she moved toward the couch to seat herself.

"Want something to drink? I know I do."

"Yeah, sure. Why not."

Zoie was expecting water or iced tea. She hadn't been asked to choose. Lena disappeared into the kitchen for a few minutes and returned with a couple of drinks in tall frosted glasses on a red lacquer tray. She placed the tray on the glass table and sat at the far end of the sectional.

It was early for alcohol, not even eleven. With her nerves frayed, Zoie took a sip of her drink, a vodka tonic.

"So you want to talk about Mr. Khalfani?" asked Lena. "What did he do now?"

"I'm trying to figure out whether he did anything."

"Look, I'm not that man's keeper. I like Jahi, but he's a big boy, and I don't butt in."

That's not the way their relationship seemed at the charity dinner that night, Zoie thought. She bit her lip and let Lena talk.

Lena said, "Jahi and I went to school together. You know UDC. All I can tell you is that the brother is for real. He's on a mission."

"You're talking about the Shelter and fighting for the homeless being his mission?"

"That's right, as well as making sure the little guy gets a fair shake."

"You've confirmed what others have said about him."

"Sounds as if you have your doubts," Lena said, peering over her glass to gauge Zoie's reaction.

"Maybe. I mean I don't know." Zoie explained some of her doubts without going into the intricate details about the Shelter's financing through the Foundation, holding back the most damaging information and not mentioning the Ray Gaddis connection at all. Lena listened intently, throwing in a question here and there to prompt Zoie to go deeper. It was dangerous talking to a reporter, especially one who was Jahi's friend.

"Mmm, doesn't sound like the Jahi I know," Lena said. "If you really want to know what's going on, why ask me? Go directly to him. Be straight with him about your suspicions. I'm sure he's got a reasonable explanation."

"I've tried, but he's gone incommunicado."

"I'm sure everyone is after him. You know he was in the news today."

"I heard, but I don't know why."

"He's announced his candidacy for the city council. That search committee with the ministers finally talked him into it. They've been trying to get him to run for years."

Zoie looked surprised. During the steamy summer nights they spent at the townhouse of his friend, Jahi never mentioned political aspirations. When he talked politics, it was about politics pertaining to the homeless. She thought that he was totally committed to working on behalf of the homeless. The DC Council was so *establishment*. Not Jahi. But then what did she know? Obviously, he hadn't confided in her. And what else of importance had he failed to disclose?

"And you knew he was planning this?" Zoie asked.

"Yeah," she answered smugly. "Nothing was ever definite. He's been thinking about it for a while. He was torn. This week he was going to decide. So I guess he did. He never said anything to you?"

Zoie sat blank faced and silent.

"I guess not," Lena said, answering her own question. "Well, that's Jahi for you. The strong, silent type—unless he's preaching for his cause."

"Jahi is running for the DC Council," Zoie said with amazement.

"Yeah. And in regard to all that stuff you told me about the Shelter and the Foundation, you really need to talk to him. And do it right away. Bad press about this stuff could ruin his election chances. The primary is only six weeks away."

Zoie grimaced. "Damn. He's not making it easy. I've tried to contact him."

"I guess you figured that he and I had a thing," Lena said, swirling the ice in her glass.

"I guessed. I wasn't sure. He never said anything."

"He wouldn't," Lena sighed. "Well, it was off and on again. Always more off than on, if you know what I mean."

"Uh-huh," said Zoie, taking a sip of her drink.

"And you and Jahi?"

Zoie hesitated. *How much should I confide? How jealous is this woman?* "We've had a few dates."

"Hey, give me credit here. I know this wasn't merely business-related curiosity. Look, the Jahi I know is a straight shooter. Let me give you some insight. He and Sister Te were hooked up for a long time. Have you met her?"

"Sister Te? The name sounds familiar."

"If you've been to the Shelter you might have run into her."

"I think I know who you're talking about," Zoie said, sitting up with new energy. Sister Te was absent the day she visited the Shelter. Her absence was the reason Zoie was barred from the women's section. "Does she run the women's part of the Shelter?"

"I'm not sure, but if you ask me, that's not all she runs. She and Jahi were a thing for many years. She went to UDC with us. She and her friends took Jahi in when he was homeless. Have you heard that story?"

Holding her glass steady, Zoie slumped back into the couch. She felt Lena's glance relishing in her discomfort.

"You didn't know about that either, huh?" Lena asked.

"I knew the part about his being homeless." Zoie went quiet. Of course, Jahi lived a full and complete life before they met. She never let herself dwell on his past relationships. It was the summer of knowing this man and at the same time not knowing him at all. But then she hadn't spelled out her whole past to him either. "Were he and Sister Te married?"

Lena took a deep breath before answering. "Sister Te is Ethiopian or Eritrean. I get that mixed up. Anyway, I think he said something about having a commitment. I wasn't too worried about it. Our relationship wasn't going anywhere. So it didn't matter."

"My God, he never said a word."

"Well, how long have you known him? A few months? Been sleeping with him a couple of months?"

Zoie's jaws went tight.

"I don't get you," Lena said, her tone "home girl" curt. "You come here, all prim and proper, accusing your man of messing up, being involved in fraudulent activity. For what?"

"Wait! I said *maybe*," Zoie interjected.

"Well, you're one of many who wants something from that man. He's trying to do good for his community. So make up your mind. Why did you come here, anyway?"

Zoie searched for an equally powerful retort, forgetting for a minute that she had promised herself that she would not go toe to toe with Lena. Two women yelling at each other would not accomplish anything. The fragile moment was blessed by an interruption, the beeping from Lena's cell phone. Lena gave Zoie a cutting stare and then rose from the couch to retrieve the device.

Zoie rose too, deciding it was long past time to go.

Lena scanned her latest message. It read, "Ray Gaddis, head of Crayton Foundation, found dead at his home in Potomac. Call in. Need you to cover background. Pete."

"Oh, Jesus," said Lena.

"What happened?" Zoie asked.

"Honey, you better sit down so you can tell me."

"Is it about Jahi?" With fear in her eyes, Zoie backed up and again sat on the couch.

"My office just texted. Looks as if your boss is dead. Wow! Did you know that? Is that why you're here?"

"Oh no!" Zoie gasped with hands to her mouth.

"Look, stay here. I've got an important call to make. Don't go anywhere. This may involve you," Lena said.

Oh shit! Zoie took a large gulp of her drink. Liquor in the morning had turned out to be most appropriate. She sat frozen while Lena disappeared from her sea of white. *Folks at the office must be going crazy*, Zoie thought. If Lena was being informed by the *Washington Times*, then all of the main media were involved. Zoie was surprised that so far no one at the Foundation had thought to call her. She dialed Regina. The call rolled to her assistant's voice mail. Zoie surmised that everyone was probably gathered around Milton's office. She scanned her contact list and found Milton's cell number. It rang a few times before he answered.

"Oh, Zoie, I'm glad you called in. I was going to call you. Did you hear the terrible news about Ray?"

"Yes, I heard, but no details. What happened?"

"When he didn't make his morning meeting or answer his phones, we had Sam Moxner from the Bethesda office go to his house to check on him. Sam found him. He was floating face down in the pool," Milton explained.

"Ugh. How horrible. Did he drown?" Zoie's head was spinning.

"No one is sure. We need to put out something official from the Foundation." Milton choked for a moment. Zoie envisioned him fighting back tears. "I have to call all the Board members before they hear it on TV. The place is crawling with Crayton-headquarter types. I'm preparing a statement now. Can you get here right away?"

"Sure. I'm on my way," Zoie said, ending the call. She took a minute to contemplate the news. *Ray dead!* She wanted to tell Milton that she'd been to Ray's house last night. She wanted to explain how she had waited outside his house and felt disgusted that he'd stood her up.

Zoie headed after Lena, and the two almost collided at the kitchen door.

"I have to leave," Zoie said. Her heart was pounding.

"I bet you do!"

"I just talked to my office."

"Do they know how he died?"

"He was found face down in his pool. Could've been an accident. They don't know yet."

"Could be murder," said Lena in a low voice.

"Anything is possible at this point."

"You said that as if you know something. Look, maybe someone needed to shut him up about the stuff you were telling me. And if so, maybe you're in danger too."

In truth, Zoie hadn't thought that far ahead to consider her own safety. She considered the possible damage to the Foundation's reputation and possible damage to her career, should she fail to come forward. But physical danger hadn't crossed her mind. White-collar crime was different, usually bloodless. No blood on anyone's hands, just dirt from dirty money. Then she remembered Rosen's allegation, how his client had felt strong-armed. She remembered Carmen Silva's insistence that she not be at all involved. There'd been real fear, not just annoyance behind Carmen's insistence.

"Are you going to tell the police about your suspicions?" Lena asked.

"What choice do I have? It's out of my hands. I was trying to work something out with Ray, so..." She stopped cold. She'd already told Lena more than she should have.

"So Ray Gaddis went bobbing for apples and never came up for air."

The two stood quiet for a minute. Zoie was coming to grips with the depth of her quandary.

"Look, I'd like you to help me figure out what's going on. I mean I'd hate to see Jahi get in trouble if he's truly an innocent party," Zoie said.

"So you're going to spill the beans?" Lena cocked her head to the side and smiled. "You actually care what happens to Jahi?"

"Yes, I do. And the Shelter."

"Strange, he does have that effect on us."

Zoie didn't respond.

"I actually think Jahi's innocent of whatever you think he might have done," Lena said. "Perhaps I'm being naïve, but I think he's the real deal."

"Then you're going to help?"

"Don't know what I can do. But, hey, you've got spunk. I was having a hard time envisioning Jahi with a 'Ms. Goody Two Shoes.'"

Zoie turned to leave. "I've got to go home for some things then head to the office."

"Wait. Yeah, I'm in. I just need to ask that I get an exclusive on whatever we find out."

Zoie thought for a second. "Okay, agreed, at least for myself. I can't make any agreements for the Foundation. In the meantime you can't say anything about what I've told you here today. This whole discussion was strictly off the record."

Lena thought for a moment. "Okay, that's fair."

"And you've got to agree not to print a word until I give you the go-ahead."

"Hey, we reporters are used to dealing with confidential sources. Speaking of confidential"—Lena grabbed a paper and pen and scribbled her cell number—"we'd better keep this on the QT. It's best if people don't know I'm in the loop. Right?"

"Right." Zoie reached into her pocketbook and brought out one of her business cards and handed it to Lena. "I'll call tonight. There's a lot I haven't told you."

"I bet!" said Lena. "I bet."

CHAPTER 29

I KNOW HOW TO FIND YOU

Zoie grabbed a cab from Lena's place and went back to her apartment. The day's macabre events and the too-early vodka and tonic were taking their toll. News of Ray's death left her in semi-shock. Ray, the poor man, was no longer an impediment to going to the Board. If Ray was murdered, the situation was truly dire. She should be talking to the police.

It was sad that Ray Gaddis was dead, but in truth, he wouldn't be missed—not by her and probably not by others. That sleazy smile of his was a turnoff. An image of Ray and Milton's *alleged* copy-room encounter drifted through her mind. Although she hadn't witnessed the episode, Silva's account was enough to activate Zoie's vivid imagination. She shook off that image, but it was quickly replaced by a gruesome vision of Ray's body bobbing in the pool. *What a way to go!* Zoie shook her bowed head.

"You all right, lady?" the cabdriver asked. His dark eyes had been peering at her in his rearview mirror.

She didn't answer.

"If you're going to throw up, I want to pull over. I just cleaned this car."

Zoie glanced down at the discolored taxi license posted behind his seat. It bore the driver's face and an unpronounceable name. On most days she would have asked the driver, what country are you from? or, how do you pronounce your name? But today too many other things occupied her mind.

"No problem. I'm okay," she finally answered, looking up. Their eyes met in the rearview mirror, and he turned his attention back to the busy street.

Zoie's brain was trying to make sense of it all. What could have been going on in Ray's house while she waited outside? Was he already dead while she sat in his driveway? He could have drowned just that morning. The cause of death could have been a suicide, an accidental fall, or a heart attack. Or was it murder, as Lena had speculated? Ray could have been distraught, fearing the exposure of his dirty dealings, causing him to commit suicide. Somehow Ray didn't seem the suicide type. The scenarios of what went down were endless.

When the cab slowed in the heavy Connecticut Avenue traffic, she became conscious of the early lunch crowd. Where was Jahi? She thought of looking at the throng. Had *he* heard about Ray? Once again she tried to contact him. Her attempt went to voice mail with one ring, as had all of the other attempts. Irritated, she left no message. *It's time to move past worrying about Jahi Khalfani,* she thought. Despite what she told Lena, Zoie felt no obligation to protect Jahi or his budding political career. She wouldn't withhold information on his account. Too much else was at stake.

She had legal obligations as the Foundation's attorney and the Board secretary. There would have to be an internal investigation. She would have to disclose everything she knew to the police and others, including her attempt to meet with Ray on the prior evening about the Shelter's funding. Her personal relationship with Jahi couldn't be a barrier to telling what she knew.

As they neared her building, Zoie noticed that a nervous sweat had taken hold and left unsightly underarm stains on her silk blouse. She needed to retrieve her papers and make a quick wardrobe change before heading to the office.

"When we get to the building, I want you to wait for me," she blurted to the driver.

"Lady, I can't just sit and wait," he said with pleasantly accented English.

"Please, I just need to run in for a few minutes. Look, I'll make it worth your while." She rooted through her pocketbook and pulled out a twenty-dollar bill. "See?" she said, waving the bill like a flag so he could view it in the rearview mirror. "This is the tip if you wait."

"Then where do you want me to take you?" the driver asked.

"Back downtown to K Street."

Unlike the continuous stream of cabs that cruised New York City's main thoroughfares, DC cabs were few and far between. She'd been lucky to hail this cab in the southwest area of DC. Today Zoie didn't want to deal with the Metro and the heat. The cabdriver mumbled under his breath as he considered her request. When he stopped in front of her building, he turned to her with a noncommittal shrug. "I don't know, lady," he said.

Zoie raised the twenty-dollar bill again for him to see. Twenty dollars for twenty minutes seemed fair to her.

"Okay," he responded, although his agreement to the arrangement was less than enthusiastic. "But you pay me now. I'll wait for twenty minutes. But no more."

"Whatever," Zoie said in a low tone. She paid him the fare she owed from Lena's, plus the extra tip. "Okay, how about you give me your cell phone number. I'll call you if I have to be longer."

"Lady, already you're changing the deal," he protested.

"No, I'll call if I don't need you to wait. Look, I'll make it worth your while."

The driver found a business card and, with a stub of a pencil, scratched a number on the front and handed it to her.

"Thanks. Now I know how to find you," she said half-jokingly and somewhat ominously.

"Okay, lady. I got to feed my family. Twenty minutes only," he reiterated as she backed out of his cab.

Zoie keyed into her apartment building, whizzed past the door clerk (who seemed oblivious to her entry), and checked her watch as she entered the waiting elevator. The clock was ticking.

Once in her apartment, she headed straight for the kitchen, grabbed a bottle of water from the refrigerator, and then entered her bedroom to find a different outfit. While flipping through her clothes rack, she put in a call to her assistant.

"Regina! Good, I got you. I've been trying to reach you. Where have you been?"

"They pulled us into the boardroom at ten thirty to tell us about Ray," Regina said, sounding anxious. "You heard, didn't you? Ray's dead."

"Yeah. I talked to Milton." Zoie was solemn.

"It's crazy around here. Arleen's been balling nonstop, and Milton's freakier than usual. I asked him whether I could leave. He told me we all had to stay. If you ask me, he needs to shut this place down. Ain't no work getting done here today."

Zoie let out a heavy sigh. Her young assistant failed to realize that today would be one of the Foundation's busiest days.

"Zoie, can I leave? They're letting Arleen go home," Regina continued.

"Regina, wait until I get there. Then we'll see."

"And, Zoie, they've been looking for you."

"Who's the *they*?"

"Corporate, corporate legal, a couple of Board members, and a couple of grantees," said Regina.

"Damn!" Zoie stopped shuffling through her closet for a replacement outfit to consider what Regina had said. So the Board members had already found out. And maybe one of the grantees calling was Jahi, though Regina would have mentioned that.

"Which grantees called?" Zoie asked to confirm her thinking.

Regina rattled off the names of several people, none of whom had anything to do with the Shelter. She added, "I told them that you were out this morning on personal business."

"That's fine. That's all you need to say." Zoie paused. "I'm sure Milton has told them that I'm on my way. What else?"

"London is supposed to be here, and I heard he's bringing another attorney from corporate to help out."

"London, huh."

From Regina's account the Foundation's office sounded like a zoo. Zoie knew her young assistant tended to exaggerate, but this time she believed her. If Averell London, Crayton's chief operating officer, and his entourage were putting in an appearance, well, who knows what. London usually shied away from the Foundation's business. He let Ray run his own show. After all, the Foundation was a separate entity. The additional legal assistance from corporate made sense. An emergency Board meeting had to be called, and a myriad of other things would need to occur.

Changed from her summer suit into long pants and a fresh blouse, Zoie took thirty seconds to freshen her makeup. It would be a long evening. For a moment her thoughts shifted to Nikki. It was good that her daughter was out of town. The coming days would be hectic: the funeral, efforts to ensure continuity, police questioning, the emergency Board meeting, and God knows what else, once she told the Board her suspicions.

As the clock ticked down on her twenty minutes, Zoie picked up the pace of her movements. She grabbed her pocketbook and keys from the bed then headed to the living room to grab her briefcase from between the couch and a small table. But other than the large fichus plant, the spot where she usually kept her briefcase was empty. A nearby stack of magazines lay toppled on the floor. Anxious, her eyes scanned the room. She was disgusted that she had misplaced her bag at such a crucial time. But her eyes returned to the spot where she'd last seen her briefcase, where her carefully stacked magazines had mysteriously collapsed. She checked the other side of the couch. No luck. Her eyes went to the table where she expected to see her laptop in its usual place on a placemat. The placemat was there but no laptop.

"Okay, Zoie, get a grip," she told herself. She moved around the room, this time being more surgical in her search. She checked all corners and then went into the bedroom. No luck. Could last night's phone call with Nikki have left her so off kilter that she'd taken her laptop and briefcase into the bathroom? They weren't in the bathroom or the kitchen. In the kitchen she noticed that her usually neat pile of bills on the side counter had been rifled.

"Oh my God! Someone's been here!"

Panic was setting in. Could the burglar still be there? She knew she had to keep her wits about her. With eyes closed, she took a deep breath. Reason conquered her initial fear. What else had the thief taken? This was about Ray and the Shelter. Someone wanted the information on her laptop and in her briefcase. Things were clearer now. For sure Ray had been murdered. Now they were after the information she'd compiled on the Shelter. She took a quick mental inventory of what she knew to be in the briefcase and on her laptop. Even though the laptop was corporate, it held quite a bit of personal information. With a few clicks, anyone could access her personal e-mail.

"Damn," she said, wondering what else had been taken. Whoever entered her apartment could do it again. Her apartment wasn't safe. A chill came over her. She needed to leave immediately and get in touch with the police. In the midst of her panic, her cell phone rang. Without looking at the caller ID, she answered. "What is it, Regina?"

"Hello, Ms. Taylor." It wasn't Regina.

"Who is this?"

"You don't need to know that. I trust you found things in order." The caller's voice was low and deliberate.

Zoie's panic subsided as she realized she was talking to the burglar. "What do you want?"

"We want your silence."

"Silence? Silence about what?"

"About what you *think* you know."

"You murdered Ray, didn't you?"

"Mr. Gaddis was a foolish man. However, you are much smarter."

"Who are you?" she asked again in frustration. "If you've got my briefcase and laptop, you have what you want."

"Not entirely. We need assurances. Death raises suspicions. We'd rather not bring more attention…with another one."

Zoie shuttered. "Leave me alone."

"That can be arranged," said the voice.

"I…I…" she stuttered. "I won't tell anyone what I know."

"It's best you remember that you don't know anything. Right, Ms. Taylor? If you forget that, we know how to find you." The caller hung up.

Zoie's heart pounded. Her knees felt weak. She clung to the table where her laptop once sat to steady herself. She had the presence of mind to check her incoming call record. The last call was listed as caller unknown. She considered immediately returning the call but thought better of it.

She found the taxi driver's card and called the number. "Uh, you still waiting?"

"Yeah, lady, but you're time has been up. I was about to leave. I gotta make a living."

"Listen, I really need you to wait."

"It's going to cost you another twenty."

"Yeah, just stay there. Please, please. I'll be right down."

The mysterious caller had said "we." How many were there? It didn't matter. It only took one crazed individual to pull off a murder and burglarize her apartment. He had her cell phone number and knew her address, where she worked, and God knows what else. He'd gotten past the feeble lock on her door. Staying in her apartment was too dangerous.

Zoie pulled out a large denim bag and stuffed it with underwear, a few jerseys, pants, sneakers, and cosmetics. With the bag and her pocketbook over her shoulder, she headed out the door. In a reflex action, she turned the lock on her door and then wondered why she'd bothered. Obviously, the person or persons who had broken in could come and go from her apartment at will. She'd deal with a locksmith later.

Outside, the cab was parked a few spaces down the street. She scurried toward it.

"Thank you—thank you for being here," she said somewhat breathless. She stuffed the denim bag into the cab's back seat and then climbed in beside it. Inside the cab she felt a little safer. She took a deep breath and collapsed into the seat.

The driver's radio blasted some exotic music. He turned it down and gave her a strange look. "K Street, right? Where on K Street are we going?" he asked as he pulled the car into the Connecticut Ave traffic.

"No, not K Street. I've changed my mind. We're headed up New York Avenue."

CHAPTER 30

WHO CAN YOU TRUST?

Zoie's taxi driver seemed none too happy having waited for his passenger. She handed him the promised twenty dollars sweetened with another ten.

His scowl morphed to a bright smile. "Thank you."

Zoie's decision to go to the Shelter instead of the Foundation was a last-minute change. But then circumstances had changed. Corporate higher-ups were waiting at work. She should have directed the driver to take her straight to the office or better still to the police to report the burglary of her apartment and the threatening call. After all, the caller all but admitted to killing Ray. But she felt trapped. The phone threat had done its job—it had secured her silence. She was part of a complicated and dangerous mess with no easy way out. For now she couldn't contact the authorities. She'd have to take another tact.

"Lady, where on New York Avenue?" asked the driver, breaking into Zoie's thoughts.

"Umm." Her brain was scattered. She couldn't remember the Shelter's address or the cross streets. "I know it's a ways up New York. Just a second." She dug deep into her pocketbook.

"I've got the address." Her search produced a crumpled business card made of recycled paper. It was Jahi's. She pressed the card against the seat to smooth it out. More than ever she needed to find him.

"Lady, help me out. Which way am I going?"

She handed the driver the card. "It's a homeless shelter in Northeast."

He glanced down at the card. "Way up there?"

"Good. You know where it is," she snapped back.

"Yes, I think I know that place."

As the taxi made its way through the afternoon traffic, now and again she found the driver's dark eyes peering at her from the rearview mirror. Each time she caught them, they quickly turned away.

"By the way, what's you name?" she asked boldly.

"I am called Muwakkil."

She looked at the taxi license. His second name was very long, with two z's and several r's. She concentrated instead on the first name, repeating his pronunciation of it. "*Mu-wa-kkil*, Muwakkil. Does it translate to a meaning in English?"

"Of course. It means 'one who can be trusted.'"

The name impressed her. "I hope that's true, Muwakkil, about your being trustworthy."

"Oh, yes, of course. If that is my name, it means I have those qualities," he said. "Parents always give a child the correct name. And I must live up to it. I cannot disappoint my parents or go against my destiny."

"I sure hope you live up to your destiny," she said under her breath as she played with the fabric of her denim bag. She wondered whether her mother had researched the meaning of Zoie or maybe had chosen it simply because she liked the way it sounded. As a preteen she looked it up and discovered that her name was Greek. It meant "life." She never thought to ask Jahi what his name meant after he explained why he'd changed his name. For sure his parents had no say in choosing that name. *Jahi* was a name he'd bestowed upon himself, its meaning corresponding to what he thought of himself or some attribute he aspired to. Too bad the name *Muwakkil*—"the one who can be trusted"—was already taken.

When they arrived at Mahali Salaam, the place was bustling. A small white van was double parked in front of the Shelter. Two young men with hand trucks were unloading the van's contents. The Shelter's heavy doors were propped open. Some of the homeless men milled around in front of the Shelter, pacing slowly in the sun, while others anchored themselves against the building in the little bit of shade the structure provided. Dinnertime was hours away, but these folks would be first in line to get a good meal.

From the looks of things, the Shelter was getting a delivery. Zoie wondered why the van hadn't gone around to the Shelter's rear loading dock.

The taxi driver pulled around the van and stopped farther down the block. Would Jahi be there? She was taking a gamble. He couldn't avoid her forever. She mumbled a litany of profanity, a preview of what she'd say to Jahi when she found him. She exited the taxi, her free-form denim bag in tow. When she threw the bag over her shoulder, the irony of the moment hit her. She looked like some bag lady in front of the Shelter. And tonight she needed to find a place to stay. At least she had options.

Zoie rifled in her pocketbook for the money to pay her fare and had second thoughts about letting the taxi go. "Muwakkil, can you wait for me again?" she asked.

"Sure, lady. I know you will make it worth my while," he answered.

Now it seemed he trusted her. "Muwakkil, you catch on fast."

"And I can be trusted," he said with a smile.

"Then I'm leaving my bag, so you know I'll be back." She threw the cloth bag in the back seat and left the amiable taxi driver leaning against his vehicle, with folded arms. With the front doors wide open, she entered behind several men carrying unmarked cardboard boxes from the truck. Another man followed them, navigating a hand truck with four boxes. She watched the procession for a few seconds as they made their way past the Shelter lobby and down an adjacent corridor before she approached the clerk at the main desk. "My name is Zoie Taylor, from the Crayton Foundation. I'm here to see Jahi Khalfani,"

The desk clerk was not the hearing-impaired guy, who'd failed to notice her on her last visit. This clerk was middle aged and blond, and his biceps—adorned in blue ink—matched his tank top. "You know, I'm not sure Jahi's around. I don't think I've seen him today. But let me check. Is he expecting you?"

"Yes," she lied, slightly hesitating, looking at her watch to appear casual.

The clerk picked up the phone and punched in a couple of numbers. "Tell Jahi he's got someone here from the Crayton Foundation named…"

"Zoie Taylor."

"Zoie Taylor," he repeated. He hung up. "It'll be just a moment."

Awkwardly Zoie pressed against the high desk as she waited for Jahi to show. A new batch of boxes passed by them, on the way to the back. She turned to the desk clerk and asked, "Are those the new pillows?"

"Nah. Are we supposed to be getting new pillows? I believe that's donated stuff for the women's section, probably clothes. I'm not sure. It's not my department."

"Oh," she responded nonchalantly, remembering that she'd missed seeing the women's section of the Shelter during her visit.

"Jahi should be here in a few minutes," the clerk told her. "You can have a seat over there." He pointed to one of the church pew benches.

She was about to sit down when she saw a young man emerge from the corridor and head in her direction. "Ms. Taylor, good to see you again," he said, offering his hand. She recognized him as the young man who completed her tour of the Shelter when she was there weeks ago.

"You're Tarik," she said, shaking his hand, his dark eyes like pools, his physique still reminding her of a long-distance runner, slight but strong.

"Good memory, Ms. Taylor. Our meeting was many weeks ago, and you still remember."

"I'm here to see Jahi," she said right away.

"Unfortunately, he's not here today."

"So where is he?" she asked without equivocation.

Tarik appeared a little startled by her directness. "I'm not exactly sure. He checks in though. You know he's running for the city council. The campaign keeps him away a lot."

Zoie frowned in disappointment.

"Ms. Taylor, Jahi depends on me to run the day-to-day operations. Whatever you need, I can probably help," Tarik said.

"And I'm sure you're doing a wonderful job." Her tone was almost dismissive. "Perhaps I could talk to Hank, the cook."

Tarik looked offended. "You mean Hank Townsend? Why him?"

"We had a nice long talk in the kitchen the last time I was here. And this is personal."

"Hank? I believe he's off today. I think he's helping Jahi on the campaign."

Zoie remembered the waiting taxi driver. She was batting zero. What should she do next? Where would she sleep? What was she going to tell the Crayton folks waiting at the Foundation? She checked her watch again.

"Ms. Taylor, I can give you any information you need."

"This is *not* about you, Tarik! I need to talk to Jahi! Preferably in person!" She looked over to see the desk clerk's look of horror. She was being nastier than she'd been with anyone in a long time. Furious with Jahi, she was now taking it out on Tarik, though he had been a little too smug.

Tarik winced and ran his hand through his tightly curled hair. "You're upset. I really wish I could be of more help. Things must be difficult at the Foundation with Ray Gaddis's death."

"What! What are you talking about? How do you know about Ray?" Zoie blasted.

She caught the entire room's attention. Tarik's dark eyes widened. "Ms. Taylor, the story of Mr. Gaddis's death is being covered on radio and TV. I'm so sorry."

"Ahh, you tell Jahi Khalfani that Zoie Taylor is looking for him!" she shouted, pointing at him as she headed to the doorway, just as another stream of mysterious boxes made their way in. Focused on Tarik, she backed straight into a woman who was attempting to squeeze through the traffic at the entrance. The woman was slim, dressed in tight-fitting jeans, wearing a snug blue-and-white head wrap, which was knotted on one side. "Watch out!" the woman cried.

"Oh, excuse me," Zoie said, realizing only a part of what had happened. At a minimum Zoie unwittingly elbowed the woman in the chest, stamped on her sandaled foot, and shoved her into the pile of boxes on a handcart. Realizing what she'd done Zoie locked eyes with the woman for a fraction of a second. The woman's eyes were fierce and so forceful that no one could have stared into them for long. Zoie was the first to turn away. The woman sucked her teeth in disgust.

"I'm so sorry," Zoie said, sincerely apologetic. The woman, however, didn't look at her again and didn't respond to her apology. Instead she helped the man with the handcart restack his toppled boxes. Tarik witnessed the whole thing but said nothing.

Zoie rushed outside. She looked down the street. Her waiting taxi and its driver were nowhere to be seen. For a moment she experienced that stomach-dropping sensation like being on a roller coaster. Had her driver left her hanging? Absconded with her things? With all that had happened that day, this was the last straw. Everything she needed for the next few days was in the taxi's back seat. Angry words turned into tears of frustration as she scanned the street, half-blinded by the bright sun. There was no taxi. She was about to give up on her self-proclaimed trustworthy driver when she noticed him at the end of the block. She squinted to see him better. He waved at her from the midst of a crowd of men who were gathered around a crate of bottled water, in the shade of the building. He hustled down the street toward her with an offering—a bottle of the water.

"It's pretty hot out here," he said, not apologizing. He didn't know that his potential disappearance had added to her stress. He didn't notice her tears.

She calmed herself, then wiped her eyes with the back of her hands and took a long swig of the water. "Where's your car?"

"Around the corner." He pointed down the street in the opposite direction.

"I was worried. I thought you left."

"Ye of little faith…" he said with a serious face. "Since I am Muwakkil, the one who can be trusted, I would never do that."

"Right."

"So where to now?"

"Let me think."

"You know, lady, it would be cheaper if you hired me for the day."

"I don't know. I got to think," she answered. For now she was just happy to not be alone.

CHAPTER 31

ON GUARD

Queen's second-floor bedroom was at the front of the house, two doors from Mrs. Woods's bedroom, at the back. At night she was close enough to hear the older woman's coughs and labored breaths, sounds that could be heard despite the incessant chatter and canned sitcom laughter from the old TV.

Queen had retreated to her own room to see *Days of Our Lives* while her charge sat up in bed, engrossed in *Wendy Williams*. In the comfort of her lounge chair, Queen sipped the last of her ginger beer and used a wet finger to collect the crumbs from her plate of her spicy meat-patty lunch.

The hum of her oscillating fan competed with the TV. The monotonous drone could grate on a person's nerves, if one had the mind to let it. It had been that way all summer. But for Queen the extra sound no longer registered on her conscious mind.

Days of Our Lives was at its cliffhanger point when the usually quiet dog next door let out a high-pitched howl followed by nonstop barking. "Now what?" Queen asked herself before her attention drifted back to the final minutes of the program. But the dog's incessant barking could not be ignored. Queen turned down the TV, shut off the whining fan, and moved to the window to look and listen.

No one was on the street, and the same cars she'd noticed earlier in the day were parked in their same spaces. She heard rustling in the bushes below. Someone or something was out there. Was it two legged or four legged? Perhaps it was just another dog or a cat. Queen knew that raccoons or deer often wandered out of nearby Rock Creek Park. She once saw a raccoon for herself, and Mrs. Woods often talked about the deer that sometimes paraded down the middle of the street. But today all she could see were the cars going to and from Broad Branch. And the dog kept barking.

Bam! It was a crash like a metal garbage can being overturned. The sound came from close by—maybe from the side of the house, an area with a small porch off the kitchen. "Oh, Lawd," Queen sighed. She slipped into her leather scuffs and descended the staircase. "Whoever messin' around here gonna be sorry." At the front door, she retrieved the baseball bat from the umbrella stand. She remembered that there were big knives in the kitchen as she peeked out the clear glass panel in the front door, hoping no one would peek back. The front porch was empty. With the baseball bat raised ready to strike, she tiptoed to the kitchen. The dog's rant got louder as she neared the part of the house nearest to the neighbor's fence. Outside there was the squeal of tires. Someone was making a fast getaway.

Not counting on the person's being gone, she continued with slow, deliberate steps. Her heart pounded in readiness as she neared the kitchen. The sound of crackling wood and the smell of smoke hit her senses in unison. Fire was confirmed by its glow through the half-glass door off the kitchen. Queen got a better look. The wooden lattice, which blocked the view from the neighboring house, was a wall of flames. Flames licked at the nearby brick.

"Oh Lawd!" she screamed. For a second she hesitated. Should she try to extinguish the fire? No extinguisher was around. She didn't open the door but grabbed the kitchen phone and dialed 911. "The house is on fire! Someone set fire to the house!"

"What's the address?"

Queen rattled off the Brandywine address. "Hurry!"

"Get yourself and everybody else out of the house immediately," the operator instructed. "The fire department is on the way."

Bat still in hand, Queen bolted up the stairs two steps at a time. She found Mrs. Woods snoring, with the TV chattering in the background.

"Wake up, Mrs. Woods! Wake up! We got a fire," shouted Queen, shaking the woman.

"Huh. Huh." Frances Woods was disoriented. "What's happening?"

Queen wasted no time explaining further. She dropped the bat and scooped her confused charge from the bed like a rag doll. Heading down the stairs, she secured her footing on each step before proceeding. Clearly frightened, the older woman grabbed loose fabric on Queen's dress and buried her face in the larger woman's chest.

Smoke was coming into the house.

"Hang on, Mrs. Woods. I got you."

On the front porch in the bright sun, Queen could see the haze of lapping flames coming from the side of the house. Frances Woods saw it too. "Oh, God, my house is burning," she cried. "How did this happen?"

"Dogs and deer don't set fires," Queen answered. "Somebody got it in for us." Queen sized up her next challenge: the long uneven stone steps going from the porch down to the street. Queen had carried Mrs. Woods down those steps before but never in a rush. She stood for a second to catch her breath and to adjust the weight of her load. "Okay, we're going down again," she warned.

"Don't drop me!" Frances Woods commanded.

"Let me help you," said a man making his way from the street. He looked sincere but too frail to be of any help.

Queen recognized him as a neighbor but wouldn't hand over her charge. "I got her," she assured him.

"You okay, Mrs. Woods?" he asked before turning to head back down. "I called 911."

"Then we both did," Queen said.

Reaching the sidewalk, Queen realized that her arms ached. Frances Woods was a small woman but, nonetheless, a load to carry. Queen sat her charge on the short stonewall that lined the front of the property. From that vantage point, the threesome looked up at the house to see billowing black smoke from the bonfire consuming the side of the house, but neither Queen nor the neighbor was going back up the stairs to check.

"All these years, nothing like this has ever happened to me," Frances Woods said, her voice solemn. She gathered her flimsy cotton gown around her and rested her hands across her chest. Queen put an arm around her and let the older woman lean into her.

"I wished they'd get here," Queen said.

Minutes later sirens sounded in the distance. "Here they come," said the neighbor.

A few more neighbors emerged onto the street to watch the firemen do their job. One or two of the neighbors came over to Frances Woods to offer assistance. Queen didn't know them. No neighbors had come to visit since she'd been working there.

The firemen made short work of the blaze. "Not much damage," reported a fireman who seemed to be in charge "Looks to me to be intentional. There's got to be follow-up from the arson squad. Did anyone see anything?"

Queen explained how she'd heard the dog barking, the crash, and then squealing tires.

"I'd advise not staying here tonight," said the fireman. "The damage isn't too bad, but the house needs to air out, and I'd be worried about whoever did this coming back."

"She can stay with us," offered a neighbor.

"Queen, I need to call Zoie," Frances Woods said. Her voice trailed.

"Sure, Mrs. Woods. I'll call her, and I'm calling my brother to look at the damage," Queen said.

Frances Woods began to cough her awful cough. Both the fireman and the neighbor frowned. "Perhaps you should go to the hospital, ma'am," the fireman said.

"No! No! No hospital!" Frances Woods insisted. Breathless, she squeezed Queen's shoulder to get her to do the talking.

Queen got the signal. "She's got medicine for that cough. I'll call her granddaughter to come for her. In the meantime I'm taking her to my house."

CHAPTER 32

THOSE YOU CAN TRUST

With no breeze the smoke from the abandoned cigarette rose straight to the porch ceiling. A distance from the cigarette, Jahi sat alone in a weathered rocking chair. Murray's family cabin was an ideal spot for a getaway. In a communications dead spot, it was perfect if one wanted to be isolated. Inside, his Marine Corps buddies had started their infamous poker game without him. For Jahi, being out of touch when he was kicking off his city-council run didn't make sense. Now his decision to leave the city for a few days bugged him. His decision to run for office at all bugged him more. Alas, the deed was done. He'd made promises to his campaign backers. Oh, what had he gotten himself into?

Other than the narrow winding road and the gravel parking pad, now covered by four vehicles, only green, a calming green surrounded the place. Exhaling, Jahi could feel his blood pressure drop. In this moment of serenity, he contemplated his situation. Deaths in his family had left a hole in his world. Two tours with the US Marines had kept him away from home for many years. Changing his name also added to the distance from family and those he loved. He didn't plan for his new name to sever him from the past. But somehow it did.

Then there was Tesfaneshe. They met at UDC. An exotic beauty with brains and boundless energy, she filled some of the void in his life. She saved him from the street when he was at his lowest. The truth was he could have saved himself, but he wanted to be saved by her. So Te and her young son became his family. She introduced him to her friends and relatives in the United States. Within her group, he—not she—was the immigrant. A community of Ethiopians—hardworking, joyful, and caring. They made sure he was fed and stayed healthy. Made sure he was loved. Te and he shared a bed for many years. Her son, then a wide-eyed boy, looked to him as a father.

But his relationship with Te wouldn't last. He had strong feelings for her but could never fully enter her world. He couldn't be Ethiopian. Indeed, he didn't want to be. Te's dark eyes hid her world and experiences. She'd lived through things he couldn't fathom—things she either would not or could not explain. He would always be the outsider, albeit a cherished one. Still, he owed her his allegiance for her years of devotion, even if he couldn't give her all that she hoped for. Alas, he came to realize that allegiance and love were not the same.

The gang at the cabin was from his Marine Corps unit. They'd served together many years ago in Desert Storm, the war CNN covered for the world, the war he got to see first hand. He could reminisce with the gang, count on them, and even trust them with his life. Warts and all, they were as much his family as anyone. Though he didn't see them often, when they were together, they fell back into a comfortable groove. Except to Hank, there was no *Jahi* here. To his Marine Corps buddies, he was still Sarge.

A pair of squirrels rustled the otherwise still foliage, interrupting his reverie. Snoop Dog Two turned up the volume on his boom box, blasting his medley of old rap cuts. Jahi barely tolerated the sounds. Hip hop wasn't his thing. Maybe it was because he was older than these guys.

Over the racket a voice in Jahi's head filtered through. *Remember what you've left behind in DC: the Shelter and the city-council race.* Taking time away wasn't the most prudent thing to do, but the get-together with his Marine buddies had been planned for months, well before he made the decision to run for the city council. The next get-together probably wouldn't happen for a couple of years. After all, everyone led busy lives and had jobs, businesses, families, and the like. Only he and Hank hadn't married. It was just as difficult for the others to separate from their obligations for three days as it was for him. What was he missing back in DC anyway? A couple of fundraisers? A radio interview?

Hank had twisted his arm before the trip. "Look, you can let a few things go. Tarik's got the Shelter covered, and Cheryl 'what's her name'—your campaign manager—can handle things with the press, community, and church folks. So you miss a few functions. Big deal!"

It didn't take much arm-twisting to convince Jahi to come. He needed to get away. His mind was clouded in the days leading up to his decision to run. He never envisioned himself with a career in politics. Didn't his strength lie in being on the outside, agitating for change from the perimeter, rather than in drowning inside the bureaucratic cesspool? But he succumbed to the pressure. Reverend Simmons, of Canaan Valley Methodist, along with a few others of the same ilk, had been *very* persuasive. "We need your fresh thinking. We need your energy to make things happen in this city," Simmons told him. "It's time to turn the heat up from the inside. Being on the city council, you can bring about the change you've been talking about more directly."

At the time it sounded good. And Jahi had partly believed Simmons. Now he wasn't so sure. The past week had been such a whirlwind. In the confusion surrounding his decision to run, he hadn't even bothered to tell key friends and allies that he was running. Jahi looked out over the switchbacks of the winding road that ended a little past the cabin's gravel driveway. He sighed. "Without my phone I can't call them now."

Snoop emerged from the house, Budweiser in hand. "Need another beer, Sarge?" he asked, pointing to Jahi's empty can on the railing ledge.

"No, thanks," Jahi answered. "I'm okay. But why don't you blast something mellow?"

Snoop grinned wide, showing his perfect white teeth. "Mellow, huh. I forgot you're not into my groove," Snoop said, giving the request some thought. "That's okay. I'll change it up. I know just the jams."

Snoop reentered the house and within less than a minute, the harsh rap sounds were replaced by the smooth sound of the Isley Brothers' "*Summer Breeze.*"

"Hey, Sarge! Thank God you got Snoop to turn off that noise!" came the call from the house, accompanied by boisterous laughter.

Snoop came back to the porch and leaned into the railing; within seconds he was followed by Murray, their weekend host.

"By the way, Sarge, if you need to use a phone, I've got mine," said Snoop.

Jahi's new iPhone had slipped from its holster and into the stream, where they'd gone to fish. The plop of the phone hitting the water caught Jahi's attention right away. Cursing himself, he managed to retrieve the phone before it embedded itself in the stream's silt bottom. The water had done its work, entering the device's cracked screen and rendering it dead.

"Hey, Dog, we all got cell phones to lend him," Murray interjected from just inside the door. "But Bro having a phone ain't the point. Have you checked your signal lately?"

"Nope, but I always have good coverage," Snoop replied with cocky confidence.

Murray laughed. "Dog, just check it."

With raised eyebrows Snoop looked at his phone's signal strength. Zero bars.

Watching the look of disbelief on Snoop's face, Murray snickered.

Snoop held his phone up in one direction and then the other. He then moved to the other side of the long porch, trying to pick up a signal. "Damn! Ain't this some shit! I'm supposed to get coverage *wherever.* Jeez, no wonder I ain't getting no calls," he moaned.

"Hey, Dog. You expecting a call from one of your shorties?" Vince Tilman called out to him from the house. Tilman's comment brought on a wave of frat-boy hoots and howls. Jahi alone was quiet.

"You're all just wrong," Snoop said. "Trying to get me in trouble. And I will be in trouble if my wife calls and she can't get ahold of me. Could be something with the kids. This ain't funny."

"We got your back, Dog. We'll explain to Lu that you were here with us," Tilman said.

Each of the other three checked their phones. No one had a signal. "No surprise here," Tuney said, "I checked as soon as we got here."

"Sorry, guys. I don't think anyone will be getting any calls unless it's by satellite phone. See that mountain over there," Murray said, pointing ahead in the distance. "That piece of landscape is blocking cell coverage." The men looked in unison at the rounded peak in the distance. Mt. Noble, as it was called, was a stump by Colorado standards but, nevertheless, presented a mass of Pennsylvania rock. "Yeah, the cell tower is on the other side, gentlemen," continued Murray. "For all intent and purposes, for the next couple of days, we're incommunicado. No cell signal, radio, or TV. My wife's family is too cheap to put in a landline or cable. You can stand it for a couple of days, can't you? It makes it a real 'off the grid' retreat."

There was a chorus of curses and groans.

"Brothers, don't panic. There's a landline three miles down the mountain, at the ranger station," Murray explained. "And if you drive a couple of miles past there, you'll pick up a cell tower, no problems."

"Ooh! Isolation," Snoop said. "For real."

"Sarge, you're awful quiet over there. Hope you've got insurance on that thing," said Tuney, referring to Jahi's dead phone. "And speaking of dust," Tuney said, invoking the group's cue to change topics originating from their time in Desert Storm.

"Dust what?" Murray butted in, pretending to be confused with the instruction. "Who said anything about dust?"

"Okay, speaking of whatever, I learned last week that Ace Henderson passed," said Tuney.

"Aww, man, not Ace," Murray said, moaning. The smile vanished from each man's face. There was a long, heavy silence before the questions of how and why Ace had died came rapid fire.

Tuney explained that he found out from Ace's daughter, who'd found out that her father died two whole weeks after it had happened. In the last years of his life, Ace had been homeless.

"Damn," Snoop said, shaking his head in disbelief.

"Sarge, did you know about Ace's situation?" Murray asked.

"No, I didn't know," Jahi answered solemnly.

"Ace, may you rest in peace," Tuney said with a bowed head.

"Yeah, rest in peace," they all chimed in.

There was a long silence and a chill in the summer's heat. News of Ace's demise put a damper on the group. No one knew what to say.

"Hey, Sarge. Hank says you're running for DC Council," Murray said, changing the subject.

"Are you 'speaking of dust' again?" Jahi asked rhetorically.

"Yeah, Sarge. I'm having a hard time digesting you as a politico. I don't see you in a suit," piped in Roger. "Will they let you wear camo and combat boots to meetings?"

They all laughed, breaking the tension of the somber news of Ace's passing. But little did they know that Jahi actually owned two suits and that he even rented a tux on occasion, all in the name of helping the homeless. He wished that Hank had kept his mouth shut. He meant to ask Hank to keep his candidacy on the QT. But somehow that thought got away from him on their drive up. Their conversation got stuck on subjects like what was needed back at the Shelter's kitchen, their days together in Iraq, and an obvious question mark: Should he be running for an elected office at all?

"Hank's got a big mouth," Jahi said flatly. Hank was not there to defend himself. He was inside cooking up the fish they'd caught that morning.

Moments later Hank poked his head onto the porch and announced, "Lunch in twenty minutes."

With the announcement of food, most of the group filed past Hank, lured by the smell of frying fish.

"Hank, got a minute?" Jahi asked.

"Don't want to burn our catch. But what's up?" Hank answered, stepping on to the porch, still clad in his white apron, a dishcloth slung over his shoulder.

Jahi waited until Tuney went inside before speaking. "Hank, I'm thinking I need to get back." His voice was low.

"No!" whined Hank. "You can't be serious!"

"Yeah, I'm feeling guilty. And I got a strange feeling something is going on back there."

"Something is always going on back there. The question is, do you need to be a part of it?" Hank was clearly frustrated. "I thought you said that Tarik had things under control. I thought you 'cleared the calendar.'"

"I think Tarik does have things under control. I'm talking about the campaign."

"Cheryl *was* pretty upset that you were taking a hiatus with the election only six weeks away. Look, I have to get back to the food. Let's talk after lunch."

After stuffing themselves on lunch, the group was mellow and full of self-praise. After all, they were eating what they had caught.

"Hank, that was a great lunch. Now whatcha gonna fix for dinner?" Murray asked while his lunch settled in his belly.

The others all chimed in with praise for Hank's culinary skills.

"Dinner, huh. I'm not sure. But as I told you guys, I don't mind doing the cooking—I hate cleaning up, though."

"No problem. I brought my rubber gloves," Snoop said. "Radio Roger and I got this one."

Roger looked up from his guitar, surprised that he was being drafted for the cleanup crew.

As the others headed back to the poker table, Jahi pulled Hank back out to the porch.

"I thought about the situation some more," Jahi said, biting his lip. "I think I better leave. Do you mind? This is your reunion too. I hate to ask you to leave because of me, but you're driving. In a way I'm at your mercy."

Hank frowned. "Yeah, it's a long walk down the mountain."

"Tell you what: just drive me to the train station in Philly," Jahi continued.

"Here to Philly! That's halfway home."

Jahi looked sheepish.

Hank rubbed his neck and sighed. "Okay, Jahi, you win on this one. But you owe me. Might as well leave now. We'll be back in time for dinner at Mahali."

Jahi smiled and patted Hank on the back. "Thanks."

Shaking his head, Hank stomped away. "I knew being here was too good to be true."

Jahi announced to the group that he and Hank would be leaving. "Duty calls," he said.

"Man, we sure hate to see you go," Snoop said.

"Yeah, cause that means you will have to not only do KP but also cook for yourselves," Hank said.

Several men groaned.

"It's a shame. We don't have any contractors here for those kinds of jobs," Tuney said. They all laughed.

"So, Sarge, now that you're going to be a big-time politician, are we going to hear about you on the news?" Snoop asked half-serious.

"Maybe," Jahi answered. "I haven't won yet."

"But what we hear will only be the good stuff, right?" Roger said.

"That's the plan," Jahi answered.

A couple of the guys tried to talk Jahi into staying one more day, but he'd made up his mind. The group said its goodbyes, and Jahi and Hank loaded up Hank's late-model Jeep Cherokee. Hank gave strict instructions for them to not mess up the steaks he was leaving in the freezer. Among those who remained, Tuney was the next best cook. "They're a quality cut," Hank shouted from the driver's side window before starting the engine.

Five miles down the winding road, Hank's phone picked up a cell signal. "Jahi, here, take it. Now you can make your calls."

"Nah," Jahi said. "I need at least another two hours of radio silence before the world settles in on me."

"I sense from what you said earlier that you're changing your mind about this city-council gig."

"Nah. I told them I'd run. Now I've got to go through with it. Who knows? I might luck out and lose."

Hank kept his eyes on the road. "Buddy, don't set yourself up for failure," he said. "Well, *speaking of dust*, I guess Katherine is going to be surprised to see me two days early."

"Maybe you ought to call her. You don't want to walk in on any surprises."

"Now, Jahi, what are you suggesting? You know that ain't happening."

"Sorry, and I know you're right about that." There was a long stretch of silence. Then Jahi asked, "Why is it that you and Katherine never got married?"

Hank and his girlfriend had been together for fifteen years. They were husband and wife in all but the paperwork. They seemed perfectly compatible, considering that Hank's Shelter job was low paying, and Katherine, a registered nurse, made considerably more.

"Marriage? We don't need to," Hank answered. "There's nothing to inherit. No children to worry about. She knows I love her, and I know she loves me."

"I envy you that," Jahi said. "That bond. That trust."

"Seems that once upon a time, you were on that track. Why did you and Sister Te never take the next step?"

"There was never a next step. We backed up and decided it wasn't going to work."

"I get the feeling you made that decision. And she just went along with it. I can tell...she still has a thing for you."

"Oh? What makes you think that?"

"Things I've heard. I have my sources," Hank said.

Jahi was quiet. He figured that Tarik might have said something or maybe even Te herself. But that was unlikely: Te was very private. "Maybe years ago she felt that way. But not now. *Not still.* Too much water under that bridge."

"If you say so. So what about what's her face, the Foundation attorney?"

"Zoie Taylor."

"Yeah, how's that going?"

"Gee, Hank, you sure got your nose up in my business today."

"Hey, don't answer if you don't want to," Hank said, lifting his hands from the steering wheel for a second. "You started it with questions about me and Katherine."

"Okay, that's fair. Yes, I have a thing for Zoie."

"Is she the one?"

"Umm, could be."

"Let me guess: you're afraid...can't commit."

"Hey, man! It's only been this summer. Anyway, I'm not sure how serious she is."

"Jahi, don't let her get away. I can tell she's not like your other ladies."

"For sure she's not."

CHAPTER 33

CLOSE LIKE FAMILY

Zoie lost her cool at the Shelter. She didn't meltdown often, but under the circumstances she had a right to be angry. She needed to calm down. Her encounter with the dreadful woman with the head wrap had drained her. There'd been enough venom in the woman's glance to bring down an elephant. And then there was Tarik—Jahi's protégé was certainly no help. She found his demeanor to be both arrogant and patronizing. He had set her off. Now her gut told her that Tarik knew more. He knew where Jahi was but wasn't letting on. *What did Jahi see in the little bastard, entrusting him with the Shelter's business?* Yes, Tarik was capable, all right. The question was, capable of what?

Thank God, she thought as cool air from the taxi's air conditioning finally made its way to the back seat. Her eyes met Muwakkil's deep black eyes in the rearview mirror. They'd been sitting there for quite a while in silence as she collected herself.

"Where to now, lady?" he asked again, his tone not irritated or pushy like some New York cabbies. This driver was in no hurry. One way or the other, he knew he'd get paid.

The cost of what she was doing crossed her mind. On a per-trip basis with waiting time, she was running up quite a tab.

Perhaps it would be cheaper to pay this guy's daily rate, as he suggested.
Muwakkil was an African businessman, but she knew how to bargain as well.

"Not quite sure," she answered, mentioning nothing of price
negotiations. She was waiting for him to bring up the subject of
the daily rate.

"Lady, you going to want me to wait again?"

"Probably," she responded with a sigh.

"You going to have more stops after that?

"Perhaps."

"Then I think you should go with my day-rate proposal. You
would be better off."

"We could do that...if the price is right," she answered.

Still parked around the corner from the Shelter, they hag-
gled to arrive at a fair daily rate. In setting his initial price,
Muwakkil mentioned the high cost of raising three kids, city
fees, and how expensive gas had become, of course. When she
balked at his price, he responded in his best pleading voice,
claiming that she was taking advantage of a poor immigrant.
Zoie fired back using her lawyer tactics. After all, she was a
guaranteed ride. And he wasn't considering the generous tip
she'd add or that she could pay in cash—once she stopped at
an ATM. After a few minutes, the deal was struck. They settled
on a rate half the price of his original proposal. He'd be her
driver until 6:00 p.m.

"Lady, you drive a hard bargain."

Zoie squelched a satisfied smile and shrugged. Haggling had
been invigorating. It had given her a much-needed shot of adrenalin, lifting the depressing fog clouding her brain. Someone had
stolen her stuff and threatened her. Someone was out to silence
her. She wouldn't let fear paralyze her. If she was ever to feel safe
again, she needed to find Jahi and get some answers.

"Okay, lady, I'm all yours. Where to now?"

What was the plan? Zoie hesitated before she answered. At the Foundation a contingent of Crayton's upper management was hovering. Milton, poor Milton, was waiting for her. Already she'd broken her promise to quickly come to the office. But right now she had to follow her gut. The Foundation would have to wait.

Maybe Jahi's friend at the café, the place where Jahi opened up to her, would know how to get in touch with him. The place was close by, but exactly where was it? Weeks ago they walked there together. Jahi had been in the lead. Focused on his every word, she didn't pay attention to their route. Back in the present, Zoie gave the driver some vague directions and hoped that by circling the nearby streets they'd find the place.

She thought of Jahi's other name—Oswald Smoot. The name usually tickled her funny bone. But today nothing was funny. Was Muwakkil right? Do parents, inspired by God, always pick the right names for their offspring? Who was Oswald Smoot, also known as Jahi Khalfani? What qualities did those names imply?

On the first try around the block, she spotted the bright-yellow sun on the Sunrise Café's sign. The café occupied a narrow slice of storefront situated between a cleaners and a nondescript store with a refrigerator in the window.

"Stop here," she said. "Remember, my stuff's in the back."

The street in front of the Sunrise Café was quiet, except for several passersby, who probably chose to take that route because of the shade. Under the café's awning, two men played a game of chess at a small folding table, while a third man seated on a crate watched. The setting was the same as she remembered from many weeks ago.

Focused on the board, the players didn't bother to look up as Zoie passed through the open door and into the dimly lit café. Inside overhead fans whirled to keep the place reasonably cool. In the second booth from the door, where natural light could reach their table, an elderly man and woman sat enjoying a meal. They glanced up from their food as she made her way to the rear.

"Hello! Anyone here?" Zoie called from the end of the long counter. The man she was looking for emerged from a doorway shielded by a beaded curtain.

He was grayer than she remembered, but he had pep in his step. "Well, hello, pretty lady," he said, greeting her with a large grin. He wiped his hands on his bib apron before pressing her extended hand between his large palms. The two-handed greeting was the same one Jahi used. "It's good to see you. It's been a long time."

"It's Stan, right?" she asked, smiling and hoping that she got his name right.

"That's what my friends call me. Stan the Man. Pretty lady, you've got a good memory. I must have made an impression." He smiled even wider. "Now what can I do you for? Did you stop by for some pie?"

"No thanks, Stan. Maybe another time."

It was lunchtime, and the little café was almost empty. Perhaps the place made all of its money from the morning crowd, hence the name Sunrise.

"Where's Brother Jahi? Is he with you?" Stan looked past her to the open door as if expecting to see the much larger Jahi enter the restaurant.

"Sorry, Stan. No Jahi this time…actually, Jahi is why I'm here. I was hoping *you* could tell me where I could find him."

"Hmm." Stan grimaced and put a finger to his lips, imposing his own silence while he pondered his answer.

"Stan, it's important that I find Jahi. I've just come from the Shelter. They were no help."

"That's strange," Stan finally said. "Did you talk to Tarik? He ought to know Jahi's whereabouts. Jahi lets him run the place.

I get the feeling they're always in touch. That Tarik is a smart young man, a chip off the old block." Stan laughed.

"I don't follow—a chip off the old block?"

"Did I make a generational faux pas?" Stan laughed again. "You know the sayings 'chip off the old block' and 'like father like son.' Oh, here's another: 'The apple doesn't fall far from the tree.' Yeah, that Tarik's smart as a whip. Just like Brother Jahi. Except Tarik takes himself a little *too* seriously. He'll come around. Jahi raised him well."

Zoie stood dazed, only partly believing what she was hearing. Was Tarik Jahi's son? It didn't make sense. The two didn't look alike. She couldn't remember Tarik calling Jahi father or any father derivative. Jahi never mentioned having a son or anything like that. Not mentioning that Tarik was his son was a major omission, especially since she already knew Tarik. There'd been plenty of time for such introductions at the Shelter. Fathers don't hide their sons in plain sight.

Zoie took a deep breath and pursed her lips. Surprises, not the pleasant kind, were coming at her left and right. Stan knew a lot evidently. She contemplated pursuing a line of questioning about Tarik's paternity, even if it meant revealing to Stan that the man she'd been sleeping with hadn't bothered to share major pieces of his life—major pieces like running for a city office or, now it seemed, having a son. Feeling confused and incredibly stupid, she proceeded. "Is Tarik any relation to Jahi? I thought he was just his protégé."

"Hmm. I don't like getting into Brother Jahi's personal business, the little of it that I know." Stan lowered his voice, his eyes narrowed, and his smile vanished. "I'm not one to tell tales out of school, if you know what I mean."

"Sure, I understand." But Stan's warning didn't stop Zoie's needing to know. What was there to hide? She persisted. "Is Tarik's being Jahi's son some sort of secret?"

"No. Guess not. Matter of fact, I think it's pretty common knowledge. At the Shelter anybody would tell you that Tarik is Jahi's boy." Stan laughed for a second. "Now I know he don't want to be called boy." Stan stroked his chin as he considered whether he should say more.

"I'm just being curious. Stan, I think you've got the wrong idea about Jahi and me. We're business associates. I work for the Foundation, which provides some of the Shelter's funding."

"Oh, well, now that news just makes it worst. I'm sure Jahi don't want his business in the street. Seems I've said too much." Stan turned away to wipe crumbs from a table in a nearby booth. "You best get Jahi's personal info straight from the horse's mouth."

"Stan, don't get me wrong. Jahi and I *are* friends. Did he ever tell you otherwise?"

Stan stopped brushing the crumbs from the table and turned to her again. "Huh, he don't tell me things about his lady *friends*. But to answer your question, he spoke very highly of you."

"Oh, yeah?" Zoie's attention focused like a laser.

"Yeah. He said something about you just after you were here. I was the one that asked him about you. He said you were both beautiful and smart."

Zoie rolled her eyes but couldn't contain a slight blush. Stan was turning out to be a charmer just like Jahi. And he was smiling again.

"So you *can* tell me about Tarik and Jahi, right?"

Stan seemed only partially convinced. "Well, guess there's no harm in explaining what I know to you. You seem pretty levelheaded," he said, rubbing the stubble on his narrow chin. "Seeing that this is common knowledge, guess my telling you don't qualify as telling tales out of school, right?"

"Right," she answered in encouragement.

He turned away but continued to observe her from the corner of his left eye. "Where to begin?

"Begin wherever you want."

He rested against the counter. "Do you know Sister Te?"

"I've never met her, but I know of her. I know that she and Jahi once had a relationship. And I know she works at the Shelter," Zoie said, feeding Stan the bits of information she'd learned from Lena only that morning. "And, Tarik, you were talking about Tarik and Sister Te."

"Ugh. Yeah. Sister Te was Jahi's ex. She's the big cheese for the women's shelter. Didn't have no women at that place when I stayed there. I never did care for her much. She rubbed me the wrong way a few times. But that's water under the bridge, so to speak."

"Go on."

"Yeah, Sister Te and Jahi go way back." Stan rubbed his chin again. "As far as I know, Tarik is *her* son. But Jahi always treated him like *his* son. Everybody knows that. From when he was a little boy. Don't have to share blood to be family, right?"

"Right," said Zoie, taking another deep breath and trying to act unconcerned as the revelations about Jahi's life unfolded. More questions were queued in her brain. She waited for an opening so she could ask them without being pushy. She wanted desperately to ask Stan what he meant by "ex." Had Jahi and Sister Te been married? But what did it matter? A long-standing relationship was a long-standing relationship, official papers or not. After her years of living with Elliot, his leaving had been horrible. They had a child together. Could a real divorce have been worse than that breakup? She thought better of further prying for details. No use making Stan any more defensive.

"Can you give me a clue as to where I might find Jahi? It's very important that I get in touch with him. This has to do with the Shelter's funding."

"Mmm, let me think. That brother doesn't let grass grow under his feet." Stan scratched his head. "Well, the last time I saw Brother Jahi, he came by to tell me that he was going to announce he was running for DC Council. Which he did."

"Yes, I heard."

"One way or another, those preachers were going to make a politician out of him. Anyway, he wanted me to spread the word with customers to vote for him on primary day."

"I see," Zoie said. She tried to digest the information. She rubbed the back of her neck where the pricks of his words had settled. More and more she felt like a fool. She knew little or nothing about the man she'd been sleeping with all summer. The man who'd captured her heart. Jahi had let both Stan and Lena know that he was running for the city council before the official announcement. And she had to find out that bit of information from a newscast. It was clear that she wasn't part of his inner circle. The people he chose to confide in were longtime associates: Tarik, Stan, Lena, Hank, and probably this Sister Te. They were his family. Things were a blur, but she tried to listen to Stan.

"Who would have thought it—Brother Jahi...a politician? I never liked politicians, but I want him to win. I expect this political stuff's gonna change him."

Judging by Stan's expression, Zoie didn't think Stan's prediction of Jahi's change meant a change for the better.

"Do you know how to contact him? I've got phone numbers, but he's not answering."

"Maybe that's because he doesn't want to talk to you," Stan replied bluntly.

Zoie responded just as bluntly. "Stan, as I've told you, it's not that kind of relationship. This is about the Shelter. If he wants to keep the Foundation's money for the Shelter, he needs to talk to me ASAP."

"I hear you, pretty lady." Stan rubbed his chin again. "I suspect he's working on his campaign. He's what you call a late entry.

He could be at that campaign office. And if he ain't, they'd likely know where to find him."

"Fair enough. You wouldn't happen to have the address for that office, would you?"

"Hold on." Stan went into the back and returned a minute later with a yellow campaign flyer with poor-quality pictures of Jahi and several other Democratic hopefuls. There was an address of a place on New York Avenue. "I don't know why the folks at Mahali didn't give you one of these. I've been to this place," Stan said, pointing to the address on the flyer. "Had to check it out. It's next to the dentist office. You can have this."

"Thank you for your help, Stan. I know you want to do what you can for the Shelter." She gave him a hug and left.

Under the shade of the café's awning, it took a few seconds for Zoie's eyes to adjust to daylight. When they did, she spotted Muwakkil leaning leisurely against his cab halfway down the block. She waved to get his attention, and he stood up. The men playing chess turned to look at her, and one of them tipped his hat. She smiled. Then she heard the faint tone of her phone signaling an incoming call, coming from her bag. She took out the phone and looked at the caller ID before answering. It indicated an unknown caller. She let it continue to ring until the missed-call message appeared on the screen. It didn't look like a local area code, but then so many new area codes had been added over the years. Something told her to not call back. She pulled out the contact numbers Lena had given her. She had yet to enter Lena's numbers into her cell phone. There was no match. Perhaps it was another threatening call.

Before she could check to see whether the caller had left a voice message, the phone rang a second time. Once again the caller ID indicated an unknown caller. This time, though, the number was different. Who was trying to get her? She let the call ring through the four-ring cycle, until her phone registered it as another missed call. Maybe it was Jahi. Had he heard that she was looking for him from either Tarik or Stan? Was he finally responding to her barrage of voice messages? Maybe the news of Ray's death had caused him to surface. The person or persons who had burglarized her apartment and who had made the earlier threats on the phone would not leave a message. When she looked up again, she saw Muwakkil backing down the street. Muwakkil, the one who could be trusted, was coming for her. *Thank God*, she thought, because her knees felt a little weak.

Swallowed in a borrowed plaid robe, Frances Woods sat on the small couch in Queen's living room. Queen's brother, Mason, sat in a recliner to one side, his eyes glued to a soccer match on TV. Mason was a male version of Queen, though younger and with lighter skin. Frances Woods's eyes shifted nervously from the TV screen to her surroundings. She certainly didn't understand the game of soccer. So instead of watching the match, with hands hidden in the folds of her borrowed apparel, she let her eyes settle on Mason. She wasn't sure which team he was rooting for, since he reacted exuberantly to most every cheer from the TV.

"I wish I had my own clothes," Frances Woods said, talking to herself.

"You say somethin', Mrs. Woods?" Mason asked.

"Just that I wish I had my own clothes." This time she was louder. The statement alerted Queen, who came from the small kitchen.

"I wish you had your own things too, but what you had on smelled like smoke."

"Oh, God, my house!" Frances Woods said. The horror of the fire was settling in. Tears welled up in her eyes.

"Don't go getting upset," Queen said, bending down to give her a hug. "Mason, you're going back over there. Check the place, and board up the kitchen-door area."

"Yeah, sure," Mason answered, his eyes never leaving the TV. "I got to see the rest of this match. When it's over, okay."

"Look, Mrs. Woods," said Queen, "I tried to call your grand-daughter at her home number, and I tried her mobile."

"Did you leave a message?"

"No, I didn't. I'll try again in a bit."

"Call her office," Frances Woods said, sounding irritated.

"Calm down, Mrs. Woods. I don't have that number."

Frances Woods turned to Mason. "I know it's a foundation, but I can't recall the name right now." She was flustered. "Mason, when you go back to my house, get the blue book on the side of my bed, near the phone. It's got the number for my insurance company."

"Sure, Mrs. Woods," he answered, though his eyes remained glued to the screen.

In a sudden outburst, Mason jumped from his chair and pumped his fists and yelled, "Yeah! Yeah!" A corresponding uproar occurred on TV. Frightened by the suddenness of it all, Frances Woods shrank into the oversized robe.

"Don't worry," Queen said, patting Francis Woods's arm. "This match will be over soon, and then he'll go. When he gets back, I'll go there and get you some clothes."

Frances Woods sighed. "Guess it's in the Lord's hands."

CHAPTER 34
WHERE'S YOUR CANDIDATE?

Campaign headquarters for Khalfani for Councilman was a storage room in the back of J&J's Barbershop on New York Avenue, next to a dentist office, just as Stan had described it. Plastered to one side of the shop's window, Zoie spotted a poster that read, "Vote Khalfani for Ward 5," and next to that was the same yellow candidate flyer that Zoie held in her hand.

Two of the shop's three chairs were occupied. A third customer yakked away while presumably waiting for one of the chairs to free up. Being as small as it was, the place couldn't hold more people without their bumping into each other. The two barbers, likely J-one and J-two, were busy at their craft.

"Here goes nothing," Zoie said under her breath as the tinkle of an old-fashioned bell atop the door announced her entrance. The older of the two barbers, a good-looking man in his fifties or sixties, with neatly groomed facial hair, looked up and nodded a greeting. The waiting customer nodded a hello as well. Without a word Zoie smiled and raised her yellow flyer.

The barber pointed her to a door at the back of the shop. "They're back there."

"Thanks," Zoie said. Through a rear door, Zoie found a storage area lined with cardboard boxes on metal shelving. The area opened into a space much larger than the barbershop itself. There were several desks and a wall lined with posters of Jahi and for Beatrice Meyer, who was running for councilman at large. Stacks of envelopes were piled on a long table. Another wall displayed a gigantic map of DC with the Ward 5 boundaries outlined in dayglow orange. The makeshift office seemed to be administered by two women. One was seated at the long table and stuffing envelopes, with a cell phone wedged between her head and her shoulder. The other one was sitting at a desk, busily checking one list against another.

"Ooh Lord!" said the woman talking on the phone. Her conversation just got louder. "I got to go. The cavalry has arrived. We can go to lunch."

Images of Jahi stared at Zoie from every corner. The bold face of "a candidate who'll stand up for what's right." *Humph!* But no Jahi in the flesh. Zoie rolled her eyes, disappointed that she hadn't found him, but she was also relieved. What would she do when she did find him?

Zoie now had the attention of the woman closest to her, a senior citizen with a brassy red wig, a sallow complexion, and a dayglow orange blouse.

"Hi. I'm Zoie Taylor. I'm looking for Jahi Khalfani."

"Ain't everybody looking for that man," answered the woman from across the room.

"Angie, behave!" the older woman commanded before turning her attention back to Zoie. "Did Pastor Dykes from the Redeemer send you?"

"Sorry. I don't know a Pastor Dykes. I'm trying to track down your candidate, Jahi Khalfani."

"Are you from the press or something?" the older woman asked, peering at Zoie over her rhinestone-crusted reading glasses.

"No. But I am here in an official capacity." Zoie handed the woman a business card identifying her as an attorney at the Crayton Foundation. "It's very important that I speak to Mr. Khalfani. I've been to the Shelter and several other places, and I've been calling him all day."

"Uh-huh. The case of the missing candidate," said the younger woman before turning back to a new phone conversation. Her counterpart was not amused.

"I need to talk to him about his Shelter's grant," Zoie explained. "It's a time-sensitive matter."

"Uh-huh. Well, I haven't seen him in a few days, but I'm not here all the time. The person who should know his whereabouts is his campaign manager, Cheryl Daniels."

"She's the one who gets paid," piped in the younger woman. "We're just volunteers."

"And proud to be helping. *Right*, Angie?" the older woman said, scolding the other.

"Oh, I like to help—but I'd be prouder if they fed us."

This time the older woman ignored her.

"How can I get in touch with this Cheryl Daniels?" Zoie asked.

"I can't give out her number, but I'll call her for you," the redhead said, trying to be helpful.

"If you would, that would be great."

Zoie's eyes scanned the desk as she waited for the redhead to locate Daniels's phone number from a paper in the desk drawer. There was a small pile of bumper stickers and a basket of campaign buttons. Some of the buttons bore Jahi's image; others just said, "Khalfani, my choice for Ward 5."

The redhead dialed the number from the landline on the desk.

"Cheryl, sorry to bother you, but I got a woman here looking for Jahi. Says she's from the foundation that gives grants to Mahali."

Zoie waited as Cheryl Daniels (presumably) gave instructions to the redhead.

"She wants to talk to you." She handed the receiver to Zoie.

Zoie introduced herself and repeated her situation and the urgent need to find Jahi.

"Well, Ms. Taylor, I wish I could help you. My candidate has taken a few days off from the campaign trail. A prior commitment has taken him out of town on a personal matter. I sure wish he'd told me about this commitment sooner. I had to cancel his appearance at the senior citizens' residence, in a radio interview, and at a rally at the community center. He's got to get back for the debates at MLK Library in a couple of days."

"I've been trying to contact him. I've left a bunch of messages, with no response," Zoie explained.

"Don't feel special," Cheryl said sarcastically. "He's ignoring my calls as well. He's got people handling the Shelter while he's away. Why don't you try there again? And I'll be sure to let him know that you're trying to reach him when he calls in."

It sounded as if things weren't going well on the campaign trail, and the campaign had just started.

When the call ended, Zoie thanked the redheaded volunteer.

"No luck, huh?"

"Not yet."

She picked up the basket and offered Zoie a campaign button. "Just got these in. These are two dollars apiece or three for five dollars."

Zoie tried to smile and resisted an incredible urge to spit. "No thanks," she answered. "I don't live in Ward Five."

CHAPTER 35

WHAT'S GOING ON, BABY GIRL?

"Enough of this!" Thoroughly disgusted, Zoie climbed into her commissioned cab. *So Jahi is officially MIA.* Even his campaign crew was miffed. He wasn't just avoiding her—he was avoiding everybody. In light of Ray's death and the likely criminal activity at the Shelter, Jahi's disappearance was even more suspicious.

"Enough of what?" Muwakkil asked.

"Nothing. Forget it," she answered.

"So, lady, where to next?" he asked.

"Downtown to K Street," she instructed. Then she mumbled under her breath, "I need to get to my office before my employers fire me. But maybe getting fired wouldn't be such a bad thing."

Muwakkil ignored the mumbling.

Preoccupied with her problems, Zoie stared out the window. How could she not go to the police? She couldn't return to her apartment. Where would she sleep? Maybe she'd go to her grandmother's. Or maybe she'd stay at Tina's. After all, she had the keys to Tina's apartment. Muwakkil scooted through DC traffic and got her to the K Street area in no time.

"Do you want me to wait again?"

"I think so," Zoie answered. "I still have several hours on this daily tab thing, right?"

"Yes, lady, you do."

"I'm going to my office. If I have to stay there, I'll give you a call."

Muwakkil pulled onto the K Street service road, and Zoie directed him to drive farther down the block, to her office building. She was trying to decide whether she should lug her denim bag into the office when she spotted Regina. Her young assistant was with a man who, at least from the rear, looked like Tarik. After a few seconds, the Tarik look-alike changed his position, allowing Zoie to see his face. It *was* Tarik—Regina and Tarik. And they were definitely together. Regina leaned into the building in a sultry stance as Tarik hovered over her, his hand pressed into the wall as a brace.

"My God. What's that little bastard up to?" Zoie said to herself. "And what's Regina doing with him?" She stared for a minute longer before ducking away from the taxi's window to avoid being seen.

"Lady, are you coming or going?" Muwakkil asked.

"I've changed my mind. Drive around the block," Zoie ordered.

The taxi tour around the block in heavy traffic took more than ten minutes. En route she spotted the homeless duo making their way to their usual spot. The wild one had his shopping cart loaded with his green bags. Carrying no possessions, the other one followed a few yards behind. *Maybe his stuff is in the wild one's cart*, she thought.

"Please stop here. Just for a minute," Zoie instructed her driver.

Muwakkil pulled over. "Lady, I can't stay here."

Down the street Zoie could see that Regina and Tarik were no longer loitering at her building's entrance.

"I'm leaving my bag with you," Zoie told Muwakkil.

"Okay, lady," he said. "But I can't double park." He pointed to the parking sign.

"Then move to where you need to move. I'll try to be back in thirty or forty minutes. I'll call first."

When her taxi drove off, Zoie looked to the sky. "God, send me a sign," she said under her breath. Usually Zoie wasn't much for calling on help from the heavens, but then nothing was usual these days, and she sure needed help. She approached the man who'd been supplying uncommon wisdom. Today, of all days, she hoped for some clue of how to get out of the jam she had stumbled into.

"Good afternoon, Simon."

The man nodded.

"You got a message for me today?"

From several yards away, the wild one turned when he saw her approach Simon. He grimaced.

"Of course, my dear." Simon reached into his pocket and pulled out a small rumpled paper bag. He pulled a folded piece of paper from the bag and handed it to her. It looked the same as the other messages she'd received over the summer. She hoped this message wouldn't be as cryptic.

Zoie tried to give Simon a five-dollar bill, but he wouldn't take it. "Give it to him," Simon told her, pointing to his companion.

In a startling move, the wild one stepped forward and snatched the bill from Zoie's hand. He grinned, his smile exhibiting his yellow teeth.

While she no longer feared the wild one, she found him unpleasant to be around. Zoie palmed her new message and walked away. She'd read the message once she was settled in her office.

Entering her building, she wondered what lies she'd have to tell her colleagues at the Foundation. Even though she didn't want to go to the police about the break-in at her apartment, at some point she'd have to let the Foundation know that her laptop—*the Foundation's laptop*—was missing.

Inside the Foundation's large suite of offices, many of the staff were congregating near the reception desk. The conversation was in whispers. Regina was not among them.

"Hello, everyone," Zoie said solemnly. "It's been a rough day."

"We can't believe it," said Lindsay, a young assistant and one of Regina's buds. "Ray was here yesterday. I saw him alive. Now he's gone."

"Do you know where Regina is?" Zoie asked.

"She went for donuts," Lindsay answered. "But who feels like eating?"

Howard Metts, a burly man and one of the grant administrators, came over and touched Zoie's shoulder. "You missed the Crayton big wigs. I don't think Averell London has stepped foot in this office in two years. Everyone was wondering where you were."

"I told Milton I'd be in later. Anyway, I'm here now," Zoie said, shaking off Howard's obvious criticism of her absence. She never liked him. "Is Milton in his office?"

"I think so. Poor guy, he's taking this hard."

Zoie found Milton in his office. He was trying to focus, but she could tell he wasn't having much success. He looked up from the papers on his desk. His red puffy eyes indicated that he'd been crying, and his milky skin, which was more translucent than usual, made him look sick.

"How are you doing, Milton?" she asked gently, settling into the chair at his desk.

"Hanging in there," he answered with a sniffle. "You missed London and his entourage."

"I heard."

"They intend to name me the acting head of the Foundation." He waited for her response to this news, but Zoie was silent. "That's just until they vet candidates to present to the Board," he continued.

"Okay," she finally said.

"We need you to do the acting paperwork. Did you see the announcement about Ray we e-mailed out?"

She hadn't seen it and didn't have a laptop to take a look. But she wasn't going to bring up the missing laptop now. She was just happy that *so far* Milton hadn't asked about her morning whereabouts.

"I'm still in shock about this whole thing," Milton said. "A Montgomery County police detective called about an hour ago. He said Ray's death looked real suspicious."

"Suspicious how?"

"The drowning might not have been an accident or a suicide." Milton grabbed a tissue and wiped his nose.

"Oh!" she said, feigning surprise.

"They're are going to want some of Ray's papers. We'll have to send some boxes of his stuff up to Crayton's headquarters. Could you give Arleen some guidance on preparing those boxes?"

"Sure."

"That is, if she can pull herself together tomorrow," Milton said.

"Yeah."

"And they want some of us to go up to Gaithersburg to make statements. Since you are the Foundation's attorney, I think you should be present."

Zoie winced. Milton, having lowered his head, missed her reaction.

"Sure, if that makes sense," she said. "I'll probably have to make a statement as well."

"I promised them our full cooperation. Hey, we've got nothing to hide, right?"

"Right," she answered, thinking of all she was hiding already.

"Who would have wanted to kill Ray? This whole thing doesn't make sense."

Actually, it did make sense, but Zoie couldn't tell Milton what she knew. She took a few notes about calls to the Board and plans for an emergency Board meeting, plus other odds and ends, things that she would suggest to him. Milton wasn't only grieving. He was overwhelmed. When she left him, he was sitting with his elbows on his desk, cradling his face, and trying—through misty eyes—to focus on some papers.

Zoie stopped by her office to grab a few papers and check Regina's cube. *Still no Regina.* Needing a computer, she installed herself in a guest cubicle. But before logging on she took a deep breath, unfolded the small paper, and read Simon's latest prophecy. "What you want to know is through a place men dare not go."

"What the hell?" she said under her breath. She read the prophecy two more times. "I don't get it."

"Don't get what?" said a breathless Regina, who popped her head into the cubicle. "Zoie, why are you sitting here?"

"I left my laptop at home."

"Oh," Regina said with a bewildered look. "Anyway, I brought donuts, if you're interested. Oh, some woman's called you a couple of times. Something about your grandmother."

"What about my grandmother?" Zoie demanded.

"Sorry, Zoie. I couldn't follow her accent. I told her you were due here any minute."

"If someone calls about my grandmother, you call me right away," Zoie instructed.

"Gee, *sorry.* I figured you'd walk in the door right after I hung up with her. I was distracted by all those Crayton execs. The phone call skipped my mind until just now." Regina sounded truly contrite.

Yeah, distracted by that skinny-assed boy. Zoie's jaws were tight, but she took a deep breath to calm herself. She wasn't going to mention Tarik unless Regina did. Zoie whipped out her phone and called her grandmother's house. The phone rang a number of times before shifting over to voice mail.

"I can't get my grandmother on the phone. God, I wonder what's going on. She's not answering. Queen's not answering."

"Who's Queen?" Regina asked.

"My grandmother's caretaker—probably the woman whose accent you couldn't decipher."

"Oh."

"Look, I have to leave. It might be a medical emergency. Tell Milton."

"Okay."

"I'll check in later."

"Zoie...may I just leave? Ain't nothing going on here."

"No!"

Regina was none too happy. She sucked her teeth, rolled her eyes, and stomped away. Her behavior reminded Zoie of Nikki, except Nikki was six and Regina was twenty-something.

Zoie shook her head and called Muwakkil. "Meet me outside... now."

Foundation business would have to wait.

CHAPTER 36

WHO'D WANT TO BURN DOWN YOUR HOUSE?

M uwakkil pulled up behind the fire department's wagon, which was parked in front of Frances Woods's house on Brandywine.

"My God! What's going on?" Zoie said as she stretched to see ahead from the taxi's back seat.

"Doesn't look good," Muwakkil replied. "Do you need my help?"

"No. Stay here," Zoie ordered.

She grabbed her pocketbook and bolted from the taxi. The smell of smoke filled her with dread. She looked up at the house, which sat some seventeen steps above the street, and then wasted no time bounding the steps to the front porch. There she found a uniformed officer, who was wearing examination gloves and busy scanning the porch's banister with a magnifying glass.

"Who are you?" the officer asked, coming forward to greet her.

"This is my grandmother's house. Where is she?" Zoie said, trying to catch her breath. "What happened?"

"The older lady who lives here was taken away earlier today."

"What? Where?"

"Calm down. Nobody was hurt."

"But what happened? Where is she?"

"We were told she went to a friend's house. There was a fire here earlier. As far as I know, the two ladies who live here are okay."

"Thank God," Zoie said, finally exhaling.

"You best go around the side. That's where the damage is. You'll find the officer in charge. He'll fill you in."

Zoie made her way down three steps and off the porch, to the level portion of the steep yard. The low-cropped ivy, which had overtaken the stone pavers, had been trampled by recent activity. At the side of the house, she found a uniformed police officer and two uniformed men, who seemed to be fire investigators. Mason Hall, Queen's brother and her grandmother's sometimes handyman, were also there.

"Zoie, we've been looking for you all day," Mason said, coming over to her.

"Mason, where's my grandmother?"

"Don't worry. She's safe. She's at my sister's place." Mason's accent was not as thick as his sister's.

"How did this happen?"

"Not sure, but my sister said she heard some noise. She came downstairs and smelled smoke and then saw flames outside the kitchen door. The smoke was coming in under the door. Wasn't nothin' she could do, so she grabbed your grandmother and got out."

"But how's my grandmother?"

"Doing well, considering. What a scare."

"Thank you for taking her in."

"Well, she wasn't going to the hospital—she made that clear. Her nerves are bad. Look what's happened to her house." Mason shook his head and pointed to the large swath of blackened bricks and the charred remnants of the side porch. "I'm taking pictures to show her. When these guys give me the okay, I'll board up this door. Can't leave the place open like this."

One of the fire investigators came over to Zoie. "Are you related to the owner?"

"Yes, I'm Mrs. Woods's granddaughter. Can you explain how this happened?"

"We're still working on it." He wiped his brow. "But we're pretty sure it was arson. Around 1:15 p.m., a 911 call came in to respond to a fire here. The call came from one of your grandmother's neighbors. A preliminary investigation of the fire scene indicated arson. The firemen were able to put out the fire, which caused little damage. Looks as if the kitchen, though, is going to need some fixing." He pushed open the charred kitchen door with its broken window to reveal the inside damage. Zoie stuck her head inside and coughed. The place was black with smoke.

"You said arson?"

"Yeah, we're pretty sure it was arson." The investigator directed her attention to labeled items in clear plastic bags, which were all spread out on a large tarp. "We found melted plastic from a milk container. The perpetrator probably filled the container with gasoline and used it as the igniting device. The technique reminds me of fires caused by Thomas Sweatt. He set side porches on fires."

"I'm sorry, but I'm not familiar with that man."

"I thought everybody knew about that guy. He set fires all over DC and PG County some years back. But this ain't him. Sweatt's doing life at a federal pen."

"Oh, I just recently moved back to the area."

"I see. Well, we've had a few copycats since then…I didn't get your name."

"Zoie Taylor."

"Ms. Taylor, I'm going to need to get your grandmother's insurance information, and I'm going to want to get her statement and the statement of someone named Queen Fleming."

"Queen Fleming is her caretaker and Mr. Hall's sister. I'm sure my grandmother wants him to board up the place until we can get the insurance company in here and the repairs made. My grandmother's frail."

"We'll go wherever she is to get the statement. We've already interviewed several of the neighbors to determine whether they noticed anyone casing the place or just anything. After we talk to your grandmother and Ms. Fleming, our report will be ready in a few days. She'll need that report for the insurance adjustor. He handed Zoie a business card."

"Thanks."

"Ms. Taylor, do you know who might've wanted to hurt your grandmother?"

"No, not off hand," Zoie lied.

"Why would someone want to torch her house out of all the houses on the block? These things usually aren't random."

Zoie's eyes widened. She shrugged.

"Well, we'll get to the bottom of it."

"I hope the people who live in that house are okay," Muwakkil said when Zoie entered the taxi. He'd been watching the action from down the street.

"Yes, thank God," Zoie sighed. She leaned back into the seat and closed her eyes.

"Okay, lady, where to now?"

"Back to the Northeast," she answered. Then she handed him the bit of paper that she had been holding—Queen's Brentwood address.

Queen's house was a small structure that could have been a row house since its distance from the neighboring houses was about the width of two persons standing shoulder to shoulder. With a chain-link fence and a screened front porch, the place looked sealed up. Zoie passed through the fence, went up a few stairs, and rang the doorbell. Queen opened the door before the bell stopped ringing.

"Mason said you were on your way here. Thank God you finally got my message," Queen said in her singsong fashion.

"So sorry that I took so long."

"I've been calling you on your mobile."

Some of the calls I didn't answer must've been from Queen. "Sorry. I've been having phone problems all day," Zoie explained with a lie. "When I got to work, they told me that you called about my grandmother, so I went to the house."

"Didn't your secretary tell you to call here? I left the number."

"Unfortunately, no. Things are crazy there today. The head of the Crayton Foundation, where I work, was found dead at his home this morning. But enough about that. How is she?"

"Come see for yourself."

"Zoie! Zoie!" said Frances Woods, who was sitting on the couch in the small living room, which was filled with furnishings that seemed bloated in comparison with the room's dimensions. Frances Woods looked lost in the oversized couch. But there were plenty of pillows stuffed behind her and a small stool for her feet.

Zoie sat next to her grandmother and hugged her.

"I'm so glad they found you. How's the house? Did you see it?" Frances Woods asked, grabbing Zoie's arm.

"The house will be repaired. A lot of smoke-related damage, but it's a sturdy brick thing. As you used to tell me when I was little, 'The big bad wolf can't blow our house down.' Gonna take some work to fix it, though. Mason is taking pictures. He'll be back soon. But how are you?"

"Still alive," Frances Woods answered with a shrug. "Still alive, thanks to Queen here. God don't give you more than you can bear. Though I guess I'm homeless for a while."

"The arson investigators are going to come and talk to you and Queen."

"I'm not going to be able to tell them much. Why someone would want to set fire to my house, I don't know."

"Well, Grandma, I'm going to have to leave. Things are crazy at work,"

"Crazier than this?" Frances Woods asked, her tone sarcastic. She wheezed a bit and started to cough.

"My boss was found dead this morning at his home. The police are speculating that it wasn't an accident."

"Lord, Lord," Frances Woods exclaimed.

"So you see things are crazy there. But I'll be back."

"Zo, this has nothing to do with that guy you were upset about, does it?"

"I sure hope not."

Frances Woods grimaced. "You stay safe. In the meantime I guess I need to find some place to stay until my house is livable again."

"Mrs. Woods, you're welcomed to stay here until your house is ready," Queen said. "Now I think you need to stop talking before you bring on one of your spells."

Frances Woods gasped for air and then coughed again. She wanted desperately to continue talking and to question her granddaughter about the troubles at her job, but her body wasn't cooperating. "Zo, stay safe," she managed.

"I'm trying." Zoie went to the door and whispered to Queen, "Thank you so much for having my grandmother stay with you."

"Not a problem. I'd be taking care of her at her house anyway. I'll put a little TV in the spare room. She can sleep there," Queen said

"Okay. I'll be in touch."

CHAPTER 37

THE SISTERS' BOND

Zoie said goodbye to her grandmother and Queen and went outside to find Muwakkil. Snippets of a plan began to percolate in her head. Leaning on the chain-link fence of the small Brentwood house, she called Lena.

"Just heard about another downsizing at the paper," Lena said, sounding sober.

The paper was none other than the *Washington Times*, the politically right-leaning, second-banana DC newspaper. The changing world of digital newspapers, blogs, and news feeds, plus the 24-7 cable news, played havoc with hardcopy news readership and its advertising revenue. Like a dinosaur in the ice age, print media was in a fight for its very existence. Would the *Washington Times* survive? Zoie doubted that it would in the long term. Lena was surely thinking the same.

"Sorry to hear that," Zoie said, stifling the urge to immediately spill the tale of her own tribulations. "Have you been affected?"

"Don't know yet." Lena sucked her teeth. "The rumor mill is cranking. Unfortunately, the rumored layoff is probably true. Guess I'll hear something official in a few days," she said.

"You'll be okay," said Zoie in an attempt to encourage her.

"From your lips to God's ears. And what about you? Did you locate our golden boy?"

Golden boy, also known as Jahi. "No!" Zoie replied in disgust. "Our 'golden boy' is still MIA. But a lot has happened since we talked this morning."

"You mean Ray Gaddis's death isn't enough drama?"

"It's too complicated for a phone conversation. I'm a wreck. I need your help."

"Hmm," said Lena. "Don't know what it is or what I can do. As far as the Gaddis situation, I'm sure you're way ahead of me. I've turned in my background research on Ray to the City Desk. It's primary on this story."

"Wait until you hear what I've got to tell you. It's bad."

"Hmm, sounds interesting," chirped Lena. "You're cheering me up. I hate to admit it, but when someone else is worse off, I get to count my blessings. Meet me back at my building in about thirty minutes so you can cheer me up some more."

Again in Muwakkil's cab, Zoie considered her options. How could Lena fit into what she was planning? She had to tell someone what was going on. She hadn't thought it all out. Before going to Queen's house, she toyed with the idea of going back to the Shelter to snoop around. Whoever was threatening her, whoever had stolen her laptop and briefcase, whoever had murdered Ray, and now whoever had set fire to her grandmother's house had to be connected to the Shelter.

As for finding Jahi, she'd all but given up on that quest. Was he really out of town as his campaign manager had told her? Perhaps this out-of-town jaunt was cover for more sinister activities. She no longer knew who or what to believe.

Getting into the Shelter wouldn't be easy. The powers that be, likely Tarik, would never let her in to look around. Being on Foundation business wouldn't help either. No, this time the official route wouldn't work. Something was telling her to checkout the women's section, the area that she'd skipped during her tour. "Where men could not go" fit Simon's latest prophecy.

As the cab headed down North Capital Street, she spotted a homeless man heading in the opposite direction, with a shopping cart stuffed with plastic bags. Seeing him triggered thoughts of Maynard and Simon—the quiet one and the wild one with the head of unkempt dreads, a haunting laugh, and the sudden, threatening moves. *The lamb and the wolf. What a pair.* Then a thought came to her, crazy as it was. A thought that made her pulse quicken. *What if I go to the Shelter undercover? What if I go as a homeless person?*

"Something wrong, lady?" asked Muwakkil, peering at her in his rearview mirror.

"No, I'm okay," she answered. "On to Southwest, where you first picked me up." Zoie glanced at the time on her cell phone and hoped that Lena would be on time.

When she arrived at Lena's building, she instructed Muwakkil to find a place to park. "I'll be about forty minutes. You know the drill."

"Whew! You're sure one busy lady," he said as she slid across the back seat.

This time she took her overstuffed bag as she exited the cab.

Muwakkil exited as well and leaned on the open driver's side door. He eyed her big bag with a grimace. "Don't you want me to watch that bag for you like before?"

Zoie glanced down at her possessions. "Oh, I see. You're worried that because I'm taking my things, I won't return and pay you."

"A man can't be too careful," he responded with a broad smile. "I'm trustworthy, but I am not sure about everyone else."

"Trustworthy but not stupid, huh? Look, you know where I live and where I work. You even have my cell number. I'll be back. At the end of the day, you'll get your money...okay?"

"You're right, lady. But it's a crazy world. I need to be careful. I'm just a poor workingman. You've been my sole passenger for the day. All my money for today is riding on you. I worry for my family's sake. Nothing personal."

"No offense taken. And thank you again for trusting me," Zoie said with a half smile.

Zoie beat Lena to the building. After providing the desk clerk with a brief explanation as to whom she was there to see, she sat on the worn leather couch in the small lobby and used her wait time to scroll through her phone's recent-call listing. Her eyes fixed on three unidentified calls. At least one of them had to be from Queen. The early call was the threatening one, and the other one was a mystery.

Lena arrived five minutes later, damp with perspiration and a little out of breath. "Sorry. I hope I'm not late; traffic was horrendous," she offered before turning to give a nod of recognition to the desk clerk.

Lena was quiet, even pensive, as she guided Zoie to the elevator and up to the seventh floor and then down the hall to her apartment. Inside, Zoie followed Lena's lead, shedding her shoes in the small foyer, before wading barefoot into the living room's plush white carpet. A movement in the carpet caught Zoie's eye. For an instant she thought her eyes were playing tricks on her. But quickly she discerned that the moving carpet was actually a fluffy white cat. The cat was performing a belly stretch in almost perfect camouflage. It rose and greeted Lena with a whine. Ignoring Zoie altogether, it followed close to Lena's bare heels as Lena entered the kitchen.

Abandoned in the sea of white, Zoie waited with her big bag in the living room. She wondered whether the cat had been hiding in the carpet that morning.

Lena returned, bearing a tray on which she balanced two large vodka tonics, plus a big glass bowl of potato chips. With the addition of the chips, it was a repeat of the before-noon drink offering. This time Zoie felt no guilt indulging. She guzzled her drink and downed the usually forbidden chips. A small bag of nuts and the apple bran muffin thrust on her at Queen's place were all she'd eaten that day.

"When I come home, I need time to get my head together," Lena said after a long sip of her drink. "That place can suck the life out of you." Lena studied Zoie's face. "You look exhausted."

"I am," responded Zoie. She finally felt comfortable enough to lean into the white couch.

"What did you find out at the Foundation?"

Zoie considered for a minute how to summarize the day's events. She decided to include the events of the previous night at Ray's house, information she'd held back before. She knew she had to make her story concise; otherwise, they'd be there for hours.

"Look, Lena, I'm going to tell you everything I know. You'll be the only one, besides myself, to know the entire story…at least the part of the story that I know."

"Okay." Lena leaned back into her sofa with folded arms. "Is this on or off the record? You didn't forget? I *am* a reporter…at least for now."

"I get it," Zoie answered. "For now I have to ask that everything I tell you be *off* the record. If things work out or if I end up dead like Ray, well, either way you'll have your exclusive."

"Sounds ominous."

"I have a plan formulating here. First, though, I need to bring you up to speed. And I need you to hold your questions until the end, or I'll never get through it. Okay?"

Lena looked puzzled. She picked up her drink and swirled the ice in her drink with her finger. "It's gonna be difficult to hold questions. But okay. May I use a recorder?"

"I guess so. Remember, I'm trusting you with my life—literally."

"Huh? You're not gonna die on my account." Lena was back in a second and placed a small device on the table. "Okay, I'm ready."

"Last night I was at Ray Gaddis's house," Zoie began.

Lena was wide eyed. She gasped and put a hand to her mouth to stifle the torrent of questions waiting there.

Zoie explained how she was supposed to meet with Ray to discuss the Mahali Shelter situation, the irregularities, and her suspicions. She described how, at Ray's behest, she prepared a briefing for the Foundation's Board. She went to Ray's house to go over the presentation. Ray had never admitted any guilt in the situation, but he was acting strangely and at first resisted the idea of bringing the matter before the Board. Zoie explained how she had waited outside his house but that he never answered his door or his phone.

"Do you think he was already dead?" Lena asked. "Sorry—I'm supposed to wait on questions. Go on."

"Likely," Zoie responded. "But what did I know?"

She told Lena that she'd been angry with Ray for standing her up. She described the burglary at her apartment that morning, her missing briefcase and laptop, the threatening phone calls, the incident at the Shelter with Tarik, the mysterious woman, and her lack of success at tracking down Jahi, who was (according to his campaign manager) out of town.

"Goodness!" Lena's hands covered her chest to keep her heart from popping out.

"There's more," said Zoie, trying to remain calm as she continued the litany of events leading up to that hour. She explained the arson at her grandmother's place and how her grandmother was now staying temporarily at her caretaker's place. And seeing Tarik with her assistant outside the Foundation building. There was so much to tell that she was sure that she'd left things out.

It was Lena who took a long deep breath as though she'd been doing all the talking. For once she seemed at a loss for words. "Well, girl, you have me beat on trauma-drama…I'm confused. Want another drink?"

"Don't you want to ask me any questions?" asked Zoie.

"Yeah! My first question is, what are you going to do?" Lena rose from the couch. "Sounds to me like you're a candidate for the witness-protection program."

"I didn't see anyone murder Ray. And I don't know who's calling me. I can't identify anyone."

"Seems to me you can link A to B. You know too much. You're a danger to someone or a group of people. Hell, so I'll ask again, what are you going to do? Hold that thought. I'm getting a refill. Sure you don't want one?"

Zoie shook her head.

Lena clicked off her recorder and headed to the kitchen.

Zoie nervously patted her knee and then looked at her watch. It was four o'clock. Her eye caught the small chrome recorder on the coffee table. How could she have been so foolish as to let everything be recorded? The device was digital and similar to one she'd used in the past. With several strokes on its touch screen, she managed to delete their conversation. She quickly placed the device back on the table.

"This is incredible," said Lena upon her return. "You *do* realize you're in serious danger, right?"

"Right, Sherlock."

"So back to my question, what are you going to do?" Lena took a sip of her new drink and seemed unconcerned about the recorder. "I have some reliable police contacts—guys I trust, who don't play around."

Zoie bit her upper lip. "Remember what I told you. In that threatening call, the guy warned me about contacting the cops. Somehow they seem to know what I'm doing."

"You said 'they.' Do you think there's more than one?"

"Could be."

"Okay, no cops. So now what?"

"I've decided to go back to the Shelter...uh...undercover."

"What!" Lena cried, almost spilling her drink. "Honey, you just might be stupider than I thought."

" Look, I know it sounds crazy, but I need more evidence before going to the police. And I want you to help me."

"Jeez! You're kidding!" Lena made a weird face.

"If I'm ever to have a sense of peace and safety again, I need to do this."

Lena squinted and stared at Zoie. "Maybe you're just crazy enough to pull this off."

"Listen to me—I need to look like a homeless person. And I need to move quickly. Can you help me?"

It took more convincing to get Lena to commit to helping, but when the reluctant reporter finally came around, she seemed to be all-in. Lena supplied a tattered gray jogging outfit. Zoie put it on and sniffed at the armpits. "A little ripe, isn't it?" Zoie said with a frown.

"What? You got a problem with my body odor? Just think of it as 'eau de Lena,' very authentic," Lena said with a sly smile. "Now let's get that makeup off your face and that polish off your fingernails and toes." Lena took Zoie into the kitchen. Within ten minutes, she had Zoie looking thoroughly washed out. Lena seemed to be having fun dressing Zoie down. Zoie let Lena have her way but drew the line when Lena brandished a pair of scissors.

"Your hair is too perfect," Lena said.

"Hey, no cutting!" Zoie commanded.

"Okay. There's more than one way to skin a cat. I should have been a movie makeup artist. That could be my next profession if I get laid off," Lena said proudly as she mussed Zoie's short bob with gel and dust from a dust mop, turning Zoie's "perfect" hair into a perfect mess.

"What do you think?" Lena asked, giving Zoie a hand mirror.

"Oh, God. Ugh! Well, I guess it's good," Zoie said with a grimace as she admired her new look.

"Let's add some finishing touches." Lena retrieved a flowerless flowerpot from the kitchen window and shoved Zoie's fingers deep into its dark soil. The process left dark residue under Zoie's nails, making them look as if Zoie hadn't cleaned them in a month.

"Ick," Zoie said, wiping the excess soil from her hands into the sink.

"There. You look like you've been living outdoors." Lena looked pleased with herself. Then she found a pair of old white tennis shoes with crushed backs. They were dirty and a little too big for Zoie, but they did the trick. "You'd fool me," Lena said, standing back for a better look at her creation. I don't think all homeless folks are bums, but you fit the stereotype.

In the rush to look the part for her undercover operation, Zoie hadn't hashed out the details of how she would actually get into the Shelter. She called Muwakkil to inform him that she was running late. To accomplish her goal, she had to move quickly. In forty-five minutes the Shelter would start its dinner service and its intake for beds for the night. Being summer, the place was unlikely to be crowded. But thinking through her next steps, she hit a snag. All of her assumptions were about the dorms for the Shelter's men. She knew nothing about how things worked on the women's side.

Mahali's annual report glossed over the operation of the two-year-old women's program. She remembered that homeless women accounted for less than fifteen percent of the Shelter's overall operating costs. Zoie had wanted to follow up on the program with Jahi and to ask some other questions about Mahali, but it seemed that when they were together, one thing led to another, and they never got around to discussing Foundation business. *So much for mixing business with pleasure.*

"What do you know about the women's part of the Shelter?" she asked Lena, who was busy cleaning up the makeover mess in her kitchen. "It's almost as though that part of the Shelter doesn't exist."

"It exists, all right," Lena said as she patted some eyebrow powder under Zoie's eyes with her pinkie to create dark circles. "Yeah, the women's center, or whatever they call it, exists…and Sister Te is its queen bee. I'm sure Jahi just turned that whole operation over to her." Lena stopped her patting and primping for a moment. "Huh…now that I think of it, I do believe Jahi is a bit of a chauvinist. I can't ever remember his mentioning homeless women."

Needing details on how to gain entry, Zoie asked Lena to call Mahali and pretend to be a social worker wanting to send someone over who needed a bed.

"I have a better idea. My Delta sister, Karen Upshaw, is a social worker for DC's Department of Human Services. I bet she knows the rundown on Mahali's section for women," Lena said. She made the call.

Karen explained that Mahali's facility for women, though still considered an emergency shelter, operated differently than the men's section. While men could only stay overnight, the women's section allowed its residents to stay for up to two weeks. During that time they were supposed to find more-permanent accommodations. Mahali's facility for women had twenty beds. The allowance for longer stays meant open beds were tougher to come by.

Lena asked her friend Karen to make a few calls, telling her sorority sister that a girl of twenty-five, named Anna, needed a place to stay because the streets had become too violent.

"No, she hasn't been raped!" Lena bellowed into the phone, at the concerned social worker. "Not yet, anyway. But that might happen if we don't get her off the streets."

Zoie's eyes grew big as she listened to Lena's half of the conversation. What was she getting into? Dressing like a homeless person was one thing; acting like someone who'd lived on the streets was quite another. She could be tough and streetwise if the need arose. For this jobperhaps she'd be better off acting withdrawn and depressed. The less she had to say, the better off she'd be. And why did Lena make her twenty-five? Her make-down made her look older, not younger. One thing for sure is that she couldn't be Zoie Taylor—the smart-mouthed attorney.

Balancing her phone under her chin, Lena washed her hands and walked into the winter-white living room. Zoie followed, trying to keep up the one-sided conversation.

"No space at Mahali, huh," Lena said, sounding disappointed and rolling her eyes. "You're sure? Uh-huh...that's too bad."

In her disappointment Zoie felt her adrenalin wane. A fatigue was taking hold. She wanted to crash on Lena's couch. But Lena's arctic-looking living room called out to her. "Don't do it," it said.

Had all the costuming and makeup been for naught? Perhaps she'd have a better chance at getting into the Shelter disguised as a man. Quickly sizing up her frailties and vulnerability, she dismissed that thought. Simon's prophecy specifically said, "What you want to know is through a place men dare not go." She had to go through the women's section.

"Call the Shelter again and beg," Lena urged her sorority sister. "Tell them you've tried other places. Tell them the young woman was attacked last night and almost raped. Now she's terrified to be on the street...yes, it has to be Mahali. Look, I'll explain why that shelter later. Just trust me on this. And, Karen, don't forget that my participation in this has got to be on the QT. If anyone asks, this girl called you directly...okay, girl. Call me back." Lena completed her call and said to Zoie, "We Deltas support each other. Don't worry. Karen will come through."

Zoie hoped Lena's confidence in her sorority sister would be enough. The two women stood in eerie silence in the sea of white. After the flurry of activity to disguise Zoie, they considered the prospect of a gigantic letdown. Now there was nothing to do but wait.

Finally Zoie broke the silence. "The women's section at the Shelter must be the Four Seasons or something. Booked."

Lena responded with a tired shrug.

Zoie smiled at the irony of it all. In truth, tonight she would be homeless. She was too afraid to return to her apartment after the burglary, and since her grandmother's house was uninhabitable, staying there wasn't an option. To sleep that night, she needed to depend on the goodwill of others or simply hit a hotel. She probably could stay with Lena, although she hadn't asked, and Lena hadn't offered. She had the key to Tina's condo. She could go there, but being alone was not that appealing. Right now *nowhere* felt safe.

The two women returned to the kitchen to wait. Lena made herself a third drink. Zoie declined another round, feeling she needed to keep her wits about her.

"We've got to have faith," Lena said as she busied herself cleaning up dishes in the sink.

It seemed like forever, but finally Lena's phone rang. Lena answered it gingerly and this time looked up at Zoie and smiled. "Mahali's going to let you in tonight," Lena whispered, holding her hand over the phone. "They can set up a cot. A woman who's been there for a while is leaving in two days. Zoie, you're in."

With a lot of help from Lena, it looked like phase one of Operation Mahali was going to be a success. Zoie wasn't inside yet, but she had the green light to enter.

Lena thanked her sorority sister profusely and finished her conversation by saying, "Girl, I owe you." Then Lena turned to Zoie with a satisfied smile. "Well, I guess that's it. Anna, my little street girl, you're on,"

"Guess so," said Zoie, who was less than enthusiastic as the full weight of what she was about to undertake came down on her. *At least Nikki is safe in Ohio,* she kept telling herself. "Tell me, Lena, where did you get the name Anna and why on earth did you make me twenty-five? Do I look like a twenty-five-year-old?"

Lena fingered her chin. "Well, you're in good physical condition. You must work out. I just thought the powers that be would be more likely to rush to the rescue of a young thing rather than a hardened thirty-something."

Perhaps Lena was right about the age thing, though it was sad to think of things that way. "And the name Anna?"

"I don't know. It just popped into my head. Anna sounds sweet and innocent. Don't you think so?"

"I guess Anna will do."

"You better start thinking up a last name and a backstory. The staff at the Shelter are going to ask you questions. You need a life. Oh, by the way, your social worker is Karen Upshaw, my Delta sister. Just say you got her phone number from one of the cards the police hand out to the homeless at the park."

"Lena, I don't know how to thank you. You've thought of everything."

"No problem. This is gonna work out for both of us. I still think you're crazy to do this."

"But there is one more thing I need you to do for me." Zoie bit her bottom lip.

"What now? Take you to a shrink to have your head examined?"

Zoie smiled. "No, not that…I need you to contact my grandmother in case something happens to me."

"Girl, don't talk like that!"

"Just if you don't hear from me in forty-eight hours."

Lena turned away. "At least you know this is dangerous. There's hope that you're still thinking rationally. And what about Jahi? I thought you were looking for him."

"I was but not anymore. If he turns up, *fine*. Otherwise, *damn him*."

"I see," said Lena.

"Look, Lena, I can't protect Jahi any longer. I don't know whether he's involved in this or not. No doubt his Shelter is involved. For all I know, Jahi might be in this up to his eyeballs. If I find out that he is, I'll make sure he goes down with anyone else involved."

"Boy, you're one tough cookie all of a sudden. As for Jahi I say he's not involved," Lena said. "This ain't him. But then I've been known to be wrong about men."

"Me too." Zoie looked at the kitchen's immaculate white tile floor and then looked into Lena's eyes. "Listen, this is serious. If I don't make contact within forty-eight hours, I want you to call the police. Tell them all that you know and that I went to Mahali undercover." Zoie thought of how she had deleted Lena's recording. She hoped that Lena would not be too upset once she discovered that there was no recording of the conversation.

"Okay," said Lena reluctantly.

"Then I need you to let my grandmother and my friend Tina know what's going on. Right now there's just me, my grandmother, and my daughter, Nikki. My friend Tina is Nikki's designated guardian should anything happen to me."

Lena winced and turned away. "Zoie, I don't like this. This just went from being a game to get a sensational story to something *way* too dangerous."

"Lena, I have to be practical. My little girl is depending on me. Thank God she's out of town right now." Zoie's eyes were tearing up. She pulled out a small picture of Nikki from her wallet and showed it to Lena.

"Cute kid," Lena said, staring intently at the photograph. "She needs her mother."

"I know," said Zoie, returning the picture to her wallet.

"I hope all of this is in a will or something. You can't expect me to remember all this stuff." Lena gave Zoie a piece of paper, and Zoie copied a few numbers from her cell phone's contact list and handed the paper to Lena.

"Remember to wait forty-eight hours before calling anyone. I wouldn't want to worry folks needlessly."

"So for forty-eight hours, I get to be the only one who knows where you are. I get to be the one that worries about what's happening to you," said Lena.

"Yeah, and you get the exclusive for your newspaper. Let's hope I find something to put an end to this. I'm not sure at this point whether I know what I'm looking for. But I do know that I can't live my life looking over my shoulder for a bogeyman to strike out at me or those I love." For an instant Zoie's thoughts shifted to Carmen Silva, the former Crayton Foundation employee. Most likely what Carmen knew went way beyond the tryst between Ray and Milton.

"I'm not pushing it," said Lena, "but if you find something interesting, snap a few photos with that cell phone when no one's looking. Something for page one."

"Okay."

"Hey, let me get a picture of you all dolled up right now. It will be good for the story, and I might need it for the police ID. You know...in case you don't show."

"Have you ever thought of changing careers? Becoming a comedian or something?" Zoie said.

"You think I'm joking? I'm serious as a diaper rash."

Lena took a picture of Zoie. Then with tears in their eyes, the two women hugged. The hug was genuine, like the hug between long-lost sisters. The jealousy (or had it just pettiness over Jahi?) seemed to vanish.

With her cell phone in her pocket, contact info for Karen Upshaw, no wallet or other ID, and a white plastic bag with a pair of panties and a bottle of water, Zoie left Lena's apartment to find Muwakkil. "God help me," Zoie said, sighing as she emerged into the hot sun as Anna, the homeless girl.

CHAPTER 38

ARE YOU GONNA GO?

Muwakkil was down the street from Lena's building, parked in a shaded spot. Zoie headed in his direction with urgency, hindered only by her ill-fitting borrowed footwear. She made a mental note: *Remember, girl: you can't run in these shoes.*

Time was almost up on her all-day chauffeuring arrangement. Surely Muwakkil would want to be paid and to go home. Zoie hoped that with a little finesse, she could talk him into another hour or so of service, for an additional fee, of course.

Zoie reached into the pocket of Lena's jogging suit and felt the wad of cash she'd pulled together to pay Muwakkil, some of it borrowed from Lena. If she were to drop dead at the Shelter without ID, she could only be identified as Anna.

Keeping the phone was risky. The latest model Blackberry certainly wasn't something a homeless person would possess. But she figured she might need it to communicate with Lena or the police should things get hairy. The phone was on but set to vibrate.

As she approached the taxi, Muwakkil was leaning against the driver's side door, engaged in a loud, animated phone conversation in a language she couldn't identify. In all the riding around they'd done that day, she'd been too engrossed in her own problems to ask where he was from. Other than the meaning of his name, information that he'd volunteered, she knew nothing about him. And Muwakkil in turn had respected her anonymity. She hadn't told him her name, nor had he asked. He never questioned the why or wherefore of their circuitous comings and goings. He'd only asked the important question, "Where to now, lady?"

Zoie stood a few feet from him, but Muwakkil didn't immediately respond to her presence. She waved her hands to get his attention. His acknowledgment was to shoo her away and turn his back to her. Obviously, he didn't recognize her. The disguise was working. She was about to tap him on the shoulder but thought better of it. If startled, he might take a swing at her.

"Hey, it's me," Zoie said. "I'm ready to go."

When he turned around, she was still unknown to him. "Sorry, girlie girl. No free rides okay," he said, shooing her away again.

Having failed to get a positive response, Zoie raised her voice. "Muwakkil...Mr. Trusted One! Remember me? Your all-day passenger! Let's get a move on!"

"Oh, oh, look at you!" he shouted, breaking into a hearty laugh. He quickly ended his phone conversation and turned to address her. "What happened to the nicely dressed lady I was driving? Forgive me, but you look a mess."

"Thank you for your assessment. I *am* a mess," she said as she primped her gunked hair and smoothed the jacket zipper of her borrowed jogging suit. "One day, Muwakkil, we'll have lunch, you and I. Then I'll explain this whole mad day to you...once I figure it out for myself."

"So messy. So mysterious," he said, scratching his head.

"Today I'm just being practical. Now let's go."

He opened the door to the back seat, and Zoie climbed in.

"Where to now, Ms. Practical Messy Lady?"

Zoie smiled and instructed Muwakkil to take her back to K Street, near her office. She received a text message, the sender unknown. It was from her nemesis and conveyed a clear instruction: "Keep your mouth shut." She stifled a gasp. Thank God her grandmother was safe with Queen. Thank God Nikki was safe in Ohio.

Traffic was heavier as the early rush hour was underway. When they rounded the corner of Fifteenth Street, she spotted the familiar homeless pair in a shady spot against the building. Muwakkil pulled into the access road, and Zoie instructed him to go slow and come to a stop a few car lengths from where they were camped. "Leave me here," she ordered. "Drive around the block or something. I need about twenty minutes."

"Okay, lady," Muwakkil responded. "You know your time is up at 6:00 p.m."

"I know," she answered, checking the large digital numerals of the Citibank clock. It read a little after five. "Be back in twenty minutes. We have one more stop."

She waited for Muwakkil to drive away before approaching the homeless men. Before she could make her way across the sidewalk, she spotted Regina, who was accompanied by another employee. The two were coming out of the building that housed the Foundation. Regina was finally getting to go home.

As the chatting women passed near Zoie, they looked in her direction. Zoie avoided their eyes. They were oblivious to her presence. Even if they'd looked directly at her, neither of them would have recognized her. Zoie had become one of the streets' ghost figures, the human beings that other human beings often looked through.

Good. The disguise is working.

"Sheee's baaack!" announced the wild one from his cardboard mat as Zoie approached. "You can dress down, but your air is still high and mighty. I can smell arrogance a mile away."

"Hello," Zoie said, her tone steady and calm in the face of his verbal attack.

The wild one looked startled, suddenly at a loss for words.

"Hello, my dear," said Simon, who was seated on a little stool nearby.

Zoie had grown somewhat accustomed to the wild one's initial thank-yous followed by a tirade of crass remarks, both of which usually came after she would leave a donation. She reminded herself that after all, he'd saved her life. His wiser, gentler companion had a velvet voice, a voice that mesmerized her.

"You both knew it was me right away. How come?" she asked.

"Despite your disguise and hard shell, your true self beams through."

She thought about his words for a second. "Hard shell, huh? Simon, I need your help," she said. A few feet away, the wild one looked on quizzically.

"How can I help?" Simon asked. Again his tone was soft and inviting. Like a whisper carried on a whirlpool, it swirled around her head. Zoie shook her head to reset her hearing.

"Earlier today you gave me a fortune, or a prophecy, or a clue, or whatever you call it. I think it's pointing me back to the homeless shelter. I'm…"

The wild one had been listening. He sprang to his feet, did a little jig, and chanted, "Shelter, shelter, helter skelter. Ha ha! Stay away from that damned Shelter!" People walking near took note of the drama and kept their distance.

"Maynard, calm down!" Simon commanded. His tone was direct, though still soothing. "Let the lady finish telling us how she needs our help!"

She glanced over at the wild one, fearful that her words would instigate another outburst. Like a scolded child, Maynard pouted and moved his mat away from Zoie and Simon, but he remained well within pouncing range. Zoie turned back to Simon, still keeping a watchful eye on Maynard in her peripheral vision.

"I want to get into Mahali. I need to look around. I believe that someone there is threatening me and my family."

Simon groaned and gave her a blank look.

"I want you to come to the Shelter with me this evening. Perhaps together we can uncover something."

"Something?" Simon responded.

"Yes. Something that will help me protect my family. I believe someone from the Shelter tried to burn down my grandmother's house."

"Oh my," moaned Simon. Wide eyed, he stroked his chin with his thumb and forefinger. "You do have a predicament. Are you sure you want to do deal with it this way?"

"I can't go to the police. I must do something to prove that that place is the center of my trouble. Something is there. I know it. Please help me," she pleaded.

"Too much *Law and Order*. Too much *Law and Order*," Maynard called.

"You're in deep, aren't you?" Simon asked with a frown.

"Looks that way," she answered, shrugging.

"Well, if I go, then he's got to go too." Simon pointed to Maynard. "In fact, it's him you need, not me. He's the one that knows that place."

"Isn't he a little *off*?" Zoie asked, keeping her voice just above a whisper.

"By *off* were you referring to the adverb, adjective, or prepositional definition of that word?" piped in Maynard. "And by the way, my high-and-mighty sister, I speak English. I also have superpowered hearing. So ha!"

"As I said, I can't go without him," repeated Simon. "He's my charge. He needs my help just as you do. In truth, *he*—not I—is the one who can help you. Mark my words. Don't be put off by his tomfoolery," Simon continued. "He's very intelligent. A scientist. A biochemist, I believe. He worked at Aberdeen Proving Ground before that terrible gas leak. You see that accident had some effect on his mind. But don't let him fool you. When he's focused, he can be of great help."

Zoie had heard about Aberdeen, the military's testing facility in northern Maryland, not far from Baltimore—the place where the military tested its biological and chemical weapons and housed deadly concoctions capable of wiping out whole populations.

She considered this new information and looked at Maynard sitting on his mat. No matter how much education this guy had, he still posed a risk. His current stance, arms folded and lips in a pout, did not inspire confidence. She judged him a liability. She turned to Simon again. "Scientist or not, I don't think he wants to help me or anyone else. He's too angry. How can I trust him?"

"You're right. He's angry—but with good reason. You have to see things from his point of view. The real question is, can *he* trust you?" Simon said. "Trust is hard to come by when you've lived his life. If you want his help, you need to first respect him and then ask him."

Zoie looked down at her worn tennis shoes, digesting what Simon had advised. Originally she'd envisioned going to the Shelter alone, but when the idea of a homeless guide occurred to her, she thought about Simon and *only* Simon. Relying on this other unstable man was a stretch. He could prove to be a major liability in an already-dangerous undertaking.

"Tell him you will help him with something he wants. Tell him you will help him recover his binder. The last time he was at that Shelter, something happened to him," Simon explained. "I believe it was there that his binder was stolen."

Zoie shivered at the thought of approaching Maynard again.

"Go. Talk to him," Simon repeated. "He's a lot of mouth. But he wouldn't hurt a fly. That is...unless the fly bit him or something. Then there'd be no telling what he might do."

Great. Zoie found Simon's fly analogy less than reassuring. With arms folded Maynard seemed unlikely to cooperate. Perhaps this unstable person could help. "Nothing ventured, nothing gained," her grandmother used to say. Zoie took a deep breath and took the five long steps over to where Maynard now sat brooding in the lotus position. His arms were still folded tightly against his chest. He flinched as she squatted on the cement next to his mat. A second later a generous passerby dropped what looked like a five-dollar bill in Maynard's can.

"Go away!" Maynard blurted. "Get your own spot." Then, like an ape, he swung his lotus-positioned legs with his long arms to the opposite edge of the mat and repositioned his donation can. "This place is taken. We're not partnering. Get it?"

"Okay, I understand," said Zoie in a calm, polite voice. "I don't intend to stay. I'm headed to Mahali. And I want you and Simon to come with me."

"Going to the Shelter—whoa! That's not gonna happen, Alice! You better be checking in with the White Rabbit about your plans. No special guests, meaning me and Simon, are allowed along when you go down that hole."

Zoie decided not to let Maynard's creative but crazy responses deter her. She needed the two of them with her in the Shelter. The thought of going alone to snoop around, as her plan had once called for, no longer seemed possible.

"From what I hear, Maynard, you're a pretty smart guy," she said, hoping to appeal to his intellectual vanity, something shared by most brilliant people. "A high IQ, huh?"

But Maynard wasn't falling for the praise bait, at least not immediately. He winced at the sound of his name and reacted as though physically attacked. When she was quiet, he perked up. His wisecracking took on a less crazed tone. "Yeah, you're right. I'm smart, too smart to go back to that damned Shelter. That place is hell for the homeless. Simon knows it. He believes what I tell him. If you're not careful, you'll get to meet the devil... personal-like."

"I believe you. You're smart all right. You recognized me right away, even in this getup."

"Never forget a face. Never forget a face. Got a photographic memory. I record the bone structure. Measure the width between the eyes, nostril size, distance between the eyebrows, and angle on the curve of the lip. Details. Details." He released his folded arms and pointed to his head. "All the measurements are up here. In millimeters."

"I see," Zoie said, hoping the unfolding of his arms signaled that she was making progress. She looked over at Simon's confident face and kept prodding. "Then maybe you know what's going on at the Shelter. Since you remember stuff."

"No *maybe* about it. Humph. God's on my side, and I memorized everything, even if I don't have my binder to write it down. I write things down to clear my database. It gets a little crowded up there," he said, again pointing to his head.

"I understand that it's important to write things down. What if when we go to the Shelter, I help you find your binder? That's where you lost it, at the Shelter, right?"

He cackled. "Silly woman! Getting something stolen *ain't* the same as losing it...get my drift?" He cocked his head to the side in a quirky pose and stared at her with a devilish grin, showing a mouth full of yellow teeth. She was repulsed but not afraid. "Start from the beginning," he continued. "Hear me! Check your facts. Can't jump to conclusions about my binder or anything else about me. Humph! Truth is, you don't know *jack shit*."

"You're right about that," she said, responding to Maynard's animated response. Under the circumstances she thought it best just to agree. Seeking help, she glanced over at Simon, who watched the whole encounter while sitting on his low stool. Simon raised his chin in a signal of encouragement. Perhaps she *was* making progress. One thing for sure, her twenty minutes was just about up; Muwakkil was due back. "Perhaps you can explain the truth to me. I believe I can trust what you say."

"Do I sense some sense?" Maynard snickered. He finished laughing at his own joke and seemed to calm down.

Zoie and Maynard talked for a few more minutes. Maynard did most of the talking. He rambled, his thoughts mostly lucid, about his binder and the evil looming at the Shelter, although he gave no details as to just *what* evil he meant. In a roundabout, up-side-down way, he confirmed that something funky was going on at the place. Perhaps what she was looking for was documented in that binder. But who would believe someone like Maynard without corroboration? She told him that she needed help to fight the evil and to save her life and the lives of her grandmother and little girl. Fear for her family seemed to resonate with him.

After a few minutes, Maynard became contemplative. He said, "Okay, I'll go to the Shelter with you and Simon. You must listen to what I tell you. I know what I'm talking about. I get my directions from God, and God tells me how to stay alive. He's going to help us." He looked to the sky. "We'll need his help when we enter the devil's pit."

CHAPTER 39

THE PLAN

It was a quarter past six when Muwakkil dropped them off several blocks from the Shelter. Zoie didn't want to be seen getting out of a taxi with her companions right in front of the place. "See, nothing to worry about," she said, handing Muwakkil a wad of cash amounting to the agreed-upon price for his services, plus a generous tip.

"Many thanks," Muwakkil said with a satisfied smile, stuffing the wad of bills into his pocket. "I knew you were a lady of your word."

"For a while, though, you doubted me."

"Just a little," he said sheepishly.

Maynard and Simon had moved away from the curb. Zoie looked around to be sure that her soon-to-be guides hadn't abandoned her. Maynard, who was farthest from the taxi, worried her. Head down, he seemed to be inspecting his feet. So much was resting on Maynard's keeping it together. But the chances of his keeping it together dwindled when he began to chant. He circled his meager pile of belongings in what could only be called a rhythmic warrior shuffle.

"Oh, God, he's preparing for battle." Zoie's heart sank. "This is going to be a disaster." She gave Simon a pleading look, but Simon simply shrugged.

Rubbing his chin, Muwakkil watched Maynard's shenanigans. Initially he'd refused to let Maynard into the taxi. "Am I going to have to delouse this cab?" Under Zoie's pressure he finally caved. "Lady, I know you're trying to do a good deed, but you need to be *careful!*" He let Maynard put his belongings into the trunk. Simon didn't have anything. When Zoie climbed into the passenger seat in the front, Muwakkil said, "There's more room back there, but I can understand why you don't want to sit next to him."

"You have a point. Actually, with the two of them, there's no room without a squeeze," she said.

Muwakkil looked at the back seat and seemed bewildered. He scratched his head. "Whatever you say, lady."

Maynard mumbled a lot during the ride, but Simon remained silent.

Now Muwakkil pointed to Maynard as he did his warrior-inspired dance and ignored Simon completely. "I've seen his kind before. He could turn *real* nasty, *real* quickly."

"Yeah, I get it. He's stinky, but I think he's harmless," she replied, trying to believe her own words. "I'll be all right. But thanks for the warning."

"You have my number should you need me again," Muwakkil said. He was no longer smiling. "You might need me again."

"We shall see," she said. Needing Muwakkil again wasn't in her plan. But in truth, she had no plan. Beyond disguising herself to get into the Shelter to snoop around, she hadn't thought much further.

Muwakkil drove away, leaving the ragtag crew on the corner.

During the ride from downtown, Simon shared the back seat with Maynard and remained perfectly quiet during the trip.

Now he stood with his hands loosely clasped behind him, rocking slowly on his heels, watching Maynard's warrior dance. As soon as the taxi disappeared into the traffic, Maynard ended his performance.

"Thank God," Zoie said. "Are you sure you and Maynard can get in the Shelter tonight?"

"Folks want to sleep under the stars on nights like this," Simon answered, looking up at what was still the summer's daylight. "There'll be plenty of beds."

"Huh, I had to have a reservation...but we should strategize."

"Strategy is his domain," Simon said, nodding in Maynard's direction. "There's your man."

Simon's words signaled Maynard to resume his dance, shuffling in tightening circles.

"Not again!" Zoie gasped. Despite the litany of degrees Maynard supposedly possessed, she found it difficult to believe that *Maynard* was the man for this job—*any* job, for that matter.

"I know what you're thinking," Simon said. His voice again lulled her rattled nerves. "Remember to not let his buffoonery fool you. Listen to what he has to say. Trust him."

Trust him! Right! Men she'd loved and trusted had failed her: her father, Elliot, and Jahi Khalfani, to name the most recent. She was being advised to trust a fool. And the man counseling her to do so while seemingly so young to be so wise was also a mystery.

She took a deep breath and went over to where Maynard performed his dance. He stopped but didn't look up. "I hear you're the strategist for this undertaking," she said.

"Glad you recognize my qualifications," he snarled. "And you, lady, might be smarter than *I* thought." His body language was no longer threatening.

"So tell me something. Once we're in there, you and Simon will be in the men's section, and I'll be in the women's. How..."

"You mean what's the plan? The plan. The plan." With his head cocked, he looked like a whacky pirate, more comical than menacing. "What's the plan?"

She nodded vigorously.

"I guess we have to meet up, so I can take you to the *secret place*."

"What secret place?"

"Aha! Now you get it. It's the place I know about that you don't."

"Yes, definitely that place. How are you going to get me there?"

"That's where they've got my binder. The one they stole from me. No one thinks I know, *but I remember*." Maynard beckoned her to move closer, but she could only get so close without tripping over his green bags.

"But how?"

He whispered, "After the lights are out, find a window that looks to the rear. I'll shine a light in the courtyard as a signal. You meet me out there." He reached into his bag and retrieved a flashlight. "Look for this beam." He shined its beam into his hand. "I'll wait until late…midnight or later."

It was the sanest-sounding string of words to come out of his mouth thus far. Perhaps he was on to something. What was this "secret place"?

"But how do I get to the courtyard?" she asked in a tense whisper.

"Calm down, Ms. Smarty Pants," he said, sucking his teeth. "You'll figure it out."

"Okay, okay. I'll wait for your signal—a flashlight shining into the courtyard, right?"

"Bingo."

"Then I will meet you outside…after I figure out how to get outside."

"Better figure that out before I give the signal."

It was a plan of sorts. The best she could expect from the likes of Maynard. She could see that questioning her enigmatic guide any further would get her nowhere. In fact, questioning him more might rile him. She'd have to rely on her wits to find a way to the back of the Shelter. She remembered seeing a loading dock and an inner courtyard from her tour of the place weeks ago. The courtyard was the view from Jahi's office window. If she could get into the place, surely she could get out.

"Did bulbs come on for you, hmm?" Maynard said, laughing. "I was beginning to worry. Didn't know whether your brain was engaged."

He's worried. What a joke.

At the Shelter's entrance, some men mused about, though not nearly as many as there'd been earlier in the day. No one paid the trio any attention.

"This is where I leave you," said Simon, stopping about five feet from the door.

"What do you mean? Leave us!" Zoie said with panic in her voice.

With a sorrowful expression, Simon did his best shrug ever.

"I told you she was a little slow," Maynard said in a loud whisper as he leaned into Simon. Maynard turned to Zoie. "He *never* goes into that place. He's too smart for that. Shh, I wouldn't be going back in there if it wasn't that he had asked me—very nicely, I should say—to help you."

Simon shrugged again, this time with raised palms, which seemed to grow in size right before her eyes.

"We'll probably see him tomorrow or the next day. Never can tell. He's got bigger fish to fry," said Maynard, chewing on a plastic straw. "Hey! This talk of fish is making me hungry. I could use a meal." Maynard looked to the sky. "God, I'm counting on you." And with those words, Maynard took a deep breath, yanked open the Shelter's heavy door, and entered.

The door closed behind Maynard, leaving Zoie with Simon outside. "I'll wait until you go in before I leave," said Simon.

"Big help you are!" She was angry. She didn't know whether to cry or just stomp away and abandon the plan. *If not this, then what?* She was crushed. Her arms and face went limp. Her plastic bag almost touched the ground.

"Have faith, dear." It was Simon's soothing voice again wrapping around her jittery anger, smothering those feelings of fear and disappointment like a damp cloth on a small blaze. There was a sparkle in his eyes as he talked to her. "Maynard will do what he said he would. He said he would guide you, and he will. Maynard has summoned all his courage to do this. Crossing that threshold on his own accord was a big deal for him. He hates that place. This is quite a test for him...and for you."

She felt almost in a trance. "If you keep your head," the voice continued, "you'll find what you're looking for."

Simon added his strength to hers to pull open the Shelter's heavy front door. "Into the pit," Zoie said with a fatalistic sigh. Once inside she turned to say goodbye to Simon as the door slowly closed behind her, but through the door's narrowing gap, she could no longer see him.

In the familiar lobby of the Shelter, someone new was behind the high counter. Her eyes scanned the half-dozen men parked on the pew-style benches that ringed the room. Where was Maynard?

"May I help you?" said a deep voice from behind the counter."

"I'm...I'm here to stay at the women's section," said Zoie.

"Your name?"

Zoie said, "Anna." She didn't recall being given a last name.

The man at the desk picked up the phone. "A young woman named Anna is here for you."

Young? How young? Perhaps she'd passed the first test.

"Someone is coming. Have a seat." He pointed to an empty bench.

Sheepishly Zoie sat down on the bench. The occupants on the nearby benches seemed oblivious to her arrival. One man nervously rubbed the side of his head with his palm. Another bench sitter stared into the distance in a kind of stupor. Another man rummaged through a paper sack in search of something, mumbling to himself all the while. Where was Maynard? He'd passed through the same door only a minute or two before her.

Zoie sat like a frightened schoolgirl, clutching her white plastic bag. She was in full costume for this act, but her nervousness was not feigned. Discreetly she sniffed at her armpit and grimaced. Lena's funk and stale perfume now mixed with Zoie's nervous sweat.

It wasn't long before a middle-aged woman in a long sack dress appeared from the dark passageway. She looked soft and pudgy but had a kind smile. She approached the bench and touched Zoie's arm. "Welcome, Anna. I'm Lois. I'm a volunteer here." Zoie had already gathered the woman's name and volunteer status from her blue-and-white name tag. "Follow me, dear," she continued. "We'll get you settled in."

Zoie responded to the woman with a half smile and then looked down at her arm where the woman had touched her. Though she knew it was meant to be a caring gesture, she found it condescending and much too personal. No one would have ever touched Zoie Taylor in such a manner. The disguise was working.

Zoie followed the woman's slow steps through the twisty corridor she had once toured as Zoie Taylor, the Foundation's attorney. "The men's dorms are back there," Lois explained as they passed a fork in the corridor. "One of these days, we'll have our own entrance connected directly to the outside. Then we won't have to come through the men's corridor at all."

After a final right turn, they were standing before the black double-door entrance to the women's section. Since Zoie's prior visit, a plaque had been added to the door. "No men allowed beyond this point," it said. Lois rang the bell and gave Zoie a patronizing smile and pat.

The woman who opened the door could have been Lois's twin. Zoie followed the two women into the world behind the double doors. She wasn't quite sure about what to expect in this world, but for one thing the color scheme had changed. The institutional pea-green walls had disappeared and become a palette of delicate pastels: orchid, pale sky blue, and buttercup. Pictures and posters with tranquil landscapes and seascapes adorned the walls. In some of the rooms, she could see curtains at the windows.

Zoie followed the two women to a small office crowded with unopened boxes and filing cabinets. "Bea is going to get you signed in," explained Lois. "Remember that when coming and going, you always need an escort. I know it's a pain and it does limit your freedom somewhat, but those are the rules. Believe me, the rule is for your protection. Bea will fill you in on the other rules, and I'll ask one of the other ladies to show you around." Lois left.

Squeezed behind the desk, Bea—the less smiley version of Lois—pulled out a packet of forms and placed them in front of Zoie, then invited Zoie to sit in the room's only other chair.

Here comes the creativity, Zoie thought, seeing all the blanks she'd have to fill in. The only pieces of misinformation she'd come prepared with were her new first name, age, and Karen Upshaw's phone number. She stared at the form.

"I hate forms myself," said Bea, interpreting Zoie's stalling as something else. "Take your time. I'll leave you to fill it out." Bea squeezed by Zoie and the desk once again, on her way out.

When Bea was out of earshot, Zoie let out a long sigh. *So far so good.* Thank God. She hadn't run into Sister Te. At least the look-alike volunteers seemed to accept her. Zoie focused on the form and began to fabricate her life as a homeless person. Her new name was Anna, and she used the version with two n's, as her great-grandmother with the same name had done. Now all she had to do was remember to answer to that name when called. Her age, also predetermined by Lena, was twenty-five. For her date of birth, she used her real birth month and day, quickly calculating the appropriate birth year.

So far those were the easy blanks. For a last name, she wrote Jackson because the lyrics of the song "Nasty" came to mind: "Janet, Miss. Jackson, if you're nasty." The words to the song made her smile to herself. Making up a new identity would have been fun if the whole situation wasn't so scary. She hadn't gone through the consequences of being caught impersonating a homeless person. It wasn't as if she'd stolen someone's identity. She began to mentally tick off the legal ramifications but realized that Bea would soon return, so she brought her focus back to completing the remaining blanks.

The blank calling for her last address was a stumper. *Something out of town will be appropriate,* she thought. She wrote down her late father's last known address, a tenement building on South Broadway in Baltimore. She had visited the place a couple of times with her mother. That had been quite a while ago. She wondered whether the building still stood. For her current employment, her answer was easy: unemployed. For previous employment she entered "waitress at IHOP," a job she'd actually held one summer while in college, before her serious internships kicked in. For her Social Security number, she concocted a string of numbers using the same prefix as her own SSN for a bit of authenticity. She quickly filled out the rest of the blanks about health, education, and next of kin, making herself a healthy high school dropout with no next of kin. She reviewed her new identity. It was a fictional life that she was glad she didn't have.

When Bea returned, she gave the forms a quick review and then groaned. What in the fictional Anna's life could be so egregious to cause the negative reaction?

"Ms. Anna Jackson, huh," Bea said, "may I see some ID?"

"Sorry, my ID was stolen with the rest of my stuff in the park… when I had to run."

"Hmm…" Bea said, looking skeptical.

Zoie had expected a different kind of reply, something like "sorry to hear that" or "what a shame you lost your stuff." There was no sympathy coming from this woman.

"You say here that your last address was in Baltimore. This could be a problem. Here we serve DC residents. And we refer Maryland residents back to the Maryland shelters."

Zoie had to think fast. In her attempt to provide an authentic address, she'd miscalculated. "Nah, I'm a DC girl," she answered quickly. "I've been living here for a long time. Lately I don't have a DC address. I've been going from place to place around Adams Morgan and Petworth. I live with friends until they throw me out. That Baltimore address is where I lived with my father for a couple of months until he died. But I went to school here—Anacostia High School—until I dropped out."

"Hmm." Bea didn't look convinced. "Well, I'll let the social worker handle this. In the meantime we've made special arrangements to accommodate you for tonight and tomorrow," Bea continued. "I'm sure you've heard we're at capacity. You're really not supposed to be here."

If only this woman knew how true that is.

"I don't know why this Karen Upshaw," Bea said, reading the social worker's name on the form, "couldn't get you into Naylor Mission House or the McCaffrey Dorms." She ended her mini-tirade with an accepting sigh. "Well, you're here now, so we'll make the best of it."

By Bea's reaction it seemed as if Zoie had already broken one of the Shelter's rules. A part of her wanted to thank the woman for making the special accommodations. A thank-you might smooth things over and limit further friction. The last thing Zoie needed was additional scrutiny. Part of her wanted to address the woman's condescending attitude. After all, this was no way to treat a person who was supposed to be a needy soul from the street—the operative words being *supposed to be.* So Zoie kept her mouth shut.

Having let off some steam, Bea let her features soften. She gave Zoie a yellow sheet outlining the rules for the women's section—twenty dos and don'ts in all.

Zoie skimmed the sheet. There were expected things: rules forbidding alcohol or drug use and restricting smoking to a designated area. Other rules governed residents' comings and goings, imposing a 9:00 p.m. curfew. If a female resident didn't return to the women's section by the curfew, she'd be locked out for the night. And then there was the rule requiring an escort when passing through the men's section. One rule addressed starting a job search within forty-eight hours, and another one required that residents meet regularly with designated social workers. Zoie planned to skirt most of the rules. With Maynard's help she planned to be gone in less than twenty-four hours.

"You have a designated locker in the hall," Bea said, handing Zoie a key on a hot-pink plastic key chain. "Our in-house social worker is here every day—from nine to one in the afternoon and from seven to nine in the evening. I know you have a contact at DC's Social Services, but we'd like to help as well. For now, perhaps you'd like to shower and change into some fresh clothes and then get a bite to eat."

"But what I'm wearing is all I have," Zoie said, looking down at the worn sweat suit. "I had to run for my life. This is it." Zoie raised her small white bag to punctuate her point.

"Guess you don't have much…poor thing. Let's see if we can find you something clean to wear." It seemed that Bea finally got it: Anna was destitute.

Zoie followed Bea down the hall, passing a few ladies on the way. Zoie figured that these women were residents because they lacked name tags. They bore no resemblance to stereotypical homeless people. But they all looked drained.

Bea guided Zoie into a room arranged as a giant clothes closet, one complete with double racks of clothing sorted by size. Zoie wasn't sure whether she was supposed to look through the stuff or what. After a moment of hesitation, she stepped inside the door and began flipping through items on the rack labeled Petite. The clothes were secondhand, clean, and in good condition. The rack labeled Petite had the fewest selections. When Bea moved over to the racks, Zoie stepped aside.

"These will probably fit you," Bea said, handing Zoie a pair of size 6-P jeans and a rose-pink sleeveless blouse. A moment later she added some baggy black pajamas and a package of new panties to the garments cradled in Zoie's arms.

Bea then gave Zoie some toiletries wrapped in lilac cellophane, the whole package looking like an Easter basket. There was soap, a toothbrush, travel-size toothpaste, mouthwash, deodorant, and tissues. A label identified the basket as a gift from the ladies of St. Luke's Parish. Zoie's arms were full, but that didn't stop Bea from adding a fluffy white towel to the pile.

"There!" said Bea with a sense of satisfaction. "You can launder that thing you're wearing or just ditch it. These clothes should get you through the next twenty-four hours. After that we'll have to see if we can find more things that fit you."

Zoie managed a thank-you. Yes, twenty-four hours was all she needed.

CHAPTER 40

PEEK-A-BOO

Zoie waited at the door of her assigned dorm room while Bea talked to a volunteer in the hall. Whether she would actually spend the entire night in the room remained to be seen. The sooner she discovered the "thing" she'd come to find, the better off she would be. The truth was that she didn't know what exactly she was looking for, other than evidence about who killed Ray and the Shelter's financial fraud. And if what she uncovered brought down Jahi, then so be it.

As she waited on Bea, her heart thumped. She was operating out of her comfort zone, in which she typically applied left-brain analyses using facts and the law. Now she had to rely on her gut and the counsel of two homeless men—one who spoke in parables and one who was easily offended and often succumbed to enigmatic rambling. She took a deep breath.

While Bea continued to chat, Zoie surveyed her new quarters. The room had been set up like the ones she'd seen while touring the men's section. The basic sleeping arrangements for four consisted of two metal bunk beds. Unlike the men's rooms, this room had a softer feel. The walls were beige instead of institutional green. And there were other small personal touches. A magnet affixed to one of the bed frames read Praise God, and a string of paper butterflies was wrapped around one of the other posts. There were stuffed animals and magazines, both of which gave the room the feel of a college dorm. Because the place was an interim-stay facility, personal touches were permitted.

Her chat finished, Bea pushed past Zoie and into the room, heading to a narrow cot placed horizontally against the far wall. "Anna, this is yours for now," Bea said, patting the cot's thin mattress. It was made up with fresh white sheets, a peach-colored blanket, and a pillow so flat that it looked as if it could've been a Sunday issue of *The Washington Post* covered by a pillowcase.

The powers that be had placed Anna's special cot against the room's only free wall, under the window. It was a fifth sleeping place in a room meant for four. Zoie viewed the cot's placement with some apprehension. Whoever occupied the lower bunk nearest to Zoie's pillow could actually kick her in the head.

"It's a squeeze, but for now it's the best we can do," Bea said, sighing, seemingly understanding Zoie's unspoken concern. "This is very temporary. In two days you'll end up in Martha's top bunk." She patted the tight cover of the upper bunk. "That is, unless your roommates agree to switch around."

"Thanks," said Zoie, placing her clothing and toiletries on her assigned cot.

"The showers are down the hall and to the right. There's an Internet corner with three computers in the dayroom and a payphone in the booth next to it. Well, that's all I can think of right now," Bea said, checking off things on an imaginary list in the palm of her hand. "The rest about the laundry and rules for watching TV are on that paper I gave you. I'll see if I can find one of your roommates to show you around. I'll leave you to get settled."

"Thank you," Zoie said. As Bea made her exit, Zoie followed her to the door and watched her disappear back down the hall.

Alone in the room, Zoie looked to the window above her cot. Her heart slowed with Bea's exit. *Great,* she thought, moving quickly to check the view from the window. She pushed back the window's translucent curtain to discover a layered arrangement: blinds and then grimy glass and then a formidable set of iron bars on the outside. The bars had probably been installed to protect the women. Considering the sordid- and seedy-looking characters dwelling right next door, the extra precautions were warranted. But while keeping the criminals out, the bars easily trapped the women inside. *Note to self: if you need to exit this place quickly, don't plan to use this window.*

Through the hazed glass and bars, she saw Mahali's inner courtyard. The courtyard was a large expanse marked by two loading docks. It was the opposite view of what she'd seen from Jahi's office. It meant that Jahi's office had to be one of the windows directly across the yard.

This was the courtyard where Maynard planned to signal her with the flashlight, where they planned to meet so that Maynard could show her the "secret place." Deep down she had to believe that she was being led to the evidence she needed.

The courtyard was quiet. The Shelter's white van was parked next to two other nondescript vehicles. She let the curtain swing back, and it blocked out the early evening light. Her rendezvous with Maynard was hours away; she hoped that everyone would be asleep. She'd have to stage a vigil to watch for his signal. There would be no dozing for her weary eyes.

Zoie wanted to get out of her musty sweat suit and into the clean clothes. She also needed food. Until now fear and the adrenalin it produced had sustained her. Food smells were coming from somewhere in the Shelter. Her stomach reacted with an involuntary groan. Perhaps she could get a meal before embarking on her quest.

She was about to close the dorm room's door, wanting some privacy while she undressed, when she remembered one of the rules from her quick scan of the rules sheet—"Closed dorm doors not allowed." Compromising, she left the door ajar.

Zoie fumbled through the gift basket, but all the while her mind wandered to her night challenge. Her rendezvous spot with Maynard was right outside her window—an impenetrable window. How would she get outside?

She pulled back the curtain for another look at the courtyard, her eyes searching for a door. There had to be one on the loading dock. The building was large, so there should be multiple exits. The building enclosed the courtyard, except for one driveway leading out. From that window her view of the courtyard was limited, so she couldn't be sure. Many windows faced the courtyard, but all were shielded with bars. To the right she saw steps leading from the courtyard's concrete ground to the loading dock on her side of the building. The steps ended at a chain-link cage of sorts. The arrangement didn't make sense, at least from her partial view. On the loading dock, her eyes scanned past stacked crates, a load of new lumber, and bright-blue tarps in a bunch. Next to the van, two dumpsters overflowed with garbage bags.

"Bingo," Zoie said as her eyes landed on a set of double doors off the second loading dock. She'd almost missed the doors because their mahogany color blended with the building's rustic brick. Unfortunately, the doors were likely accessed from the men's side. "There must be a way to get out there from this part of the building," she said. "I've got to find a way to get back there. Maynard, you better deliver."

"You got a boyfriend over there?" said a voice behind her.

Startled, Zoie quickly turned to find a willowy young woman standing in the completely open door. Zoie had been so focused on finding a way into the courtyard that she'd let the girl sneak up on her. How long had the girl been standing there and watching her? Had she heard Zoie's commentary on the courtyard?

The young woman looked as if she'd just come from a throwback dress rehearsal for *I Dream of Jeanie*. Her red shorts hung low on her narrow hips. A shiny white halter exposed her long, lean midriff and a navel ring. Her hair was pulled into a tight bun on her head, and her ears bore enormous gold hoops that seemed painful to bear. It was difficult to gauge her age. She was a woman yet a girl who couldn't have been much older than twenty-two. The fist-sized bruise on her left cheek gave her a hard edge, dampening her genie magic.

"What's up? You seem pretty interested in what's across the way," the young woman said with a sarcastic DC drawl. With her arms folded, she leaned into the doorframe. Zoie wondered how long she'd been standing there. "The men's dorms are over there. Don't worry. They stay on their side, and we stay on ours."

"Yeah. And that's a good thing," Zoie finally responded. She was glad that the young woman had dropped the boyfriend theme.

"Have you seen some of those creeps?" the young woman asked, squinting for emphasis.

Zoie's eyes widened. "Uh-huh. Last night in the park...a couple of creeps chased me." She wondered whether the young woman had heard her mention Maynard. Thank goodness that the line of conversation continued to drift elsewhere.

"Well, you're safe here. I've had my own run in with freaks," said the young woman, her tone matter of fact. She gingerly touched her bruised cheek and winced.

"Ooh, that looks nasty. Are you okay?" asked Zoie

"Yeah. It happened a few days ago. It was a lot worse."

Zoie noticed more bruises on the young woman's arms. "Who did that to you?"

The young woman hesitated. "Rico, my pimp. Humph. I should be saying that the muthafucka *was* my pimp." She snorted. "Those days are over. He don't own me no more."

"Oh," said Zoie.

The woman's tight bun and chiseled cheekbones accentuated her hard look, not to mention that she'd just identified herself as a hooker. Or was it as a former hooker?

"So you're the one they're squeezing in," said the young woman, straightening up to her full height and finally entering the room. She flopped on a lower bunk.

Zoie was going to respond to the "squeezing" comment but didn't get a chance.

"Hey, don't get all defensive. It's not a problem with me. Ain't like we pay rent here."

"You like it here?" asked Zoie, no longer wanting to stare at the woman. She went back to sorting the things on her cot, looking for the thin cloth robe she'd been given.

"It's not the Hilton, but it beats the streets. Anyway, I'm Jasmine. Folks call me Jazz, like the music. This is my bunk." She patted the sleeping place where she was sitting. There were a pile of magazines and a small stuffed bear, brown with a pink ribbon that read Hot Mama. "Cruz sleeps on the top here. She's still at work," Jazz continued. "And Martha and Tanisha are over there," she said, pointing.

"I'm Anna," said Zoie, extending her hand with businesslike etiquette.

At first the offer of a hand seemed to rattle the girl. She stared at Zoie's outstretched hand, seemingly clueless about how to respond. It was an awkward moment. But then she sat straight up and moved closer, reciprocating with a firm handshake. "Bea sent me to show you around."

"Thanks," said Zoie, "but do you mind if I change and shower first? I've been in these same clothes for several hot, sweaty days."

The lie rolled smoothly from Zoie's tongue. It had only been a few hours since Zoie's transformation into Anna, the homeless girl, but somehow it seemed much longer.

"No problem," Jazz replied. "Peeuuuw! Yeah, girl, go ahead and wash. Don't you hate it when you can smell your own crotch?"

"Yeah," replied Zoie with a cringe. Disgusted by the last comment, she now more than ever wanted the shower. She could only imagine what other horrific and uncomfortable things Jazz liked to talk about.

Zoie thought her request for time to change and shower had been a not-too-subtle request for privacy. She expected Jazz to go away and come back. But Jazz had other ideas. The young woman settled on her bunk, her legs crossed. She pulled a magazine from her pile and thumbed through it with her eyes alternating between the magazine pages and Zoie.

No time for modesty today. Moving quickly, Zoie proceeded to undress.

"Hey, nice undies you got there. Ooh, it's a matching set." Jazz's eyes were now firmly fixed on Zoie.

Ooops!

"They look expensive. You bought those undies living on the street?"

Immediately Zoie was aware of the faux pas in her undercover get-up. Her deep rose-pink satin bra and matching lace boyshort panties were none other than Calvin Klein. Her weakness for high-quality underwear, the designer stuff, was only second to her weakness for expensive shoes.

"Yeah, I like nice things...when I get the money," Zoie responded, trying to find her own hard edge, as she quickly slipped into the thin robe to cover up her faux pas and head to the showers with her new soap and towel. "I haven't always been on the street."

It took only an instant. Jazz spotted Zoie's Blackberry. The device had wormed its way out of the jacket pocket on Zoie's sweat suit. Now it lay on the cot in plain sight. Jazz sprang from her cross-legged position and grabbed it.

"Hey! Look at this! An expensive phone too. Bet you need to keep in touch with customers," Jazz said, inspecting it. "I need one of these."

Zoie snatched the phone from Jazz, surprising herself and leaving Jazz in shock. "Sorry—this is not for sharing," Zoie said, clinging to her phone. This little episode meant that she would have to keep the phone locked away in her assigned locker.

"Hmm," Jazz said. Her eyes narrowed. "Okay, be that way." She backed away and glared back at Zoie. "Check you out. Pricey undies. Nice new phone. I want me a phone like that, except with rhinestones." She settled back on her bunk, put a finger to her mouth, and gave Zoie a once-over. "You know...somethin' ain't right with this picture. Hmm. You ain't no ordinary homeless person."

Zoie choked. It had taken this true street person a matter of minutes to figure out that she wasn't authentic. "What's ordinary? Homelessness can happen to anybody."

"Yeah, you right about that. Everybody had a mother at one time or another, even if that ain't true now. Hmm. I'm guessing you're 'anybody' is either a drug dealer or a hooker, like me. No track marks, no bruises."

Zoie had to think fast. But this girl seemed to be doing all the thinking for her. She decided to play along. "You may be right."

"Then I'm guessing it's a hooker. Huh, I should know. Drug dealers don't wind up in places like this. Neither do hookers... unless they're running from something or somebody."

"No, I'm just down on my luck. I didn't put enough away for a rainy day. But I'll get back on my feet. In the meantime I can't lose my contacts."

"So you're one of the prissy-appointment kind. Independent, huh?" Leaning back on her elbows, Jazz was smiling a twisted smile, seemingly pleased that she'd guessed correctly about Zoie's identity. She gave Zoie another once-over. "You're like one of those escorts or a call girl. You sure ain't been out on Fourteenth Street. Hey! If you were walking those streets or anywhere near there—shit—I'd have seen you."

Zoie couldn't believe she was letting this girl concoct Anna's backstory. But so far it was working. She needed friends, not enemies, in this place. Being too coy about a made-up past could sabotage her plans, and she really didn't want to tangle with Jazz. Undoubtedly, Jazz knew her way around the Shelter, which meant she knew how to get into the courtyard.

"You can give it whatever fancy name you like," Zoie said. "My tricks paid pretty well." Zoie surprised herself: "tricks" had rolled off her tongue as if it were part of her everyday vocabulary. She only knew the word in the context of a movie. She clung to the towel and held the robe closed as she continued to work the new theme. "For a while I was sick. I couldn't work. When I couldn't pay my bills, my butt was put out on the street."

"You done let yourself go," Jazz said, continuing to look her over. "You got to keep up your looks. Ain't nobody gonna pay big bucks for that.

In light of Jazz's critique of her appearance, Zoie looked down at herself. *Well, at least the disguise is still working.*

"Why didn't you ask one of your customers for some cash? An advance payment." Jazz asked. "Didn't you have a special John, someone who always comes back and gives you something extra?"

"Yeah, but I was trying to be independent, to not be beholden to any man. If they give, they want something in return. They think they own you. I didn't want anyone to own me."

"I know that feeling. I want to be independent too. Bet you advertised on Craigslist. Rico paid my bills, kept a roof over my head, and kept the money I made. That mutha' got all the nookie he wanted free of charge. Then he'd slap me around if I said I needed a bigger allowance. One day I opened my big mouth and said something about going independent. That muthafucka went crazy! But that didn't even matter. I didn't even have to say something like that to get him going, 'cause he'd rough me up just for the hell of it. That muthafucka is an ignorant fool! He didn't even mind that after he beat me, I was too messed up to work. Laid me up with my face all swollen and my ribs hurting. Then I saw the 'writing on the wall.' Took a while, but I 'smelled the coffee.' The rest of his girls kept getting younger and younger—fifteen, fourteen, thirteen. Soon he'll be running twelve-year-olds. Baby bitches. He said his 'bidniz' model was changing." She sucked her teeth in disgust. "What the fuck was that about? I wasn't pretty enough to work the hotel bars. I had to stay out on the street corner, freezing my ass off. He said I was a bad influence on the young ones 'cause I was always asking for stuff." She took a deep breath. "Yeah, I ran away more than once. I've been here three times. Last time I ran away, he texted me." She imitated Rico: "'Baby, you know your Rico misses you. Come on home.' After he banged me up this last time, I left. He ain't sent me no texts to come back 'cause he turned off my phone service. It's like he don't want me back. It's like he throwed me away." She sniffed. "How you like that? Good thing 'cause I don't want to be beholden to no man like that no more."

Zoie was stunned. She couldn't believe that this girl had just poured out her heart after their having just met each other. Jazz's eyes were watery, but there were no tears. Zoie truly felt for the girl. The girl had been used up and disposed of like a broken-down racehorse. Zoie had never heard of pimps putting girls out to pasture at age twenty-two or any age, for that matter, but she guessed that it happened. What was the pimpdom business model? Up or out like the military or the corporate world? No benefits, no retirement. Perhaps Jazz hadn't been cooperative enough to manage the other girls. As tough as life had been for Jazz, it was clear that it had to come to this for her to give it up. A whole other world was out there for her. She just didn't know it.

"Jazz, I'm so sorry. You'll be okay."

Jazz bowed her head and held her stomach.

"Look, I'm headed to the shower. When I come back, we'll talk some more."

Dressed in the one-size-fits-all robe and ultrathin flip-flops, Zoie headed for the showers. Luckily the bathroom was close. On her way she stopped by her assigned locker, deposited her phone inside, and made a mental note: *Remember to get the phone on the way out.*

Alone in the long, narrow bathroom, which had five square sinks and three shower stalls, Zoie had a bit of privacy. She hung her robe and towel on a nearby hook and took the fastest shower she'd ever taken. The warm water felt good as it ran down her body. She was careful to not let the force of the water ruin her matted hairdo, a Lena special. A certain grunge was a necessary part of her disguise.

She couldn't imagine that anyone would recognize her. She hadn't had any interaction with the women's side of the Shelter. Still...it was possible. Someone like Sister Te—the "Dragon Queen"—could be lurking. After all, earlier in the day, they'd locked eyes for several horrible seconds. But so far there had been no Sister Te sightings.

Zoie returned to the room. Jazz hadn't budged from her bunk. Deep in thought the young woman didn't acknowledge Zoie's return. Zoie decided to not interrupt the young woman's meditation. Zoie quickly dressed in her newly acquired hand-me-downs and replaced the paper-thin slides with Lena's holey sneakers. Jazz emerged from her trance and looked up. Her expression was serious. "Hey, Anna. I've had this idea for a long time."

"Oh, what's that?" Zoie responded while folding her towel.

"There's this guy I know."

"Yeah."

"He's not a pimp or anything." An excitement had entered Jazz's voice. "He said he'd set up a website for me. You know, one of those Internet sites where the Johns can use their credit cards and pay to watch me do nasty stuff."

"The Internet?"

"Yeah, like my own private sex channel." Jazz rested on her elbows with her legs dangling over the side of her bunk. "You've seen Internet sex stuff, haven't you?"

"Yeah, what about it?" Actually Zoie did know about the online sex trade and not just from TV reports. At Fairday and Winston, she'd reviewed a number of cases for a client who caught its employees using the company's computers to access such sites. The company's policy for such violations was pretty cut and dry—immediate dismissal. That company, as well as others, was well within its rights to restrict usage of its computing resources and misuse of company-paid time. Nevertheless, the company wanted a final legal review prior to its planned mass firing of forty-five of its employees.

"Well, what do you think? No touching. Just watching. No pimp. No stinking beer-belly hogs lying on you, crushing you. They be all sweaty and stinky. No worrying about catching God knows what or getting beat up. What do you think?"

How sad. Hooker's paradise—the Internet. Her tech person will surely take his cut and end up controlling the whole thing. Just another sort of pimp. This young woman's dream was to graduate from being a pimp-sponsored streetwalker to being a self-employed "Internet ho." Jazz might have been on the streets for years. Internet sex was her way indoors.

"Well, what do you think?" Jazz asked for the third time.

What would Anna, now deemed an independent hooker, say? Zoie had to be careful with her response. No bursting Jazz's bubble. She started her answer slowly. "Let me see. No stinky bodies, rough hands, beard burns, hands grabbing here and there, and catching those diseases."

"So?"

"Sounds as if you got yourself a plan."

Anna's approval was what Jazz wanted to hear. "You got that right!" Jazz beamed, wincing as her bruised cheek morphed as part of a large smile. "Hey, maybe we could do this thing together. You know, be available for twelve hours of airtime. Get a nice apartment. Nice clothes. Nice *undies*." She giggled.

Zoie found herself giggling along with Jazz for very different reasons. The thought of participating in an online sex show was such a stretch that she actually blushed. Never in her wildest dreams had the concept occurred to her. "Hooking without really hooking, huh?"

"Girl, you got it!" Jazz's eyes shined at the prospect of the collaboration. "Hey, if you hurry up, I'll show you around this place. Then we got lots of stuff to work out. Girl, you know I'm serious. We can be partners. In the meantime don't say nothin' to nobody about this. This got to be our secret. Just between you and me, right?"

"Right. And what I was doing prior to coming here has to be on the down-low. Right?"

"Hey, don't have to worry about me. Tell you one thing, though: later we got to fix you up. That hair thing you got goin' ain't gonna do nothin' for a camera."

CHAPTER 41

PEACH COBBLER

Hand in hand and with Jazz in the lead, the two women made their way down the narrow hall, as other women squeezed passed. Zoie could've pulled away from Jazz, but she decided to let the bonding thing happen. She needed the younger woman's help as a guide to the ins and outs of the Shelter. Still, Zoie wondered how, when the time came, she'd detach from her new *best bud*—Jazz.

The aroma of food grabbed Zoie's attention again, calling to her from farther down the hall. Her stomach's primal consciousness responded with more growls.

"Listen, Jazz—before we go farther, show me where I can get something to eat."

"Been without for a while, huh? I heard that tummy." Jazz laughed. "Don't worry. We're headed to plenty of food. I don't think this place really helps people find places to live, but they sure feed you."

Like the men's section, the women's side of the building was a maze. But Jazz knew the place. After a series of turns, they arrived at what Jazz called the Great Room, where a group of women congregated. They were young and old, comprising different sizes and different hues.

The large open space was divided into activity areas. In one area three large sofas formed a U-shaped grouping, where the women focused on a large-screen TV. They were glued to a sitcom, complete with a 1970s laugh track. In another tighter space, three rectangular tables with computer monitors formed what Jazz described as the computer center. Two computers were in use, their users facing a wall filled with notices. The TV's irritating synthetic laughter didn't seem to bother the women, who were focused on the computer screens.

"You got to sign up to use the computers," Jazz explained. There's a thirty-minute limit. Most days there's no problem if you run over, unless somebody's waiting."

Of immediate interest to Zoie was the room's open kitchen, a space defined by a long gray counter on white laminate cabinetry. Two microwaves anchored one end of the counter, and a large coffee maker and an industrial-looking toaster oven filled the other end. A large refrigerator hid all but the wide rear end of a woman who was searching for something inside of it.

"That's Cruz, our roommate. I hope she found a place to move with her kids," Jazz said. Without being asked Jazz filled in the details of the plight of Cruz and her four children. No man in the picture, no job, and no available space at the family shelter. In family shelters they could have stayed together in a room or a small suite. Sometimes it meant staying in a motel room with a hot plate for a stove, paid for by DC Social Services. At least it beat the alternatives, like camping in the park or in the lobby of the Martin Luther King Library. This time the family options weren't possible, so Cruz and her kids were split up. Her kids went to two different foster homes, and Cruz was now at Mahali. "Cruz had to do it that way," Jazz explained. "She didn't want those kids living on the street."

"Mmm."

"You can buy your own stuff and put it in the fridge, except the only cooking we can do is in the microwave or that toaster oven. We don't have to cook anyway. Dinner's brought in about five thirty every day. We get cereal, bagels, or yogurt and fruit for breakfast and sandwiches and salads most days for lunch. Not too bad, huh?"

Zoie responded with a half-hearted smile.

Dinner had been brought in a while ago. Several women still hovered over the food in the large aluminum pans that lined two tables.

Zoie's stomach groaned again. "Where does the food come from?"

"The Shelter's main kitchen," Jazz answered. "You can go around to that dining room to eat. The entrance is on the side of the building. But down there you just gonna run into the creeps. The men *gotta* eat there. And most of them ain't too clean. So who wants to eat sitting next to them? Eating here's better."

So Hank's kitchen is cooking this food. For a moment Zoie considered going to the Shelter's dining room. But then she might run into Maynard there, who might just freak if he saw her. He wouldn't like that she had deviated from their planned rendezvous later that night. And if Hank was around, he might recognize her. But Hank wasn't supposed to be there at all. At least that's what she'd been told earlier in the day.

Then there was Jazz to consider. She wouldn't go for eating with the "creepy men." The trauma of Jazz's life on the street had clearly turned the young woman off to any direct contact with men. Behind the doors of the women's section and her being in front of an Internet camera while engaging in provocative activities were the only places where Jazz would feel safe.

"Plates and cups over there," Jazz said, pointing to a stack of Styrofoam dishes and plastic utensils.

The food was picked over. Still, there was plenty left: baked chicken, green beans, macaroni and cheese, corn on the cob, a tossed salad, rolls, and a half pan of peach cobbler. "Check this out." Jazz pointed to the cobbler with her fork. "Save room for that. We get the cobbler every few days. I think they're trying to make us fat."

Peach cobbler meant that Hank *was* around. During her tour of his kitchen, Zoie was told that only *he* knew the secret ingredients for his famous cobbler. Even if others did the prep work, only he added the special ingredients to his signature dish.

Damn!

Zoie took small portions of food from each pan. Jazz, on the other hand, piled her plate high. Zoie wondered how the tall slender woman could eat mass quantities and maintain her slim waist and toned tummy. At a picnic-style table, Jazz plopped down, across from Zoie.

Zoie counted fifteen other women in the great room. Other than Jazz, though, none of the women approached her. No greetings or welcomings. No hellos, byes, or anything similar. Other than the background noise of the TV at the other end of the room and the occasional whine of the microwave, there was no hum of conversation. Each woman seemed to dwell in her own world, oblivious to those around her. Zoie didn't want to explain her fictional life on the street, so other women's distancing themselves was for the best. Still, she found it strange. She asked Jazz, "Is everyone keeping to themselves, or is it just me?"

"Yeah, people keep to themselves," Jazz answered with her mouth full of food. "They want to keep their business private. Know what I mean? They'd rather be in their own places or wherever. It's bad enough you got to share a room."

"They're depressed?"

"Guess you could call it that. They're busy thinking about how they gonna find a place when their time here is up." Jazz put down a chicken bone and licked her fingers. "You don't stay here 'cause you love it."

Zoie understood, at least as much she could, having lived a relatively privileged life. From the moment she entered the place, she'd been both fearful and creeped out. Communal bathrooms, communal sleeping, and communal dining—all privacy was lost. Living in a shelter wasn't exactly a voluntary arrangement like being in a college dorm or at a summer camp. In those situations folks found new friends, romped, and frolicked. Jazz was right. No one wanted to be in a shelter.

"Of course you got your nosey folks. There's one or two around here. They'll talk to you until the sun comes up. Now them you gotta watch," Jazz said, raising her pinkie for emphasis.

The large clock on the wall over the computer area read a few minutes after seven. One of the volunteer women began covering the food pans with heavy aluminum, preparing to put those pans away. Zoie could tell that it was going to be a long evening. Remembering her ultimate goal, she scanned the room for a possible exit to the rear courtyard. There had to be an exit or some sort of escape route for safety reasons. The windowless Great Room made it difficult for Zoie to get her bearings with respect to the courtyard. The room was like the hub of a wheel, with the spokes being the four corridors leading away from it. Zoie knew what was down one of those corridors, since it was the one by which she and Jazz had entered the room.

As she finished her meal, chatty Jazz turned quiet. The initial excitement of recruiting a partner for her web-based sex business seemed to wane. "We still need to do some serious talking," Jazz whispered.

"Sure," Zoie answered, still playing along.

"We can talk later. Want a cigarette?" Jazz asked, producing a flat pink enamel cigarette case. It was half-full.

Zoie hesitated. She'd smoked a few times during the exam week of her last year of law school. Smoking calmed her nerves but later produced a headache. Now she detested smoky places, but she resisted the urge to pooh-pooh Jazz's offer. "So there's a place where we can smoke?"

"Sure. This place is strict, but even in jail you get to smoke." Jazz seemed to speak with authority about incarceration. She opened her cigarette case. "Go ahead; take one. There's a place to smoke we call the Pen. It's out on the loading dock. Come on—I'll show you."

Bingo. This is the way out—the way to the courtyard. "Yeah, I'll take one," Zoie said, taking a cigarette.

Jazz was about to close the case when Zoie put her hand over it. "Wait. May I have another one? One for now and another one for later."

"Hey, girl! You must think I'm the store or somethin'."

"Sorry. When I ran from the park, I had to leave all my stuff behind."

"So as my grandmother used to say, 'You ain't got a pot to piss in.'"

Zoie shrugged and smiled. Her grandmother used to say the same thing.

Jazz smiled back with a bit of a wince from her bruise. "No more parks or street corners for us. Right?"

Zoie nodded in agreement.

"Okay, then. Take two cigarettes. Take three. Just remember you owe me. And when you get your emergency check, remember it's Salem Ultra Lights."

Zoie took another cigarette. A plan had percolated in her head. Once she knew how to get to the outside smoking area, the second cigarette would serve as her excuse to go outside later that night. She rolled her extra cigarette in a napkin and put it in her pocket and held the other in her hand.

While disposing the remains of their dinner, someone caught Jazz's eye. "See that woman?" she said, directing Zoie's attention to a thin brown-skinned woman with a stately air, who'd just entered the room. "That's Sister Te. She runs the place."

Ugh! Just my luck. It was the woman from Zoie's earlier ugly encounter in the Shelter's lobby. It was Jahi's ex and Tarik's mother. In the distance Zoie could see Sister Te's chiseled cheeks. She was a haughty beauty with an air of the exotic and an air of all business. *So this is Jahi's type.* Zoie felt no jealousy. Like a week-old bouquet of flowers, her feelings for Jahi were dying at the rate of a bloom an hour. Now all she felt was anger and disgust. As Sister Te moved in their direction, Zoie looked away.

"Do you have food left?" Sister Te asked the volunteer who had placed a final pan onto a stainless-steel cart.

"Sure, and peach cobbler," answered the volunteer. "The ladies aren't that hungry today."

Sister Te took a Styrofoam plate from the stack and crouched effortlessly in her tight jeans to peek under the aluminum lids.

"Come on. I'm gonna introduce you," Jazz said, grabbing Zoie's arm.

"That's okay," Zoie said, holding back. "I'll meet her later... maybe after we have a smoke."

"We got to do it now. She ain't gonna be around later. Come on. She's a good one to know. She'll help you get your emergency cash."

"Oh," said Zoie, taking a deep breath. *Here goes nothing.*

They went to stand near Sister Te, who had found a piece of chicken and was now chatting with two of the residents. She turned to Jazz. "Hello, Jazz," Sister Te said. "Who's your friend?"

"This here is Anna."

"Welcome to the women's section of the Shelter, Anna. I'm Makeda Tesfaneshe, one of the Shelter's directors, but everyone calls me Sister Te." Her accent was faint. Strangely, she didn't offer a hand, though only one hand held her plate. Perhaps her free hand had touched the greasy chicken. "You're the one who arrived today, aren't you?"

"Yes, "Zoie replied, keeping her voice low. She didn't look directly at the woman, but she could feel Sister Te give her a once-over. Zoie knew that if she locked eyes with those evil eyes, she'd be recognized.

"Yes, Bea told me about your situation," Sister Te said. "I guess you know we're at capacity. Under these circumstances you're fortunate to be here."

"I know," Zoie replied flatly. "Thanks for making a place for me."

"Have you stayed here before? I never forget a face. Hmm. There's something familiar about you."

"No. I've never been homeless."

"Well, don't despair, dear. Homelessness can happen to anyone. It's nothing to be ashamed of. It's what you do with the opportunities to improve your situation that counts. Let's see how we can help you." Then Sister Te directed her attention back to Jazz. "And how many times have *you* stayed here?"

"Three," replied Jazz soberly.

"Hmm. I think it's more like four. And this will be the last time, right?"

Jazz shrugged.

"We've got to find you a permanent, safe situation. Right?"

"From your mouth to God's ears," Jazz answered.

"Anna, we'll talk some more tomorrow. I'm glad Jazz is helping you get settled."

Sister Te walked away, stopping briefly to speak with a few residents as she exited the Great Room. When she disappeared down the hall, Zoie was relieved. Though Sister Te had failed to recognize her, the woman was clearly suspicious. Soon this woman would recall their prior meeting. Surely Tarik had told his mother that the woman she'd collided with near the reception desk was the brash lawyer from the Crayton Foundation, who was in search of Jahi.

But the infamous Sister Te didn't seem like the monster Zoie had imagined. Those eyes that had met hers earlier in the day were intimidating. A monster? Sister Te had an air of authority, even dominance. But making her a monster was a stretch. Still, she couldn't envision Jahi romantically connected to this woman. But then she couldn't envision a lot about Jahi. How could she have been so wrong about him?

Jazz guided Zoie through a door next to the computer center. Zoie spotted the door when her eyes originally scanned the Great Room. But since there was no exit sign, she believed the door to be a closet. Jazz led her down a short poorly lit hall and past a crowded storage area complete with windows. The final door to the outside *did* have an exit sign. When she passed through that door, the hot evening air hit Zoie in the face in the form of a puff of smoke. The sun had just dipped behind the tall trees leading out of the courtyard, but there was still plenty of daylight. Two women finishing their smokes leaned on the brick wall. They introduced themselves as Beverly and Janet. Jazz seemed to know them but was strangely quiet until they left.

The Pen, as it was called, was an approximate thirty-by-twelve-foot chain-link enclosure situated on the loading dock. It was built like a cage; one side consisted of the Shelter's brick wall, and the other sides, including the high ceiling, were formed by heavy chain link. At one time, perhaps, it had served as secure outdoor storage. Now it served the women of the Shelter as their protected smoking area.

Surely no one could get in or out of the Pen without either going back through the Shelter or leaving through its chain-link door. That door, which led to the steps and the courtyard floor, was shut and probably locked. One could always cut through chain links with special tools, but that would require a local hardware store and a man with muscle. Zoie wondered how, when the time came, she would make it out to meet Maynard. Jazz offered her a light.

Zoie took a drag but avoided inhaling. Somehow she managed not to choke. Leaning against the brick wall, Jazz gazed at the sky as if she were dreaming. Then she just began to talk. She'd been thinking a lot about this online sex business. Her ideas flowed like a stream of consciousness: the use of PayPal, Craigslist, and cameras that allowed for interaction with the customers. Naughty video chats. Jazz knew about all this from her techie customer, the one who would set up the operation and maintain it. Zoie wanted to ask what percentage of the business this tech guy wanted. Then she thought better of bringing up the money end.

Jazz kept rapping to the sky about the whole deal. Zoie grunted a few agreements but listened with half an ear. Her mind was focused on her most immediate problem: how to get out of the Pen and down to the courtyard.

In the courtyard the two older-make cars were still parked, along with the Shelter's van. In the latest annual report of the Shelter, the van was supposed to be a recently purchased and "gently used" model. In contrast, this van had indeed endured a hard life, riddled with dings and tires that looked rounded by road wear. In the courtyard off the far end of the Pen, an insect swarm hovered in the last beam of sunlight, above the overflowing garbage dumpster. Zoie was glad that the insects seemed content on their side of the chain link.

While Jazz was preoccupied puffing on her cigarette and chatting at the sky, Zoie decided to verify her assumptions about her escape options. Nonchalantly she moved to the chain-link door and applied downward pressure on the lever-style handle. As she suspected, the door was locked. It needed a key to open it.

"Hey! What are you doing?" Jazz asked, waking from her reverie.

"I just wanted to make sure it was locked," Zoie replied, moving away from the door.

"Yeah, they better keep it locked. Sometimes you can see those creeps from the men's side out here. One time one of those freaks came up and stuck his finger through this hole." Jazz demonstrated by sticking her finger through the chain-link fence. "He said, 'Give me a cigarette, sweet cheeks, and I'll give you some of this.' Then he shook his dick at me."

"Were you scared?"

"Yeah! I was out here by myself. But don't worry. They keep it locked. They can't get in."

"Good," replied Zoie. *And we can't get out.*

CHAPTER 42

I SEE THE LIGHT

With no more Sister Te encounters, the rest of the evening at the Shelter was without incident. And with Jazz glued to Zoie's side, the other women at the Shelter kept their distance. It was as if Jazz was a Shelter enforcer who'd claimed Zoie as her personal charge. Theirs was certainly an odd relationship, one that Zoie found no reason to challenge.

The Great Room's TV was tuned in to a marathon airing of the housewives of some city or another. Zoie settled down to watch the program from a second-tier chair behind the couch. The ever-present Jazz was beside her. Though Zoie's eyes were directed at the screen, her mind was focused on her plans for later that night, when hopefully the other women would be asleep. She found it ironic that the Shelter residents enjoyed a show about self-absorbed women living in mini-mansions. No matter the situation, hope for a better life reigned eternal.

In a half-lucid moment, Zoie promised to let Jazz give her a makeup job and style her hair. She agreed to the makeover so that the young woman would cease pestering her about fixing the "mess" that was her hair. Little did Jazz know that Zoie was counting on not being around for the grand makeover.

Zoie was beginning to feel guilty about lying to Jazz. She truly liked the young woman, even though she considered her plans for a future career in online sex misguided, at best. Jazz was looking for a friend, and Zoie momentarily filled the need. Hence a one-sided bond was established, creating a relationship that far exceeded Zoie's expectations. Earlier in the Pen, Jazz shared the intimate details of her previous life. Zoie listened in horror as the young woman revealed her abusive past: How she escaped an incestuous relationship with her father, which started when she was six. How her mother eventually rejected her, choosing to believe the husband rather than the daughter. How, after leaving home at thirteen, she ended up in the clutches of yet another abusive man. Now, many years later, Jazz had broken ties with her pimp. However, exactly who'd broken up with whom was a bit murky.

Most of the folks in Jazz's life had betrayed and misused her. While the women in the picture were not without fault, the main culprits had been men. It was no wonder that Jazz feared men. Why Jazz seemed to trust this technical wiz, who promised to help with the porn site, Zoie couldn't fathom. If Jazz had her way, no man would ever touch her again. In her vision for a new life, sex would still serve as her meal ticket, relegated to a contained fantasy, a virtual service to excite men from a protected distance— thanks to technology. After what Jazz had been through, who could blame her? Jazz's miseries made Zoie's own mishaps with men seem trivial. When Jazz finished her disturbing account of life, Zoie hugged her and promised a brighter future for both of them.

Now Zoie was about to be the next one to betray the young woman. Jazz was both brave and naïve to open up her painful life to a stranger. Zoie, however, had her own serious troubles. *Her* life and the lives of her loved ones were being threatened. Ending that threat was the reason she'd come to the Shelter.

Unfortunately, the young woman had become emotionally attached to her. Learning that Zoie had used her would be another cut in Jazz's already-scarred life. Zoie hugged Jazz and whispered promises of a better life, but all the while she was thinking of the coming betrayal.

Sorry, Jazz.

⚜

It was tight in Zoie's assigned dorm room, with five women and the extra cot. After checking the situation, she and Jazz stayed in the Great Room until the others were in their bunks before returning to the room.

"Cruz found a shelter that takes families. Now she can be with her kids," Jazz told Zoie. "She'll be gone tomorrow."

So will I, Zoie thought.

In the tight room, the women talked for a while about their day, the Shelter's new social worker, and the oppressive heat outside. "Thank God this place is air conditioned," said one of the women. None of the conversations were deep or soul searching. It was as if discussions of prospects for permanent housing were verboten. Usually inquisitive, Zoie kept quiet. The other women reciprocated by not asking their newest roommate any questions about how long she'd been on the streets or what had happened to put her there in the first place. No one even asked whether she had kids. Perhaps those questions were topics for the morning. Discussing life's next steps required energy. Now they were all tired.

According to the Shelter's rules, the dorm's lights were to be out at 10:30 p.m. The women drifted off to sleep seemingly glad for the silence and the sense of solitude in the tight space. Only Jazz stayed awake, flipping through her celebrity magazines, aided by a clip-on book light. In the silence she mouthed the song being piped into her head through her earbuds.

An air-conditioner vent was right above Zoie's cot. Still dressed in her latest street duds, Zoie pulled her covers up to her neck as a shield against the draft. At least the cold would help her stay awake. She didn't know how long she'd have to wait for Maynard's signal. If the signal came before she was free to look into the courtyard, she might miss it. After all, Jazz was still awake. Then again, Maynard's signal might be hours away. She'd just have to remain vigilant through the night. For a moment Zoie thought that crazy Maynard might not come through. Dismissing the thought as defeatist, she hoped that Jazz would soon join the others in slumberland.

Zoie detected a soft snore coming from Jazz's bunk.

Finally!

Jazz's book light fell to the side. Both the light and the attached magazine hung precariously on the edge of the bunk, the light illuminating the floor. Jazz, unaware, rolled to her side and faced the wall. Zoie sat up in her cot and checked the status of each of her other dorm mates. She could only see lumps under blankets in the two top bunks, and the woman who occupied the lower bunk opposite to Jazz had been asleep for a couple of hours. Erratic sleep sounds were coming from the four bunks. Zoie played mind games with the snoring sounds. Each sound was different in intensity and rhythm. Amazingly, the sounds didn't collide. Concentrating on the snoring was enough to keep her awake.

Assured that her roommates were asleep, Zoie pulled back the curtain to peer through the blinds. With the dark room behind her and the courtyard lit by the moon and lights beyond, things looked clearer. A few lights shone in the men's section. Directly across the yard, a light was on in what she thought to be Jahi's office. In that window a large male figure paced back and forth with what looked to be a phone to his ear. The head of dreadlocks was unmistakable.

Jahi!

Zoie felt a new anxiety. Though she hadn't completely removed Jahi from her mind, somehow she'd nullified him as a distraction and relegated him to neither good nor evil. A nothing. Unable to affect her. *Or so she thought.* She hadn't expected to see him. Now, even with the distance of the courtyard and the cover of the dark separating them, she was chilled. His being at the Shelter could be a complication. His presence was more likely to hurt her than to help. She'd hoped he would be gone. Perhaps he'd returned her many calls. She'd find out when she retrieved her phone from the locker. Mesmerized, she watched as Jahi continued to pace unaware that she was watching from across the courtyard. He finally sat, putting his back to the window and his feet on his desk.

What now? She had to recalibrate.

Zoie drew back from the window, leaving Jahi and whatever he was up to for someone else to watch. She got up and turned off Jazz's book light and then put it and the magazine at the foot of the young woman's bunk. The room's red night-light provided enough light to navigate the room. Back in her cot, Zoie buried her face in her blanket and let silent tears stream down her cheeks. How could she let herself be hurt again?

Time moved ever so slowly as she waited for something to happen. It had been a long time since Zoie heard any sounds coming from the hall outside her dorm room. The snoring sounds continued to tell her that her roommates were in deep hibernation.

Without her phone she had little concept of time. She figured that at least twenty minutes had passed since she last looked out the window. This time when she looked out, the light in Jahi's office was out. In fact, except for the moonlight and the soft, dim glow from the lamppost at the corner of the driveway, the courtyard was completely dark. "Come on, Maynard!" she whispered. "Where are you?"

At last there it was—the signal. The beam of light. In fact, there were two beams crossing each other to form a tall thin X, ending in two circles of light on the courtyard's ground. The lights made her think of the Batman signal in the sky over Gotham, minus the insignia. But before she could take it all in, the light was gone. She almost panicked. "Wait!" she whispered a bit too loudly. She closed her eyes and again looked out in the courtyard. Thank God—the signal had returned.

Zoie slid into her broken sneakers and peered into the dark hall. Other than an emergency light here and there, the hall was dark. Light streamed from the bathroom, but it was in the opposite direction of the Pen. She turned quickly and groped for the book light at the end of Jazz's bunk. She clipped it to her jeans but kept it off; then she left the dorm room.

It was difficult to tiptoe in her scuff sneakers, so she proceeded barefoot, with the laces of the dangling sneakers wrapped around her hand. The hall was dim, but she could see more light ahead. An overhead beam illuminated the Great Room's TV area. The clock over the computers read 1:45 a.m. exactly. She headed quickly for the unmarked door that led to the Pen. *Thank God that it's not locked.* She entered the short passageway leading to the outside door and closed the interior door behind her. The passageway was black. She praised herself for thinking to bring the book light and then turned it on. In the massive darkness, her light was like a firefly, but it sufficed. The door to the outside groaned when she pressed the metal bar to open it. Outside, the moon provided enough light, so she no longer needed the book light.

A tinge of cool and damp air mixed with the still-warm air of the late night. Zoie quickly put the sneakers back on and moved close to the chain-link fence to look for Maynard in the court-yard. "Give me a sign. Please be here," she whispered. Even if he was out there, how could she get to him? She could go no farther. She was trapped by the Pen's security. At least if anyone should come out and question why she was outside so late, she had her alibi—the now partly crushed cigarette in her pocket. Alas, she hadn't thought to get a match or lighter. "Maynard, where are you?" she whispered. Had she put on this charade and come to this point only to be foiled by a locked chain-link door and an unstable assistant? She took the book light off her belt, turned it on, and waved it back and forth, hoping that Maynard would see her signal.

"Damn, turn that off, oh ye of little faith!" said a whispering and snickering voice from overhead.

Zoie's head jerked up. Someone was on top the Pen.

"Turn that off!" the voice commanded again in a loud whisper. She complied. It was Maynard, and he was perched on the chain-link cage and peering down at her. His body was spread across the chain-link ceiling like a giant spider. With his much brighter flashlight, he lit his face. His illuminated yellow-toothed smile lasted a few seconds; then he extinguished his light.

"Oh, God. You scared me," she said, keeping her voice low. She caught her breath.

He said, "Shhhhhhh!"

In a low whisper, she asked, "Can you help me get out of here?"

"Humph!" Maynard responded, forgoing his typical sarcasm. Instead, he went straight into action. The next thing Zoie knew,

Maynard was gone from overhead. The whole structure of the Pen shook with his weight as he climbed down from its roof, relying on the strength of his fingers to lower himself. He landed on the loading dock in front of the cage door.

Zoie had moved against the brick wall until the Pen stopped shaking. She now came closer to see what Maynard would do next. He retrieved some sort of tool from the nest of matted hair on his crown. The instrument looked like something she'd seen in a dentist's office, but it was too dark to really tell what it was. Without further illumination Maynard used the tool to work on the lock. In about thirty seconds, she heard the click of the lock's release.

"Well, that seemed simple enough," she said with a sigh of relief and a new confidence in the skill of her curious guide.

Maynard didn't seem to appreciate her half-hearted compliment. "Shhhhh," he said and signaled to her to follow him into the dark courtyard. She complied, being careful to gently close the Pen's door behind her.

With the moon illuminating their way, they descended the five stairs from the loading dock to the courtyard's ground. Zoie mimicked Maynard's crouched position as they crept around the edge of the courtyard, moving in stops and starts, with quick steps and then painfully slow ones. They moved away from where the cars were parked and then scurried past the smelly dumpster. Proceeding along the building wall, they stopped at the building's edge. From that point a driveway led out of the courtyard. Zoie had difficulty moving quickly in her too-large sneakers. Considering the courtyard's crumbling pavement and other sharp objects that might be in their path, she dared not remove her shoes.

Where the driveway began, a lamppost marked the opposite end of the building. The pair hung close to the building's shadow.

"Where are we going?" she whispered as they leaned into the bricks.

Maynard pointed to a freestanding brick structure some fifteen yards down the driveway. Windowless, the structure looked like a utility building, like something PEPCO might use to house wiring, albeit considerably larger. "My binder is in there," Maynard said in a whispered growl, "along with enough shit to keep you singing for days."

"What!"

Zoie was confused but dismissed his comment as another Maynardism. Having seen him in action, she knew that questioning him would only lead to an argument.

"Shhhh!" Like a thief in the night, Maynard darted from the safety of the shadows and into the light, scurrying down the driveway until he reached the doorway of the small building. Zoie took a deep breath and followed him. At least the doorway of the small building was in the shadow.

Once again Maynard retrieved his tool from his matted hair. This time there were two locks to pick. He knelt in front of the door with his small flashlight awkwardly wedged between his shoulder and cheek and worked the locks. These locks were stubborn. Several times he grunted in frustration. Zoie thought to offer her assistance, thinking she could at least hold the flashlight. But on second thought, she dared not ask. Except for his connection to Simon, Maynard was an independent operator. Her offer of help would be viewed as interference. They'd teamed up to find evidence and his binder, but their collaboration had definite limits.

Zoie watched Maynard work the locks, wondering how often he'd unlawfully entered a building. He certainly had the skill to be a burglar and certainly the economic incentive. She pondered her role in their escapade. Escaping from somewhere was one thing; breaking into a place was something quite different.

But then murder, arson, theft, and intimidation were all very different too. She was in deep. Legalities, in light of the danger she and her family faced, no longer mattered. After several uncomfortable minutes, first one lock and then the other gave way. Maynard wiped his forehead with his sleeve. Zoie breathed her second sigh of relief.

Inside the building the beam from Maynard's flashlight was dwarfed by the room's deep darkness. It was the kind of darkness in which Zoie couldn't see a hand held close to her face. Zoie's fear of the solid darkness, however, was overpowered her revulsion to the room's strange smell. Pungent and disgusting. "Ahh!" said Maynard. "Shit! At least it's not the smell of death."

"A cheerful thought," Zoie said. She turned on the book light, held her nose, and took several careful steps into the room.

Maynard closed the door behind them. She heard the locks click.

"Hey! Why did you do that?" Zoie said, feeling trapped.

"And you did graduate work? Simon said you were an attorney." He sucked his teeth. "I do wonder. I do wonder."

How did Simon know that she was an attorney? She didn't remember telling either of them that in their abbreviated conversations. Now she was locked in a dark room, away from earshot of potential help, alone with a man who was both shifty and unstable. What had she gotten herself into?

"How did Simon know about my being an attorney?"

"Humph. You got to ask that? Now you're really showing your ass," Maynard said with a snicker. "Ain't Simon the one been giving you those prophecies?"

"Well, yeah."

"Then duh! He don't say much, but he knows everything. Simon's the man, even if he's sometimes a little too goody two shoes for my liking."

"Okay, I get it. Simon's the man. Please, though, let's leave the door open."

"Look, Ms. Smarty Pants Attorney, you want to find whatever it is you're looking for and don't want to be caught—right?"

"Right."

"So if someone comes and finds the door unlocked, they're gonna know that someone's been here and might be here right now. Get it?"

"Okay, okay. Let's just hurry and look around so we can get out of here."

"I don't like it here any better than you. But I gotta find my binder. *You* gotta find my binder."

Maynard shined his flashlight around the room. In the intense darkness, Zoie's book light looked like tiny Tinker Bell. Inching forward, she stumbled against a crate and almost fell. Viewing her near accident, Maynard sucked his teeth and then shined the flashlight beam on the floor and rolled a second flashlight to her. "Here, Ms. Clumsy, take this."

"Thanks," she said, immediately turning it on. "Aren't there more lights?"

"Yeah, fluorescents." Maynard shined his light at the ceiling to reveal long industrial bulbs. "But we ain't gonna turn them on today."

Zoie didn't want to argue. "Hey, how do you know about this place?"

"In scary dreams, one night, the devil's minions caught me off guard. They dragged me in here to have some fun at my expense. He's a smart one, that devil. He could send his disciples back here at any time."

"Great! Who is this devil, and who are his minions?"

"Come on, lady. You got to know the answers to your own questions. No religious training either, huh."

"You mean Lucifer, the devil, the fallen angel."

"Mmm. I give you a B-minus for that answer."

"Then who are these minions?"

Maynard hesitated. He seemed upset by the question. "I don't know for sure. Those buggers keep changing. They're shape shifters—some days men, other days women. They could be any-body. You never know. Even you could be a minion. I thought so at first…except Simon gave you the thumbs-up."

"Thank God!"

Zoie turned back to search, not knowing what exactly she was looking for. She found a floor lamp and turned it on. Maynard groaned at the additional light, but it was too late. The lamp-light was already giving her a better view of things. The room was large. Styrofoam coolers were everywhere, and there were two restaurant-sized refrigerators. A long and tall worktable sur-rounded by several stools consumed most of the room's center. On the rough table, she found plant remnants—twigs and leaves, some fresh looking and some dried. There were boxes of Ziploc bags and several pairs of pruning shears. At first glance the table looked like something a gardener or florist might work on. But then it came to her.

"My God! It's a marijuana operation," Zoie said, thinking out loud. Behind her she heard Maynard's low, deep cackle. She sniffed the leaves. The plant material was the source of the room's overwhelmingly putrid smell. She sniffed again. The smell was not the smell of marijuana. She checked the refrigera-tors. With the exception of several vials and one wimpy branch of the plant, they were empty. Staying near the door, Maynard chuckled nervously as Zoie searched. Every so often he shushed her and signaled her to stop and listen.

The drugs intrigued Zoie. Who was the devil, and who were his minions? Was Jahi the devil or someone from the Shelter? The sign outside the door clearly labeled the building as prop-erty of the Shelter.

"What's this stuff?" she asked, fingering the pieces of brown-and-red leaves.

"Thought you'd never ask. *Catha edulis*."

"What?"

"*Catha edulis*, otherwise known as khat."

"Huh." Zoie had heard about khat. She knew the stuff was illegal. And she'd heard it was a favorite of Middle Easterners. Otherwise, she didn't know much else.

"Everybody wants to chew this stuff. Makes you *crazy*," Maynard continued.

Zoie found it ironic that Maynard would use the word *crazy*, considering the state of his own mental health. But then in his mind, he was the sanest one of all.

"You knew this was here? All this time you knew about this operation."

"Yeah, and I also know that the moon on average is 238,857 miles from the earth. Really helps to know this information if I plan to go there."

"Can you be serious?"

"Lady, I'm as serious as the e-coli on your fast-food burger. This place is dangerous. Now stop trying to be cute, and keep your end of the bargain. Find my binder, and let's go!"

Strangely Maynard hung by the door. From that position he guided his flashlight beam into the room's various corners. He didn't want to venture farther. Zoie thought, *Something must have happened to him in this room.*

"You're afraid, aren't you?"

"Yeah, and you best be afraid too."

At least she now knew. She'd have to search alone. Maynard would stand guard by the door. She could ask no more of him.

The drug operation was beyond what she had expected to find. She was looking for evidence of the Shelter's misappropriation of the Foundation's funds and the Shelter's connection to Ray's murder. Perhaps this was it. Perhaps the misdirected funds bankrolled the drug operation. And the illegal operation was enough to close the place down and put those responsible in jail. Beyond the hanky panky with the Foundation's funds, she now wondered whether Ray had known about the khat operation. Was he profiting from it, or was he just tied up in grant kickbacks? How in God's name had Ray gotten himself trapped in the whole thing? Greed, of course. He *was* a bit of a sleazebag. But there had to be more to it. "Because he knew all this, they had to kill him," she said.

"Kill who? Who's about to be dead?"

"My boss was killed. Possibly because he knew about this operation."

"See...I told you this place was evil."

Talk of killing set Maynard off. He started his circling dance in the small space near the door. The beam from his flashlight rounded the walls as if it were being chased. Following it was enough to make a person dizzy. Zoie tried to focus. She moved past the high table and farther into the room. Her light caught a desk against a wall, in the corner. She carefully made her way to it. There she found piles of papers, including one pile that had an orange and blue ring binder near the top.

"Hey, Maynard! Is your binder orange and blue?"

"Yes! Yes! My Syracuse colors."

"Did you go to Syracuse?"

"No, silly woman. I taught there."

"Oh." Zoie flipped through the pages of the three-ring binder. Each page was carefully hand done in a combination of what looked like hieroglyphics, Cyrillic lettering, and gibberish words." It was Maynard's own code spelling out his secrets, inaccessible to all but him.

"Hey, don't read that! You haven't been cleared!" Maynard bellowed from across the room. "Humph! You can't read it anyway. Thank you, God."

"Okay. Okay. You're right. I can't read it."

Maynard laughed nervously. "Bring it to me. Bring it to me. Let's get out of here."

"Just a second. Maybe my laptop and briefcase are here," Zoie said. She looked around the desk and in the drawers. The drawers were stuffed with twine and thin wire. Some files were on the desk and in its drawers. She wanted to go through the files, but Maynard fidgeted near the door. She was afraid he'd bust a gut. She should have been afraid, but the stuff on the desk was intriguing—a folder full of invoices from Kenya Airlines and KLM. "Oh, God. This is how they're shipping this stuff."

"Ms. Smarty Pants, they're gonna be shipping our bodies if we don't get out of here."

"Hang on just a few more minutes. *Please* try to calm down."

She shuffled through some folders on a table close to the desk. Then she saw her laptop. "Look, Maynard, I found my laptop! But where's my briefcase?"

"They took something from you too?"

"Just this morning they stole my laptop and briefcase from my apartment."

"Hmm. Now they know everything about you. The devil may be evil, but he's no dummy."

Maynard was right. Everything had happened so fast. The laptop had personal as well as Foundation information.

"Come on, Ms. Smarty Pants. Get your stuff. Bring my binder. Damn, we got to go. Let's get out of here...wait!" Maynard said, freezing. Like a mime he cocked his head toward the door and put a finger to his lips. "Shh!"

Zoie could now hear what Maynard heard. Faint voices were on the other side of the door. She quickly moved to the floor lamp and turned it off. The voices became louder. With his flashlight guiding him, Maynard left his guard post at the door and darted into the room. He grabbed his binder and then Zoie's arm and yanked her behind a double stack of wooden crates piled high at the back of the room. The two crouched low and turned off their flashlights. In the room's inky blackness, they heard the door locks give way. Maynard gave her one more "Shh!" before the door swung open.

Through slits in the crates, they had a view to the open door. The distant street lamp provided eerie backlighting for the doorway's shadowed figures. In an awkward crouch, Maynard pressed low to the ground, maintaining his view while protecting his precious binder. He chewed at his shirt and trembled. Zoie also had landed in an awkward position. Her otherwise healthy haunches screamed pain. She dare not move as terror trumped pain. She was about to find out who was behind everything. But what good would that knowing be if she ended up dead?

CHAPTER 43
MAYNARD FINDS HIS MANE

Backlit by the moon, two slender men, one slightly taller than the other, stood in the doorway of the Mahali outbuilding. The shorter of the two switched on the fluorescents. With a flicker and a crackle, the overhead lights responded in harsh brightness.

"This place gets messier with each shipment," the taller of the two said, disgusted. "Asad, can't you get your crew to clean up after themselves?"

Asad, the shorter and older of the two, groaned. With his foot he pushed a Styrofoam ice chest out of his path.

"So you left those messages as I told you?" Tarik was curt. "And you used the voice-distortion device?"

Asad responded begrudgingly in his thick Somalian accent. "Sure, my brother, I did all that. This woman is not answering. Everything goes to voice mail."

"Then I hope she listens and heeds our warning. And, of course, you made these calls with burner phones?"

"Yeah, sure," Asad said, bristling. He didn't enjoy being interrogated by the arrogant younger man. But he had to endure. There was little work for someone in his circumstance—certainly none as lucrative as the khat business. He preferred this to spending his nights babysitting cars in a downtown garage or his days circling the busy city in someone else's cab. For now this was better, even if it meant submitting to Tarik's badgering. He had a much younger wife, one small child, and another on the way.

Asad had signed on to work the khat operation, a business he knew well. But lately Tarik had asked him to do other things—things not connected to the smuggling operation. The cocky boy and his mother had other illegal business dealings. He had been expected to follow their orders without explanation, as if he were some child. He found himself being dragged deeper into the muck. For these crimes his punishment, if he were caught, would be more severe. Rather than a slap on the wrist or deportation, he could face life behind bars in a US prison.

Tarik brushed the khat debris from the plank table and into a small flat box. "Then, Asad—my trusted associate—tell me something: the Taylor woman is not answering, but do you at least know where she is? Remember…I also asked you to keep tabs on her."

"I know you wanted me to keep track of her. In truth, I have not had time to find her," Asad replied.

Tarik frowned and shook his head. Then he said with a sigh, "How did I know you would not follow through?"

Tarik's English was perfect. He spoke English as if it were his first language. He'd come to the United States from Ethiopia at age three. When his mother received her papers to come to the United States, she refused to leave him behind with relatives in Addis Abba, as other mothers before her had done. There was no shame in leaving children behind to wait until the family was established, but his mother would not hear of it. She'd already lost her husband and refused to be separated from her child.

Tarik wished that Asad, the husband of his cousin Mihret, spoke Amharic like the rest of the family. So close were their peoples in the motherland, yet the distance between their tongues was the width of an ocean. English, the language of business, was now their common tongue. Asad's not knowing Amharic was more than a little disadvantage when it came to dealing with their customers. He'd made little effort to learn his wife's tongue. Why, even Jahi spoke some Amharic. Still, the Somali had proven trustworthy, even if he *was* slow to follow through. It would not have been Tarik's choice to use Asad, but his mother insisted. "Better to keep our dealings in the family," she had said.

Asad did have positives. He knew the khat operation from back in Somalia. In DC he had learned quickly to deal with their airport contacts and the distribution model for the Ethiopian establishments along Georgia Avenue, U Street, and Eighteenth Street. He knew the customers in the DC cabbie community. With DC having the largest concentration of Ethiopians in the United States, their business was set to grow. Plus, he was the link to the fledgling Somalian community in DC, a population not on par number-wise with Ethiopians but likely to grow fast. Asad knew only superficially about the family's other ventures. And Tarik and his mother had determined early on that it was best to keep it that way—to keep their businesses compartmentalized.

Tarik knew that if he relied solely on Asad, he would indeed be blindsided. A khat user, Asad was often "indisposed." The leaves should have made his cousin more alert and more of a risk taker. Perhaps because Asad had been chewing the stuff for so long, he needed to chew greater quantities for longer periods to achieve the desired boost. So Tarik used other eyes sometimes to tell him what he needed to know.

"I know the Taylor woman was at the Foundation's office earlier today. Downtown they're in a knot over that pig Gaddis." Tarik rolled his eyes and then stared at Asad to gauge his reaction. "The Taylor woman knows about the fire. That should keep her quiet."

"Yes, the fire was good thinking on your part, Tarik. And this time nobody had to die."

"Asad! Asad, my brother, you are too sensitive. We do what we need to do, not for the fun of it. This is business. If necessary, I have other means to ensure the Taylor woman's silence...means that will be even more effective."

"What do you intend?"

"I will let you know if we have to take that route." Tarik went over to where Zoie's laptop was found. He didn't seem to notice that the laptop had been unearthed from the pile and was now sitting very prominently in the middle of the desk. "I know where her daughter is. Anyway, enough about this woman. She is the least of our problems. We have another serious situation."

"What now?" Asad said, his attention piqued for bad news.

"I just received a text from Frankfurt. Our shipment has been intercepted."

"I was supposed to pick the shipment up from our contact at Dulles later this morning. Before you called me here, I was going to pick up one of our guys at the twenty-four-hour joint near the airport.

"Asad, be careful. You don't know who's watching those places. Anyway, we still have the shipment coming in from Amsterdam this evening. But that means we'll have no fresh product for today's distribution. We will have a lot of disappointed customers."

Somewhat bewildered by the news, Asad quickly calculated the effect of this setback. No khat for distribution meant no money for him. Plus, no fresh khat for his own consumption. Khat sharpened his wits and eased his fatigue, though the brown juice often stained his clothes. A day without the potent khat would not be the end of the world. But it was a nasty sandstorm.

"Do you realize that this is the first time in the thirty months of this operation that we have had a glitch like this?" Tarik asked.

"Our contacts in jeopardy in Frankfurt are thinking this is more than what you call a 'glitch.'"

"True. True. Sad. We'll have to cauterize that arm of the operation. But don't worry," Tarik said with an air of authority. "We are insolated triple times over. They don't know where the stuff actually comes from or where it winds up. Ahh!" He sighed as if the weight of the world were on him. "So many palms to grease. It's a wonder we make any profit from this operation. In fact, we will make nothing today. As we go forward, the price for our product must go up to be in line with our risk."

"Tarik, the price has always fluctuated."

"No, this will be different. For the next shipment, there will be a big increase."

Asad scratched his head. He decided not to comment, though he couldn't contain a groan.

"Customers are satisfied with the product, right? Its freshness?" Tarik continued.

"Well, yes." Asad didn't know what price the khat market would bear. Even for him there was a cutoff price, though he had become dependent on the stuff to stay alert, even as a boy in Mogadishu. Tarik had organized the operation, which expedited the product from the growing fields in Ethiopia's Haare Province to the DC area. No longer was DC dependent on New York and Philadelphia for its supply. Coming straight to DC meant the product was fresher. Now most of the Ethiopian establishments in the area relied on Tarik's operation. The fresher the product, the more potent; thus, it was more valuable.

"We have always had the freshest product. And for that our customers should be willing to pay more."

"Have you told Sister Te about Frankfurt?"

"Let me worry about my mother. Look, I want you to get your boys and go to New York."

"New York?"

"Yes, New York. Buy the product from our competitors. Bring back what you can to sell here later today."

"But the stuff will not be fresh. You just said we sell the quality stuff."

Tarik put his hands to his temples as if to contain his brain and calm his temper. He spoke slowly. "I know what I said, but I also don't want our customers seeking alternate suppliers when we don't come through."

"Okay." Asad dreaded the long drive up to New York and back in the dark, even if he could sleep part of the time. "I need money for the purchase."

"Wait just a minute. I'll get you some cash."

"And the woman?"

"You are relieved of that assignment. I'll take care of the problem."

From her squatted position behind the crates, Zoie couldn't see either man's face, but she knew from the first words that came out of the younger man's mouth that one was Tarik. As for the one called Asad, he was an unknown. His thick accent made it difficult to follow his end of the conversation. She was able to decipher enough to know it was trouble indeed. Each time they referred to her as the "Taylor woman," she cringed. And when Tarik mentioned that he knew where to find Nikki, it was all she could do to stifle a gasp.

They were worried about where to find Zoie, but, lo and behold, she was right under their noses. If they had considered her to be a danger before, what threat level was she now?

Her haunches burned as she maintained her squat without shifting her position. Her muscles were locking under the stress. Maynard was contorted low to the floor. She could feel his quivering leg pressed up against her thigh. He'd been quiet as a mouse, but then he started to whimper. His first whimper was barely audible, but the next was louder.

"What was that?" Tarik asked.

"I didn't hear anything."

"Listen, do you hear it? It sounds like a dog."

As if Tarik's words were a cue, Maynard sprang from his hiding place, knocking down crates around him in the process. With his binder pressed to his chest, he bolted for the door, taking a route that put the long plank table between him and the two men. At the door he fumbled to release the locks with his free hand. But it was not enough.

"What the fuck!" shouted Tarik in shock.

They were after him. Maynard turned and sprang like a jackrabbit from the floor to the tabletop.

"How in the hell did he get in here?" Tarik demanded.

"I don't know!" answered Asad.

Maynard ran down the tabletop to its opposite end. Stunned, the two men watched in amazement as Maynard performed his weird ritual dance accompanied by hoots and caws. In all the commotion, Zoie shrank farther behind the fallen crates. Luckily she hadn't been exposed. The jumble of fallen crates gave her more cover and a larger peephole through which to witness the happenings.

"Get him! Get him!" Tarik shouted to Asad, who stood paralyzed by the surprise. The two went into action to restrain the intruder.

Sure footed, Maynard jettisoned back and forth on the eighteen-foot-long table, dodging his pursuers, who scrambled like a comedy team around the table's edge. A number of times, Tarik and Asad tried to fake him out. Maynard read their fakes and escaped their flailing attempts to grab his legs. At one point his weight at the table's end caused the thing to tilt and almost cap-size. But like a tightrope walker, he maintained his balance.

"Asad, get the broom!" shouted Tarik.

Asad picked up a nearby broom. With its straw end, he tried to swat Maynard like a fly. When that tactic didn't work, he gripped the broom's handle like a bat and delivered a power-ful blow to Maynard's shins. The swift move caused damage to Maynard's legs. Still clutching his binder, Maynard howled in pain. He could no longer jump or stand erect. He keeled over like a stiff statue, falling to the floor. His two assaulters squashed Maynard's struggling on the ground. But still he howled. After several tugs Tarik ripped the binder from Maynard's grip and tossed it on the table. Asad pounded Maynard with the broom handle while Tarik sat on the man's legs to ensure he could not rise.

From her hiding place, Zoie tried to watch, though strick-en with horror. She couldn't see everything, but she heard Maynard's screams and then moans. She saw Asad's arms rise and fall with each strike of the broom. She held her breath and closed her eyes. It was vile. Closed eyes didn't prevent the sounds of Maynard's beating from reaching her ears. Part of her wanted to help Maynard, but she knew she'd be no match for the two. For so many years, she'd fantasized about being Wonder Woman— but she wasn't. Getting herself caught would do neither of them any good.

Asad stopped his pounding and wiped his brow. "Who is this guy?"

Tarik was standing again and looking down at his captive. "He was here a few weeks ago. He's the kook we made chew the leaves. Remember how freaked he got? Looks as if he came back for his book."

"You mean that stupid binder with the strange language?"

"Yeah, that." Tarik wiped his mouth and motioned to the binder that had landed precariously on the table's edge. "But what I want to know is, *how* did he get in here? And *who* has he told about this place? And *who* left the door open?"

"Not me," Asad said. "I am always careful."

The moaning stopped. Zoie wondered whether that was a good or bad sign. Was Maynard still alive? For a minute she considered that it would be better if he were dead. If alive, he might easily break under interrogation and give her away. She quickly erased any wish for his death from her thoughts. It was wrong to wish anyone dead, even to protect herself.

"What do we do with him?" Asad asked.

Her ears, now acclimated to Asad's accent, she fully understood the question. But what she didn't know was whether the "him" was a live person or a dead one.

"Let me think. Let me think. Just what we needed, another glitch."

"You still want me to go to New York?"

"Yes, damn it! But first you have to help me get rid of him!"

Eyes closed, Zoie prayed. *Please, God, I'm sorry for what I was thinking. I really don't want him to be dead.* It had been a long time since she'd prayed. She'd almost forgotten how. She prayed for Maynard. She prayed for Nikki. She prayed for her grandmother. She asked to be delivered safely from her predicament. Then she heard the groan of a person in pain.

"He's coming around," Asad said. "Have you decided what to do with him?"

"This is too dangerous. We need a permanent fix. We can't have him continuing to show up here to snoop around."

"I understand," said Asad.

"But it's got to look like an accident." Tarik looked down at Maynard. "Hey, fellow. Why didn't you stay away when we let you go last time? You kook!"

"How's it going to look like an accident?" Asad asked. "Look at him. Clearly he has been beaten."

"Yes, you did quite a job on him."

Asad smirked.

"Not to worry. Homeless folks get roughed up all the time. Tie him up," Tarik ordered.

Asad stood over Maynard for a moment, pondering the damage his broom-handle strikes had inflicted on the man. He sighed and then retrieved a roll of heavy twine from a utility bin beneath the table and bound Maynard's hands and feet as Tarik had bid. In the meantime Tarik searched for something in the almost-empty refrigerator.

"I thought we had more heroin? Did we use it all on Gaddis?"

Through the crates Zoie couldn't see everything, but she'd certainly heard Tarik's confession. She pressed her fingers to her mouth. *So that is how they did it. They overdosed Ray.*

"Aha! I found it," Tarik said, coming forth from the refrigerator with a small vial. "Whose idea was it to put this in the freezer?"

Asad did not answer.

"We used two vials of this concoction on Gaddis," said Tarik. "But I think one vial should do the trick. Asad, you get going to New York. Get Wasie and Mulu to dump the body. They can leave him in some doorway downtown. Sprinkle him with liquor for effect. No one will miss him. His death won't even make the evening news."

Tarik filled a syringe with the contents of the vial and injected Maynard with the extremely cold solution.

Looking on at the execution, Asad swallowed hard. He'd seen much worse in Mogadishu—beheadings and the like. Escaping the violence was one of the reasons he'd left his homeland. But here he was facing violence again. "Okay, so I'll pick up the same two guys who were going to go out to Dulles, and then I will head to New York. I need money."

Tarik went to the corner of the room and pulled aside a large paper shredder, which hid a floor safe. He opened the safe and removed a wad of bills and then locked it. "Five thousand should be enough," he said. "It should handle buying the product and gas. You are only buying one day's worth of product. Beyond tomorrow the leaves will be just garbage, only good for tea, not worth the money."

"Right."

"And remember, Asad, you're going to the wholesaler in Queens, near JFK airport. The place I took you a couple of times. You know where I mean. And don't hang around trying to see your New York relatives. This trip must be quick."

"Sure," Asad said, taking the stack of bills and wrapping it in cellophane from the table. He didn't want to offend Tarik. He'd count it later. Asad placed the wrapped money on the table and bent down to feel Maynard's pulse. "Tarik, I think he is gone."

"I told you. The combination of heroin and vodka works fast."

Asad pulled a tarp from under the table and covered Maynard's body. He had taken part in the man's death, but he found no joy in it. "I will call you from the road," he said, his tone more solemn than usual.

Zoie saw Asad take the cash and leave the room. There was nothing she could do. A tear rolled down her cheek. *They did it. They really did it. They killed him.* Maynard was gone. If Maynard had stuck to his guns and refused to come with her to the Shelter, he'd still be alive. She'd talked him into this misadventure. She'd led him back to the place that he so feared. Sadness and guilt washed over her, feelings quickly overshadowed by the reality of her situation. If caught, she would be their next victim.

CHAPTER 44

FINDING HELP

Tarik lingered after Asad's departure. Behind the jumbled crates, Zoie waited too, hoping Tarik would leave so that she could escape. A muscle in her right leg cramped, but she willed herself motionless. Perhaps Tarik was waiting for his goons to come to remove Maynard's body. At least multiple calls seemed to distract him. *Thank God.* He didn't look in the direction of the crates.

With a phone glued to his ear, Tarik paced back and forth beside the long table. With each loop he stepped over Maynard's tarp-draped body. He reverted to a language that Zoie had never heard. English words were thrown in the mix, but even these words were mutilated by an accent that belied his otherwise flawless English. *He's speaking Ethiopian*, Zoie thought. Then she remembered that Ethiopians spoke something called Amharic, an ancient biblical tongue. She'd gleaned that information from a *Washington Post* article. But knowing that was of no help now.

At first Tarik sounded irritated. But as the calls continued, his tone was more conciliatory. Zoie tried to guess who was on the other end of the call. Surely if he were talking to Jahi, he'd use English. He must have called the guys to dispose of Maynard's body. *Poor Maynard.* Perhaps Tarik was talking to his mother. Or perhaps he was notifying the khat dealer in Queens that Asad was on the way. *Give that schmuck a load of khat.* Who else could he be talking to past two thirty in the morning?

Who was really in charge of the Shelter's crime syndicate? What did Ray have to do with the khat operation? Based on what Zoie knew, Ray's demise still didn't make sense. She suspected that the Shelter had fraudulently used its Foundation grant. Were they paying Ray for special influence during the selection process? She heard Tarik say Jahi several times. Where did he fit in? As the Shelter's director, he had to be in on it—front and center.

Zoie had compiled suspicions and questions to be addressed. If they'd looked at the information on her laptop, they'd have realized that she knew next to nothing. Maybe she knew enough to call a special meeting of the Foundation's Board, but what she knew was certainly not enough to indict anyone. And in no way had she guessed anything about a drug operation. Now she doubted that the khat operation was the whole thing. If only she understood Amharic. She needed subtitles to follow along. But right now she needed to be rescued.

Please just leave! Don't you have things to do somewhere else? Her leg cramped again. Ever so slowly Zoie let her right hip settle to the floor to relieve her haunch's burn. With one false move, the jigsaw pile of crates would collapse. With one false move, a protruding nail could stab her. With one false move, she could end up like Maynard.

Tarik ended his string of calls and moved to search through the pile of papers on the desk, as Zoie had done earlier. In the process he mumbled to himself in a combination of English and this other language. He must have found what he was looking for because he turned off the overhead lights and exited the building.

Once again the room was in pitch darkness. Zoie heard the door locks being reengaged from the outside. *Thank God.* Still, she dared not speak or otherwise make a sound. For a while she remained as if paralyzed. Tarik might have forgotten something. He might race back at any second. After a few minutes of stillness, her fear of Tarik's eminent return subsided. Turning out the lights had been a signal that he didn't intend to return immediately. It was time to make her escape.

In the darkness she fumbled for Jazz's book light. She found it still faithfully clipped to the belt loop of her jeans. With that light she was able to find her small flashlight, which had slipped from her hand and rolled under the crates. With the beams of the two lights, she made her way through the crate pile and over to Maynard's body. His murderers hadn't bothered to lay him out straight. He was a large lump and partly propped against a wooden chest and covered by the tarp. As Zoie looked down at the covered body, something told her to look at him one last time. She squatted beside him, pulled the tarp back, and shined the flashlight in his face.

The man on the ground before her was only nominally Maynard. His features were grossly distorted from swelling. If he were alive, the swelling around his eyes would have kept them shut. Coagulated blood was caked around his nose and mouth. Blood glistened in his matted hair. She let the light drift down to see his bound hands positioned again his chest as if in a prayer.

"Oh, Maynard, I'm so sorry," Zoie said as her tears started again. "I won't let them get away with this." She pressed her palm against his swollen cheek and felt that he was still warm. The warmth wasn't unusual. After all, he hadn't been dead that long. Then she saw his chest rise ever so slightly. *Could it be too much to ask? Could he be breathing?*

Zoie checked his bound wrist for a pulse. She felt what she believed to be a pulse, though ever so slight. She shook him and called in a loud whisper, "Maynard! Maynard! Can you hear me?" His precariously balanced head fell to the side. She shook him again, but there was no response.

Yes, Maynard was alive—but barely. Surely he *would* die without treatment. She couldn't let Tarik and his cohorts return and find him still breathing. Surely they'd finish the job.

Unconscious, the strapping man, once quick on his feet, now constituted deadweight. She knew that she couldn't move him alone. She didn't even try.

She tried rousing him in terms he'd understand. "Maynard! It's Ms. Smarty Pants. You were right about the danger. We've got to get out of here before the devil's minions come back."

Her efforts to revive him were fruitless. He wasn't going to walk out of there, and she wasn't going to carry him. It was time for plan B. She thought for a second. She would have to leave him there and go for help. Though she hated to do it, she again covered him with the tarp, leaving it so that air could flow in. If Tarik and his cohorts returned, they'd continue to believe he was dead.

"Don't worry, Maynard. I'll be back. God, let him hang on until I can get help." Although Tarik had locked the door from the outside, fortunately it could be unlocked sans keys from the inside. Zoie peeked out the door to check the path ahead before venturing on to the driveway. She closed the door, but now it was unlocked. Should Tarik return before she could get help, he'd know that someone else had been in the khat room. She had to move fast. Without the aid of the flashlight, she scurried up the driveway and toward the Shelter. At the lamppost she could see the full courtyard. It was quiet, and the three vehicles parked there earlier were gone. She surmised that Asad had taken one of them to New York, but she had no idea whether Tarik had taken another one or whether he was inside the men's Shelter. Rather than skulk along the courtyard's perimeter, she took the courtyard straight on, moving as fast as permitted by her over-sized shoes, darting across the open space.

Zoie found the Pen's chain-link door shut but unlocked as they had left it. *Thank God!* The exterior door to the women's section was also still unlocked. With her flashlight guiding her, she made her way back through the short dark hall to the Great Room. The clock over the computers read a quarter to three. She'd been out of the building for over an hour.

The room was quiet, except for the intermittent hum of the refrigerator's motor. She needed help, but something told her not to rely on the Shelter's personnel. There was no way to tell who might be in Tarik's gang or under Sister Te's spell. She thought it best to call 911 for an ambulance and the police.

Over in the business center, the phones she'd seen earlier were now missing. They probably had been put away so that no one could misuse the Shelter's account during the night. She headed to get her cell phone from the locker. On the way she searched her jean pockets for the locker key and then remembered that she'd left it in the robe pocket after taking her shower. She quickly made it back to the dorm room and peeked in. Her roommates were still asleep, but what looked like a body now occupied her cot. The body's face was turned to the wall, and the covers were pulled high. She felt her stomach sink. Perhaps it was Sister Te waiting for her.

She had to get the key. Summoning her courage, she tiptoed farther into the room and aimed the flashlight's beam at what seemed to be the person's head. The person turned over.

"Jazz!" Zoie said in an irritated whisper. "What are you doing in my bed?"

"Good, you're back," Jazz whispered. "Went to see your boyfriend, huh?"

"No! But why are you in my bed?"

"I forgot to tell you. Annette, the night counselor, does bed checks. She'll be back around in the next hour," Jazz answered. "This place is like DC jail."

"I wouldn't know," Zoie said, irritated but at the same time relieved that it was Jazz and not Sister Te. It did make sense for someone to stay the night with the women, but was this Annette person involved in the illegal goings-on? Who could she trust?

Jazz had wrapped herself like a mummy in Zoie's blanket and had arranged her own bunk to look as if she were still in it. "Take that damn light out of my face," Jazz ordered, shielding her eyes.

"Shh," Zoie insisted. She aimed the flashlight at the floor. "Okay, Jazz, I get it. You're trying to help me."

"Yeah, that's what we do. We ladies have to stick together. That's the only way to survive." Jazz loosened her wrap, sat up, and swung her legs over the edge of the cot. "Can't have you getting into trouble your first night here. You got to be careful, or they'll kick you out."

If only Jazz knew how much trouble I'm already in. "Thanks. Now I really need your help."

"What's up?"

"It's a long story and a matter of life and death. Come out in the hall, where we can talk, and I'll explain," Zoie said. "You have to hurry."

Zoie grabbed her robe from the floor under the cot. She found the locker key in the robe pocket where she'd left it. Then she rushed out of the room and went a short way down the hall, to the lockers, and retrieved her Blackberry. A barefoot Jazz donning baby-doll pajamas was right behind her.

"Now can you tell me what's going on?" Jazz asked in a quiet voice. "Oh, God! You're all bloody."

"Shh!" Zoie hadn't even noticed the blood. Maynard's blood was on her hands, face, and shirt.

"Oh, Anna, did he hurt you?" Jazz tried to stroke Zoie's cheek, but Zoie batted Jazz's hand away. "Be that way," Jazz said, her feelings hurt. "Anyway, I hope you got him good."

"It's not like that, Jazz," Zoie said. "A friend of mine is badly hurt. We have to help him." With all that had happened that night, Zoie could no longer keep up the charade. She hadn't planned to reveal herself just yet, but she just suddenly blurted, "My name is not Anna."

"Huh?" Jazz looked confused.

"I promise. I'll explain it all. Now I need your help. It's really serious. Come on!"

Zoie grabbed Jazz by the hand and pulled her into the Great Room. Dumbstruck, Jazz let herself be led. In the kitchen area, Zoie found a steak knife in a utility drawer. "We might need this," Zoie said.

"Girlfriend, you're serious! You're gonna finish this guy off?" Jazz asked in horror.

"Shh. No. I told you. It's not like that. Let's go."

Back outside and in the Pen, Zoie breathed a sigh of relief when she saw that the cars hadn't returned. She hoped that no one had returned to the little house in her absence and found Maynard breathing. Still confused, Jazz clung to the chain-link fence and peered out into the courtyard's eerie darkness. "Stay here," Zoie ordered as her attention was directed to her cell phone's alert that she had about fifteen missed calls. *Probably more threatening calls*, she thought. She wondered who else could have called. But the immediate crisis had to take priority.

Zoie dialed 911, but before the call could go through, her phone went dark. She'd started the day with her phone fully charged, but in the locker the phone's futile search for a signal must have drained the battery.

"Damn—don't crap out on me now," she told her phone. "Damn! Damn!" She stomped her feet.

"You're gonna get us both thrown out of here," Jazz said as she hugged herself against the slight night breeze.

Zoie sighed and tried to think. "There's no more time. I know what we've got to do," she said. "Come on." But when she opened the chain-link door to exit the Pen, Jazz freaked.

"Where we going? The creeps are out there."

"Look, Jazz, you'll be okay with me," Zoie said, trying to coax the young woman to venture outside the Pen. "You're going to help me get my friend to safety."

"I can't go out there like this, without shoes."

Until now the fact that Jazz was barefoot hadn't registered. Zoie directed the light to the girl's curled toes. "Okay, take these," she said, taking off the broken-heel sneakers. "They ought to fit you." With a cringe Jazz complied, slipping her feet into the shoes, which fit her better than they had Zoie.

"Come on," Zoie said again, grabbing Jazz by the hand. The courtyard was paved, but grit and gravel debris slowed them down. With Jazz in tow, Zoie stayed on the balls of her feet to avoid putting the full weight of her body into each step. At one point she stopped to remove a small stone that had wedged under a middle toe.

"We're headed to the small house down the driveway," she told Jazz as they stopped at the corner of the main building near the lantern. "Have you ever been in there?"

"Uh-huh," Jazz said, acting coy. "Once."

"What? You're part of this scheme too?"

"If you're talking about that chewing-weed business, yeah."

Zoie wanted to scream, but she willed herself to remain calm.

"No big deal," said Jazz. "Sister Te asked me to help cut up those vines and put them in plastic baggies. I'd never seen that shit before. She gave me $150 for three hours of work. Not bad money, but I didn't like it. The stuff smelled awful, and I didn't like how those guys chewed it with all that green-and-brown mess drooling out their mouths. Like babies eating rotten peas. Disgusting! And one of those guys wanted me to do something else besides cut vines. He smelled as bad as the homeless creeps. Worse than most Johns. You know them Africans don't bathe every day. Of course, I didn't tell Sister Te, seeing she's African and all. She's been nice to me, and she doesn't have BO.

"While I worked, I know they talked about me, but I couldn't understand a word they said. I just told Sister Te I didn't want to help no more. At first she was a little huffy about it. Then she told me it was okay. I didn't have to go back there, but she said I sure better keep my mouth shut about what I'd seen, if I knew what was good for me. No hard feelings. She even let me work at her store on Georgia Avenue for a few days. Only ten dollars an hour for that. I told you Sister Te's a businesswoman. So I've kept my mouth shut...til now."

Jazz's confession was amazing, but it was taking up time. The clock was ticking on saving Maynard. The thugs would return soon. Zoie wanted to know enough to determine whether she could still trust Jazz. "When was the last time you were in that building?"

"Last year," the girl answered, hugging her bare arms, as they stood at the corner of the building. "Why you asking me all these questions? Did they ask you to work there too?"

"No."

Zoie felt relieved by Jazz's story. She concluded that her new friend had played an insignificant role in the drug operation. It was also clear that Jazz quickly developed attachments, and one such attachment was to Sister Te, who must have figured that since Jazz was a hooker, she knew how to keep her mouth shut. The question now was whether Jazz would go running to her patroness or to one of her patroness's goons. Zoie's gut told her Jazz would not.

"Okay, now I understand. Thanks for explaining," Zoie said. Holding Jazz's wrist, she made the remaining distance to the door of the small building in a sprint.

"Who's in there?" Jazz asked.

"Nobody, except my friend, I hope." Zoie took a deep breath and opened the door. "Thank God," she said, looking into the darkness.

"Ooh, this is spooky. Turn on the lights," Jazz said.

Zoie closed the door and directed the flashlight in search of the light switch. The fluorescents took a second but finally responded with their bright light.

"Ugh! Still smells awful, just as I remember," said Jazz. "Where's your friend? Ain't he supposed to be here?"

"Over here, on the floor. But I don't know whether he's still alive." Zoie went over to the large blue lump on the floor, crouched down, and pulled back the tarp."

"Oh! Look at him," Jazz said, peering down. "He's one of those homeless creeps."

"He's homeless, and he's my friend. Those bastards beat him and then shot him up with dope. He only came in here to get the binder they'd taken from him."

"He looks dead," Jazz said.

"I hope not. Please, God, let him be alive," Zoie said. With two fingers she checked his pulse at his neck. The pulse was there but very weak. "Okay, he's still alive. Look, we have to hurry. You have to help me get him out of here." She unwrapped the steak knife and cut the heavy twine bindings from his wrists and ankles.

"I'm glad your friend is alive, but he's too big to carry."

"I know. We're going to put him on this tarp and drag him out of here." After Jazz heard the plan, her eyes widened. "We have to move," continued Zoie. "They may come back anytime."

Space by the table was tight. Zoie spread the tarp in the room's entryway, close to the door, leaving enough space for the door to open. She lowered Maynard's head to the floor, straightened his body as best she could, and then grabbed his heels and pulled him with all her might. "Sorry, Maynard," she grunted. "This is the only way to get you out of here. Jazz, do something. Hold that tarp straight."

Jazz responded as if waking from a dream. Straining, Zoie pulled Maynard onto the tarp, and Jazz maneuvered the tarp to go underneath him. Zoie rose from her stooped position, holding her back. "He's one heavy dude."

"I'm really scared," Jazz said. "If they come back and find us, they'll kill us, right?"

"Right, because we know too much."

Initially Jazz was reluctant to touch Maynard. With more prompting she finally pitched in and helped Zoie arrange Maynard on the tarp. "Do they know about you? Do they know your name ain't Anna?"

"Yes, and they know my real name. They killed a guy I know because he knew too much, and they set fire to my grandmother's house so I'd keep my mouth shut. They also robbed my apartment."

"Hey! You still got an apartment?"

In the heat of the moment, Zoie had made another slip. Her undercover persona was unraveling like a loose thread on a sweater's hem. "Yeah, I still have an apartment," Zoie admitted, still portraying her original lie as a minor inaccuracy. "I have an apartment, but I haven't been able to go back there because these characters might be waiting for me. So I have nowhere to stay."

"Oh," Jazz said, accepting that explanation.

"They're very dangerous. And now you see, Jazz, selling khat is not all they do. They'll get rid of anyone who gets in their way."

"Hmm. Well, I don't want to be in their way. Now I remember. Cat is what they call those leaves. *Cat*, like kitty cat. African people love this stuff. I don't see any regular black folks who want to chew a mouthful of leaves. For anybody that wants to, more power to 'em. Sister Te says it ain't like coke, crack, smack, or weed. She says it shouldn't be illegal 'cause it just gives you a buzz…like too much coffee."

Zoie refrained from commenting on khat's classification as a minor drug. For one thing, Zoie didn't know much about it. And she wanted Jazz to focus on their task: getting themselves and Maynard to safety.

So far Jazz hadn't really reacted to the revelation that her new best friend's name wasn't Anna. And the young woman hadn't even asked for her real name. Jazz seemed more bewildered by these revelations than upset by them. It was as if the young woman were operating with a seven-second delay. Zoie was fully expecting that Jazz's next big question would be, who are you really? In the meantime Zoie wasn't volunteering a full explanation. Once their deadly misadventure was over, Zoie intended to provide Jazz with a complete explanation—that is, if she still had breath to do the telling and if Jazz was still alive to listen.

Sister Te had clearly convinced Jazz that the khat business was about the same degree of moral transgression as prostitution—in other words, no big deal. And for sure less of an offense than selling hard drugs. In any case, Jazz must have witnessed plenty of drug dealing on the streets.

"Okay, let's get out of here. We've got go!" Wasting no time, Zoie retrieved Maynard's binder from where it still sat precariously on the table's edge. She secured it under Maynard's butt. "He'll want this when he wakes up."

"If he wakes up," Jazz added.

"Let's be positive. Come on—help me." Zoie wrapped the knife in a towel she found under the table, and she put the wrapped knife and the cut bindings in the tarp. Working quickly, she pulled the two corners of the tarp together, partly covering

Maynard's head, and bid Jazz to perform the same maneuver at his feet. Working in tandem, they pulled Maynard out of the building. Zoie turned off the lights and closed the door.

"Where we taking him?" Jazz asked.

"Somewhere where they can't find him. Somewhere where he can hold out until an ambulance gets here." Zoie wiped her brow with the back of her hand and thought for a second. "I've got an idea."

In the tarp Maynard's body formed a wide U as the two women struggled with his deadweight. Zoie kept her end of the tarp lifted so that his head wouldn't bump along the ground. Jazz did a similar thing at her end, near his feet. Maynard's side took the brunt of the rough journey along the concrete. The women huffed and puffed as they dragged him up the drive's slight incline and then across the middle of the courtyard to Zoie's target location—the dumpster near the Pen. The courtyard debris dug into Zoie's bare soles, but fear enabled her to put up with the discomfort.

"We can stick him behind this," said Zoie, finally stopping in front of the bin. "They'll never think to look here. Let's do it quickly!"

The dumpster's overflowing bags provided a tunnel of sorts in the crevice between the dumpster and the loading dock. There was just enough room to put Maynard in that space. The overflowing garbage bags provided cover in case anyone looked down from the loading dock. The garbage stank, but at least the swarm of flying insects Zoie had seen earlier had retreated for the night. With the flashlight to guide her, Zoie crawled into the crevice and pulled the tarp from her end. It wasn't the best of places to put him, but she told herself that at least he was out of the khat house. Considering the beating he'd taken and the drug injection, he was lucky to be alive. He still could have internal bleeding, but it was promising that he hadn't died within minutes of the lethal injection. Maybe that meant that he had survived the worst of it. As Jazz stood by the dumpster, Zoie scanned the courtyard with her flashlight and used her bare feet to wipe away any trail that dragging the tarp had left.

"God, I'd like to see their faces when they find out that he's gone."

"Not me. I don't want to see their faces at all," Jazz said.

"You're right about that. Okay, Jazz, let's get out of here. But first I'm asking you—just as Sister Te asked you—*please* don't say anything."

"Sister Te never asked me. She told me. She said keep my mouth shut. She never even said please."

Zoie hugged Jazz and then put an arm around the young girl's waist and led her up to the loading dock and inside the Pen. Exhausted, Zoie wiped her forehead with her bloodied shirt and took several deep breaths before taking a minute to brush the bits of courtyard grit digging into her soles.

"Want your shoes back?" Jazz asked.

"Later. Let's just get inside. I have to call 911."

"Then we got to deal with police." Jazz frowned and shook her head. "They'll lock me up. I got a rap sheet."

"Look, Jazz, you don't have to be part of this. I won't say anything about your helping me. I won't say anything about your working with Sister Te."

"Anna…oh, I mean whoever you really are."

"What, Jazz?" It was truly weird. Jazz still didn't seem to be bothered that Zoie's name wasn't Anna. She guessed hookers had their real names and their street aliases. So maybe the whole name thing was, as Jazz would say, no big deal.

"Girl, you better give me back my book light!" The spunky, streetwise Jazz had returned.

Zoie knew that Jazz was only feigning anger. "Sure. Thanks. It was helpful." The light still clung to her belt loop through everything. She detached it and handed it to Jazz.

"Are you still gonna be my partner with the website?"

For a second Zoie took a deep breath and closed her eyes. In her head she heard her grandmother's voice. Her southern cadence would become warm but forceful when she meant to give a warning or life advice. The voice conveyed the old adage about the appropriateness of a lie: "Remember, Zo, sometimes the truth is overrated. Not everybody's ready to hear the whole truth at any given moment."

Zoie squeezed the young girl's hand. "Of course, Jazz," Zoie said. Alas, her deception had to persist. There would be no apologies or explanation. The truth was for later. This lie was for now.

CHAPTER 45

IS HELP ON THE WAY?

Zoie and Jazz leaned against the Pen's brick wall, sweating and exhausted after moving Maynard's lifeless body across the courtyard and stowing him behind the dumpster. Even in the perceived safety of the chain-link enclosure, their adrenaline pumped.

"I need a cigarette," Jazz said, wiping her runny nose with the tail of her flimsy pajama shirt.

"Yeah, and I need a drink," Zoie said as she leaned forward and braced herself with her hands on her knees.

A car beam from down the driveway called them to attention. Without a word they hustled inside the Shelter. In minutes Tarik and his crew would learn that Maynard or what they thought to be his dead body was missing. Zoie led Jazz down the passageway to the still-quiet Great Room. "Please, God, don't let them find Maynard," she said.

"Please, God, don't let them find us," Jazz chimed in.

"I thought no men could come into this section."

"Those are the rules, but now I don't know."

"Quick, Jazz, where's a phone?"

Jazz thought for a second. She seemed confused. She was proving that she didn't operate well under stress.

Zoie wanted to shake her. "Pull yourself together, Jazz!" she commanded in a loud whisper. "Stay with me now. Think! Where's a phone?"

"Umm...there's a phone in Annette's office," Jazz finally offered. "But she may be in there, and when she's not, she keeps her door locked."

"Think again!" Zoie demanded. "What about the other women? Does someone have a cell phone?"

"Yeah, Cruz. But she's asleep."

"We'll just have to wake her."

With Zoie in the lead, the two women rushed through the dimly lit halls, heading back to their dorm room. Jazz pointed out Cruz, who was sleeping on the lower bunk opposite to Jazz's. Zoie peeked at the dark courtyard. Both cars had returned. Four men now stood next to an opened trunk. Jazz peeked through the curtains at the window's other end.

"Okay, we have to get that phone," Zoie whispered loudly. "Do you know where she keeps it?"

"Yeah, in her locker."

"Damn!" Zoie shined the flashlight in the woman's face and gently shook her. "Cruz, wake up," Zoie whispered, trying not to disturb the top bunk's occupants, Martha and Tanisha. Cruz's eyes opened and tried to stare into the flashlight beam.

"What's going on? Is there a fire or something?"

"No, Cruz. But it's an emergency. I need to use your phone to call 911."

The woman sat up and rubbed an eye. "What's the emergency? Why can't Annette call?"

"Shh. Keep your voices down!" Zoie commanded in a loud whisper. "Cruz, it's a long story. Right now we need your help."

Jazz whispered, "This is serious stuff. We can't ask Annette to help."

"But why?"

"Roomie, you need to trust me on this one," Jazz answered, finally sounding engaged.

Zoie looked back at Jazz. So Jazz did know more. She knew that Annette was in on the drug operation. It made sense. The night counselor worked directly for Sister Te. She lived at the Shelter and ran the place like a benevolent warden—but a warden, nevertheless. That meant that Tarik *could* gain access to the women's section. Yes, Jazz had known all along, but she hadn't mentioned the Annette link. It wasn't as if Jazz had withheld information. It was that Zoie had failed to ask the right question: Who else is involved?

"Come on, Cruz," Jazz begged. "We need your phone. Didn't I lend you fifty dollars to take your kids to the movies?"

"Okay, okay." Cruz swung her bare legs to the edge of her bunk. She grabbed her standard-issue robe from the foot of her bunk to cover her bra and panties sleepwear. Zoie and Jazz followed Cruz to her locker and watched as she retrieved her basic flip phone and turned it on.

Seeing the phone's display light, Zoie grabbed it from Cruz's hand. She moved past the bathroom and to the darkest part of the hall to distance herself from her roommates. Taking a deep breath, she dialed 911.

This time when a 911 operator came on, Zoie was able to give her the Shelter's name and approximate location. "Yes, there's a seriously injured man here. He's hidden behind the dumpster out back...his name is Maynard...no, I don't know his last name...he was beaten and injected with a drug overdose...yes, I witnessed the whole thing...I'm not sure what the drug is...the men who beat him are still around. They're in a little house in the back of the Shelter...yes, I'm a resident at the Shelter...what's my connection? Witness, concerned citizen, and friend of the victim...yes, I'm calling from the Shelter. I'm here inside the women's wing. The men who did this are very dangerous...look you need to hurry. If they find him, they'll kill him...there's at least four of them. Tell the police and the ambulance to come down the drive in back of the Shelter. Please hurry!"

Just as Zoie finished the 911 call, a person who could only have been the infamous Annette appeared at the other end of the hall. Even from a distance, Zoie could tell that the woman consumed healthy meals and exercised with more than padded wrist weights. Zoie stuffed Cruz's flip phone into her waistband, next to the battery-dead Blackberry.

"Ladies, what's going on?" Annette asked as she neared Jazz and Cruz. The boom of her voice matched her muscular physique. She didn't seem concerned that she might wake the other residents. "What's with the hall convention at this hour?"

Jazz and Cruz huddled together like children waiting to be brought to task.

"Ladies, give me the short version! What's going on?" Annette bellowed.

Cruz said, "We were helping our new roommate."

Slouched with arms wrapped behind her, Jazz bit her bottom lip. Her gaze shifted nervously—right, left, and then to the floor.

"Oh, yeah, Anna something or other," Annette said. "Is that cramped space bothering you, ladies? I thought it was a bad idea to force another cot into that tight space. Is that what's going on?" Annette directed her question to Jazz. "So what's Anna's problem?"

Tilting her head, Jazz shrugged. "She wasn't feeling well."

Cruz was about to pipe in to offer volatile information about the night's events, but Jazz poked a finger in her roommate's side, squelching any extra commentary.

"So why didn't she come and see me?" Annette asked. "Does she need a doctor or something?"

Jazz shrugged again. Cruz, confused from having received the message to shut up, observed the silence with a shrug.

"Hey, Anna. Are you okay? Can I help you?" Annette called down the hall. As Annette approached, Zoie moved into the light, pouting and feigning discomfort. "So, Anna, what's the problem?" Annette asked in a tone of true concern. "Oh my goodness! Look at the blood on your face and your shirt! What happened?"

Amid the night's pressing events, Zoie forgot all about the blood evidence on her clothing. Her feigned malady had to match the symptoms. "I had a nosebleed," she said. The survival-mode lie dripped from her lips like melting ice cream. She'd become adept at conjuring tales to fit the situation.

Annette towered over Zoie. She lifted Zoie's chin for a cursory inspection of Zoie's nose. "Humph. I don't see any blood or crusting in your nose."

"That's because I washed it off in the bathroom."

"Umm," said Annette, releasing Zoie's chin, "do you know what caused it? Do you have high blood pressure?"

"I'm not sure, but I still feel a little dizzy."

"Should I call an ambulance?"

"No. I'm better, really," Zoie said quickly.

"Well, let's make sure it's stopped. A cold compress stops a nosebleed. Let's go to the kitchen and get you an ice pack. And you should see a doctor later today. I'll give you a referral for Dr. Clark. He's just down the road. That way you don't have to go to the emergency room."

Annette put her arm around Zoie and led her slowly down the hall, toward the Great Room. "You ladies should go back to bed," she told Jazz and Cruz, as well as the other women who were now standing in their doorways. "I can handle this."

As she passed her two roommates, Zoie shared a knowing glance with Jazz. *How long will it take for the police and ambulance to get here?*

Zoie hadn't known the Shelter's exact address. She was counting on the Shelter being in DC's emergency-response database. As she held the ice pack that Annette had given her for the feigned nosebleed, her thoughts went to Maynard, who probably was still unconscious and behind the dumpster.

"Are you feeling any better?" Annette asked. "You seem a little spacey."

"No, I'm better, really." Her nose was cold, and she started to think that if she held the ice pack to her sinuses any longer, she'd suffer brain freeze.

Each minute of waiting seemed like an hour. At least the thugs weren't storming the women's section in search of Maynard. Zoie's brain cycled through what Tarik and his cohorts must be thinking. He was probably scratching his head and trying to figure out how the man he'd beaten, drugged, and left for dead managed to escape. Had he walked out? Someone had to have opened the door from the inside. Had Tarik discovered that the binder was also missing? Only the beaten man would've wanted the binder. Were the coded messages valuable to someone else? So far, *thankfully*, they hadn't called Annette. If they did, she'd make the connection between the bloodstains and Maynard.

"I think I want to lie down," Zoie told Annette, who'd stopped flipping through a magazine and now looked half-asleep.

"Let me get that voucher for Dr. Clark." Annette took off for her office and was back in several minutes with a slip for the Shelter's on-call physician. Zoie thanked her and gave her back the blue ice pack.

"Tell the volunteers in the morning to get you some clean clothes. I doubt the blood is gonna wash out."

411

Zoie hurried back to her dorm room. The room was dark, but all the women were awake. Jazz was the first to pop out of her bunk, and Cruz followed her, went straight for the window, and looked out it. Zoie tapped Cruz on the shoulder and handed the woman back her phone. "Thanks."

"You okay?" Jazz asked, stroking Zoie's arm like a mother hen.

"Yeah. Do you see anything outside?" Zoie asked.

"Not yet," Cruz said. Jazz must have filled her in on the night's happenings.

"Those guys must still be in the house. You know Annette works for them," Jazz whispered as if the Annette-Tarik connection were news.

"Jazz, thanks for warning me about Annette, and thanks for all your help tonight. We may have saved a life."

"Look, they're here," reported Cruz from the window, where she was joined by Martha from the top bunk.

Zoie moved to the window. Two police cruisers eased their way into the courtyard without sirens but with their dome lights flashing. Behind those vehicles came a fire-department ambulance.

"Anna, are you an undercover cop?" said a cool voice in the dark. Tanisha remained perched on her high bunk, while her dorm mates crowded at the window.

"I'm no cop," Zoie answered. She patted Jazz on the shoulder.

Jazz leaned close to Zoie's ear and whispered, "Don't worry— I won't tell them what you really do."

Zoie left the women at the window and headed back to the Great Room and then out to the Pen. Jazz and several other women weren't far behind.

Outside, homeless men had already gathered on the loading dock. Two cops were shining flashlights behind the dumpster.

"He's here, all right," yelled one of the cops. "I can't tell whether he's alive. Get the EMTs over here."

At least ten women congregated in the Pen, pressing their bodies against the chain-link fence for a better view of the courtyard happenings. Zoie, still barefoot, made her way down the steps to the courtyard. She spotted an officer standing by his cruiser. He was communicating through a shoulder mic. Compared with the others, he was older and seemed to be orchestrating things.

"I'm Zoie Taylor," she said. "I'm the person who called 911."

While the EMTs attended to Maynard with oxygen, Zoie gave the officer an abbreviated account of what had transpired that night in the small brick house—the beating and the drugs. She didn't mention the connected crimes: Ray's murder, the fire, the break-in, and the suspected financial fraud. The whole story (or at least what she knew of it) would have been too long and confusing. She didn't try to explain how she'd come to be at the Shelter in the first place or how she knew Maynard. As far as this officer was concerned, she was just another Shelter resident.

"Well, if you saw all this happen in the house," the officer said, "how did this guy get behind this dumpster? Did his attackers put him there?"

"No. They thought he was dead. Tarik, the ringleader, was going to get some other guys to move his body. They were going to put him on the street and make it look as if he'd been attacked and died there."

"Then how did he get behind that dumpster?"

"I was hiding when I witnessed the attempt to kill him. After Tarik left the house, I moved Maynard behind the dumpster."

"And whose blood is that on your shirt? Are you hurt?"

"No, it's his blood."

"You say his name is Maynard?"

"Yes."

"And you were able to move him unassisted?"

"Yeah, I dragged him using that tarp," Zoie confirmed, pointing to the piece of the blue tarp protruding from the gap. Part of her wanted to give Jazz credit for helping. She caught sight of Jazz pressed against the chain-link fence, looking scared. She'd promised Jazz that she would keep her out of it. "Officer, don't let my size fool you. I'm stronger than I look."

"Hmm. You must be."

Beyond the ambulance was a backup force. Three officers from that contingent made their way up the driveway, leading four handcuffed men. One of the handcuffed men was Tarik. Zoie didn't look in his direction. Even in handcuffs Tarik still frightened her.

The EMTs removed Maynard from behind the dumpster and placed him on a stretcher, an oxygen mask still attached to his face. Zoie went up to the stretcher and touched Maynard's arm. "How is he?"

"His breathing is very shallow. He's hanging on by a thread. He may have a couple of broken ribs. He could have a punctured lung. He's lucky to be alive," the woman EMT answered. "Someone was looking out for him...are you the one who called in?"

"Yes."

"Do you know what drug he took?"

"He didn't *take* anything. The men who beat him injected him with something. I think I heard them say heroin and vodka. I'm not sure. The needle might still be in the house...where's his binder?" Zoie asked. She ran over to the dumpster. With little explanation she instructed one of the officers to point the flashlight as she crawled back into the gap and retrieved Maynard's binder for a second time.

Zoie gave the binder to the female EMT. "This thing is precious to him. He must have it with him when he wakes up," Zoie told the woman.

The EMT agreed to guard it.

"We've done all we can do for him here," said the second EMT.

"Where are you taking him?" Zoie asked.

"To the level-one trauma ward at Washington Hospital."

They loaded Maynard into the ambulance, turned the vehicle around in the courtyard, and took off. *What now?* Zoie could hear the siren's whine fade in the distance.

Maynard, hang on!

CHAPTER 46

THE SECOND CAVALRY

The ambulance left with Maynard and a woman, and a formidable-looking man ambled down the long driveway to the rear of the Shelter.

"Jesus, it's Lena," Zoie said.

It was Lena sporting her brand of sexy casual—khaki shorts that showed off her shapely legs and a low-cut peasant top that accentuated her bosom. She was ready for work with a notebook and serious-looking camera, which hung around her neck on a thick strap. She displayed a necklace badge that identified her as a member of the press.

"Thank God you're okay," Lena said, running over and embracing Zoie. "Girl, I've been calling and calling. You had me worried. I kept wondering whether I'd have to use those emergency numbers to give your family bad news." Wide eyed, Lena surveyed the scene, taking in the assemblage of uniformed cops, police vehicles, and onlookers. "What happened? And what's with the blood?"

"Oh," said Zoie, looking at her blouse and hands. "It's not my blood. It belongs to the guy they tried to kill. The ambulance just took him. He's the one you ought to worry about."

"This is exciting—I mean serious," Lena said, her expression morphing from glee to one more fitting with the situation. "You got to fill me in."

"I will. But first, what are *you* doing here?"

"Remember, I said I had friends on the force?" Lena touched her companion's arm. "Zoie Taylor, meet Charles Bender—Detective Charles Bender."

"Call me Charles," he said, extending his hand.

Zoie shook it reluctantly.

"Based on Lena's account of what's going on, I'm glad to hear the blood's not yours," he said. "You're mixed up in some dangerous business." Detective Bender's freshly pressed clothes and fade cut said he cared about his appearance and never missed a barber appointment. He turned to the officer in charge and introduced himself. "Detective Bender, Narcotics, Seventh District." He flashed his shield for confirmation.

"You're a ways from home base, Detective," said Officer Frankle. "Did you get a call about this?"

"No, actually my presence is unofficial. I'm here with my friend, who's doing a story. And I don't want to get in your way, Officer."

"Mmm," Officer Frankle said as he considered the matter. "If you have information that can help us understand what went down here, I'd appreciate your sharing it."

"Indeed, I may have some," answered Detective Bender. Having been given the green light to add his counsel to the situation, Bender began to disclose what he knew. "There's a lot going on here. This assault may be connected to a probable homicide of a prominent DC businessman in Potomac yesterday. The Montgomery County boys got that one. And you may need to bring in the white-collar crew to look at the Shelter's books."

Zoie didn't track all of the conversation. Her mind was consumed with thoughts of Maynard, who was in route to the hospital, stubbornly clinging to life. He had never wanted to come back to the Shelter. He'd proclaimed it evil. But she'd wrangled him into it—that is, she and Simon. And where was Simon? She had to let him know that his friend was in serious condition. Zoie took a deep breath. What a strange turn of events. Her plan had been to find evidence of likely Foundation kickbacks. No progress there, but she'd uncovered so much more. Lena's showing up with the cavalry after the fact hadn't been part of the plan.

"Lena, I'm glad to see you, even though I asked you *not* to set off alarms unless you hadn't heard from me." Zoie took a deep breath. "So what brought you here?"

"Zoie, cool out. After you took off in that getup, I got nervous about this whole scheme. So I called Charles and filled him in on your plan to infiltrate the Shelter."

Zoie frowned. *Infiltrate?* Why had she ever believed that she could share things with Lena in confidence?

"Now, Zoie, don't be mad," Lena continued. "I know I wasn't supposed to tell anyone. But you'll thank me later. Charles is a really good guy."

"I'm not mad," Zoie said with an expression that did not match her words.

"Wow, let me explain. When I talked to Charles, he thought you were crazy to try this on your own. But he promised not to interfere. Now I didn't ask him to, but being the detective that he is, he did some checking around. And he came up with info pointing to some really funky happenings here tonight. Then he got a tip from an informant who seemed to know that you were here. Your cover was already blown."

"But how could that be?"

"Maybe somebody recognized you. I don't know. But when Charles found out that a 911 call came in reporting an assault at Mahali, he figured your being here undercover and the assault report were too coincidental. He swung by and picked me up, and here we are."

"So Charles knows more?"

"Girl, I'm not sure what he knows. I know that he's one of the good guys."

"Like Jahi, huh?"

"Look, sometimes I'm wrong."

"And Charles?"

"Hey! We're talking about the police here. Anyway, Charles will have to tell you what he knows. In the meantime you gotta fill me in. *Remember* that you promised me an exclusive."

Zoie laughed to relieve the tension. She was exhausted, and her knees felt like they were about to buckle. "Someone out there knows how this all fits together, and it ain't me," Zoie said.

"Girl, you've cracked a case," Lena said. "Hold on a minute— I need some pictures." Lena backed up and starting snapping, first capturing Zoie in her bloodied clothes against the backdrop of the police cruisers, then taking a shot of the homeless onlookers congregated on the loading dock.

At Detective Bender's behest, Officer Frankle gave Zoie and Lena the okay to sit in the back of his cruiser. Feeling safe, Zoie let her head fall back against the seat. She closed her eyes and mumbled, "Lena, there's so much to tell you. There's more going on here than I ever suspected. There's a big-time drug operation running out of this place. These criminals beat my homeless contact without mercy. I heard them talking about going after me. I'm sure they're responsible for Ray Gaddis's death and the break-in at my apartment. My laptop and briefcase are here." Zoie's voice trailed off.

"My God! What you did was so dangerous. Hopefully the madness stops here, now that the police have them in custody."

"They only have *some* of them," Zoie said, sitting up again. "I'm still afraid. I don't know how wide or how deep this goes.

I don't know how many people who work in the Shelter are involved. It even goes to the residents. More folks are involved, more than those four thugs. Even my assistant at the Foundation may be involved."

"You're kidding."

"I wish I were. And Sister Te's in this for sure. She's got to be one of the ringleaders, along with her son."

"And Jahi?"

Zoie felt a chill at Jahi's mention. "Lena, you tell me. How could he *not* be involved? How could *all* this criminal activity go on under his nose and he not be in the middle of it? For all I know, he's the grand pooh-bah of the whole operation."

"Ooooweee! Mr. Wannabe City Councilman. Sorry to hear that," Lena said with a moan. "I held high hopes for that man-child. I had him pegged for one of the all-time good guys. Gee, too bad. How could I have been so wrong?"

The courtyard was somewhat lit by police lights. Someone turned on the lights on the men's loading dock. From the cruiser window, Zoie watched as two officers stuffed a handcuffed Tarik and his cohorts into a police van.

"I need some air," Zoie said.

Zoie and Lena emerged from the cruiser. As Lena moved around the crime scene snapping pictures, Zoie braced herself against the cruiser and looked back at the Pen. Filled with women pressed into its fencing, it reminded Zoie of a scene from a concentration-camp documentary. Although the Pen's door to the courtyard was ajar, none of the women ventured out into the yard. But someone was coming into the courtyard from another Shelter door. It was Sister Te, late to the party and accompanied by none other than Annette. For a few minutes, Zoie had forgotten about these second-tier characters. In regard to Annette, her appearance was very late. Zoie expected to see the night counselor swoop in long before this. But Annette had taken her time, probably so she could alert Sister Te. The two had probably needed to coordinate their alibis before showing their faces to the police.

Sister Te and Annette descended into the courtyard, and Zoie latched on to Lena's arm. Sister Te and her accomplice went straight over to Officer Frankle. They ignored Zoie and Lena.

"I understand you have arrested my son. I'm not sure why you have taken him into custody, but may I speak to him?" Sister Te said to Frankle.

Lena dragged Zoie back a few yards, far enough away that Zoie missed hearing Officer Frankle's reply to Sister Te's request. Zoie knew that if Sister Te had a chance to speak to her son, she'd do so in Amharic. She'd feed him the "communal lie," and the police would be none the wiser. While Zoie was focusing on trying to hear what was being said, Lena was having her own panic. She redirected Zoie's attention to the latest addition to the courtyard's loading dock—Jahi Khalfani. He was near the double-door exit from the men's Shelter, speaking to several of the men assembled there.

Zoie, feeling that she needed some independent protection, was glad that Detective Bender was close by. *How are these fast talkers going to get out of this one?* Zoie beckoned Detective Bender. "What now?" she asked, her voice defiant.

"I told Frankle who you are and explained that you were here as an unofficial undercover investigator, working on behalf of your Foundation. Just so you know, the men who attacked Maynard are now under arrest."

"Thanks, Charles, but what about the whole khat operation? What about the rest of the skullduggery going on here?"

"Is there someone else that you can identify as being involved?"

"Where do I start?" Zoie answered with disgust. "There's Sister Te, the woman over there with Frankle. She runs the women's section of the Shelter, and there's Jahi Khalfani, director of the entire Shelter."

"Now that dude's name is familiar."

"That *dude* is all in the news. He's running for the DC Council. And let's not forget Sister Te's sidekick. Her name is Annette."

"Whew!" Detective Bender exclaimed. "If all of this is true, they're going to need another paddy wagon. Did you witness their involvement in the assault or drug operation?"

"Well, no…not exactly. I overhead their names mentioned by Tarik, one of the guys they just caught. He was discussing his illegal activities on the phone. And by the way, Tarik is Sister Te's son."

Charles rubbed his clean-shaven chin. "Zoie, you're a wealth of information, an investigator's dream for providing all of these leads. But I don't know."

"What don't you know, Detective? I know what I heard. Oh, there's another man named Asad. He's on his way to New York City to pick up more khat from a Queens dealer. He's the one who beat Maynard with a broomstick. I witnessed that beating from where I was hiding. In fact, Asad probably took the Shelter's van for his drug run. You see that the Shelter's van isn't parked here."

Charles jotted notes on a small pad and then looked up. "Okay, Detective Taylor. Got it. I'll let these guys know."

"And can I get my laptop and briefcase back? They stole it when they broke into my apartment this morning. It's in that house where they beat Maynard. I saw it."

"Yes, ma'am. I'm sure you'll get your things back at some point. But for now I think you're gonna have to wait. Most likely they'll go into evidence as stolen property."

Discouraged, Zoie sighed.

"Zoie, I need to give you some more disappointing news. It's unlikely these other folks you're naming will be arrested tonight."

"What?"

"Now hold it. You should know the drill. They'll either be brought in for questioning or be asked to come in to give statements. Until there's more evidence to incriminate them, they'll end up in that vague category known as 'persons of interest.'"

"A criminal attorney, I'm not." Zoie was indignant. "But 'persons of interest'! I'm telling you what I overheard! You guys need to take them off the street before they hurt somebody else. My family and I won't be safe until they're locked up."

"Was this conversation that you overheard on speakerphone?"

"Well, no."

Charles rubbed his lips in thought. "Look, I hear you. But here's my unofficial opinion, for what it's worth. What you overheard was only one-half of a phone conversation, right?"

"Right."

"Okay, so what you heard lacked full context. And was the whole part of what you heard in English or in some other language that you comprehend?"

"Well, parts were in English, and the rest was in their language."

"Their language. Well, there it is."

Too furious to acknowledge the truth of Charles's statements, with her jaw locked, Zoie remained silent. The truth was that she couldn't really remember what Tarik had said or say that she understood it, except that in the course of his conversations on the phone or with Asad, he mentioned Jahi and his mother.

Charles continued but with a gentler tone. "Khalfani and this Sister Te person, as far as everyone knows, are upstanding members of the community, right?"

"And your point is?"

"Get real, Zoie. That dude is running for the DC Council. He runs a homeless shelter, and Sister Te helps him. These uniform types all know them. They patrol this district. I wouldn't be surprised if on occasion they've eaten in the Shelter's dining hall. They 'shoot the shit' with this guy. You've heard the term *police-community relations*. That's what's going on here."

Zoie frowned. "Hmm."

"So you see, without clear evidence of specific wrongdoing by those individuals, these Fifth District guys aren't going to move on them tonight. And by the way, since last I checked, having a guilty relative doesn't make a person guilty. If the law worked that way, I'd be in jail a few times over."

Zoie didn't like that Charles was lecturing her about the law. Still, she recognized that he was giving her the straight scoop.

Having ended his conversation with the men on the loading dock, Jahi descended into the courtyard. His baggy jeans and a sloppy long T-shirt told Zoie that he'd dressed in haste. With dreads pulled back in a ponytail, his full face revealed a frightening anger. He looked ready to fight. She'd seen that expression once before, during the gum-in-hair incident at the movies at the beginning of the summer. That time the threat had been an adolescent prank. He'd been ready to do battle. This time his Shelter and its employees were under siege. He joined Sister Te and Annette, who were still engaged in an animated exchange with Officer Frankle. When Jahi joined them, Charles moved away. The only bit of the conversation Zoie could pick up was Sister Te's anguished cry. "Ja', they've arrested Tarik!"

Fists clenched, Jahi lowered his head as if in silent prayer. The stance seemed to calm him and soften his expression. He looked up in Zoie's direction. His anger had dissolved. For a moment it seemed as if their eyes would meet. But it wasn't so much that he was looking at her as through her, as if she were some ethereal being outside his realm of comprehension. His neutral reaction indicated that he didn't recognize her. The eerie encounter lasted only seconds, but the Jahi Zoie saw gave her chills.

Perhaps Officer Frankle failed to mention that a woman named Zoie Taylor had made the 911 call, which resulted in Tarik's arrest. It could be that her disguise was still working: without heels or even shoes or makeup, she wasn't the Zoie whom Jahi had come to know. He'd seen her in the raw when they made love. Those times his eyes had been opened. He knew what she looked like unadorned. Here she was out of context. Zoie...at the Shelter...in the middle of the night. It didn't make sense. To Sister Te and Annette, she was just Anna, a homeless woman they'd crammed into the women's section.

It's just as well he doesn't know me.

Jahi turned to Zoie again and looked right past her to acknowledge Lena. "Lena! What are you doing here?"

In what seemed like protective positioning, Lena moved closer to Jahi, blocking Zoie from his line of sight. Lena smiled and drummed her nails on her plastic press badge, which now adhered to her damp bosom. For a moment the badge drew his eyes.

"Hey, Jahi—you know me. I go where the news takes me," Lena answered whimsically. Then her tone turned serious. "Unfortunately, lover boy, today Mahali is where the news is... and I got to tell you—the news ain't good."

Jahi responded with a grimace and went to Sister Te's side.

Charles pulled Frankle aside, leaving Jahi and Sister Te to commiserate about their child. Frankle had denied the pair's request to talk with Tarik in private. "He's not a minor," Frankle told them, his tone apologetic. "You'll have a chance to speak to him at the precinct, after he and his cohorts are booked."

Sister Te was pissed. Jahi held her back.

Minutes later Charles told Zoie and Lena that he'd worked out a special arrangement for her. Frankle would allow Zoie to leave the crime scene under the stipulation that Charles would deliver her to the Fifth District station by 10:00 a.m. to give her statement.

"Since you don't have ID, I vouched for you," Charles explained, cocking his brow. "Vouched" meant that Charles put his reputation on the line. With that came the unspoken admonishment: *Don't let me down.* "I trust Lena completely, and she says you're okay." Charles turned to Lena, who couldn't contain her one-hundred-watt grin. "Lena, baby, you've got some wild friends."

With a weak smile, Zoie thanked Charles for his efforts on her behalf. She'd never mastered gracious gestures, like admitting when she was wrong. She wasn't sure she even liked Charles. She resented how he'd taken charge of the situation without consulting her. Decision making was her purview, something she'd always done on her own. Elliot's departure from her life ended the necessity to confer with anyone when making important decisions. But this time Zoie was exhausted, too exhausted to exert dominance in her own life. *Let this "knight" in shining armor take charge*, she thought. What would be the point in resisting? Hadn't Charles handled the situation just fine? As a DC detective, he probably knew the territory and how to negotiate around the police department's bureaucracy. With Charles there she could avoid a direct confrontation with Jahi. In her peripheral vision, she tracked Jahi's movements.

"If this Maynard had died, things would be different," Charles said. "Then this would be a murder scene, and they'd take you right down to the station. And from what I gather, this homeless fellow is not out of the woods yet. Let's hope he makes it."

"Am I a person of interest?" Zoie asked.

Charles scratched his head. "Zoie, you got to admit that this whole scene and your involvement is pretty flakey."

Lena had been quiet. She now piped in., "Charles, what's the problem? I've already explained why Zoie came to the Shelter. I even helped with her disguise. Weren't you listening?"

"Whoa! Cool down ladies," Charles said. "You never know about these things."

"I think he's right," Zoie said quietly, followed by a long sigh. "Lena, you don't know everything."

Lena bristled. "What do you mean?"

"I'll bring you up to speed later," Zoie told her.

Charles said, "So far they've got the broom handle they think was used as the assault weapon and plenty of evidence about the khat operation."

"I bet the guys in this district knew this was going on," Lena said.

"Now, Lena, we don't know that," Charles said, his tone scolding. "Be careful with your accusations."

"Hey, don't get all 'police brotherhood' on me. I'm just saying. I'm being honest between we three."

"I don't know who knew what or how," Charles sighed. "All I know is that khat is a Schedule I narcotic when it's fresh. Most of the time, though, it's not treated as such. I can't say we heavily pursue enforcement of the stuff. Not in the way we go after cocaine or heroin. All I know is that African cabdrivers love it. They claim it keeps them alert. Most of them picked up the chewing habit back home. The stuff's addictive. And from what I know, it's difficult to get the good stuff here."

"What's the good stuff?" Lena asked.

"By good, I mean fresh. It's got a short shelf life. And when it's no longer fresh, they dry it and make tea. It loses its potency and is downgraded to Schedule VI when it's dry, which most jurisdictions consider to be no big deal."

"So which one is this—a big deal or no big deal?" Zoie asked.

"I don't know yet. Anyway, congratulations, Zoie. You may have uncovered a prime khat-distribution point for the city's Ethiopian, Somali, and Yemeni populations. This bust is gonna interrupt their supply. At least for a while. Cabbies aren't gonna be happy."

"Well, so be it," Zoie replied. "These drug dealers are killers."

"If khat is Schedule I, which is up there with coke and heroin, why isn't it treated more seriously?" Lena asked.

"Good question. I guess it's because it's not really considered a street drug. Africans and Arabs seem to have restricted its use to their own communities. And the habit doesn't cost hundreds a day like those other drugs. So these folks aren't knocking over grocery stores to support their habit."

"No, they're just *killing* folks," Zoie said sarcastically.

"And their *little* community ain't so little anymore. What used to be all black Shaw around Ninth Street and U Street is now Little Ethiopia. Don't get me wrong—I love the food," said Lena.

Charles was well versed in narcotics. After all, narcotics was his beat. Maynard had known about khat as well. Their take on the drug matched the spiel that Sister Te had given Jazz. On the scale of harmful substances, khat, though harmful, ranked below marijuana in the eyes of crime fighters. Trying to stop its distribution was an afterthought.

"Taking a man's life isn't a petty crime," Zoie insisted. But Charles had already turned away, his attention directed to his fellow officers.

Zoie was ambivalent about delaying giving her statement. While she certainly needed to get cleaned up, part of her just wanted to get the statement over with as quickly as possible. At some point she'd have to explain her visit to Ray's house, a visit that might have coincided with his murder. Explaining the probable fraudulent ties between the Shelter, Ray, and the Foundation grants wasn't going to be simple either. Nor was how she'd come to suspect her own assistant's involvement in the criminal dealings. When the time came, she didn't know whether she'd tell them about the uncorroborated info concerning Ray's in-office sexual indiscretions. Would she mention Jazz's name in connection with Sister Te and the drug operation? She'd *promised* Jazz that she wouldn't involve her. Zoie wanted to be truthful, but at the same time, she didn't want to inflict collateral damage, if it could be helped.

What she knew and what she suspected whirled in her brain, merging into a convoluted plot. Everyone at the Foundation or Mahali was now suspect. She wondered whether there'd be enough evidence to connect all the dots. It was far too early for her to breathe a sigh of relief. The crisis wouldn't be over until all guilty parties were behind bars. Until then she and her family would be in danger

Zoie considered the particulars of her own situation. In a zealous rush to wrap up cases, sometimes the police made terrible mistakes—mistakes that dragged down innocent parties. Even though she might obtain vindication ultimately, a prolonged investigation might ensue, which could screw up her life for months, even years. Once the giant wheels of the criminal justice system got rolling, they sometimes crushed innocent people in their path. The damning aspect of her situation was that she'd been involved with Jahi, one of the Foundation's clients.

Zoie fanned her face. *I have nothing to worry about.* There was plenty of evidence pointing to her innocent involvement in any criminal act. After all, hadn't she been the victim? There was the break-in at her apartment and the arson at her grandmother's house. What could be clearer? This gang wanted to keep her quiet, not so much about the khat operation, which she had yet to discover, but because she'd figured out the connection between Mahali, fraud, and Ray's murder—a connection she still didn't fully understand.

Yes, her delaying her statement to the police looked more and more appealing. She needed time to gather her thoughts before she spilled her guts. She also needed to retrieve her pocketbook and ID, to change out of her bloodied clothes, and to get shoes for her bruised feet. High on the list of things that she didn't need was an encounter with Jahi. Now she had to admit that she was grateful for the delay that Charles had arranged. She so wanted to sleep but certainly not back at her apartment. She doubted, though, that sleep anywhere would be possible that night.

"We're taking you back to my place," Lena said, almost as if she could read Zoie's mind. "And remember you owe me that exclusive."

"Lena, I know what I promised. And I plan to fulfill it," Zoie said, her tone irritated.

Zoie looked back at the Pen. Jazz's pink baby-doll pajamas pressed against the chain-link fence and stood out like a neon sign amid the others' drab attire. Zoie couldn't read her roommate's expression but imagined that it registered bewilderment and disappointment. Zoie mouthed a hushed "Sorry," but the distance between the two women was probably too great for Jazz to read Zoie's lips.

"Come on. Let's get out of here," Lena said. She grabbed Zoie's arm and signaled to her detective escort that they were ready to leave. The three exited the crime scene, maneuvering past the patrol cars, and headed down the driveway. No one from the Shelter tried to stop the two strangers who lead Zoie, also known as Anna, a Shelter resident, away. As far as Zoie could tell, Jahi was still unaware of her true identity. Perhaps he'd failed to even ask who placed the 911 call, which brought the hoards of law enforcement to his beloved Shelter. With his arm around Sister Te's shoulder, Jahi was too busy comforting his ex to notice that the homeless woman who'd been integral to the night's happenings was leaving the scene.

With Lena in the passenger seat and Zoie safely in the back, Charles navigated his late-model Cadillac Escalade through the empty DC streets and to Lena's Southwest apartment. Wound tight, Lena chattered about Jahi almost the whole way. Slouched into the soft leather of the back seat, Zoie tried to ignore her.

"I think this Mahali drug operation has scuttled his political career," Lena pronounced. When no one offered any comment, she said, "Hey, you're mighty quiet back there."

"What's there to say? I agree with everything," Zoie responded, though she wasn't sure what everything was.

Charles, who'd been quiet, finally chimed in, offering an unsolicited explanation of how he had known that something funky was going down at the Shelter. One of his informants had tipped him off that a woman possibly fitting Zoie's description had arrived at the Shelter in the early evening.

With this new line of conversation, Zoie's interest perked up. "And who might this informant be?"

"I'm not at liberty to say," Charles answered. "I wouldn't be a good cop if I told you anything about this informant. Let's just say Narcotics has eyes all over the city."

An informant, huh. Charles was being careful. He wouldn't even give a pronoun clue to identify the informant's gender. Arms crossed, Zoie sank back into the seat and considered the possible informant suspects. Who would have known that she was at the shelter? Of course, there was the enigmatic Simon. Maynard had said that Simon was the one who knew she was an attorney. Then there was Muwakkil, the taxi driver who'd chauffeured her for most of the day. He knew what she looked like before *and* after changing into her homeless getup. He also knew where she lived. For laughs Zoie put Jazz on her suspect list. Having been on the streets, Jazz would be a good source of information for the police. If Jazz were indeed the informant, the girl would surely deserve an Oscar for the best portrayal of an abused woman in the role of an undercover informant. Zoie guessed that Jazz was smarter than she seemed. And then it could have been anybody else at the Shelter, someone who'd been watching her from afar. Bea, the volunteer, perhaps? Tanisha or Martha? In the end Muwakkil stood out as the most plausible. *Muwakkil, huh? The one who can be trusted?*

"Yeah, Muwakkil can be trusted, all right. Trusted to do what?" Zoie said under her breath.

CHAPTER 47

THOSE THINGS
MOST PRECIOUS

In the wee hours, going from Northeast DC to Southwest DC, through the semi-deserted city was a fifteen-minute ride. Charles pulled into the no-parking zone in front of Lena's building and stuck a placard on his dashboard, identifying his Cadillac as a police vehicle. Lena hopped out and keyed a code into the digital pad next to the main door. Still barefooted, Zoie took her time maneuvering the short gritty sidewalk to the building.

The young desk attendant knew Lena. "Good evening, Ms. Christian. Or is it morning? Please have your guests sign the visitor register."

"No need," Charles said, stepping forward and flashing his police shield.

If you liked the macho type, Charles is your man, Zoie thought. The threesome proceeded to Lena's seventh-floor apartment. When Lena opened her door, all eyes focused on Lena's carpet, a sea of white as threatening as the Rubicon. Lena shed her shoes. Obviously accustomed to the shoe routine, Charles followed suit.

Zoie had no shoes to shed. Her bare feet were strangely cold, a bit numb, and filthy, having picked up God knows what from the Shelter's courtyard. Until now neither Lena nor Charles had seemed to notice her bare feet. Zoie was about to ask Lena for some plastic bags to cover them when Lena noticed Zoie's problem. "Poor thing," Lena said, looking down at Zoie's feet. "Wait here. I'll get you something to clean them." She scurried toward the kitchen.

"Lena, let's make this easy!" Charles called after her. Zoie had no time to mount a credible objection before Charles swooped down, lifted her slight frame, and deposited her in a kitchen chair.

In the kitchen Lena was ready with a pan of warm, soapy water and a towel. "There," she said proudly, placing the pan at Zoie's feet, clearly happy that her carpet was no longer in jeopardy.

Zoie thanked them profusely and placed her feet into the warm water to soak. She would examine her feet for scrapes later. For now she just wanted to enjoy the water's warmth.

Accompanied by Lena, Charles went into the living room and made himself comfortable.

While her feet soaked, Zoie spotted the paper on which she'd written her emergency-contact numbers. Lena was to get in touch with these people if something happened to her at the Shelter. Thank God that Lena hadn't needed to use them. She folded the paper into a tight square and stuck it in her pocket. "Soon this will be all over," she said, sighing. Soon she would bring Nikki home. For now her daughter was safe in Ohio. Zoie pondered asking the Benjamins to keep Nikki for an additional week, until things settled down.

After Zoie ensured that her feet were clean enough to pass through Lena's carpeted areas, her host showed her to the apartment's second bedroom. The small room, like the rest of Lena's home, was immaculate. It was done in eggshell tones. The sofa was adorned with animal-print pillows, and the Queen Anne desk was covered in tidily stacked documents. Lena had already moved Zoie's denim bag and pocketbook into the room. "All I want is to get into my own clothes and get a few hours of shut eye," Zoie said.

"I'll pull out the sofa bed for you," Lena said with a sigh. "Let me get some sheets, and you probably want to take a shower to get the crud off. By the way, do you think we can do that exclusive interview after you talk to the police? I let my editor know that I'm expecting a hot story." Lena waited anxiously for Zoie's response.

"I guess. Yeah, sure." At some point Zoie would have to contact the Foundation, and surely she would have to go with the police to her apartment, which should now be considered a crime scene because of the break-in and the theft of her laptop and briefcase. She didn't know what she would be allowed to tell Lena with a murder and attempted-murder cases pending.

Zoie dug through her things in search of her all-important Blackberry charger. In her rush to leave her apartment after the break-in, she'd failed to pack the charger and a robe. Lena lent her a terrycloth robe and found an old Blackberry charger, which luckily worked with Zoie's phone. Zoie stripped off her bloodied clothes and put them in a plastic bag for Charles. It seemed the bloodied clothes constituted evidence and "Sir" Charles was accountable for this evidence. It was a stipulation of the grand bargain that Charles had made with the Fifth District officers to keep her from being marched off to the precinct.

"This isn't what you were wearing when you left here," Lena said, making the clothing connection. "Guess my jogging suit is history?"

"Sorry. I'll reimburse you," Zoie said.

"I'm not worried about it. Mmm, I have some fond memories of what I was doing in that thing."

"Too much information," Zoie replied with a half smile. "Please ask Charles to check on Maynard. They took him to Washington Hospital Center."

Lena passed on the request for an update on Maynard's condition to Charles, who in turn called out from the living room. "Zoie, do you know this Maynard's last name?"

"No! All I know is Maynard!" she responded.

In the next half hour, Zoie was feeling a bit saner. She'd showered, ridding herself of the remaining blood, sweat, and dirt from the night's ordeals. Donning the borrowed robe, she joined Lena and Charles on the white sofa. Sipping beer, Charles looked quite at home.

"Your friend Maynard is still critical but breathing on his own," Charles reported.

"Thank God," Zoie said.

"Thank yourself," Charles said. "Moving him was a smart thing. It kept him from further harm. The hospital has the report on the drug those thugs used on him. Seems if the drugs didn't get him, the internal injuries from the beating could have done him in."

Lena said, "See, Zoie—you're a hero. This is gonna make a great story."

Zoie wasn't seeking praise. She was just relieved that Maynard had survived. And she was very, very tired. "Thanks, Charles. I needed to know that. Now I'll try to get a few hours of sleep."

"Okay. But remember that I'll be back at nine to take you to the station."

"That soon, huh?"

"Got to get this over with."

"If you mean getting the statement over with, well, yeah, that's good. But you and I know this is far from over. There are more of them out there. They didn't finish off Maynard, and they didn't get me...this time, anyway. But they might try again."

"Goons don't take those actions on their own. I think we got the ringleaders."

"I'm not sure about that."

"Then you have legitimate concerns for your safety. Do you want me to see if I can arrange protection?"

Zoie closed her eyes and nervously rubbed her forehead as she thought. It was only a few hours until daylight. And at 9:00 a.m. Charles would be back. All she wanted to do was to get a little sleep.

"We've got the guy at the desk downstairs," Lena offered, trying to be helpful.

Zoie opened her eyes and laughed. "Did I tell you how easy it was for me to get past your security yesterday? And the front desk of my building is manned twenty-four hours too, but that didn't stop them from breaking into my place. She turned to Charles. "Look, maybe the police can arrange something later. The truth is I'm afraid to return to my apartment."

"Charles, is Jahi Khalfani still at large?" Lena asked.

"'At large' sounds so ominous…" Zoie said.

"If Khalfani is behind this, as you suspect, then it is ominous. I'll check on his status before I leave."

"Please check on Sister Te's status as well."

"You ladies make a great team," Charles said. He went off to the kitchen to call his precinct contact. He was back in a few minutes with an update. "Khalfani and this Sister Te are at the Fifth District station. They're not being held. They're just giving their statements. And my contact says Khalfani wants to arrange bail for one of the guys they arrested."

"That's got to be Tarik," Zoie said.

"Well, I can tell you that there'll be no bail tonight, no bail until after arraignment, and maybe no bail even then, depending on what he's charged with."

"Okay, I can deal with that," Zoie said. "Right now I want to check my messages and then close my eyes. I'm exhausted." The adrenalin rush had come and gone. She was crashing.

"You've got my number," Charles said, turning to Lena. "If anything looks fishy, call me right away."

Lena walked Charles into the foyer. Heading to the kitchen for a glass of water, Zoie looked back to see their bodies press together in a sultry embrace. Earlier Zoie had noticed Charles's gold band. *Another case of an affair with a married man.* Anyway, who was she to judge? Lena was a single, thirty-something, professional black woman in a city infamous for its unfavorable ratio of black women to black men—unfavorable for women that is. Under those circumstances it was difficult for an educated woman to find her equal. And it appeared that Lena had chosen not to look beyond her own race. But then she'd just reconnected with Lena. What did she know about Lena, really?

The two must have sensed Zoie's eyes. They exited to the outside hall to conclude their farewell.

Sipping her water, Zoie sat on the sofa bed, scrolling through her missed calls while her Blackberry charged. Many of the calls she didn't recognize. She figured the unrecognized calls to be more of the threatening variety. She sure wasn't going to upset herself further by listening to those messages tonight. In fact, they could wait until she sat with the police. Several local area codes came up in the list. She figured that these calls were from folks at her office and maybe even from Jahi, though his cell number didn't appear in the list. A number of calls bearing a 419 area code grabbed her attention. Some were clearly identified as from Celeste. A few had a 419 area code but provided no names. The last missed call from that area code was at 1:30 a.m. Why would Celeste be calling at that hour? The Benjamins usually turned in before the late-night news.

Zoie took a deep breath and called Celeste. After two rings Celeste answered with a weak "Hello."

"Celeste, this is Zoie. Sorry to call at this ungodly hour. I saw you'd tried to call me several times. I figured it must be important."

"Oh, God! Zoie, we've been trying to contact you for hours."

"My cell battery went dead. What's wrong? What's going on? Is Nikki okay?"

"Oh, Zoie, Nikki is missing."

"What do you mean—Nikki is missing?"

"Since this evening she's been gone. We can't find her."

"Where have you looked? Have you looked in the closets and under the beds? Have you looked in the dryer?" Zoie said in rapid fire. Zoie was now standing, stretching the cord that tethered the device to the wall outlet. "Check the dryer! She hid there once when she was three. She's a master at hide-and-seek."

"Yes, yes, Zoie. We've looked everywhere. She was supposed to be with the neighbor kids to watch a movie. But…" Celeste's voice trailed off. Zoie could hear sobbing.

"Did you leave her over there? Was it after dark?"

Celeste was no longer answering. All Zoie could hear was the woman's muffled sobs.

"Celeste! Celeste! Get it together! You're telling me that you lost my child?"

The next voice to come on the line was Phillip Benjamin.

"My wife is too upset to talk now." Zoie could tell that he, too, was shaken, but at least he was still coherent. Zoie heard him say, "Celeste, sit down before you pass out."

"Phillip! Phillip! Are you still there? What's going on?"

"Zoie, I'll explain what I know. The Perrysburg police are here. They've been listening on the other phone in case this was a ransom call. "It's Zoie Taylor, Nikki's mother," he told someone in the room.

"Ransom call? Do they think she's been kidnapped?"

"Right now nobody's sure. We tried to call you at home and at your office…wait. They want to talk to you."

Zoie could hardly speak. All kinds of things were going through her mind. At the top of the list was the ugly conversation that she and Nikki had when they last talked. Then she remembered the threat that Tarik had made about her daughter. She had figured that Nikki, being in Ohio, was safe.

"Hey, what's going on?" After seeing Charles off, Lena returned. "Who are you talking to at this hour?"

With the phone pressed to her ear, Zoie directed a loud "Shh!" at Lena.

Lena grimaced and backed away and waited by her desk.

"I'm so sorry, Zoie. I'm going to put the police on. They can explain what they're doing," Phillip said.

Zoie was suddenly talking to a Perrysburg detective named Marconi. The detective explained that they'd already searched the neighborhood and were planning to do a more thorough search at light. They were also checking all of the registered child sex offenders in the area. As Zoie listened, her heart sank.

"What? What?" said Lena, who couldn't hear the other end of the conversation.

"We think she might've run away," continued the detective. "Seems that the puppy she was very attached to is also missing. The Benjamins told us that they had sold the puppy to a man who planned to pick it up next week. We're trying to locate this person so we can talk to him. You know animals are sometimes used to lure children away."

Zoie gasped.

"We don't know if that's what happened. But we have to consider all possibilities." The detective went on to explain that they were working with a picture of Nikki and the puppy, which the Benjamins had provided, and that the FBI branch in Toledo was now involved. They planned to issue an Amber Alert within the hour. "Is there anything you know that can help us with the search? Sometimes things you think are ordinary can be helpful clues, like what foods she likes."

"Give me a moment to think," Zoie said, almost stuttering. Her usually sharp mind was unresponsive. There was plenty she could tell them, but none of it could be categorized as ordinary. How does she tell them about a crime syndicate out for revenge? *Oh, Nikki, you were supposed to be safe in Ohio.*

"Ms. Taylor, are you still there?"

"Yes…I'm here."

"This must be quite a shock. I want you to know we're doing everything possible to find your daughter. The FBI can send an agent to interview you. Sometimes an interview can generate clues." There was a long pause. "But in my experience I think it's better if you were right here. You're the mother, and when we find her—and we *will* find her—she's going to want her mother. I suggest you try to get here as soon as possible."

Where could she begin to tell them about the events of the last forty-eight hours? And if she did tell them, would doing so help or hinder the return of her daughter? "I understand," she said. "Detective Marconi, please put Phillip back on the line."

Phillip must have been standing right there. Without delay he was on the line. "Zoie, as Detective Marconi said, we're going to find her."

"Phillip, is it true? Did you sell the puppy that Nikki wanted?"

"Well, yes, Zoie. This guy gave us a seventy-five-dollar deposit. The dog was supposed to be a surprise for his kid's birthday. He said he'd come back with the rest of the money in ten days. By then Nikki would be home with you. The arrangement was going to work out all the way around."

Phillip's matter-of-fact explanation set Zoie on boil. If it weren't for the fact that the phone charger tethered her to the wall, she would have run from the room screaming. It was that and the knowledge that if she lost her cool, Phillip, like Celeste, would simply shutdown. Accordingly, she struggled to control the tone of her remarks. She needed Phillip to keep talking. She needed information to determine whether the Shelter's crew had kidnapped Nikki or something else had transpired. Had she run away? Zoie clenched her fist and articulated her every syllable. "Did Nikki know that you had sold the dog?"

"No…at least I don't think so," Phillip answered, sounding very unsure. "She did ask what would happen to Biscuit when she left. We told her we would find the puppy a good home."

"Well, how did she act when you told her that?"

"She was quiet and sad, but that was to be expected."

Despite efforts to maintain her control, Zoie unleashed her anger. "Damn! Damn! Damn you, Phillip!"

Her outburst obviously startled Phillip because there was an eerie silence on the Perrysburg end of the call. Phillip finally responded in the calmest voice he could muster. "Zoie, getting angry is not going to help find Nikki."

"Phillip, you knew how attached Nikki was to that dog!"

"Don't put this on us, Zoie. You made it clear to all of us that the dog was not going home with Nikki."

"But you didn't have to be *stupid* about it!" she screamed.

"Zoie, I'm going to hang up now. You need to calm down." The Ohio end of the call went dead. Zoie glared at her Blackberry as if the device itself were to blame for the disconnection. She slammed the phone into the bed, jerking its charger from the wall.

Lena, having witnessed the whole thing, sprang forward with a slew of questions. "Okay. This is serious. What's going on?"

As though in a trance, Zoie slowly sat on the bed. Her eyes were glued to the phone. She tried willing it to ring so that she could finish thrashing the Benjamins for losing her daughter. But the phone lay silent.

"Zoie! What's going on?"

Zoie turned to address Lena. In the matter of seconds, her demeanor had gone from utter rage to something Zen-like. "Lena, not now...Nikki is missing."

After a few minutes, Zoie regained her equilibrium. She quickly dressed into her own things—jeans and a jersey. Her change in demeanor cued Lena to resume her questioning. Zoie responded but only with curt answers.

"God, Zoie! This is awful. What do you think is going on?"

"Lena, I don't know. How many times do I have to say it? I don't know. I don't know. All I know is my daughter is missing." Not stopping to look at Lena, Zoie shoved her possessions into the overnight bag. She retrieved her phone from the bed and disconnected it from the charger. The phone had little or no charge, but what juice it had would have to do.

"Can I borrow this?" Zoie asked, holding up the charger.

"Sure."

"Do you think the thugs from Mahali snatched her? Jahi wouldn't do something like that. Taking a child?"

"He's surprising us all, isn't he?"

"Charles said Jahi and that *bitch* are still at the precinct," Lena offered. "How could..."

"Don't be silly! They've got phones. They've got goons. They could call in a kidnapping as easily as ordering takeout."

"Well, I guess," Lena said, indicating that she wasn't completely convinced.

Had Lena changed her mind? Could it be she no longer considered Jahi guilty? Zoie slung her stuffed overnight bag over one shoulder and her purse over the other. She grabbed her running shoes and headed to the living room. Lena was hot on her socked heels.

"Wait! Where are you going?"

"To where my daughter was last seen."

"But that's out of town! What about your statement to the police? Remember that Charles will be here in a few hours. Don't we want to let the police know what's going on?"

"Maybe, maybe not."

"What do you mean? Charles is putting his reputation on the line for you. You at least have to show up at the station. Surely he can help with this other situation." Lena was pleading.

"Lena, this *other situation* is my daughter's life! All other deals are off!"

"Well, of course, of course, but…"

Zoie took a deep breath. "Lena, I don't expect you to understand. After all, you *don't* have a child."

The look of horror on Lena's face told Zoie that the no-child remark hit its target. Zoie guessed that Lena wanted a child. So far she just hadn't hooked up with the right guy or made the decision to go it alone. Zoie knew her remark was insensitive, but it accomplished her intention—to shut Lena up. Brutal truth had a way of doing that. Zoie also knew that as soon as she walked out the door, Lena would call Charles. Zoie wasn't sure whether Charles would try to prevent her from leaving town, but for a moment it occurred to her that Charles actually might be helpful. Then on second thought, she decided not to chance confiding anything more in him. What if Jahi's crew were holding Nikki as the ultimate leverage? If so, more involvement with the DC police wouldn't be good. Zoie sat on the small bench in the foyer pushing her feet into her shoes. Since Phillip hung up, no one from Ohio had called back. She'd call them again when she was out of Lena's earshot.

"But where are you going? It's four in the morning."

"Reagan Airport to get the first thing flying to ah… Pittsburgh."

"Pittsburgh?" Lena said. She was somewhat bewildered.

"Remember that I told you Nikki was in Pittsburgh with her grandparents. I've got to meet a cop there." Like the lies she'd told at the Shelter, Zoie found the Pittsburgh lie easy to tell. It was another lie of necessity, one concerning life and death. She remembered her grandmother's old saying "The truth is overrated."

"Oh, I guess you did say Pittsburgh," Lena said sheepishly. Lena was talking again, but the sting of the no-child remark had siphoned her usual reporter's spark, or perhaps she was ashamed. In the face of a missing child, she'd tried to pressure Zoie by using Charles's reputation and her "exclusive." Luckily Lena hadn't made the connection between Toledo and the phone numbers no longer in her possession. Zoie was glad she'd retrieved the paper with her contacts. She didn't want anyone calling Ohio and revealing things that might further jeopardize Nikki's safe return.

"Do you have the number of a cab company?" Zoie asked.

Still subdued, Lena gave her the number of the cab company she used and supplied the building address for the pickup. Zoie ordered a cab to take her to Reagan Airport.

Lena accompanied Zoie down to the lobby. The cab was already waiting.

"Look, I am grateful for all your help," Zoie said. "I owe you a lot...not to mention the money I borrowed. And you will get your story at some point. Now, though, I'm focused on my daughter. I'll be in touch."

Neither offered a parting hug. As Zoie entered the cab, Lena said, "Stay safe. I'll pray for your daughter."

Maybe Lena would pray, but Zoie knew for sure that she would immediately call Charles, so Zoie didn't bother to ask her not to.

CHAPTER 48

NEAR THE TUNNEL'S END

Zoie's cab was heading toward the entrance to the freeway when she said, "I've changed my mind. I don't want to go to the airport."

"Huh? Then where to, lady?"

"Just don't get on the freeway! Let me think."

For a moment she considered going to Jahi's apartment, not to the Capitol Hill place he'd been house sitting. She'd been there once. There she could face him and negotiate for her daughter's safety. That is, if he actually had something to do with Nikki's disappearance. But Jahi was still likely to be at the police station, still consoling Sister Te. She envisioned the pair wringing their hands over Tarik, plotting to cover up their tracks in the multiple crimes. Or in an even more evil scenario, the two could be directing Nikki's fate. *My poor baby.* A tear rolled down Zoie's cheek. No, she needed to get to Perrysburg to search for Nikki.

"Take me to Columbia Road and Seventeenth Street," she told the driver. She figured that Charles and company would trace her movements to the airport, but it would take hours for them to figure out that she hadn't taken a flight to Pittsburgh or anywhere else. By the time the DC cops figured out that she wasn't at the airport or the train station, she'd be long gone. Of course, they could trace her cell and identify her last call to the Benjamins in Ohio. There were records at her home and information on her laptop being held in evidence. Charles could easily figure out her whereabouts. Hopefully he'd understand her plight and cut her some slack. Maybe he had children and could sympathize with her actions more than Lena had. He'd have to hold off the DC cop's need for a statement. Perhaps Maynard would regain consciousness and explain what had happened. Thinking of Maynard, she sighed. He would give a cryptic account of the night's horrific events, blaming it all on the devil's nameless disciples.

In the cab's darkness, Zoie turned off her phone to preserve its remaining charge. She felt inside her pocketbook for a piece of braided lanyard. Nikki had made the short rough chain just before they left New York. Zoie rubbed the lanyard between her thumb and forefinger, remembering Nikki's pride in producing the complicated box style. "Here, Mommy," she had said. "I used your favorite colors, pink and silver."

Such a bright child. Such a lonely child. All she wanted was a puppy for company, and I couldn't even allow that bit of happiness. Zoie realized that she'd taken her own failings out on the Benjamins. Every emotion conceivable fired on her every nerve: guilt, shame, dread, and anger. Silently she called on God, the fleeting presence in her life.

There was a chance that Nikki hadn't been kidnapped. There was a chance Nikki's disappearance had nothing to do with Jahi and his gang. Was that good news or bad? Zoie wiped tears from her cheeks. Since the puppy was also missing, there was a chance that Nikki had been so upset about leaving the puppy that she'd taken off on her own. To go where? Somewhere her daughter was alone. Scared.

"Please, God, keep Nikki safe," she whispered.

Zoie exited the cab at the corner of Seventeenth Street and Columbia Road and hustled up the hill to Tina's building. In the dark rear lot of Tina's building, the BMW was waiting. She unlocked the car, threw the denim bag onto the back seat, got in quickly, and locked the doors. The car was hot and stuffy, but something told her not to open the windows. With her heart pounding, she started the car.

The bottled water she'd left from the previous night was in the cup holder. She took a swig of the piss-warm liquid and splashed some on her face. Tired or not, she knew it was time to hit the road.

She couldn't remember the Benjamins' address, and without a charged Blackberry, she couldn't access her contacts. She took a deep breath and finally figured out how to use the BMW's GPS. She set the device for Perrysburg, Ohio and followed its instructions. Once on Route 270, Zoie turned on the radio. The stoic announcer rattled off a litany of overnight events: a shooting in Southeast DC, a truck overturned in Langley Park, and a fire at a store in Georgetown. There was no mention of an assault on a homeless man at a homeless shelter or of a khat drug bust. For a minute Zoie considered that her harrowing night might have all been a dream. But it was real. She'd indeed uncovered a drug operation and saved a man's life or nearly caused his death, depending on how one judged such things. And the Perrysburg police had confirmed that Nikki was missing.

With decent traffic and a few short rest stops, Zoie figured she could make it to Perrysburg in ten hours. In Hagerstown she got off the highway for gas and was directed to a twenty-four-hour Walmart. There she purchased a Blackberry car charger. In the parking lot, she plugged in the phone and prayed for divine intervention. Promising herself that she wouldn't blow a gasket, she took a deep breath and called the Benjamins. It took several rings for Phillip Benjamin to answer.

"Phillip, it's Zoie. What's happening? Have you found Nikki?"

"Zoie, I'm glad you called back," he said, sounding down. "I'm turning you over to Detective Marconi."

"Phillip, wait!"

It was clear that Phillip didn't want to talk to her. Was it because of more horrendous news or their earlier clash?

"Please, God…please, God," she whispered as the seconds ticked before Marconi took the phone.

"Ms. Taylor, Marconi here."

"What news do you have for me? I'm headed there."

"Good, you're coming. I'm told the child's father is also on his way."

"Oh!"

Elliot in Perrysburg? Of course.

It was no surprise that the Benjamins had called their son. Zoie fought to shake off this latest curveball. Her priority was Nikki. She could hear her grandmother's voice. "Now, Zoie, don't be petty. That petty stuff can boomerang."

"Ms. Taylor, are you still there."

"Yes, yes." She gathered her wits and listened intently to Marconi's account of the search efforts.

"We've got thirty men out on the street and searching down by the river." Mention of the river gave Zoie chills. She knew about the Maumee. She'd walked along it with Elliot. "We located the man who put the deposit on the puppy," Marconi continued. "Nothing there. That trail's a dead end."

"So that's good news?"

"I'd count this update as neutral. As far as kidnapping suspects, I'm inclined to cross him off the list. There are other kidnappers out there. The FBI is making the rounds of the registered pedophiles in the area."

Zoie cringed. "Oh, God! Pedophiles, close by?"

"Ma'am, they're all over, unfortunately. We're hoping your daughter's a *runaway*. But if she isn't being held, then she's out there alone. That's mighty dangerous. Someone with ill intentions could still find her before we do. Ms. Taylor, is there anything else you want to share about your daughter that could help us?"

Zoie wanted to say, "Yes, there's the possibility that a drug ring has grabbed her," but she held back. If the drug crew did have Nikki, saying too much might jeopardize her further. "Well, yes. I know she was upset. Upset about having to leave the puppy in Ohio. And you should know she's very smart."

"Yes, we know those things from the grandparents," Marconi said with a matter-of-fact tone.

"Then…there is nothing else I can think of."

"Okay, if you think of anything else, call right away."

When the call ended, Zoie checked her phone. If the drug crew did have her daughter, wouldn't they be trying to contact her? Demanding something? Perhaps her silence? There was one missed call and a text message, both from Detective Bender. The message read, "Lena filled me in. Hope u find ur child. Shelter biz can wait but still needs settling."

Charles did have a heart.

The road was long and boring. Zoie tried listening to the radio, but she wasn't having much success in blocking terrible visions of what might have happened to her daughter. She pictured Nikki's body down by the river or her huddling somewhere. She was probably scared and hungry, wherever she was. When she dismissed *those* thoughts, she relived Maynard's beating. Her visions were soon replaced by the dread of seeing Elliot again. Even in the emotional distress over her missing child, the feeling of hurt and anger over Elliot's betrayal seemed as fresh as the day their relationship ended.

The last time she'd set eyes on Elliot was in her attorney's office. He'd come to sign the child-custody agreement, giving up his parental rights. He'd been jittery, saying little else than, "Where do I sign?" He babbled about wanting the marathon poster that he'd left at their apartment. At one point he offered a weak "Sorry." Having signed the document, he let out a deep sigh of relief. Elliot wanted out. He wanted a fresh start. No responsibilities. It was as simple as that, or was it? Months before, he'd packed his things and left their apartment. His total explanation for abandoning them was, "I just can't do it." No amount of Zoie's pleading could turn the situation around. Zoie wasn't required to be present for the signing, but witnessing his act of abandonment was something she needed to do. Until the end she'd remained in disbelief that he was *officially* walking away. Somehow her being there was meant to make it real, to jolt her into reality.

And so that's how it went down. Painful as that day was, she no longer could doubt. He didn't want the child, and he didn't want her. Nikki was only ninth months old.

At each rest stop, Zoie downed coffee and a pastry. The caffeine and sugar kept her alert, especially during the most tedious part of the drive—the Pennsylvania Turnpike. As the day wore on, other calls came in. Most of them were from the Foundation. She ignored them all but always checked to see if any of the calls were from unknown origins. She talked to Detective Marconi several more times. The last time was outside of Pittsburgh. No status change.

"Nikki, where are you?"

At 3:30 p.m. the BMW rolled up in front of the Benjamins' comfortable home. Two police vehicles were parked in their driveway. Down the block two men leaned against a van labeled WUPW Toledo. Another media vehicle was parked across the street. Exhausted and sticky, Zoie leaned her forehead against the steering wheel for a second, trying to gather the strength to face what she would find inside. She went up the brick walkway and the four steps to the porch, where a uniformed officer stood in her path to the door.

"I'm Zoie Taylor," she explained.

"You're the child's mother. We've been expecting you," the officer said with a broad grin. "It's a good day. Sometimes we get lucky, and today the angels were on our side."

"Does that mean you found her?" Zoie said, forcing a smile.

"Yeah, about forty-five minutes ago. You mean they didn't call and tell you?"

Without responding Zoie bounded for the door. Inside she called, "Nikki! Nikki!"

A middle-aged man with a beer belly and another uniformed officer came forward from the kitchen. "Ms. Taylor, I'm Detective Marconi," said the beer-belly man. "I was just trying to contact you. Based on your calls, we expected you sooner. I guess you've heard the good news."

"Yes, yes, where is she? What happened? Where did you find her? Is she okay? I want to see her."

In the midst of Zoie's barrage of questions, the Benjamins entered the room. Phillip looked well, but Celeste was an obvious mess—frail, nervous, and paler than usual. Phillip led his wife to the couch. Something else felt wrong. Where was the air of joy that accompanied the return of a missing child?

"Celeste, Phillip, where's Nikki," Zoie asked.

Elliot entered the room with Nikki sitting upright in his arms. The infamous puppy romped at his heels. Nikki looked unharmed. *Thank God.* Zoie kept her distance. She tried not to fixate on Elliot, but she couldn't help it. He looked the same. His runner's body was still long and lean.

"Hello, Zoie," Elliot said as he attempted to lower Nikki to the floor.

"Nikki, baby," Zoie said with arms wide to receive her daughter. But the solemn child clung to her father's neck. It was clear that they had a relationship—one that predated that moment. *A daughter always wants a father, even an occasional one.*

"Hi, Mommy," Nikki said as she clung to Elliot with one arm while leaning to reach for the jumping puppy with her free hand.

Zoie wanted to grab her and squeeze her and shower her with kisses, but she resisted, waiting instead for Nikki to come around. "Nikki, where have you been?" Zoie asked, her tone gentle as she focused on her child, as she tried not to acknowledge Elliot's presence.

The child shrugged in that "I don't know" way kids do. This behavior was unlike Nikki. The precocious child usually had something to say about everything.

"Elliot found her," Phillip said. "She took the puppy and hid under the bleachers at the high school's football field. She thinks you're going to be mad at her. She has no use for us either. We're the ones giving her puppy away."

Zoie had a lot of emotions, but being angry with Nikki wasn't one of them. "Baby, I'm not mad. I promise. I'm not mad," Zoie said as tears rolled down her cheeks. "I was so worried."

"I was at the place where Daddy used to run. He told me he liked to play under the bleachers when he was my age."

Elliot finally spoke. "I don't know why I didn't think of that place sooner. I took her over to that field a few weeks back when we went for a run. She was fascinated with how the sunlight filtered through the bleachers."

"I should've figured it out too," Phillip said. "Not the bleachers part, but figuring she'd run away. If I'd looked around, I would have noticed both the peanut butter and a half loaf of bread were missing."

"Phillip, you don't even eat peanut butter," Celeste said as if from another planet.

"I knew Daddy would come for me," Nikki said.

"Elliot, thank you for finding my daughter," Zoie said.

Finally, Nikki ran to her mother arms. "I'm sorry, Mommy. I had to stay with Biscuit. Mommy, I want to go live with Daddy because Biscuit can live at his house."

"Don't worry, baby. Biscuit can live at our house. I promise," Zoie said, giving Elliot a menacing glance. Plenty of issues came with that promise. She would just have to deal with them later.

Just then a young woman entered the room. She was willowy with long limbs and a swan neck, willowy except for a prominent belly the size of a small watermelon half-hidden in her flowing summer dress. She had to be at least six months along.

"Zoie, this is Cassandra," Elliot said. "Cassandra, Zoie."

"You have a very special daughter," Cassandra said with the most innocent smile. She was pretty, young, and most surprisingly black. Zoie wondered how much Elliot had told this woman about how and why their relationship ended.

"Mommy, she's got my sister in her tummy," Nikki said, running over and patting Cassandra's belly as if to do so was the most natural thing in the world.

It took a while for Detective Marconi and his small entourage to wrap up their police work. When they were ready to leave, Phillip thanked them profusely for their efforts to find his granddaughter, without mentioning that it was Elliot who'd actually come through. As the self-appointed spokesman for the family, Phillip made a statement to local news reporters, thanking the police and all the volunteers who'd participated in the search.

Nikki was one exhausted little girl. She'd spent the night with the puppy under the bleachers with a flashlight, a jar of peanut butter, and a half loaf of bread. She even remembered to bring a knife to spread the peanut butter on the bread. She was a determined little girl. It had been a warm night, and except for some insect bites, Nikki had come through her adventure unscathed. Despite the excitement over her return and her mother's acquiescing to letting her keep Biscuit, she couldn't keep her eyes open. As soon as the sun began to dip, she fell asleep in her mother's arms.

Zoie planned to take Nikki and stay the night in a nearby Ramada hotel. But Nikki's reticence to be parted from the puppy changed those plans. That left few choices, one of which was to find a hotel that took dogs. There was no way that Zoie was going to leave Nikki at the Benjamins and go to a hotel alone. The Benjamins, in their awkward way, convinced Zoie to stay. She would sleep the night with Nikki in the child's twin bed—with the puppy, of course. How could she stay in that house with Elliot and his new love? They would be right in the next room, the same room she used to stay in with Elliot when they visited all those years ago. *Nikki is safe*, Zoie told herself. *I can deal with anything for one night. Haven't I proved that at the Shelter?*

As tired as she was, Zoie wasn't ready to crash. When she was back home in her own comfortable surroundings, she'd sleep for twelve hours. With Nikki asleep in her room, Zoie sat with Celeste and Phillip Benjamin, picking at oatmeal cookies and making small talk until there was no more small talk to make. When the conversation traipsed dangerously close to topics of substance—explosive topics like Elliot—she excused herself and went to sit on the lighted front porch.

Joy M. Copeland

She settled into one of the Adirondack chairs and shook her head, marveling at how she'd endured the Benjamins. Tonight she was just too tired to fight. Her mind drifted back to the drama waiting for her back in DC. She hadn't thought about *that trouble* in many hours. The mess she'd left seemed far away and inconsequential when compared with the safety and happiness of her daughter. But it was time to reconnect to the rest of her life.

She sent a text to Charles and Lena: "Nikki found safe. Details when I return."

Soon Charles texted back. "Glad 2 see update on missing-child database. See you back here—SOON," he said.

"Wow!" she said, reading Charles's text. She realized that he'd been tracking her all along. She shrugged it off.

She checked her business messages. Everybody in the world was looking for her: members of the board, Regina, and Milton, of course. An e-mail announcing an emergency meeting of the Crayton Foundation's Board for next week had gone out. Another e-mail gave the preliminary arrangements for Ray's wake. *So quick*, she thought.

Her head was spinning. She called Milton's direct line, hoping since it was late that he wouldn't pick up. She lucked out and got his voice mailbox. She left a short message in which she apologized for her lack of communication, explaining that she'd had a major family emergency involving her daughter, and telling him to expect her back at work next week. Since she no longer trusted Regina, there was no one else to tell. After she ended the call, she wondered whether she should even go back to the Foundation. Financially she could survive until she got a new position. Would the Foundation even want her back?

Deep in thought she didn't notice when Elliot came around from the back of the house and peeked at her from between the porch balusters.

"I thought you might be here," he said. "Can we talk?"

What did he want? They hadn't talked in years.

"Zoie, please," he said, coming up the stairs and onto the porch. "Please give me a few minutes of your time."

Zoie's back went straight as Elliot approached. He sat in the chair next to her. Her fists tightened.

"Look, Elliot, today has been stressful and strange. The whole week has been strange. If what you've got to say to me is some *bizarre* stuff, I don't want to hear it." The energy reserve that had allowed her to stay awake and make the drive to Ohio was now depleted. She had no patience.

"I just wanted to say," he stuttered, "that you've done a wonderful job with Nikki."

"And you, of all people, thought I would have done otherwise," Zoie hissed. "You're telling me how wonderful my daughter is as if I don't know that." She rose and passed him, heading for the front door. He jumped up and grabbed her arm."

"Let me go!"

"Zoie, please hear me out. You have every right to be angry. God knows I put you through hell. I was a fool. I'm *so* sorry. I was crazed and still an adolescent. I was afraid of losing my freedom. Afraid of responsibility."

"You disowned your daughter, this wonderful child you speak of. How do I ever explain to her that you didn't want her?"

"I know—I know," he said, his eyes filling with tears. "Someday I must tell her I was a fool and hope that she understands. I now know I made a huge mistake. Cassandra has shown me how wrong I was. The Wall Street thing. The feeling of self-importance. It was all so silly. So superficial. So false. I got carried away. I know that now. I think I've finally grown up. Zoie, I'm ready to be a father. Is there any way you can forgive me?"

"Forgive you!" Thoroughly disgusted, she stared straight into his anguished eyes.

"Yes, please forgive me. I'm begging you. For Nikki's sake."

His face contorted with pain. Had the man-child she had once loved finally matured? Today God had returned her daughter. God had done so by way of this imperfect man, the man who happened to be her father. Zoie knew that Nikki wanted this man in her life. But it was all too soon. Years of hating him had given Zoie a strange comfort. The hate had shielded her from more hurt. Alas, it also had shielded her from knowing more love. Now she didn't know whether she could forgive him. She didn't know whether her heart could open that wide. It certainly wasn't happening today. She sucked her teeth and walked away.

CHAPTER 49

EVERYBODY'S GOT QUESTIONS

"Mommy, when am I going to see Daddy again?" The question came from the back of the BMW, where Nikki sat in her booster seat. It was the third time Nikki had asked that question or a similar one in the last half hour. Zoie's responses had been evasive and noncommittal—ones unsatisfactory for the precocious six-year-old. Zoie was running out of bogus answers. Now she was annoyed that she needed to think up more excuses for something she didn't want to happen.

"As I said, baby, your father is real busy. He may not be able to take off from work." Her latest response was a rehash of her earlier answers.

"But he said he'd come see me," Nikki insisted, using that particular child's whine designed to grate on adult nerves.

Damn him!

The morning had gone smoothly, considering the happenings of the previous day. Elliot got up early and went to a local pet store. He bought a pet carrier and a pet gate for Biscuit. He also found a booster seat for Nikki. He presented them to Zoie with a sheepish smile, as if he were seeking praise for his actions.

But Zoie had no praise to give. She managed a flat thank-you.

"Zoie, please…give some thought to what I asked you last night," he said.

Zoie refused to look at him or to answer. All she wanted was for Elliot and the whole situation to disappear in a puff of smoke."

When it was time for them to leave, the scene in front of the Benjamins' house resembled a lovefest complete with a group hug and tears. Cassandra, the new daughter-in-law, got into the act. It was as if Elliot's wife had been a part of the Benjamin clan for a decade, fully conversant in the family's idiosyncrasies. Or perhaps it was just that pregnant women cried easily. Zoie couldn't remember how she had felt carrying Nikki. The details of her pregnancy were overshadowed by the drama and hurt that accompanied it. Zoie's memory of much of it was blocked for emotional self-preservation.

As the lovefest continued, Zoie stood as a bystander, watching as love was showered on her Nikki. She couldn't participate and found it difficult to stomach it. She was still tired from the previous day's drive, but pure disgust now supplied her with boundless energy to retake the road. She politely thanked the Benjamins for having Nikki for the summer and hustled the child into the waiting car.

"Gee, Mommy," Nikki said. "Is this your new car?"

"No, baby. It belongs to your aunt Tina. I borrowed it. So that means we need to take good care of it."

That morning Celeste seemed more of her old self. She'd always been a little loony in a way some considered endearing, but last night she'd been way off the deep end.

"I hope you'll let Nikki come back," Celeste said.

"We'll see," Zoie replied, forcing a smile.

The puppy was now safe in the pet carrier, which was sitting on a mound of towels and plastic to protect the back seat. "I'm glad Tina can't see this," Zoie said under her breath. While arranging the back seat, she resolved to have the car professionally cleaned before Tina returned from Florida.

The puppy whimpered for the first hour of the trip. Nikki calmed the puppy by sticking her small fingers through the carrier's grate so that the puppy could lick them. It was an arrangement that suited them both. They were headed home, but where would home be? They couldn't go back to Zoie's apartment, not after the break-in. After telling the police what had happened, her apartment would become an official crime scene. And now there was *the dog*.

"Mommy, did you hear me?"

"I hear you, baby."

"Can Daddy come for Christmas?"

"I don't think so. Your father has his own life. At Christmas he'll probably be at the home of Cassandra's parents or back in New York." Elliot, a nonreligious Jew, never objected to Christmas. He celebrated the secular version of the holiday with all of its commerciality—as long as someone else did the holiday prep work and he got gifts.

"Then, Mommy, when can I see him? Don't you think the baby will be born by Christmas? Do you think the baby will be born on Jesus's birthday?" Nikki asked with a yawn.

"Ugh," Zoie said under her breath while rolling her eyes. She hoped that her disgust was not evident to her daughter. She hadn't inquired about Cassandra's due date. The date of the blessed event was something she didn't care to know. "I'm sure your father will be in touch. He'll let us know when he can come."

There were no follow-up questions from the back seat. All was quiet. Could those last answers have solved it? In the rearview mirror, Zoie could see her daughter slouched over and fast asleep.

So home couldn't be Zoie's Connecticut Avenue apartment, and it couldn't be her grandmother's Brandywine house, which had been damaged by the fire. Luckily Tina had left Zoie the keys to the Adams Morgan condo.

"Thank you, dear Tina."

Nikki slept on and off for about half the trip. There was no more talk of Elliot or the new baby. Now in comfortable possession of her beloved Biscuit, the child didn't seem to care where they would live. In between Nikki's car naps, the mother and daughter passed the time by counting cars by color, first red ones and then silver ones. They talked about the first grade and Nikki's new private school. They sang along to the latest pop hits. Nikki loved Beyonce's "Single Ladies" and Kanye's "American Boy." Nikki always knew the lyrics. But this time she'd forgotten a lot. The Benjamins weren't much for listening to music.

The car time together helped Zoie and Nikki reconnect. It alleviated the awkwardness that had crept between them after weeks of separation. The last several weeks had been especially strained and marked by emotional phone conversations, in which Nikki made her pleas to keep the puppy. After everything, the child had won out. She'd won by using the worst kinds of emotional extortion—guilt and playing her mother against her father. Still, Zoie was not resentful. She was just glad to have her child.

They stopped every couple of hours to let the puppy do its business. There had been only one accident in the pet carrier, though the padding did its job by protecting Tina's car. An air freshener and car detailing would handle any lingering doggy odors.

It was dark when they pulled into Tina's parking space. They had missed the rush-hour traffic. Loaded down with the pet gate, carrier, and other bags, Zoie and Nikki made two trips from the car to Tina's third-floor condo. After being closed up for weeks, the place was hot and stuffy. Zoie found the air-conditioner controls and blasted the fan. It felt a lot better once the stagnant air began to move. Like Tina, the place had a casual elegance, with its earth tones, wooden floors, and small area rugs here and there. The place was the polar opposite to Lena's frozen tundra.

Tina had furnished the place when she was still making beaucoup bucks in the financial-industry hustle, before she decided to ditch that insane work life for a more peaceful existence. Hopefully the puppy wouldn't damage anything. To make sure, Zoie would have to keep Biscuit barricaded in the kitchen, behind the pet gate. It would be a temporary arrangement.

At a nearby grocery store, Zoie purchased pet food and something for breakfast. Having slept in the car, Nikki was wide awake and rambunctious. They watched a movie and played Uno. At eleven o'clock Nikki finally faded. Zoie put her to bed in Tina's room, after explaining that in this apartment the puppy had to sleep in the kitchen.

"Mommy, tell me again why we have to stay in Auntie Tina's apartment. Why can't we go to our apartment?"

"We're having some work done at our apartment. And remember that I told you before that there's a no-dog policy."

"Oh, that's right," Nikki said. "But what about staying in Great Gram's house?"

"Great Gram had a fire at her place just the other day."

"Did her house burn down?" Nikki asked, rubbing her eyes, unable to get excited at the news of a fire.

"No, thank God. But the workmen need to fix the damage. And it's got to get cleaned up before Great Gram can move back in."

"So where does Great Gram live now?"

"She's staying at Queen's house for a while. You remember Queen, don't you? We'll go see them tomorrow."

"I like Queen," Nikki said softly. "She makes the best choco-late cake."

This latest round of questions and answers seemed to satisfy the bright child. Living alone this summer, Zoie hadn't had to answer to anyone other than herself. Nikki needed answers— but not answers that included the stories of murders, drugs, and thugs who might hurt them. No information that would give her nightmares.

Zoie kissed Nikki on the forehead and was about to turn off the light when Nikki asked another question. "Mommy, why didn't you and Daddy stay married?"

So Elliot is still on the child's mind.

"Baby, your father and I were never married. I thought you knew that."

"Kinda," Nikki said in a quiet voice. "I know people have ba-bies without being married. You had me like that?"

"That's right."

"But why did Daddy leave us?"

Zoie thought for a second. "Your father and I didn't love each other anymore. So we broke up." Her statements were simple but only half-true.

For a few long seconds, Nikki contemplated Zoie's answer. Then she asked, "But didn't Daddy still love me?"

Zoie's heart was breaking all over again. "Oh, baby, of course," she answered as she lovingly brushed back her child's hair. "How could your father *not* love you?"

"That's the same thing Grandma Celeste said." The child's voice trailed off. Her eyes narrowed until they finally closed. The question of her father's love weighed on her small shoulders. She was willing to accept her mother's response for now. She was too tired to keep asking.

So Nikki's been trying to figure this out. At least on this, Celeste and I are on the same page. They both had given Nikki a weird confirmation about her father's love, twisting the truth just enough to obfuscate its cruel reality. For now that answer seemed enough. But they'd left Nikki with a *question* to answer a question. She knew Nikki would mull over things. It would only be a matter of time before she further challenged their answers. Zoie would just have to keep on lying. She would never tell her little girl that her father hadn't her. One day Elliot would have to answer Nikki directly. Zoie hoped that when that time came, he would lie too.

Zoie fixed a straight Scotch from Tina's liquor cabinet. It burned going down, but she needed something. Then she called Detective Charles Bender.

"Sorry to contact you so late," she said, sighing afterward.

"No problem. I was half-expecting your call," he answered. "All's well with your daughter, I take it."

"She's better than I am."

"Yeah, you've had a rough few days."

"For sure."

"So you need to get this statement done. When can I take you in for that?"

"Tomorrow afternoon. First, I need to see my grandmother. And I need to find a sitter for my daughter. Otherwise, she'll have to come with me to the station."

"Okay, call me when you're done with that. I'll arrange to meet you at the Fifth District station. Remember, though, this is not my case."

"So do you really need to be there?"

"Why, Zoie, it sounds as if you don't want me there." Charles laughed. "But you're right. I don't need to be there. I'm just an intermediary…unless they want to pull me in on the drug stuff. I want to be there. I promised those guys over at Fifth District I'd deliver you for the statement. You see I'm living up to my commitment."

"Touché."

"Don't worry. The Fifth District guys aren't after you. They've had time to do some checking on your story. Remember they have your laptop. And by the way, the thug who was in on Maynard's beating, a Somalian by the name of Asad, was picked up in Queens, along with another thug. They were driving the Shelter's van, just as you said, and had a load of khat. So thanks for that tip."

"Glad to be of help. And what about Tarik? Is he still locked up?"

"Surely he won't be allowed bail until his arraignment…if then."

"And what about Jahi?"

"You mean the dude who's running for city council? He ain't going down anytime soon."

"Why not?"

"Now, Zoie, we talked about this. You're the attorney. So far there's no evidence connecting him to anything criminal. Other than the fact that their operation was going on right under his nose and that he's got to be one stupid dude not to have known about it."

"Pretty unbelievable, huh?"

"Yeah, flakey for sure. But as I've told you, those guys at the Fifth District have known Khalfani for years. If he were just a regular street dude, things would go differently. Right now, in the eyes of the Fifth District, he's one of the good guys until proven otherwise. Perhaps your statement will be the thing that helps to prove otherwise."

"And what of Maynard? The man that was assaulted?" Zoie asked with her hand pressed against her forehead.

"As far as I know, he's still at Washington Hospital and in a critical condition."

"Huh…"

As to Jahi's innocence, Zoie didn't know whether her statement would prove otherwise. Over the past days, she assumed that Jahi was involved and pegged him as the ringleader, the one behind it all. She assumed it all without hard evidence. Her undercover operation hadn't found the information on Mahali's grant fraud that she had been after originally. Instead, she'd uncovered the drug business. Perhaps Maynard knew something else. But would anyone ever believe his insane banter? She could go no further. It was up to the police and ultimately the DA. Once the police investigated the Shelter's financial misdealing, *surely* the trail would lead to Jahi.

That night Zoie curled up next to Nikki. Thoughts of her missing child and Elliot's resurrection left little brain space for thoughts about the Shelter, Ray Gaddis, or Jahi Khalfani. Tomorrow those things would again be all-consuming. Now she was so tired. With Nikki by her side, safe in Tina's apartment, she could finally sleep. She hoped she would dream of nothing.

The next morning, after walking the puppy and running a few errands for groceries and getting more puppy supplies, Zoie and Nikki drove over to Queen's house, in Northeast. They found Frances Woods sitting on Queen's sun porch, at the back of the house. With her feet up, reading the newspaper, she looked very comfortable. There was color in her cheeks, and her walker was nearby. Overall she seemed less frail.

"Zo! I was wondering why I hadn't heard from you," her grandmother said. "Hey, Nikki! Sweetie, did you have a good time at your grandparents' house?"

"Yeah," answered Nikki, moving close and instantly warming to the great-grandmother she hadn't seen all summer. "Did you know, Great Gram, that I have a puppy now? I was going to bring him with me to show you, but Mommy said I had to leave him at Aunt Tina's house."

"Aunt Tina's house?"

"Long story," Zoie said. "Anyway, I wasn't sure if Queen allowed dogs in her house."

"Baby, give your great-grandmother a big hug."

The child complied and then plopped into the wicker rocking chair on the other side of the room and proceeded to put the chair in motion.

"About your puppy, your mommy told you right. I don't know if Queen likes dogs. Not everybody likes dogs."

"I wish everybody liked dogs," Nikki said with a frown.

"Zo, why are you looking so down?"

"As I said, it's a long story," Zoie answered.

"I got plenty of time to listen. As you can see, I'm not going anywhere."

Queen entered the room, carrying a pitcher of iced tea and several glasses. There was also a small glass of lemonade. "Do you like lemonade, little one?" Queen asked.

"Yes, ma'am," Nikki said as her legs swung scissor fashion in anticipation of the sugary drink.

"Zoie, is the lemonade okay for her," Queen asked. "It's freshly squeezed."

"Yes. Thanks, Queen." Zoie turned to her daughter. "Nikki, this counts as your juice today, okay?"

"But Grandma Celeste lets me have..."

"Nikki, you're home now. So we go by *my* rules," Zoie said quickly.

"We're not *actually* home," the child said in defiance.

Zoie gave Nikki a fierce look, and the little girl wisely changed the subject. "Queen, do you like dogs?"

"Oh, yes, I love dogs. Been thinking about gettin' one myself."

"Queen, can I bring my new puppy over to see Great Gram?"

Queen was a little surprised. "Well, I guess," she answered. "If your mom thinks it's okay."

"We'll see," Zoie said.

Frances Woods laughed. She leaned over and whispered, "Zo, your daughter's going to give you a run for your money. She reminds me of you when you were that age."

"Now, Nikki, if you ask me about cats, I got to say that cats be a whole different t'ing," Queen said.

"Yeah, cats be a whole different t'ing," repeated Nikki, mimicking Queen's Jamaican accent to perfection. "Queen, what does 'whole different t'ing' mean?"

"You want to come help me make chocolate cookies?" Queen asked Nikki. "Then I'll tell you all about them cats. Them mysterious cats."

"Oh, can I, Mommy?" Nikki asked, excited about chocolate cookies and hearing a juicy cat tale.

"Sure," Zoie answered, winking at Queen.

Nikki followed Queen from the porch.

"Now, Zo, tell me what's going on," Frances Woods said. She put the newspaper aside and directed her attention to her granddaughter.

"Oh, Grandma, where do I start?"

"When I saw you the other day, you were trying to solve some mystery. I think it had to do with that guy you were seeing. *Ja* something or other," she said, waving her hand dismissively.

"Well, Grandma, I solved part of a mystery. It has to do with a drug ring being run out of the homeless shelter."

"My Lord! I read something about a drug bust at a homeless shelter in the paper yesterday."

"So it did make the press…well, those same thugs broke in to my apartment."

Frances Woods gasped and clutched the arms of her chair.

"Grandma, don't worry. I wasn't there when it happened. Thank God. But I don't feel comfortable staying there. Anyway, we can't have a dog. So for now I'm staying at Tina's place. She's down in Florida."

"Sorry you couldn't stay at my house. Queen's brother is working on getting things back in order. But I might have to stay here another couple of weeks."

"How's it going here?" Zoie asked, looking about the sunny room.

"Whew! You told me so much; now my nerves need to settle. Well, Queen's doing the best she can. Her brother lives here, and her nephew is in and out. It's a little tight. I'm paying her extra for being put out like this. I know she wishes she were back on Brandywine with more space."

"I need to go to the police precinct to give my statement about the whole thing. Do you think Queen would watch Nikki until I get back?"

"I don't know. You've got to make your own deal with her. Those two do seem to get along."

"They do."

"So tell me how you snagged those guys."

Zoie didn't want to get into the details of her undercover operation or to mention Ray Gaddis's murder. "Grandma, it's a long and *complicated* story. But one thing I can tell you is that I know those thugs set the fire at your house. They did it to threaten me."

Frances Woods put her hand to her mouth.

"Oh. Maybe I shouldn't be telling you this."

"No, you need to tell me. No, I have to know!"

Zoie sighed. "Okay, I went to Ohio."

"Yeah, you went to bring Nikki home."

"No, I went there because Nikki was missing."

"Missing! Oh, God. She looks okay."

"You're right. She's good. She ran away. She was mad that I wasn't going to let her bring that puppy home."

"Oh! But you found her. The police found her?"

"*Actually* Elliot found her," Zoie explained.

"Zoie, I'm truly confused. You're talking Elliot. Elliot, the father who doesn't want to be a father?"

"Yes, *that* Elliot," Zoie said, lowering her voice. She looked around to make sure that Nikki was nowhere close. "The very one who didn't want anything to do with her."

Frances Woods's lips were tight. "From your tone I take it he does now."

Zoie sighed deeply. "He wants to be forgiven so that he can be a part of her life."

"Oh. You did mention he'd been to see her at his parents' place earlier this summer. You said he was married and had a new baby on the way."

"He's into being a father for the baby yet to be born. And suddenly he *wants* to be a father to my daughter as well," Zoie said disgustedly. "Go figure."

"Is his wife a white girl?"

"Actually, no. Guess he's into chocolate, whether light or dark."

"At least the boy's consistent. Lord, Lord," Frances Woods said, shaking her head.

"Grandma, I'm tired of men. Men leaving. Being left by men. Men lying. What is it with men? First, my father. Then Elliot. The latest is Jahi. I don't know what his problem is. I'm just glad our relationship didn't go any further. He's a crook."

"Well, Zo, you sure can pick 'em."

Zoie buried her face in her hands.

"Zo, I'm so sorry you're going through this. I hate to see you hurting." She rubbed Zoie's arm with her arthritic hand. "That Elliot's got some nerve. You know what Ida calls him—Elliot the Idiot."

"Ida's got it right," Zoie said with a weepy half smile.

"It's tough for us women, even if we're the stronger of the sexes. But as far as men go, I also know they're not all like those fools. It's not fair to condemn them all."

"If you say so."

"Why look at your grandfather. He was a hardworking and loyal husband and father. He loved your mother and me to death. And I miss him."

"I think men like Grandpa are rare. Seems to me that men walk away a lot and that we women get left a lot. I still think it wasn't the cancer that got Mom. It was her broken heart."

"Zo, I hate to see you so down on the whole male gender. Women can be fools too." She took the deepest breath that she could and then coughed hard. "Sometimes it's the women who walk away...as I did."

"Grandma, what are you talking about?"

Tears welled in Frances Woods's eyes. "You know, Zo, that I've got my long stories too. I guess with your being my closest relative and old enough to hear it"—she paused to gasp for air—"that one day I'm going to have to explain myself to you. Got to do it before I die. I owe it to you."

"Grandma, don't talk like that," Zoie said, rubbing her grand-mother's shoulder.

Frances Woods put a fist to her mouth and started to hack. When the hacking wouldn't stop, Zoie called Queen to bring her special cough remedy: hot water with turmeric, cinnamon, lemon juice, and honey.

Through the hacking Frances Woods looked up and saw the panic in her granddaughter's eyes. She didn't have enough breath to tell her story. Her secret would have to wait.

CHAPTER 50

DO YOU KNOW WHO YOUR FRIENDS ARE?

When Frances Woods's coughing spell finally ceased, she was exhausted. The hacking had taken its toll. She was damp with perspiration; her arms were limp, and her eyes were dim. The secret she'd protected for so many years and now wanted to share with Zoie would have to wait. Wait until she could gather enough breath to string together more than ten words. Wait until she could answer all the questions that would follow. Wait until she could again find the courage to tell her tale.

Zoie, helpless to do anything, watched her grandmother's coughing episode. Thank God for Queen, who ably handled things. Nikki came running from the kitchen, clearly upset. She latched on to her mother's waist, her head pressing under Zoie's bosom. "Mommy, what's happening to Great Gram? Is she going to die?"

"No, baby," Zoie told her, trying to console her child, though she had her own fears. "Great Gram will be better when the medicine starts to work."

Queen took Frances Woods into the back room, which had become the older woman's temporary bedroom. When Queen returned to the porch, Zoie sent Nikki back to the kitchen to check on the cookie mix. Zoie had plenty of questions for Queen. According to Queen, her grandmother's coughing spells were the results of a brutal bronchitis. By all accounts she was on the mend. "The doctor says the cough is gonna stick around for a while. I can tell it's lessening."

Still, Zoie was not convinced.

"You think your grandmother is gonna keel over right in front of your eyes," Queen said. "But I can tell that ain't gonna happen."

"What makes you so sure?" Zoie asked.

"Has she passed on her jewelry to you?"

"No."

"When people are about to leave this world, they pass on their precious things. Frances Woods ain't about to give away any of her good things. Ha! She ain't goin' nowhere anytime soon."

Zoie wondered what it was that her grandmother had been about to tell her. The secret that Frances Woods had been harboring sounded ominous. Zoie knew that old people kept secrets. Decades ago society shamed folks so badly that people hid their indiscretions, things that by today's standards wouldn't be considered scandal worthy. With her grandmother's health the way it was, Zoie wouldn't prod. It was clear that Frances Woods had a desperate need to get something off her chest. Alas, her chest wouldn't cooperate.

Zoie had to go to the Fifth District station to meet Detective Charles Bender and tell her own secrets. She made arrangements with Queen to take care of Nikki while she was gone. In the absence of the puppy, Nikki had bonded with Queen.

Zoie called Detective Bender. "Charles, I'm ready."

"Okay," Charles said, sounding enthusiastic. " I'm going to call to make sure that the detective in charge of this case is around. The Fifth District is on Bladensburg Road. Do you have a way to get there? Or should I pick you up?"

"I have a car. I should be there in the next thirty minutes."

Charles took on a serious tone. "Zoie, I advise you to tell them *everything*. You've been holding back."

"Charles, you don't know the half of it. I've had to weigh what I could tell without endangering my family."

"I understand. But hopefully you needn't fear that now. Get the whole story out. They've rounded up a few more runners connected with the drug operation. The more you tell them, the faster they can get the rest."

Following Charles's advice to tell *all* wasn't going to be easy. Earlier that morning, before Nikki woke, Zoie jotted down the key points she wanted to tell them, just in case the police failed to ask the right questions. As she drove past the Shelter, she couldn't help but wonder if Jahi were somewhere inside. *He must be brooding,* she thought. *He's probably still conspiring with Sister Te to cover their tracks.* If he ended up facing criminal charges, could he continue running for the city council? She laughed to herself. What made him different than some others on the council? But then she couldn't remember any council member linked to a murder.

The police station in the Fifth District was a busy place. Charles was waiting near the station's entrance, chatting with a much shorter man.

"Zoie Taylor, this is Detective Ross. He's the lead on the assault case and the drug bust."

Zoie and Ross shook hands.

"I've heard a bunch about you," Ross said with a slight smile. He was balding and had a paunch and the pallor of someone who'd spent the summer indoors. The sparkle in his pale-blue eyes made him look compassionate and likable. "I understand you're an attorney and you actually witnessed the assault on the homeless man."

"More like attempted murder," Zoie said.

"Well, we'll have to leave the particulars about the charges to the US attorney. Perhaps what you tell us today will help make the case for the more serious charge."

"Okay," Zoie said, understanding that she'd have to leave lawyering on the back burner.

"And you also witnessed the drug dealings?"

"Not the sale exactly, but I overheard their plans for the khat. And you may have to add a homicide to your case. But I guess that would be the Montgomery County folks," Zoie said.

Detective Ross seemed skeptical. He looked to Detective Bender and then turned back to Zoie. "Well, let's get going."

Zoie's statement lasted three hours, with a couple of coffee breaks. It took place in a sterile conference room with cinder-block walls and bunker-style slot windows near the ceiling. Zoie sat with Ross and a younger detective named Erkhard, who asked few questions and essentially operated the recorder. Out of professional courtesy, Ross allowed Charles Bender to sit in on the questioning. Well aware that this was not his case and that he was outside his district, Charles remained silent.

In the end the police didn't question Zoie that much. Zoie had a story to tell. She took the lead in the discussion, weaving the facts about what had transpired that summer. She explained her relationship with Jahi. She explained how she'd come to suspect fraudulent activities around the Crayton Foundation's grant process. She told them about her meeting with Sy Rosen and how what he had told her made her even more suspicious. She told them about how she'd confronted Ray Gaddis and how he had wanted to delay bringing her suspicions before the Foundation's Board. She mentioned that she was outside of Ray's Potomac house on the night of his death. She told them about the break-in and theft at her apartment and the apparent arson at her grandmother's house, which was done by the same gang. She described the phone threats. Zoie explained how she'd come to know Simon and Maynard, the homeless duo, and how she'd convinced them to accompany her to the Shelter. She even told them about Simon's backing out at the last minute. But she left out any mention of prophecies or things that would make them doubt her statement.

"Maynard led me to that house at the back of the Shelter's property," she told them. "He'd been there before, and he was very afraid. I found my laptop and Maynard's binder back there."

Ross let her talk, only interrupting occasionally with clarifying questions. Zoie gave them her cell phone and password to access the voice messages to back up her story of how she and her family were threatened.

Ross flipped through his notes on a yellow legal pad. "I heard about this binder. Is it true you sent it with Maynard to the hospital?"

"Yes, it's very important to him."

"Do you know what's in the binder?"

"No. What I saw, I couldn't read," she answered. "It is cryptic, written in some kind of code. But that's Maynard for you."

"And you saved Maynard's life by calling 911, after you hid him behind the dumpster?" Ross asked.

"Yes," Zoie answered.

"What phone did you use to make the call?"

"One of the women in my dorm room had a phone. I couldn't find a phone inside, and I didn't trust going to the office."

"Why not?"

"Intuition, I guess. Everyone looked guilty."

Ross looked down at the papers. "In the report filed by the officer on the scene, there's a question about how you managed to move Maynard from the utility building. It's a long way from the back of the property to behind that dumpster. The victim is a big man, and you're a small person. Can you comment on that?"

"I dragged him on a tarp."

"Without assistance?"

"Yes, without assistance. God sends help when you need it." She was matter of fact in her answer. She'd kept her promise to Jazz to not involve her. In truth, it had been difficult for even the two of them to move Maynard's dead weight. Zoie just hoped that the other women at the Shelter were being as discreet.

"I grant that sometimes there is superhuman strength. I guess your adrenalin really kicked in...and, Ms. Taylor, do you have any knowledge that Jahi Khalfani ordered Tarik or this Asad to beat Maynard?"

"I can't say for sure. According to his campaign manager, Jahi was supposed to be on some kind of retreat. But I knew he was back in his office at the Shelter."

"Did you see him?"

"Yes, I saw him through the window of the dorm room in the women's section. It was late, and the lights were on in his office. I could see him in there. He didn't see me."

"And you went to the Shelter in disguise to look for evidence to support your suspicions of financial fraud?"

"Yes."

"Why didn't you go to the police?"

"By that time they'd already set fire to my grandmother's place and broken into my apartment. They wanted me to stop digging. To keep quiet. They were threatening my family."

"Okay. What fraud did you suspect?"

Zoie took a deep breath and a sip of water before answering. "I think there might have been some kickback scheme going down between Ray and the Shelter. The Shelter received considerable grants from the Foundation. Ray pushed hard for continuing their grant. Or..."

"Or what?"

"Well...it's possible they were blackmailing Ray."

"And who would be the most likely person to be doing this?"

"I know that Jahi, as the director of the Shelter and head of the Shelter's board, was Ray's contact on grant matters. But then Tarik seemed to be his second-in-command."

"What do you think Jahi or Tarik might have on Ray Gaddis?"

"Can we turn the recorder off?" Zoie asked, looking at each of the three men.

"Okay, shut it off," Ross told Erkhard.

"Look, this is speculation. But I did find out something about Ray when I started digging around earlier this summer."

"What was that?" Ross asked.

"Ray Gaddis is, or should I say *was*, a closeted gay."

"Hmm," Ross said, sitting back from the table. He drummed his fingers silently on the oval table. The whole room was quiet. "Ms. Taylor, if Gaddis was a closeted gay, how did you come by this knowledge?"

"From a trusted source...a person who wishes to remain anonymous." In the explanation of her own investigation, Zoie hadn't mentioned her trip to Florida or Carmen Silva. Zoie had no intention of implicating the woman who had explicitly requested to be left alone.

"*Ms. Taylor...*"

"My source witnessed Gaddis and a male coworker in a sexual encounter," Zoie said, looking around for some reaction. All she got was blank stares. "It happened a couple of years ago," she continued. "All I can tell you is that the encounter took place at the office, after-hours."

Zoie couldn't tell whether Ross or Erkard believed her. The information was taking a while to sink in. "Look, I know what

I'm telling you qualifies as hearsay. This isn't anything the US attorney can bring up in court. It's my speculation. Gaddis has a wife and two sons. I'm guessing he wanted his sexual preferences to remain hush hush. And I'm guessing Tarik and company found out about his secret life. They could have used the information to blackmail him. Maybe they have pictures or something. And their payoff had to come from the grants to the Shelter."

"If Ray Gaddis was paying them, why would they turn around and murder him?"

Zoie shrugged. "Perhaps they thought he was going to spill his guts to me and the Foundation. When I confronted Ray with my suspicions about the Shelter's mishandling of the grant funds, he got very nervous. Essentially, I wanted to go to the Board with my suspicions, and he was trying to stop me."

"Murray," Ross said, turning to his partner. "We've got to get Montgomery County in on this. Ms. Taylor, can we get you to speak to them?"

"Sure. Have you talked with Maynard yet?"

"We've tried," said Detective Erkhard, looking tentatively at his partner for guidance. "He's disoriented."

Zoie figured that they had gotten the full dose of Maynard. Disorientation wasn't the right word to explain his condition.

When they wrapped up, Charles came over to Zoie. "Zoie Taylor, you're full of surprises. You never cease to amaze me."

"So now what, Detective?" Zoie said, her tone sarcastic as she gathered her things. "Do I get my laptop and briefcase back?"

He watched her with a smirk. "I doubt it. Not right away, anyway. They're probably still gathering information from them. But on another note...Lena asked me to mention something about the 'exclusive' you owe her."

"Oh, that." Zoie grimaced.

"Look, she's on your side. She was counting on your story to get her some needed 'street cred' at work. Things are rough for her these days. She's worried about a layoff."

"Sorry to hear that, but life-and-death stuff trumps job loss," Zoie blurted. Then she thought for a moment. "Charles, I'm sorry—you're right," she said, shaking her head. "Lena was there when I needed help. I'm a little on edge. Telling them what happened that night at the Shelter was like reliving it. Now I'm angry all over again. I didn't want to expose Ray's little secret."

"But Ray Gaddis is dead."

"Believe me, Ray was no great friend or boss. I didn't care for the man. He was an obnoxious creep. With that said, I didn't want to expose stuff that would cause further pain to his family." She sighed. "You know his funeral is in a few days."

"Will you go?"

"Don't think so. I'm not ready to face the Foundation folks en masse. I need to tell the Board most of what I told you guys here. As a Board officer, it's my duty to warn them that the Foundation is about to be hit with big-time bad press."

"Your statement and accusations about Gaddis's misdealings won't be made public until they've had a chance to investigate. And then a police spokesperson will release the information. For now Tarik and his posse are being held for the drugs and Maynard's beating. Those things are already public and seemingly have no connection to Ray Gaddis or the Foundation."

"Charles, tell me…how did you know that I was at the Shelter?"

"Got to have eyes and ears all over the city."

"Muwakkil."

"Well, yeah. He's a good pair of eyes. We've been trying to locate the distribution point for some of the drugs for months now. When Lena tipped me off that you had headed to the Shelter and the 911 call came in, well, it all just fit together."

"Uh-huh. Anyway, thanks for being here. It was nice to see a familiar face in that room, even if it was only a face I've known for a few days," Zoie said.

Charles bowed his head in a "you're welcome" gesture. Then in a quiet voice, he said, "I wish we could've met under different circumstances."

Whoa! Zoie felt his eyes waiting for some response, some encouragement for this advance. But she was having none of it. The reasons this relationship could go nowhere abounded: First, he wasn't her type. Second, there was a little nit—he was already with Lena. Third, he was *supposed* to be with whoever had the wedding band that matched his. *This brother has some nerve.*

"Charles, just do me a favor," Zoie said. Her tone was flat and discouraging. "Tell Lena I'll call her tonight."

She walked away.

CHAPTER 51
WHAT'S DONE IS DONE

The irritating smell of industrial-strength disinfectant permeated the visitors' room at DC's central detention facility, otherwise known as DC Jail. Having been patted down, Jahi waited in the small visiting booth. In the world of the DC Jail, he was a fortunate visitor. He'd been processed through the jail's administrative hoops in record time. But then he had connections inside the jail. His main connection, one Nathan Cole, was a supervising guard. Gung Ho Nate, as he was called, just happened to be an old Marine Corps buddy. Nate greased the skids, meeting him at the entrance and escorting him past a line of desperate visitors, who might end up waiting hours for a turn to see their loved ones. Yes, the brotherhood of marines was in full operation. Despite Jahi's recent woes, there were still friends he could depend on.

Jahi was somewhat accustomed to the jail, having visited it in the past, but the place still served up a chill. He surveyed the booth's Plexiglas arrangement. There were the usual telephone receiver and several cameras hanging from the tall ceiling. At least he'd be able to see the boy even if he couldn't embrace him. He could discern whether the boy had been roughed up. Jahi wanted a frank discussion with Tarik. Nate guaranteed that their conversation wouldn't be recorded. He trusted Nate.

If the DC government had its way, the pseudo-intimate prisoner visit, with its Plexiglas barrier, would be a thing of the past. A bill pending in the DC Council aimed to transform in-person visits, except with attorneys, into video chats. The inmate and the visitor would be physically separated and get to talk to each other from special videoconference rooms located in separate buildings. Touted as cheaper and safer, the newly proposed visit process was the wave of the future—a win for the taxpayer and of little concern to anyone else, except the inmate's family. The council would probably pass the bill, and the Mayor would probably sign it. The bill would come up for a vote in the new session scheduled for next year, after the November general elections. If Jahi were going to be on the council, he'd vote against it. Jahi smiled to himself with a humph. But that council scenario was no longer in the cards. Like so many things of late, his run for the DC Council seemed to be part of the pipe dream extinguished that night when the police arrived at the Shelter. It all had fallen apart *so fast*. But had it really? Or was that night just the final scene in a drama that had been playing out for a very long time or something he'd been blind to? He had to find out.

Yes, Gung Ho Nate Cole had come through for him. Along with expediting his admittance to the visitors' center, Nate had promised to keep an eye out for Tarik's safety. But there was only so much his friend could do for Tarik, even from the inside. After all, jail was jail. Tarik had a ways to go. He prayed the boy would survive it.

Yes, Nate had proven to still be a friend. In the last few days, Jahi was finding out just *who* his real friends were. He'd walked free after the initial incident at the Shelter, but in breathtaking speed he'd fallen from grace. *And* charges could be pending, but for what he wasn't sure. Now he had his own attorney. Mahali's

Board had immediately suspended him without pay, taking action in a fashion faster than he'd ever seen them do anything. He was no longer allowed on the Shelter grounds. Hank managed to retrieve some of his personal papers from his office. Now even the continued existence of the Shelter was a question mark. And as for his political career, without pressure, he'd dropped out of the Ward 5 city-council race. On the one hand, giving up the race was a shame. A poll taken just before the police raid gave him an excellent chance of winning the primary. And in DC a democratic primary win was an almost guaranteed general-election win.

"Don't give up," urged his campaign manager, though she was thoroughly disgusted with him. "Other candidates have overcome looming felony charges and gone on to victory."

But Jahi no longer had the stomach to fight. His heart was no longer in politics. He doubted whether it ever really was.

This, too, will pass, Jahi told himself. At some point he'd be vindicated. In the meantime he needed to support Tarik. It might be too late for Te. She'd made her choice.

Jahi punched his right fist into his left palm and shook his head. How could things have gone so wrong? He thought of Tarik as a son. Surely no other child filled that special space. Tarik didn't take his breakup with Te well. How do you explain to a child that you're no longer in love with his mother? How do you explain to a child that a lack of love for the mother doesn't mean a lack of love for the child? Jahi tried to maintain a close relationship with Tarik, but the distance between them grew when they lived apart. A blood bond wasn't there to secure the fractured connection.

"I'll be nearby," he'd told Tarik as he moved out. "Remember that you can always come to me. My leaving changes nothing between us." Tarik had listened to these assurances with his same sullen demeanor. He'd always been a serious kid. At twelve he was already lanky, impressionable, and quite smart. He'd been eager to be a man, long before he needed to be, long before he needed to burden himself with responsibility. After Tarik finished high school, Te sent him to visit his uncle in Addis Abba. Tarik was excited to go. He wanted to know everything about the land of his birth—the land of the father he never knew. He wanted to nourish his Ethiopian roots. He didn't want to be one of those immigrants who came to the United States as child and knew little of his homeland. Te panicked because his visit was only supposed to be for a couple of months. Tarik ended up staying nine months before returning to start college.

The Tarik who returned from Ethiopia was a different young man than the one who'd left. Jahi noticed the boy's new sense of confidence. He'd been to his homeland, the one he'd left as a toddler. He'd met his father's family and heard the stories about his brave father from them. He told his relatives that he wanted to stay longer. They eyed him with bewilderment, asking, "Why would you want to stay here? We all want to go the US."

Jahi saw a red light flashing over the door on the other side of the Plexiglas. Tarik entered the room from that door. The guard pointed to the clock on the wall and then to his watch and went to sit at a table by the door. The cardboard sign on the wall inside the booth said, "Visits are limited to thirty minutes." After all, many others were waiting for their turn to see their loved ones.

Tarik and Jahi picked up their phones. The boy looked thin and nervous, but at least he was in one piece. If he were hurt, he was hiding it well.

Jahi pressed a palm to the glass. Tarik responded in kind with the shield between them. Tarik pulled his hand back quickly.

"How are you, Son?"

"Well enough."

Jahi forced a smile. "How are the accommodations?"

"We do better at Mahali," Tarik answered. "The Shelter is cleaner and has better food."

"No doubt, no doubt. Hank takes care of our stomachs." There was a long, awkward silence. Then Jahi asked, "Did your mother come? When I spoke to her a couple of days ago, she said she was planning to come."

Tarik smiled. It was a strange, sad smile that faded. "She told me what the Board did...to you and to her. Jahi, I'm truly sorry. I didn't mean to drag you down."

Jahi looked away. He was trying to hide his anger and disappointment with the boy he'd put so much trust in. What use would it be now to rage at the boy? He calmed himself before asking, "Why Tarik? Why?"

Tarik shrugged. "It all got away from me."

"What got away? What about Ray Gaddis? Why?"

"Ah, that one. That one was a *bushti*...a fag," he said with a nonchalant shrug.

"I know what it means," Jahi said, his jaws tightening. *When did Tarik become so homophobic?* He closed his eyes and shook his head. "So what are you saying?" Jahi asked in a heated whisper. "So what does that mean? Were you blackmailing him?"

Over the few days since Tarik's arrest, Jahi pieced together parts of the story. At the precinct Tarik remained sullen. Te had given him vague replies to his questions. She had warned him by saying, "It's better if you don't know." In frustration he'd gripped her by her delicate shoulders. He wanted to shake her until she confessed. What was really going on? He demanded to know. She hadn't struggled, instead letting her head roll back like a bobble-head doll. When he stopped, she looked at him with those dark eyes, eyes filled with a kind of hatred he didn't understand. He let her go.

"Were you blackmailing him?" he asked Tarik again.

It took a while for Tarik to respond. He looked up at the ceiling, spotting the camera, but continued to talk. "No, not at first. He was the one who proposed the kickback deal. For a cut he'd make sure we got the grant. He wanted too much. It wasn't until later we found out about his extracurricular activities. We followed him to the Bee Boy Bar on Capitol Hill."

Jahi hung on Tarik's every word, each syllable. He looked for some remorse in the boy's face, in his voice. But there seemed to be none. "But how? How did you find out about Gaddis? How did it work? And who is the *we*?"

Tarik leaned into the glass. "Jahi, Jahi, my sometimes father," he said with a smirk. "Your naiveté amazes me. For someone who's fought in a war and lived on the edge of life here in DC, how could you miss these things?"

Jahi didn't know what to say. His face was frozen. The boy, the man, who Jahi looked at through the glass was someone he didn't know.

"Oh, I know your head's been in the clouds with all that fake political shit," Tarik continued. "And then lately that woman."

"Tarik, don't make this about me." His voice was sharp but not loud. "You can't blame me for what you've done...you're right about something, though: I *have* been blind. But it's not the *what* that surprises me. It's the *who*. I trusted you. I trusted your mother." Jahi's jaw was clenched. "Tarik, how could you do this? I don't know you anymore."

"Didn't money still come to the Shelter from the Foundation?" Tarik shot back. "You're worried about the khat. Khat is nothing. It's less harmful than chewing tobacco. We had a way to bring funds into the Shelter. If your girlfriend hadn't interfered, perhaps Gaddis wouldn't have freaked. Perhaps he wouldn't have threatened to tell all and shut down your precious Shelter."

"So you killed him, and you almost killed that man at the Shelter?" Jahi stuttered. "You could have come to me. We could have found a way out of this without the killing."

Jahi's anger turned to tears.

"Humph." Tarik seemed to take pleasure in watching Jahi's pain. "You're right about one thing, Jahi: you don't know me anymore."

The trauma ward at Washington Hospital Center was quieter than the rest of the hospital. Zoie stood at the main reception desk and watched the two nurses who were in a deep discussion. One nurse stood with her hand on her hip and with several charts anchored under her arm. Zoie hoped that one of them would turn around and acknowledge her. But it seemed that they needed some coaxing.

"Hello. I need some help here," Zoie called out.

They turned to her in unison. The taller of the two women moved closer. She was dressed in a pink smock, and her hair was in a neat bun. "May I help you?"

"Yes, thanks. I'm looking for a man named Maynard. He was brought in a few days ago."

"What's the last name?"

"I don't know it. He goes by Maynard."

"I know the guy she means," the other nurse piped in. "He's the one in 806."

"Oh yeah, that guy. Are you family?" the first nurse asked.

"Obviously not," the other nurse said sarcastically. "She's doesn't even know his full name."

Zoie smiled, determined not to get into a tiff with the hospital staff. "She's right. I'm not family. I'm a friend," Zoie answered with all the charm she could muster. "Maynard's been homeless for a while. And I was with him when he was injured."

"Well, we don't usually let patients in his status have nonfamily visitors," said the first nurse.

"I doubt he'll have *any* family visiting," Zoie said. "They probably don't know he's been hurt. I'm here because Maynard saved my life—not once but twice. I need to say hello and thanks."

The nurses looked at each other in silent agreement.

"Okay, I'll walk you down there," said the first nurse.

"Thank you."

As Zoie and the nurse in pink headed down the hall to 806, Zoie asked, "Has he received any visitors at all?"

"I'm not here all the time. But I've only seen the hospital's social worker and police detectives come to this room. He was admitted by an ER doctor after being beaten, right?"

"I believe so."

"The first day he was unconscious."

"Have you seen another guy? Dark skinned, wearing a cap?"

"No...no one by that description."

"Just thought maybe his good friend Simon might've come by."

"While I've been here, no one except the social worker, cops, and you have come." Outside the room the nurse said, "He's conscious but under mild sedation. I should warn you that he gets agitated very easily."

"I understand," Zoie said with a knowing look.

"And another thing," the nurse continued, "they admitted him under the name 'Maynard.' He's conscious but not answering to that name."

"Did he call you the devil's minion?"

"Come to think of it, one of the nurses mentioned she heard him say something about Satan. And he talks about someone named Coach."

"That's Maynard all right."

Accommodations in the critical-care ward comprised high-tech private rooms, albeit with glass walls so nurses could easily view their patients. The two women entered room 806 and, from the foot of the bed, looked down at the man. He seemed to be awake. At least his eyes were open, though they were surrounded by blue-black skin. His gazed at nothing with a cold, empty stare. Open-eyed comatose. The monitoring equipment next to him indicated a steady pulse. His forehead and cheeks were bandaged, and his long, thick dreads—which gave him his fierceness—were evident on the pillow.

"Maynard," said the nurse as she adjusted the valve controlling the drip of the intravenous solution, which hung close to his head. "Maynard, can you hear me?" There was no response. She turned to him directly. "Sir, how are you feeling today?"

This time he mumbled, gritted his teeth, and then rolled his eyes.

"If you start feeling pain again, use the call button." She placed the button near his hand. "There's a visitor here for you. She says she's a friend."

"Humph."

The nurse took Zoie aside. "He's got several broken ribs, and he lost his spleen. He won't be able to exert much breath to talk. And laughing is a definite no-no, though he doesn't look in the mood for that," she whispered, looking back at him. "You should also know that he still has some residual effects from those drugs he took. He's lucky to be alive."

"He didn't take those drugs," Zoie whispered back in his defense. "The thugs who attacked him injected him with those drugs."

"I did hear that," the nurse said slowly, as if distracted. "Sorry. I'm going to leave you with him now. Try not to get him excited. Even with the sedation, I'm afraid he might pull the line out of his arm." The nurse looked back at Maynard and then turned and whispered, "Poor thing. I'd rather not restrain him."

"Does he still have the binder with him?" Zoie asked.

"Strange that you should ask. The police came by earlier. They said they didn't get much from him. They wanted to take the binder, but he made a fuss. That's when we sedated him."

"Did they take it?"

"No. It has a note attached that says, 'Must stay with patient.'"

"I gave the binder to the EMTs with those instructions when they put him into the ambulance," Zoie explained. "One of the EMTs must have written the note."

"Well, it's in the drawer next to the bed. But let's not go through that again," the nurse said. She looked back at Maynard once again and then left.

Zoie sat herself in a chair next to Maynard's left side. Then realizing it was difficult for him to see her, she stood up and leaned over to talk to him.

"Maynard, or whoever you want to be today, it's me. Remember Ms. Smarty Pants?"

Maynard didn't answer or turn to look at her.

"Thank God that you're still alive. I'm so sorry I made you go back to the Shelter. You warned me. But the police got those guys. The devil's minions are in jail."

"Simon told me," Maynard finally responded. His voice was faint and gravelly. He managed to turn his head ever so slightly to look at her. Even that bit of movement looked painful, so she moved closer.

"Simon came to see you? How does he know all of this?"

"Ms. Smarty Pants, you still don't get it."

"Yes, you're right. Guess I'm dense." She could tell that he wanted to laugh, which was a no-no. "I'm so glad you survived this. I was really worried."

"It's not over. The devil's still out there."

"Yeah, and the police still have my laptop and briefcase."

"Humph. They wanted to take my binder. Simon says you've been calling on God lately."

"Huh?"

"'Thank God…God help me.' Simon says I got to trust you, trust you to do the right thing."

"Then tell me—please—what *is* the right thing?"

"Take my binder. Keep it for me."

"Are you sure?"

"Sure," he said weakly. He closed his eyes.

Zoie took Maynard's worn binder from the bedside drawer, stuffed it into her oversized bag, and left the hospital.

CHAPTER 52

STARTING OVER

"This is quite a document, Zoie," Dylan Ross said. He leaned against the doorframe of her office, waiting for permission to enter, nervously tapping the roll of paper against his free palm. It was the document that explained the Foundation's potential liabilities in connection with Ray Gaddis's kickback scheme.

"I'm glad you found it helpful," Zoie said, her expression sullen.

"Thanks for getting it to us early. Your doing so gave us time to properly absorb it. And your presentation today was most enlightening. Gee, I don't know what to say. I'm still in shock."

"It's been a crazy couple of weeks," Zoie said with a frown.

"Yeah, it got rough in there. But you handled it...Zoie are *you* okay?"

The Board's second emergency meeting since Ray's death had just adjourned. Board members wanted to linger. They were still bewildered by the betrayal and the obvious criminality of their leader, Ray Gaddis. They wanted to commiserate, and they wanted to talk to Zoie. But she'd politely retreated to her office. Four hours talking to the Board was quite enough. She had trudged through the legal ramifications of the Shelter mess and admitted her affair with Jahi Khalfani. Now she was tired of explaining and their questions. She was embarrassed that her personal life had intersected with her professional responsibilities. Most of all, however, she was just plain tired.

With elbows on her desk, she leaned forward and beckoned Dylan to enter. "Have a seat, but first close the door."

He complied.

"Dylan, I'm fine." She sighed. "Don't fret about me. I had to retreat. I needed some breathing room."

"Of course, of course. I understand." Dylan was one of the sharper Board members—thoughtful and insightful, not like Ray's flunkies, the Board members who received a quarterly stipend to fill a conference room chair. In the past Dylan had always been her ally, a voice of reason. Plus, he wasn't hard on the eyes.

Zoie had been back in the office for two days. Her reentry after ten days away proved awkward. Milton was fine, but a few of the other staff at the Foundation seemed nervous in her presence. They couldn't look her in the eye. The office gossip was thick. The *Washington Post* carried the story of the drug bust and the speculation of crimes, which might involve the Foundation. Stuff like that always leaked. Too many people knew her story.

Both days Regina Bullock had called in sick. *A smart move*, thought Zoie, since she didn't know what she'd say to her young assistant when they came face to face. Still, Zoie hadn't told Milton about her suspicions about Regina. Part of her didn't want to be responsible for causing the foolish young woman to lose her job. Zoie also hadn't mentioned anything about Ray's recreational sex to the Board. Certainly she hadn't said anything to Milton. The investigators would have to fill in the blanks on their own. One day soon, they'd uncover hard facts about who did what to whom. As far as Zoie was concerned, she'd done her duty.

"I tried to explain it as best I could," she said.

"I'm still in shock," Dylan said again, his blue eyes twinkling in a way that grabbed her attention. "It's one thing to lose Gaddis. Tragic for his family, especially under the shadow of these allegations. It's hard to put a dead man on trial. But we have to come to grips with where the evidence seems to point."

"I have no doubts about what happened, but the investigators will have to come to their own conclusions."

"But why resign?" Dylan asked calmly but forcefully. "Why do you feel the need to resign over this? Nobody blames you. You're the one who brought this all to light."

Milton had announced Zoie's resignation at the Board meeting. His announcement came at the end of the session so that the Board could focus on her report without being distracted. The news brought wide eyes and groans. One Board member asked her, "Are you doing this because you feel you're culpable?" No one had mentioned conflict of interest. After all, she was on the Board, and she'd had an intimate relationship with a Foundation grantee. Certainly it was a situation to be frowned upon.

Alone with Dylan, Zoie took a deep breath. "I feel I need to be doing something else with my life," she said, not wanting to admit that she no longer felt comfortable working for the Foundation, knowing what she did about Milton and Ray's relationship, and having Regina around. Plus, she didn't want to help unwind the tangled mess the Foundation was in. She thought the simplest answer was the best. "It's time for me to move on."

"Move on? Gee, you've only been here four months."

"I know," she said with a shrug.

"Well, I'm here on behalf of several of the Board members, including Milton. We'd like you to reconsider. We think you're the best person to see us through the legal hoops in connection with this whole Shelter mess. You've pointed out just how much we're at risk here. You're familiar with the situation, and if you stay we won't have to bring a new person up to speed. We've got to look at our grantee portfolio and ensure that Ray hasn't corrupted our entire process."

"I appreciate your confidence in me," Zoie said with a weak smile. "But I've made up my mind. I need to move on."

"But…" he stammered.

She put up her hand, signaling him to stop.

"Okay," Dylan said with a sigh. "I hear you. Seems your decision is firm. I'll have to report back to the members that you're truly not interested in staying on."

"Dylan, I'll be around the next two weeks, working mostly from home. There are things that I need to wrap up. Crayton will assign an attorney from corporate to fill in until Milton can hire somebody."

"Well, we'll miss you." Dylan sighed again. "So I've fulfilled my official assignment, which was to ask you to reconsider." He leaned back in the chair, looking more relaxed. "Now…on a separate matter. And I'm sure there's no conflict of interest here." He cleared his throat. "Would you consider going to dinner with me?"

The following afternoon, without so much as a hello or "sorry that I'm late," Lena slid across the seat of the booth where Zoie had been waiting for her. "Well, it's done. Mahali is closed," Lena announced with a grimace.

When Lena and Zoie agreed to meet at the small Greek restaurant on Eighteenth Street in Adams Morgan at 3:00 p.m., they hoped the place would be empty in the off hours. And it was. Lena was finally going to get her exclusive.

"Crayton pulled its funding, and other contributors followed suit," Lena explained. "Who can blame them? Nobody wants to be caught funding criminals. So Mahali's Board shut it down. *Shut it down.*"

Zoie knew that the Crayton Foundation had pulled the Shelter's funding. Mahali's decision to close was the surprise. "What about the residents?" she asked, thinking mostly of Jazz and the other women she'd met at the Shelter.

"Yeah, what about them?" Lena replied sarcastically. She was clearly pissed about something. "The women probably got shipped off to other shelters. Since the men only stay for the night, there are a few other places they can go. Finding a cot for the night won't be a serious issue until winter."

"Sorry to hear it. *No*, maybe I'm not sorry," Zoie said, correcting herself. "Mahali's rot goes deep."

"Well, Charles told me they haven't arrested anyone else other than the bunch they got that night you were there, the ones picked up in New York in the van, and a few others."

"But other folks working at the Shelter are involved," Zoie said emphatically.

"So what else do you know?"

"I can't tell you exactly what I know or how I know it." Zoie was protecting Jazz and what she'd said about Sister Te and Annette, the infamous night monitor.

"Whoa! You're still full of secrets. You still think Jahi's guilty. Tell me—do you have evidence? Specific evidence?"

"No. Not about him. I'm hoping the investigation will flush out the evidence. Anyway, my source didn't mention him," Zoie answered. She wondered whether Lena had been talking to Jahi.

"Hmm. Well, I've known him longer than you have. Blackmail, drug peddling, murder. Nah, that's not him. It doesn't add up. Jahi's been a straight shooter to a fault. He may be guilty of something but certainly not those criminal things. Shoot, if he'd stayed in the council race and won, he would have made a lousy politician. He doesn't have the chops for lying."

"If you say so." Zoie was tight lipped.

"I think that kid and his ex did the dirt."

Zoie no longer wanted to discuss Jahi's guilt or innocence. The waiter's approach ended that line of conversation. They both ordered Greek custard pie and tea.

"This is de-lish," said Lena, licking her fork. "I shouldn't be eating it. But what the hell."

"Okay, I'm ready to be interviewed," Zoie said, finishing her custard pie and leaning back in her seat. "I've informed Crayton's Board. I've fulfilled my fiduciary responsibility, so now we can proceed. But first let's establish some ground rules."

"Ha! The truth is there's no need."

"What do you mean? You've been pushing for this story."

"Yes, and you owe me—remember? But…since I no longer work for the *Washington Times*, what's the point? I'm not in the mood to do a freelance piece, unless I'm assured of getting paid."

"Huh?"

"Yeah, they axed me. It happened yesterday afternoon, right after we made the date to meet. I thought we should still get together so that I could tell you in person."

Zoie winced. "Oh, Lena, I'm so sorry."

"Deep down I knew this was coming," Lena continued. "I was just hoping it wouldn't."

"I'm sorry I couldn't do the interview sooner. Do you understand why I couldn't talk to you on the record before?"

"Yeah, yeah. I'm not blaming you. Getting the exclusive wouldn't have made any difference in my job situation. The paper's mind was made up. My beat, the DC social scene, was eliminated. The City Desk lost people too. The problem is deep. It's the damn Internet."

Zoie was relieved that she didn't have to do the interview. Anyway, the bare bones of the story had already appeared in *The Washington Post* without any quotes from her.

"Guess I'll freelance for a while," Lena proclaimed. "I've got to do something to pay my mortgage."

Zoie explained her own decision to leave the Foundation.

"You're leaving of your own accord," Lena reminded her. "That's not the same thing."

"For sure," Zoie admitted. In fact, she already had leads on new positions. Information that she wouldn't share with Lena.

"This calls for a celebration," Lena said. "Waiter! Two vodka tonics for two unemployed people!"

When the waiter brought the drinks, Lena and Zoie raised their glasses. Lena made the toast. "To starting over and to finding the truth."

CHAPTER 53

CAT COW TO THE RESCUE

Zoie watched Tina drain her martini. Her friend had left her vegetarian entree untouched. The concerned waitress checked in. "Ladies, are your dishes okay?"

"Oh, yes," Tina answered. Zoie shook her head in agreement. The food was usually good at Nora's, albeit a little pricey. Organic ingredients added to the flavor and also to the cost.

Zoie picked at her chicken entrée, but unlike Tina she'd resisted filling up on alcohol. She vowed to not re-create the debilitating martini hangover she'd suffered in Florida. She'd have to relate the happenings of the past six weeks perfectly sober.

"All this drama is enough to make me start eating steak," said the committed vegetarian. The saga of the Shelter's drug gang and Ray Gaddis's murder had her head spinning. Indeed, Tina had been out of the loop. She sipped her water and promised not to order more liquor until she ate. "Zoie, I can't keep all the names straight. Who's this Lena person again? Is she the sister who works for that right-wing newspaper? And did I hear right? Your assistant was having an affair with the drug dealer?"

"Yes, and yes," Zoie answered blandly. "By the way, that paper, the *Washington Times*, laid her off."

"Too bad." Tina frowned. "So the crazy homeless guy with the book of codes gave you the fortune-cookie clues?"

"No! There were two homeless guys. You see—I knew this was too complicated to explain over dinner."

"Hold on. Okay, there were two of them. Just get me straight on a couple of points."

"Maynard, the one you're calling crazy, was with me in the Shelter. He's in a halfway house, recuperating from his injuries. And thank goodness that he's now on his meds."

"And the codebook you talked about?"

"That's Maynard's binder, and I got a guy I know who teaches high school AP math to help with that. He got a few of his students to decipher the contents. Maynard used common coding techniques, things kids use."

"So what did they uncover? Anything juicy?"

"Lots of recipes—lasagna, chili, fried chicken, and so on. *And* info on the khat operation at the Shelter *and* some damning stuff about the incompetence at Aberdeen, where he used to work."

"The biotest facility in Maryland?"

"Yep! And I haven't seen the other guy since he left me at the Shelter."

"That's Simon. He gave you the messages, right?"

"Yep. Little fortune-cookie strips."

"I'd call them messages. Wow! Well, I can't say I'm making sense of it. I missed all that, huh? Why didn't you call me?"

"You *are* joking? I tried many times to contact you. Either your phone was off, or you just refused to answer. I left voice messages. Do you ever check your voice mail?"

"Sorry," said Tina. She shrugged and stared at her cold food.

"If you want to be incommunicado, you can't ask me why I didn't call."

"To tell the truth, I don't listen to voice messages. I can't remember my password to retrieve them," Tina said unapologetically.

"It's amazing how after years of being on a telephone leash, you can just cut the ties. Anyway, you could have texted SOS or something."

"Note to self," Zoie said, disgusted, "Tina Davis only responds to texts."

An awkward silence followed. Zoie stared at her plate and pushed her cold food around with her fork. It was Tina who re-started the conversation.

"Look, Zoie, I'm really sorry. Obviously, I wasn't there for you when you needed me. I've been caught up in my own trials and tribulations."

"Uh-huh."

"So you've been playing detective all summer. Hey, when you were a kid, did you want to be Nancy Drew?"

"Never thought about it," Zoie answered coldly, not ready to let Tina off the hook.

"Sounds like Nancy Drew stuff to me."

"Nancy Drew was pedestrian," Zoie said, finally perking up. "I wanted to be a superhero actually. Wonder Woman."

"So that explains it. Well, Wonder Woman was too goody goody for me," said Tina. "Now Cat Woman was more my style… but let's get serious. You've been dealing with some dangerous characters."

"Yeah. I thought I was going undercover to investigate regular old white-collar stuff."

"Zoie, they could've killed you. Then my poor goddaughter would only have me to rely on."

"Well, maybe, maybe not."

"What do you mean? Don't tell me you've changed your mind about Nikki's guardianship?" Tina said, raising her voice. "Was my being out of touch that upsetting?"

"Tina, calm down. That's not it. Yes, not being able to con-tact you was irritating. But I'd never reverse my decision about something so important, just like that. You're still my pick for Nikki's guardian. And thanks again for letting me use your car and condo. It's just…"

"Just what?"

"Elliot's back in the picture, or I should say he *wants* to be back in the picture."

Tina rolled her eyes and signaled for their waitress. "This is getting better and better." When the waitress came to the table, Tina pointed to her empty martini glass. "Another one of these, please."

"And can you please rewarm our plates and bring me a merlot?" After the waitress left, Zoie said, "Let's back up on Elliot a minute. You haven't heard the other part of this story. While the Shelter and drug thing was going on, Nikki ran away from the Benjamins. Because of a puppy."

"No, girl!" said Tina, her mouth gaping.

Zoie gave Tina the short version of the puppy saga, explaining how at first she'd suspected the drug gang of kidnapping Nikki, under orders from Jahi. "Of course, I was wrong about that," Zoie explained. "It was all Nikki's doing. And go figure—it was Elliot who found her."

Tina's eyes widened. "No need to go to the movies. The latest dramas are playing right here."

The reheated food arrived, along with their drinks.

"So that's how I ended up bringing Nikki and the puppy home from Ohio, in your car, and you know the rest. You didn't find any dog hair, did you?" Zoie asked anxiously. "I had the car and your place thoroughly cleaned.

"They're fine. I'm glad they got some use while I was away." Tina stroked the condensation on the martini glass with her finger. "But I'm still processing all this. Out of everything you've told me, Nikki's disappearance was the only incident that didn't involve Jahi or this Tarik."

"Right. But as I told you, at first I thought both Jahi and Tarik were involved. I guess I was wrong. So far Jahi hasn't been arrested for anything."

"But why?"

"No evidence. Nothing links him directly to the drug business or to Ray's murder or to the fraud involving the grant funds. Being the Shelter's director and a Board member of the Shelter, he had fiduciary responsibility. *Soooo* I can only hope that they'll find something down the line to nail him."

"Has he contacted you? Have you talked to him?"

"No. Thank goodness. I don't want to talk to him. He's on my shit list on so many levels."

"What about junior Jahi?"

"Tarik's in DC jail. The judge denied bail. He thinks he's a flight risk. Plus, there's a request to extradite him to Montgomery County. Maryland is looking at murder charges. They've linked the drugs in Gaddis's body with the drugs found at the Shelter's drug house. And I heard that Jahi's ex, Sister Te, has gone missing. Remember she's Tarik's mother. The police think she's fled the country."

"How do you like that? She skips the country and leaves her son to do the time."

"Looks that way," Zoie answered with another deep sigh. "Nothing would surprise me at this point."

"Betcha Jahi knows where she is."

"Perhaps, but who cares?" Zoie finally took a bite of her food. "I want to talk about something else. How are things with you? You must've had a fabulous time in Florida with Bert."

"Right," Tina answered with a smirk. She flipped back her reddish-brown curls.

"What happened?"

"Bert's a freak. Actually I knew he was somewhat a freak, at least a tiger in bed. But what I didn't know was that his sexual predilections extended professionally."

"Huh?"

"Remember that I told you he was producing videos of gentle yoga for the geriatric set, like the one I'm in. Well, that endeavor turned into producing this hot new thing—yoga porn. Evidently there's a lot of money in it, and more than anything Bert wants to make money. So nude yoga or yoga porn is the latest thing."

"*Nooooo!* You didn't?" Zoie said.

"Of course I didn't. Bert was fun—for a while. I'm no prude, but it all got...*creepy*."

"Too strange."

"Dear friend, I kid you not. I didn't figure it out for a long time. Stupid me. She tapped her forehead."

"Yeah, join the 'Stupid Me Club.'"

Zoie's thoughts went to her missing friend and helper at the Shelter's women's section—Jazz. Jazz would have appreciated the business opportunities in yoga porn. Zoie never found out what happened to the young woman after the Shelter closed soon after the drug bust. Somewhere out there, perhaps Jazz was on her way to realizing her dream in the independent, online sex business. Once Zoie had looked down on Jazz's career choice, but who was she to pooh-pooh someone else's dreams? Jazz's twist on the sex business was sure better than returning to an abusive pimp. One day she'd look her up online.

"Earth to Zoie! Earth to Zoie!" Tina cocked her head sideways to glare at her friend.

"Oh, I'm still here," Zoie answered stiffly.

"Girl, you drifted off. Is yoga porn that shocking?"

"No. It's the mental pictures. I can't erase the vision of a Cat-Cow pose in the buff."

The thought of yoga porn tickled Zoie's funny bone. A contagious giddiness took hold of her, and Tina joined in. Zoie fanned her red face and took a large sip of her merlot. The sip was a bad idea. She tried to stifle her next giggle, but it was too late. The wine shot up into her nose. In a quick move to halt the embarrassing flow of burgundy liquid, she grabbed a napkin and covered her nose and mouth. Her failed attempts to control her demeanor only intensified Tina's giggles. Both women tried to muffle the sounds of their antics. Tina pressed her hand against her mouth to deaden her squeals of delight. Silliness tears rolled down Zoie's cheeks. Folks at a nearby table looked their way for a minute and then refocused on their own meals.

"No matter how bad things get, sometimes you just have to laugh," Tina said after she regained enough composure to speak.

"Oh, Tina, it's so good to have you back in town," Zoie said, leaning forward with the laughter tears still rolling down her cheeks.

It was the first time in a long time that Zoie had laughed. It was the first time in a long time that she thought that everything was going to be all right.

CHAPTER 54

SOME THINGS YOU'LL NEVER KNOW

Frances Woods looked out the bay window of her reconfigured dining room. The room now served as her bedroom, complete with a handicap-accessible bathroom. She looked down the ivy-covered hill to the street. There, in the front of the house, the view was much more preferable. When she was upstairs at night, the moonlight created eerie shadows on her bedroom ceiling. And in the day the starlings queued on the back power line, reminiscent of Hitchcock's *The Birds*. Overall, being downstairs was better. Why hadn't she thought of this change before?

Zoie had moved back to her childhood home some eighteen months ago. The once-quiet house on Brandywine was quiet no more. The move solved a number of Zoie's logistical issues. Nikki's dog had a welcoming place to live. The fenced backyard relieved Zoie of the chore of dog walking. For a modest increase in pay, Queen agreed to meet Nikki's school van and to be available to care for Nikki after school. There was no money lost on the change since Zoie was able to sublet her Connecticut Avenue apartment until its lease expired.

Since the changes Frances Woods's health had also improved. Her once persistent cough was now a bad memory. Being on the first floor, she could access the kitchen and the living room, leaving the upstairs to Zoie, Nikki, and Queen. She hadn't seen the changes they'd made to the upstairs rooms, and part of her didn't care much about what they'd done. She was content. She'd received her heart's desire—the company of her granddaughter and great-granddaughter. Life, which previously had been an endless drone of illness, was once more livable.

Frances Woods saw a man across the street. He seemed to be watching the house. He looked to be tall, and he seemed to be black. Between the cap he wore and her failing eyesight, she couldn't make out his face. "What's he looking up here for?" she asked under her breath.

She didn't notice Zoie standing in the doorway and holding a manila envelope. Zoie was dressed in a peach-colored tracksuit, and her hair was nicely coifed. The trial for the Shelter had been difficult for her. And having to change jobs in the midst of everything had been a challenge. But those days of confusion had passed. Now her granddaughter had a glow about her. It seemed that Zoie had found some peace after moving in. *Thank the Lord,* thought Frances Woods.

"Morning, Grandma. What are you mumbling about?"

"Nothing," Frances Woods said with a sigh. Now focused on her granddaughter, thoughts of the man across the street faded. She braced herself on her walker and maneuvered to a nearby armchair. "Just babbling to myself. Anyway, you shouldn't be sneaking up on me."

"Sorry," Zoie said. She plopped on the bed across from her grandmother. "You're pretty chipper this morning, already dressed and all. Is Ms. Ida coming by?"

"Yes, after church. But look at you! You're too dressed up for a run. You must be expecting Dylan."

"I am," Zoie answered with a grin that would not be contained. "We're going for a run in the park."

"I'm glad he's going with you. That park is too dangerous these days. Remember t the body of that girl they found several years back. That was when you were still in New York."

"I remember," Zoie answered with a sigh. "Just bones. All they found were bones. Don't worry. I won't go running alone. But first Dylan is going to fix us brunch."

"My, my," Frances Woods said, her tone approving. She'd learned long ago it was better to keep commentary on Zoie's love life to a minimum.

"After last night's sleepover, Tina's taking Nikki and her niece to the American Girl store at Tysons Corner. Nikki can pick out the doll she wants for her birthday."

"I didn't know that Nikki liked dolls."

"Neither did I. Do you remember that I wasn't into dolls? Maybe Wonder Woman and action figures but not dolls. I don't even think Nikki knows who Wonder Woman is. But Elliot mentioned something about American Girl dolls when he was here and promised to buy her one for her birthday. I think the real reason she's interested in those dolls is because he brought it up. *She loves her daddy.*"

"Now, Zoie, Nikki's making up for lost time. And so is he."

Zoie shrugged. "I guess."

Zoie's relationship with Elliot had changed a lot from a year ago. She could now speak his name without going apoplectic. The two had achieved a détente of sorts. Elliot had wiggled his way back into her life, for Nikki's sake. He'd made several visits to DC, ostensibly for business, but he had actually come to see Nikki. Nikki even had a picture of her baby sister, Bridget, stuck to her mirror. There was such a resemblance that it could have been a picture of Nikki at the same age. And Nikki was excited about the baby and ready for the role of big sister, even though she was just learning what it was like to be a daddy's girl.

With leads from her former colleague in New York, Zoie landed a position at a small law firm in which the atmosphere was both congenial and family friendly. Dylan Ross was now a frequent visitor to the Brandywine house. He was still on Crayton Foundation's Board, but Zoie told him that she'd rather not be kept apprised of the happenings at her former employer.

Biscuit, an almost full-grown retriever, entered the room and settled on the floor, next to Zoie's leg. "She only comes to me when Nikki and Queen aren't around," Zoie said, stroking the dog's dark coat. After the previous year's upheaval over the dog, she'd actually grown fond of the animal. As for Frances Woods, Biscuit feared her walker, which worked out since it kept the dog from underfoot.

"What's in the envelope?" Frances Woods asked.

"Oh, yeah," Zoie answered, remembering what she was holding. "I was moving things in the upstairs closet, and I pulled on a box on the top shelf. Its contents spilled out...old pictures."

"Huh," Frances Woods said. "I forgot about that box. I probably haven't touched that stuff in twenty years."

"Yeah, and I brought down twenty years of dust. There are pictures of me, Mom, you, and Grandpa. There were even a few with my father. I thought he didn't take pictures."

"There are a few around."

Zoie pressed the envelope to her chest as she thought about her mother, a woman who didn't get to see her forty-seventh year. "You've got pictures of my cousin Harriet and my great-aunt Sylvia."

"Yeah, all those folks are gone," said Frances Woods with a sigh.

"Grandma, if you want, I'll bring the whole box down. But I really wanted to ask you about this one." Zoie removed an old picture from the envelope. "I don't know this person. He doesn't look like family." Zoie handed the picture to her grandmother.

It was a picture of a young man dressed as if for church. With a hat in hand, he was standing in a formal pose, one arm resting on a Greek column pedestal. He was dark skinned and had a tall thin build. The black-and-white photo was yellow and cracked where it had been folded, before being pressed flat between the cardboard in the envelope.

"Folks always said he looked like Nate King Cole," Frances Woods said as she stared at the photo, almost dreamy eyed.

Zoie was confused by her grandmother's reaction. "You mean Natalie Cole's father?"

"Yeah."

"I remember Nat King Cole from that video Natalie Cole did with him. The two sang together. But he was dead when they made that video. Brought back to life through the wonders of technology...okay, but who's this?"

Frances Wood put a hand to her mouth as she looked at the photo. Then she said, "His name was Gabriel. Gabriel Simon. He was my very first love."

"Wow, Grandma. Let me see him again." Zoie took the picture from her grandmother. "Was he someone here in DC before you met Grandpa?"

"Well, I guess you should know the story. It doesn't make much difference now. I think all the main characters are dead. *May they rest in peace.* My telling you can't hurt anybody. The truth has its way of coming to light, as painful as it may be."

"Grandma! What are you talking about?"

Frances Woods explained how she'd been forced to leave North Carolina because she was pregnant with Gabriel Simon's child. "It was bad enough that I was with child without being married. It wasn't like it is today. My father was a good man, but back in those days, like many folks with lighter skin, he was what we called 'color struck.' He wanted to keep his family's line on the lighter side. Like you're not white but you're better than the darker folks. And if you can't be white, it was better to be the closest thing." Frances Woods turned to stare out the window but continued to talk. "I'm not saying it was right, but back in the day, a lot of good people felt that way. Some still do today."

Zoie sat stunned and speechless. She'd never heard her grandmother talk so frankly about race and color. Zoie knew about being color struck. She heard what her grandmother said, but she didn't want to believe it. Who could be raised in Washington, DC, without being aware of the not-so-subtle color line? The practices of light-skinned superiority had infected Howard University's past and had been prevalent on DC's Gold Coast, where affluent blacks shared education, position, and a lighter skin. And who didn't know about Spike Lee's *School Daze*. Yes, Zoie was well aware of the issue. Although her grandmother and grandfather were lighter than most—her grandmother a creamy-ivory tone, her grandfather Calvin a rose beige—she'd always believed her family had been spared the color-struck curse. She thought that that brand of prejudice was something that happened in other people's families—not hers. Her mother was the color of peanut butter, and her father was a few shades darker than that. Her own complexion was what folks called a permanent tan, the envy of her milk-white friends at Columbia, who had tried to achieve the desirable tone by baking in the sun. The thought that her grandmother's family, *her* family, carried the curse made Zoie cringe. She'd always considered being color struck as nothing short of self-hatred and black-on-black racism. The whole thing disgusted her.

Deep in thought, Frances Woods turned toward the window. She didn't notice Zoie's distress. And distress it truly was.

Zoie closed her eyes and took a deep breath. But a sickening feeling enveloped her. It was as if she'd just received news of the death of someone close. It was a feeling of shock, loss, and sadness. Loss of what was left of her innocence. She'd been naive about her family. After a long silence, she finally asked, "Grandma, did you feel that way?"

Frances Woods turned to her granddaughter. "Of course not. I loved him."

"Then why didn't you and Gabriel just run off together?"

Frances Woods sighed. "In those days I didn't think that way. It was more complicated...I was an obedient daughter. I was young. I wasn't brave enough."

"So Mom was Gabriel's child? And you came to DC and had Mom, right?"

"Yes, and I married Calvin. He knew my situation, and he married me anyway. I couldn't ask for a better husband. Bless his soul."

"Then what about Gabriel? Did you ever see him again? Did he ever get to see his child?"

Frances Woods frowned. "No, but we corresponded a bit through his sister. I told him that he had a daughter, and I let him know where we lived. His sister told me he'd come to DC to find us. But then..." She shrugged, looking quite pitiful, like a child lost in the woods. "I don't know what happened."

"What do you mean?"

"I never heard from him again." Her old eyes filled with tears. "His sister wrote that he never returned home. He disappeared... just disappeared."

"Wow! How weird. Did you go back to North Carolina to see your family?"

"Yes. And I asked about him. I thought one day I'd run into him. But he disappeared from the face of the earth. I always thought some ill had befallen him."

"Did Mom know about him?"

"No, I never told your mother. I didn't want her to feel differently about Calvin. It wouldn't have been fair to him. She was the only child I had and his only child too. He loved her dearly."

"Yes, and I know Mom loved him. Maybe she didn't miss anything," Zoie said with tears in her eyes. "If it had been me, I'd want to know." Zoie pondered the picture. "So this is my real grandfather...Gabriel Simon, huh. He reminds me of somebody, but I can't think who."

Frances Woods shrugged and turned back to the window. Zoie left the room and ran upstairs.

In her room Zoie let her tears flow, tears of sadness, anger, shame, and disgust. She was sad that her mother never had the chance to know her real father. Sad for her grandmother, who had to forgo her true love. Still, she was angry that her grandmother had complied with her family's wishes. Where had the grandmother she knew been, the one with a backbone? Zoie continued to feel physically ill. She was ashamed. *Color racism practiced by her own kin.* She'd done nothing wrong, but she felt that somehow her family's past tainted her.

She wanted to look at Gabriel Simon's picture again, but in her rush to get away from her grandmother, she'd left the photo. In her reverie it was doubtful that her grandmother would have let the picture go. Something kept telling Zoie that she'd seen the man in the picture before. He did look a little like Simon, the mysterious homeless man, who'd provided counsel that summer. Maynard's soft-spoken friend. But it couldn't be Gabriel Simon. That made no sense. Gabriel Simon would be ancient—well, at least as old as her grandmother.

She kept the fortune-cookie strips that Simon had given her that summer. She had collected the dozen or so prophecies, some more significant than others, and kept them in a plastic sandwich bag. Zoie wiped her tears and went to the drawer where the plastic bag was stuffed next to a jewelry box. She hadn't looked at those fortune-cookie slips since the incident at the Shelter. Her fingers sifted through the papers and pulled one out. The message was no longer handwritten. She pulled out another and then another. They all looked the same—run-of-the-mill paper strips found in fortune cookies, complete with lucky lottery numbers on the back.

"Huh," she said after checking them all. "What? How?" Had she been dreaming? Had Simon, the mystery man, wiped out the evidence of his existence? Or had she been hallucinating when she had read the strips of paper? She didn't know what to believe.

She sank back on her bed and stared into the distance. Who could she even talk to about this? She'd only mentioned it to Tina in the very beginning but no one else. She didn't talk about the prophecies, because she didn't want anyone to think she was crazy. Maynard would understand. One day she'd have to find Maynard again. Yes, he would understand.

CHAPTER 55

CHOICES

Hugging her knees, Zoie sat on the landing bench, waiting for Dylan. The bench was the very one she'd hid under as a child. She'd always felt her hiding place to be the safest place in the world. Safe from the loud, ugly squabbles between her mother and father. Safe from her mother's call to do chores, when she'd rather daydream. After they moved into the Brandywine house, Nikki quickly claimed that spot as her own, squeezing into its tight space with the dog. Zoie no longer fit in that space under the bench, but she no longer needed to hide. It was time to face life and all it had to offer.

From her staircase perch, Zoie watched the front door, pondering the mystery of the morphed fortune-cookie strips and the bombshell about her family. She wondered whether deep down her mother knew that Grandpa Calvin wasn't her real father. Her mother must have questioned why she'd turned out darker than both of her parents. Her grandmother was courageous. After all, she and Grandpa moved into the house when there were few if any other blacks in the upscale neighborhood. What would she have done if she'd been in her grandmother's shoes? Back then societal expectations were different. Could she have bucked a stern father? She had to give her grandmother some slack. She couldn't judge her based on today's norms.

Zoie's thoughts shifted to Dylan, the new man in her life. He was fun and really sweet and good with Nikki. After the Jahi debacle, she was hesitant to reengage. Who or what was she getting involved with? So she had Dylan investigated. The investigation was Tina's suggestion. Leave it to Tina to walk the line between spiritual enlightenment and practicality.

"I wish I'd checked out Yoga Bert before going to Florida," Tina confessed. "Bert, isn't he the *Sesame Street* character? All I know is that anybody named Bert should be checked out as a matter of course."

"And he would have been revealed as kinky. Then you might have gone your whole life without discovering yoga porn," Zoie said. Mentioning yoga porn tickled their funny bones. They had a good laugh.

For a meager sum, Zoie got a pretty good idea of just whom she was hooking up with. The PI's report confirmed that Dylan was indeed single, a graduate of Virginia Tech and MIT. He owned a small tech firm in Northern Virginia and lived alone in a modest, *modest* by McLean standards, two-million-dollar townhouse. He had a hefty net worth and no police record. Not even a traffic violation. He'd grown up in Virginia Beach in a middle-class family, not unlike her own, except his family were white and weren't churchgoers. The PI's report even provided a serious picture of Dylan in his senior year at First Colonial High. Yes, Dylan checked out squeaky clean. Zoie hoped that Dylan would never find out that she'd vetted him. There'd be no more crapshoots when it came to her heart. Her already-short supply of trust was exhausted.

Zoie did a mental inventory of her past relationships. Elliot was a mistake, except that mistake brought her Nikki. She'd had a few fleeting relationships since Elliot. Nothing serious. Then there was *Jahi*.

Even though her relationship with Jahi had been short lived, it was *entirely* different. There was a mystery about him. A danger. He didn't fit the mold of her usual picks: the starchy business types, the preppy graduates who'd attended the best schools, or the metrosexuals schooled in proper wine-and-cheese pairings and who knew all the best restaurants. Nor was Jahi like the ambitious workaholics she'd dated—the ones intent on setting the world on fire and racing for the bucks on the multimillionaire track.

Being with Jahi had been scary and, at the same time, exhilarating. He had undeniable magnetism, sexual or otherwise. He was strong willed but still very needy. Perhaps that was it. Was it his neediness that attracted her? Whatever it had been, she'd fallen for him pretty hard. And what had she reaped for opening her heart? Betrayal. Indifference. Damn near killed.

She never received a real explanation of Jahi's part in the Mahali debacle. Over a year ago, she asked Charles, who was still with Lena and still sniffing around, "What's the deal with Jahi?"

All Charles said was, "They don't have enough to pin on the brother. The US attorney's not interested in wasting time on a weak case."

A weak case? So Jahi was never charged. She'd run into him a few times during Tarik's trial. Tarik was convicted of murder in Maryland and of assault and battery and drug-trafficking charges in DC's federal court. The details of the kickback scheme remained the unsettled piece. With Ray Gaddis dead and Tarik in prison, to conclude that piece seemed less important. Certainly the Crayton Foundation wasn't pushing for more bad press. For them Ray's involvement was an embarrassment.

They just wanted it all to go away. But pursuing that case would either exonerate Jahi or set the stage for bringing him up on charges for bribery, financial malfeasance, or a possible civil suit for negligence.

Lena's theory was that Jahi's head had been in the "do-good-ers cloud" and that he'd believed the stories about himself and had gotten caught up in the self-importance trap. And because he hadn't been paying attention, he let Tarik get away with mur-der—literal murder.

Whether Jahi was innocent or not, Zoie figured that Jahi had left her "out to dry." He'd turned out to be just another self-absorbed man-child, a more down-home version of Elliot, who shirked responsibility when it came to relationships. She shook her head and tried to push thoughts of Jahi away.

Dylan, on the other hand, embodied all the qualities any sane woman would include on her guy-related wish list. His hefty bank account, though not a priority, was a definite plus. He was intelligent, funny, and a decent cook. Geeky but not really. And the sex wasn't bad either. He wasn't as skilled as other lovers she'd had but trainable. Most importantly, though, he'd made it clear that he cared about her. Having a man who treated her well was a top requirement.

From the safety of her bench, Zoie tightened the grip on her knees and rocked. Still, with all of Dylan's good qualities, something was missing. She couldn't quite put her finger on the thing that was supposed to fill that vacant space. Perhaps she was being gun shy about the relationship and overthinking things. Despite her liking Dylan as much as she did, perhaps the passion on her side just wasn't that strong. She remem-bered what her grandmother had said about Grandpa Calvin: "At first I didn't love him, but over time the love came." If things continued the way they'd been going, maybe that would be the way things would go with Dylan. She tried to convince herself that a life with Dylan wouldn't be just settling. But a part of her kept asking, *or would it?*

Zoie spotted movement out on the porch. She knew her grandmother was expecting Ida Bascom. Through the front door's side panel, she spotted Dylan. He was a little early. She bolted down the stairs to greet him. Biscuit came running from somewhere, wagging his tail and waiting for her to open the door.

Dylan was dressed in his track gear. "Ready for brunch?" he asked, kissing her on the forehead. Normally he would have embraced her, but his arms held two brown bags marked Whole Foods. Zoie's head reached to his upper chest. It had been that way with all the men she dated.

"I'm hungry, especially since you're doing the cooking," Zoie answered, taking one of the bags from him and wondering whether her eyes were still red from her tears.

"Hi, boy," Dylan said, bending down to give Biscuit a hello pat. "If you don't mind, I've brought clothes to change into after our run. They're still in the car," he said, referring to his BMW parked out front. "We're going to run, right?"

"For sure. After you cook, we clean up, and we give our food time to settle."

He wrapped his now free arm around Zoie's shoulder and yelled out, "Hello, Mrs. Woods," before Zoie ushered him to the kitchen. "So what've you been up to?" Dylan asked as he put his bag on the counter.

A lot is what she wanted to say. The revelation that her grandfather wasn't really her grandfather. The mystery of the fortune-cookie prophecies from a homeless man, who she had come to find out looked like her real grandfather. The news of her discovery of her new lineage would have been enough to talk about had it not been for the color issue. In a quick assessment, she determined she wouldn't—*couldn't*, actually—tell Dylan any of it.

Perhaps one day he could understand how she'd been hallucinating all that summer or how awful she felt when being told that her grandmother had been forced to abandon her real grandfather because he was too dark. She didn't have the patience to explain it all or to attempt to educate Dylan in racial issues when she didn't completely understand them herself.

"Well?" he asked, setting his bag on the kitchen counter and pushing his shaggy hair out of his face. "Something is up. You seem a little down or maybe deep in thought."

"No, everything's cool. Just waiting for you," she answered. "I've been taking advantage of the silence since Nikki is out with Tina."

That answer seemed to satisfy him. How could she explain the horror and the shame she was feeling? There never seemed to be a good way to confer her feelings when it came to black issues to a white person. That had been the case when she lived with Elliot, even with their years of being together. They hadn't been tuned into the same cultural shorthand. Sometimes she just needed to be around a person who understood exactly what she meant. Someone who'd lived in that same space.

Perhaps at some point she'd give Dylan the benefit of the doubt. But for now she was still sorting things out for herself. No, she wouldn't tell him any of it today. Maybe not for a long time.

About thirty minutes later, Ida Bascomb arrived. When Zoie opened the door, she found her grandmother's old friend with a white-gloved hand clutching the porch rail and the other leaning on her cane. She was trying to catch her breath. "When are y'all going to get an elevator to take old folks like me up and down those stairs?" she said, chuckling mildly. Ida Bascomb's colors for this Sunday were green and white—and not just any green but a deep-emerald color that would have made St. Patrick proud. As usual her attire was too large for her slight, bony frame. The large shoulder pads made the garment look as if it were still on a hanger. Her cavalier-style hat, with its foot-long white plume, would most certainly be a vision obstruction to anyone unfortunate enough to sit behind her in church.

Tail wagging, Biscuit came running to greet the latest arrival. Ida Bascomb didn't like dogs. With the slightest motion of her cane, she shooed Biscuit away. She caught a glimpse of Dylan, who was peeking into the foyer from the hall, behind the great staircase.

"I'm sure glad I don't have to climb more stairs," Ida said.

Zoie set up a folding chair for Ms. Bascomb across from her grandmother. "I'll bring some food in a little bit," Zoie told her grandmother. "Do you want some eggs Benedict, Ms. Bascomb?"

"No, child, but I'll take a piece of toast with some tea when you bring your grandmother's food."

Zoie closed the door and left them to chat.

"So the boyfriend is here, I see," said Ida in a half whisper, with a sly smile.

"Now, Ida, behave yourself," Frances Woods scolded.

"Did I say anything?" Ida bristled.

"No, but I can tell you were going to make some wisecrack. I'll say it for you. Yes, the boy is white. And he seems very nice. You got to remember things are different these days."

Ida raised her eyebrows and smirked.

An awkward moment passed.

"Well, I told her," Frances Woods said in a low voice.

"Told who what?" Ida's voice indicated irritation with her friend.

"Told Zoie about Laurel's real father."

"Oh, that. That's old news," Ida said with the wave of her gloved hand. "About time you got around to telling someone the truth besides me. How did she take it?"

"Not sure, but she seemed all right."

"As you said, things are different these days. Having a baby without getting married is a regular thing. Plus, it's easy to tell a secret when all the people who'd get hurt by it are gone." It was clear Ida was referring to Laurel and Calvin.

"I guess you're right, Ida," Frances Woods said, sighing. "Nobody is gonna get hurt. But as much as I would have liked to have the whole thing off my chest, I didn't tell Zo everything."

"For God's sake, Fran! What more is there to tell?"

"I didn't tell her that Gabe had planned to come for me and Laurel. I was going to runaway with him. Do you remember that I told you I was planning to leave Calvin?" She pressed her hands to her mouth as if to stifle the source of such a shameful confession.

"Oh, that. Now, Fran, that was a long time ago," Ida said, attempting to console her friend. "And the truth is you never left Calvin, because Laurel's father never came. No sense getting upset about 'could haves.'" Ida always made things simple.

With a solemn face, Frances Woods nodded in weak agreement. It was as if all that stored up pain was coming to the surface.

"And you never did find out why he didn't come, did you?"

Frances Woods didn't answer. Staring out the window, she thought back to those heartbreaking weeks of expectation—the weeks she expected to find Gabe standing at the door of their basement apartment in Shaw. But whatever they had planned was never meant to be. God meant for her to stay with Calvin, and only God knew why Gabe hadn't come.

Then Ida asked, "If he'd come as he said he would, would you *really* have left Calvin?"

Frances Woods sighed and, with a weak voice, said, "I don't know. I really don't know."

Queen arrived just as Dylan finished fixing brunch. Queen was glad to be back. She liked being at the Brandywine house better than being at her own place, where her brother and his grown son ruled the roost. Since the days after the fire, Queen had been like one of the family.

Queen brought food to Frances Woods and Ida Bascomb. In the kitchen Zoie and Dylan cleaned some of the mess before they sat down to eat. When the doorbell rang, Biscuit headed for the door.

"I'll get it," Queen said. "You all just get my kitchen back in shape."

Zoie knew that Queen wasn't joking about the kitchen. She rolled her eyes, and Dylan laughed. "Wonder who that could be? I'm not expecting anyone. Are you, Queen?" she asked.

"It might be my brother. I made an extra pie to bring here and left it sitting on my stove."

Queen left the two in the kitchen and went to answer the door. She looked out the side panel on the front door. There was a tall black man on the porch. He didn't look familiar. He was well groomed, and his hands were crossed in front of him. "Oh, God, I hope it ain't Jehovah's Witnesses. Nowadays even the Mormons come around. But usually in twos," Queen said. She looked over to check that her baseball bat was in the umbrella stand.

Queen held Biscuit back and opened the door.

"Hello, ma'am." The man looked as if he were about to choke. "I'm here to see Zoie Taylor. Is she home?"

Queen looked him up and down and decided he looked decent enough. "Zoie!" Queen yelled to the back of the house. "You have a visitor."

"Who is it, Queen?" Zoie came bounding from the kitchen just as the man stepped inside. She stopped in her tracks. It was as if she'd seen a ghost. It was Jahi Khalfani. He'd just been on her mind. She must have conjured him up. But something about him was different. He was thinner than the last time she'd seen him. His proud long dreads were cropped short, and instead of his usual T-shirt and jeans, he was in a starched white collar shirt and dress slacks.

He stood by the door, and Queen stood nearby, holding back an anxious Biscuit. "Hello, Zoie," he said. "I've come to say I'm sorry."

95452109R10294

Made in the USA
Lexington, KY
09 August 2018